AND SO IT

The Therengian Army kept up the advance. The Orcs increased their volleys, then the Novarsk cavalry made their appearance, riding west to destroy the threat.

Natalia countered by sending her own horsemen to reinforce the flank, followed by the tuskers—large, brutish creatures ridden by Orc hunters armed with long spears. Two years ago, they had torn through the finest cavalry in the Petty Kingdoms, the Temple Knights of Saint Cunar. Now, with an increase in numbers, and time to hone their skills, they were an integral part of her plan.

The rest of the army had yet to make contact, yet the decreased range led to more accurate volleys from both sides. Bolts and arrows flew out in greater and greater numbers, leaving a noticeable effect on both armies.

Natalia gazed east, willing Kargen and Shaluhk to get into position, but the thick forest hid their location. All she could do was trust them to do what was needed.

She held her breath as a thunderous cheer erupted from the warriors who steeled themselves for the imminent engagement, then the clash of axes and swords was all that could be heard.

The battle reminded her of a giant serpent writhing along the hill like a living thing. In the early morning mist, she'd considered a more traditional attack, perhaps concentrating her army on a single point. However, an entirely different approach made much more sense with the forces at her disposal. The key to success would be pinning the enemy in place. Yet now, witnessing the terrible majesty of it all, she doubted herself. As a Stormwind, she'd trained for this and should be revelling in the moment, but the Army of Therengia was not simply warriors—it was people, her people, and the loss of each one was a wound she would bear for the rest of her life. She closed her eyes, praying to the Saints for victory.

ALSO BY PAUL J BENNETT

MAELSTROM

THE FROZEN FLAME: BOOK FIVE

PAUL J BENNETT

First Edition: December 2021

ePub ISBN: 978-1-990073-31-1
Mobi ISBN: 978-1-990073-32-8
Print ISBN: 978-1-990073-33-5

This book is a work of fiction. Any similarity to any person, living or dead is entirely coincidental.

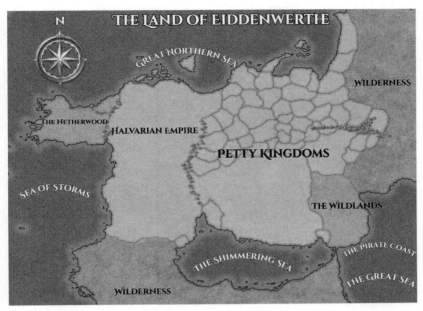

The World of Eiddenwerthe

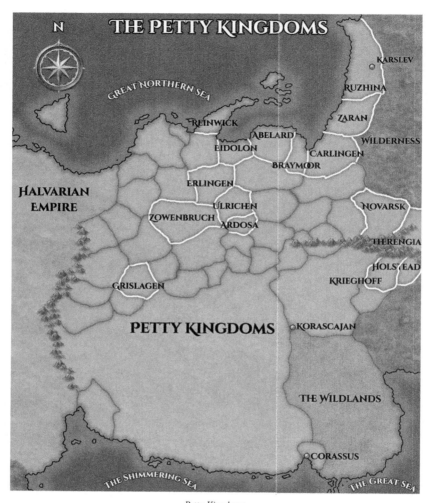

Petty Kingdoms

Therengia

Stormwind Manor

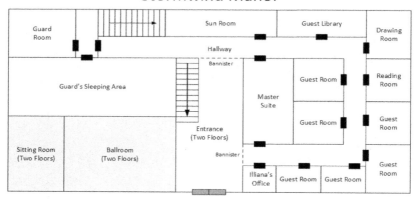

Upper Floor

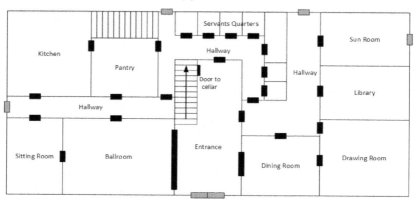

Ground Floor

Stormwind Manor

HERONWOOD

Spring 1108 SR*
(*Saints Reckoning)

Natalia surveyed the enemy lines. Rada, Queen of Novarsk, deployed her army along the top of a long hill, stretching from east to west, centred on the village of Heronwood. Her position was anchored on either side by the thick forest typical of the region. Their formation would have been imposing to a regular army but was a blessing to the Army of Therengia.

"Well?" said Athgar. "What do you think?"

"Exactly as I predicted," said Natalia. "The Petty Kingdoms never surprise me. They always use the same tactics, over and over."

He chuckled. "Which allows us to defeat them, again and again. Let's hope this time we can do so with a minimum of bloodshed."

"Are the Red Hand in position?"

"They are," replied Athgar. "And Kargen knows what to do. We need only delay them a little bit longer. What's the plan?" He was fully aware of the plan, but he knew repeating it would settle his bondmate's nerves.

"The Stone Crushers and Black Axes are on our left. They'll push north, keeping to the trees whenever possible. The idea is to draw out the enemy cavalry, what little there is of it, and force them to engage. Our own cavalry will then react, along with the tuskers."

"Are you sure that's wise? The horsemen of Ebenstadt are untested."

"Their mere presence," said Natalia, "will be a warning to Therengia's enemies that we now wield a mixed army. Whether they actually engage in battle matters little. Meanwhile, the fyrd will push forward and engage all along the line. I am, however, going to add a little twist to keep the enemy on their toes."

"This is news to me."

She smiled. "It's nice to know I can still surprise you. We shall advance at the oblique."

"Meaning?"

"I intend to concentrate on the westward edge of their line, forcing them to redeploy. That should make Kargen's part a bit easier. It will be the Cloud Hunters' job to tie down what few warriors remain in the east."

The Cloud Hunters, a new tribe of Orcs who came at the behest of Shaluhk, founded the village of Gal-Drulan in the north of Therengia, helping the kingdom claim the area. Now they sat on the eastern end of the line of battle, beside the Orcs of the Red Hand.

"Shall we begin?" Natalia asked.

"You're the warmaster."

"And you're the High Thane. Thus, I offer you the opportunity to launch the attack."

"Before we do," said Athgar, "I have a question."

"Which is?"

"Where is their cavalry?"

"They are behind the hill, on the western end of their line."

"How can you be so sure?"

"Ah," she replied. "You forget, the Cloud Hunters have a master of air. She used her magic to spy out the enemy positions."

"You seem to have thought of everything."

"I'm a battle mage; it's part of my training to consider all the options."

"Then you may begin at your leisure."

She turned to her runners, young men and women of the villages acting as her voice this day. "Relay word to commence the attack," she commanded them. The youths ran off, eager to do their part.

The advance began slowly as it often does with such affairs. The Orcs on either flank were the first to move, securing the line against any hidden threats. They were masters of skirmishing, more than capable of keeping the enemy at bay when needed. Like the Red Hand, the Orcs of the Black Axe had equipped themselves with the mighty Orc warbows Athgar had developed. Their range was similar to the enemy's crossbows but with a much higher discharge rate, especially in the hands of well-seasoned hunters.

Athgar, nominally in charge of the Thane Guard, was behind the main line today, ready to bring the elite warriors to any danger points that might develop. As hand-picked soldiers, each and every one of them was a veteran of the last two years of near-constant warfare.

They'd thought the fight over when they defeated the Church and captured Ebenstadt, but it was not to be. Alarmed by the threat of a new Therengia, warriors and mercenaries flocked eastward, eager to put an end to this upstart kingdom. Disorganized and largely ineffective, they'd easily been defeated, but then Novarsk, convinced the fight had weakened the new realm, launched an invasion of its own. Now, six months later, the Army of Therengia was deep inside the borders of Novarsk, ready to finish this once and for all.

Athgar hoped it would finally bring about peace, but he had his doubts. The war had caused nothing but misery and death. No, he corrected himself; that was not entirely true. News of the rebirth of Therengia produced a flood of new people to their realm, mainly Therengians who'd been persecuted for generations. So many came that the villages swelled beyond capacity, forcing new ones to be founded. Today's battle would firmly establish them as a power to be reckoned with, provided they survived.

The entire army was moving now, catching Athgar off guard. He berated himself for his daydreaming and ordered the Thane Guard to advance, maintaining their position relative to the rest of the army. He spared a momentary glance eastward to catch Kargen and Shaluhk disappearing into the forest, along with the hunters of the Red Hand.

Her horse gave Natalia enough of a height advantage that she could see over her troops. The distant enemy deployed their warriors in a straight line, more or less, with crossbows interspersed with more traditional footmen. At the Volstrum, she learned many ways to integrate the various arms that made up such a force. The most common was to deploy archers on either flank, but Rada had chosen this alternate arrangement, perhaps considering herself less traditional.

Arrows flew as the two armies drew closer, but few casualties happened at this range. That would change as the battle developed, yet for now, this long-range exchange was to Natalia's advantage, for her archers were well-trained and experienced hunters, far more accurate than their Novarsk opponents.

. . .

The Therengian Army kept up the advance. The Orcs increased their volleys, then the Novarsk cavalry made their appearance, riding west to destroy the threat.

Natalia countered by sending her own horsemen to reinforce the flank, followed by the tuskers—large, brutish creatures ridden by Orc hunters armed with long spears. Two years ago, they had torn through the finest cavalry in the Petty Kingdoms, the Temple Knights of Saint Cunar. Now, with an increase in numbers, and time to hone their skills, they were an integral part of her plan.

The rest of the army had yet to make contact, yet the decreased range led to more accurate volleys from both sides. Bolts and arrows flew out in greater and greater numbers, leaving a noticeable effect on both armies.

Natalia gazed east, willing Kargen and Shaluhk to get into position, but the thick forest hid their location. All she could do was trust them to do what was needed.

She held her breath as a thunderous cheer erupted from the warriors who steeled themselves for the imminent engagement, then the clash of axes and swords was all that could be heard.

The battle reminded her of a giant serpent writhing along the hill like a living thing. In the early morning mist, she'd considered a more traditional attack, perhaps concentrating her army on a single point. However, an entirely different approach made much more sense with the forces at her disposal. The key to success would be pinning the enemy in place. Yet now, witnessing the terrible majesty of it all, she doubted herself. As a Stormwind, she'd trained for this and should be revelling in the moment, but the Army of Therengia was not simply warriors—it was people, her people, and the loss of each one was a wound she would bear for the rest of her life. She closed her eyes, praying to the Saints for victory.

Kargen halted, staring out from the trees. Beside him, he felt the reassuring presence of his bondmate, Shaluhk.

"It has worked," he said. "We are behind them."

"As we should be," said Shaluhk, "but now comes the most dangerous part of all. Can you spot our target?"

"She has made it easy," replied Kargen. "Do you not see her standard?"

"Do not get... what is the word Nat-Alia likes to use? Carried away?"

He grinned. "Rest assured, I shall not. Now, come. We have much work to do." He looked over his shoulder to where his hunters waited. They all knew their task this day, and a hundred more were ready to carry on should he fall. He took Shaluhk's hand, squeezing it slightly.

"Be careful, Shaluhk. I would not want you harmed."

"Nor I, bondmate mine. Now, let us finally put an end to the designs of this Queen of Novarsk."

They advanced, moving quietly until they were in the open plain, waiting for all his hunters to clear the woods before he broke into a run.

The sun was warm, the breeze pleasant, and he felt the blessings of the Ancestors swelling within his chest. They were the Orcs of the Red Hand, and they would end this battle and the war!

The first sign of success was the sudden collapse of the Novarsk cavalry. Natalia briefly glimpsed ghostly figures fighting the horsemen before the enemy broke, scattering like an upset ant hill. Orcs streamed out of the woods on the western flank, swarming around the beleaguered Novarsk footmen, and then she lost sight of them as they disappeared behind the hill.

Before her, the fyrd fought on, making little headway but at least holding their own. She tried to spot what was happening in the east, but the ground here was too uneven, her height no longer an advantage.

Filled with a momentary sense of panic, Natalia looked over at the Thane Guard only to see Athgar safe and sound. She closed her eyes, forcing herself to slow her breathing. The battle was beyond her control now; she must trust in others to win the day.

Shaluhk slowed her pace, drawing on arcane powers to begin her spell. Kargen, matching her speed, waited for his hunters to draw closer, then spotted Kragor.

"Bring the warbows to the front," he commanded. "We shall gift the enemy one volley, then charge."

Hunters ran forward to form a scattered line. Each drew back an arrow, then Kragor gave the command, and they let fly.

Shaluhk completed her spell, and ghostly figures appeared—Orcs of old, with strange-looking armour, armed with wickedly long spears. She pointed towards the enemy, and they advanced, their feet making no sound as they trod the physical realm. The hunters of the Red Hand surged forward beside warriors of old, axes ready to bring death and destruction to their enemies.

The men of Novarsk were intent on the battle before them, where the Therengian fyrd fought for control of the hill. The Orcs drew closer, and then an enemy soldier glanced in their direction, yelling out a warning before he fell as an arrow took him in the chest.

Others turned to face the new threat at his shout, but it was too late. The Orcs of the Red Hand cut through the rear of the Novarsk line, ghostly warriors of the past accompanying them.

The sounds of fighting dimmed, and it soon became apparent the battle was over. Men threw down their weapons, fleeing to the north, only to be cut down by Orcs.

At first, Natalia felt pity for these warriors, but then her heart hardened. They had come to her home in war and were now paying the price—they deserved no less.

Athgar drew closer. "It's over," he said, "and I didn't even get to use my axe." She turned, and they held each other a moment before letting go.

"A great victory," he added. "Any word on Kargen?"

"Not yet," she replied, "but we shall know soon enough."

The army before them was now nothing more than a large mass of people milling around a hill. She could make out knots of enemy soldiers being herded into groups, but little evidence remained of the disciplined companies who had started this battle.

"Here comes Raleth," said Athgar. "Perhaps he has news?"

The young Thane of Runewald stopped a few steps short, taking a moment to catch his breath. "The fighting has ceased, and the prisoners are being rounded up."

"And their leader?" asked the High Thane.

"No word as yet, but there were signs of fighting to their rear."

Natalia, still watching the remote hilltop, broke into a smile as a trio of familiar faces appeared in the distance. "We are successful," she announced.

Athgar followed her gaze to where Kargen and Shaluhk, followed by half a dozen hunters, prodded an individual ahead of them—the now-disgraced Queen of Novarsk herself, Rada.

"We defeated the enemy," said Natalia, "and captured its ruler. Novarsk is ours, at least for the moment. But there are decisions to come, ones that fall not on the warmaster's shoulders but on the High Thane's and those who advise him."

"Where would you suggest we start?" asked Athgar.

"First, we must decide what to do with all these prisoners, then comes the fate of Rada."

"You're the one familiar with the politics of the Petty Kingdoms. What would they do if the roles were reversed?"

"That depends," said Natalia. "Were you the ruler of a Petty Kingdom, they would likely hold you for ransom. As a Therengian, however, they would insist on your execution to wipe what they see as heresy from the Continent."

"Heresy?" said Athgar. "Hardly that. I might remind you we are not the death worshippers they believe us to be. We even host Temple Knights in Ebenstadt."

"A fact I am very much aware of. Yet you asked me how I thought the Petty Kingdoms would react. I do not agree with them, only inform you of their ways so that you may consider the repercussions of your actions."

"It seems they would consider us heretics regardless of what we do."

"Also, likely true," said Natalia. "In any case, by your own commands, the decision is not yours alone. You must call a meeting of the Thane's Council and let them decide."

Athgar winced. "We need a better name for that. After all, it isn't just thanes; there are chieftains there as well."

"And shamans," Natalia reminded him, "but let us not concern ourselves with such trivial matters at this time. There are more important matters to consider."

"Finburg is already in our hands, and their capital, Halmund, will surrender rather than risk the death of their queen." He turned to Raleth. "March the prisoners back to Ebenstadt. I'll send Wynfrith and the fyrd on to Halmund, along with the Stone Crushers and Black Axes."

"And if they refuse to surrender?" asked the young Therengian.

"Then Rugg has permission to reduce their walls. That threat alone should be more than sufficient to convince them to give up. Tell them that as long as they don't resist, there will be no punishment."

"A good idea," said Natalia. "It's common practice amongst the Petty Kingdoms to sack a captured city."

"Not amongst Therengians," said Athgar. "A point we must be sure to impress upon them."

"And as to the rulership of Novarsk itself?"

"I shall confer with the council, but I'm inclined to appoint a military governor, at least for the short term."

"And in the long term?"

"That largely depends on what we decide to do with Rada." He paused a moment, looking drained of energy.

"Are you all right?" asked Natalia.

"I'm fine, just tired of having to make all these decisions. We've had nothing but war for the last two years. I feel like my life has been stripped away from me."

"It's my fault. If I hadn't claimed the name Therengia, none of this would have happened."

"Don't blame yourself," he said. "The defeat of the Church's Army could have no other outcome. At least this way, we secured some breathing room. Outsiders will now think twice before taking on the army that defeated Novarsk. Always assuming, of course, they don't see us as an even bigger threat and gang up on us."

"Even that will take time. The Petty Kingdoms subsist on a diet of subterfuge and guile. They'll not be so eager to trust their neighbours in an alliance anytime soon."

"Good," he said. "Then we'll finally have peace."

"Yes, and a chance to return to a semblance of normal life, whatever that is."

They wandered up the hill, making their way past the injured and dead. There'd been terrible carnage here, deaths that would affect people not by the loss of warriors but by the loss of brothers, sisters, husbands, and wives, for amongst the Therengians, both genders fought side by side.

Natalia, in particular, found it difficult to reconcile the loss of so many even though victory was achieved. Athgar, however, was more pragmatic. To his mind, it was better to sacrifice a few rather than the many who would be subjugated under the oppression of foreign rule. Therengians, as a people, had suffered for centuries, a forgotten folk valued little amongst the Petty Kingdoms. Here, however, they had found a home, a home they would gladly give their last breath to defend.

Finally, they found their way to Kargen and Shaluhk, only to witness the great Orc chieftain pushing Rada to the ground. Her armour was blood-soaked, yet her sword remained clean, or so it appeared as Kargen handed it to Athgar.

"I bring you the Queen of Novarsk," he announced. "Or should I say, former queen?"

Athgar stared down at Rada, noting the defiance in her eyes. "What have you to say for yourself?"

She spat at him, although he was too distant for her to hit.

"Take her away and put her in chains," he ordered. "We shall deal with her back in Ebenstadt."

AFTERMATH

Spring 1108 SR

Athgar glanced around the room. Seven thanes were present, along with the Dwarf, Belgast Ridgehand, who, this day, would represent the interests of Ebenstadt. In addition, four Orc chieftains and their shamans attended, bringing the total count to sixteen: eighteen if he included himself and Natalia, who was present in her position as warmaster.

At the moment, everyone was quiet, with all eyes on Athgar as he pondered how to begin. A loud squeal interrupted his thoughts when Oswyn ran into the room, narrowly missing the edge of a table. Behind her raced Agar, coming to a halt as he saw everyone now looking at him.

"Sorry," said the young Orc. "Oswyn got out of hand."

Athgar chuckled before rising from his seat and scooping up his daughter as she ran past.

"Are you causing trouble again?" he asked, his mood lightened by her presence.

Agar drew closer, and Athgar had to remind himself the young Orc was only four, for he was the size of a Human eight-year-old. "She keeps trying to take my axe."

"Give her your old wooden one, but keep an eye on her. I wouldn't want her to get hurt."

"Are you sure? Mother is always telling me Human younglings are delicate compared to us." Agar looked at Natalia.

"She's a Therengian," she replied, "just like her father. See that she learns respect for it."

"I shall," said Agar as he held out his hand. Athgar put Oswyn down, and she ran over to her tribe brother, placing her hand within his.

"You be good," said Natalia, "and do what Agar says."

Everyone sat quietly, watching them leave until Grazuhk broke the silence.

"He does you proud," she said, looking at Kargen. "He shall make a fine hunter one day and follow his father to become chieftain."

"Perhaps," said Kargen, "but the path is his to follow, not mine to direct."

"Would that Humans felt the same way," said Natalia. "Then we might not have to deal with the likes of Rada."

"You mean QUEEN Rada," corrected Faramund, the Thane of Farwald.

"I mean Rada," she replied. "She no longer rules, nor is it certain she ever will again. However, that decision is, of course, up to this council to decide."

"Yes," said Athgar, "which brings us to the reason for this gathering. It falls on the council to determine the fate of our prisoners, including the erstwhile Queen of Novarsk."

Wynfrith leaned forward in her chair, placing her elbows on the table. "There are many who would suggest we execute them, although that is a tad excessive to my mind.

"Or we could enthrall them," suggested Cynrith, Thane of the newly restored Ashborne.

"No," said Athgar. "There's no place in Therengia for thralls. Slavery is a vile practice, and I will not condone its presence."

"Then what would you suggest? Imprisonment?"

"I was thinking of offering them up for ransom. This war cost us greatly, not only in people but in coins. I propose we recoup some of that loss by allowing common soldiers to go free after paying their value in coins."

"You can't be serious?"

"Why not? It works for the nobility, doesn't it?" He turned to Natalia. "I would value your thoughts."

"It's true," said Natalia. "Ransom is a common and effective way to deal with prisoners of noble blood. It would also help recover badly needed funds."

"But these are commoners," said Raleth, "with little to their name."

"Then they shall pay less," said Athgar. "Details must be worked out, but the principle remains. In addition, each warrior released would take an oath never to take up arms against Therengia again, under pain of death."

"I don't like this," said Cynrith. "How can we trust them?"

"To start with, we treat them as civilized beings. We cannot continue to win over our enemies by the force of arms alone. Rather, we must make efforts to establish ourselves as a legitimate land with laws and customs understood by all."

"Are you suggesting we adopt skrolling customs?"

Athgar winced at the use of the word. "They are not skrollings," he replied. "That word marks them as outsiders. Therengia encompasses many different cultures now, not only our own. We need to learn to live with them, not spend lifetimes trying to suppress them."

"He's right," offered Belgast. "I might remind you that, by your definition, this kingdom consists of more skrollings than Therengians, or did you forget how many of us live in Ebenstadt?"

"Let us put this issue aside," said Kargen. "This bickering will lead nowhere. The matter at hand is what to do with the captured warriors. I say the High Thane's proposal has merit. I, for one, have no desire to watch over prisoners, not to mention looking after slaves. Do you?" He stared at Cynrith, and the thane backed down.

"I have no objection," the man answered.

"Then let us take a vote," said Athgar. "All in favour of this plan to ransom the prisoners?"

All hands rose.

"Then it's settled. Who would like to oversee the arrangements?"

"I shall," offered Wynfrith. "Although I need to discuss it with Natalia before proceeding, as we have to determine how to establish a prisoner's worth, and I would be interested in her ideas."

"I should be glad to help in any capacity," said Natalia.

"That brings up the matter of Rada herself," noted Athgar. "I should very much like to hear your opinions."

"We cannot let her go, even with a ransom," said Aswulf, Thane of Thaneford. "She is far too dangerous. Within months of her return, she'd raise a new army, and we'd be back to more fighting."

Everyone nodded in agreement. Athgar's gaze fell on Raleth. "You've held her in custody these past few weeks. What do you think?"

"That she's despised. There are rumours she conspired to kill her father and seize the throne. Not exactly the type of person we could trust. There's also the matter of her invasion of our lands."

"Come, you are a thane now. If the choice were yours, what would you do with her?"

"Imprisonment is the only option," said Raleth.

"Why would you say that?"

Therengia. In our case, each village, be it Human or Orc, might be considered a shire, except for Runewald, of course, since it houses both an Orc tribe and a Human village."

"And what is a reeve?"

"A person designated by the ruler to see to the administration of the region."

"But the chieftain does that."

"That's true," said Natalia, "but if the tribe were particularly large, it would be hard for him to rule over everything. Thus, he might designate someone to take on that responsibility."

"And Human kingdoms do this?"

"They do. Some even go so far as to appoint separate individuals to rule on matters of law. We call them judges."

"It is strange to think of such things," said Shaluhk, "yet the larger this land of ours gets, the more I understand the need."

"It also depends on how active the ruler wants to be. Many barons insist on doing everything themselves, while others would gladly pass that burden on to someone else."

"What of the family?" said Shaluhk. "Were they operated in such a manner?"

"In a sense, but their entire hierarchy is based on magical ability rather than birth. A powerful spellcaster will advance rapidly to the top, while someone less gifted is relegated to the lower levels for the rest of their life."

"If that is true, you would have been destined to rise high in this family."

"We refer to it as the family, but it's far from that. If anything, it's more of a loose collection of like-minded people more akin to an army than blood relatives."

"One does not need blood to make a family," said Shaluhk. "We are living proof of that."

"Indeed we are, and thank the Saints for that… or the Ancestors, if you're so inclined."

"Or the Gods," said Shaluhk. "You might as well thank them all while you are at it."

"You are getting quite philosophical," said Kargen. "Is that the right word?"

"Yes," said Natalia, "but I'm surprised to hear you say that. She is, of course, but it's not a word I would expect an Orc to use or a Therengian, for that matter."

"It is the influence of Tonfer Garul. Ever since his arrival here, I have been intrigued by his thoughts. Never before have I met a true scholar, let alone one who is an Orc."

"I've been busy of late," said Athgar, "what with the war and all. How is he doing with the archives?"

"He has spent much time with Dunstan, the bard. I believe he intends to document as much oral history as he can."

"And where is he keeping all this information?"

"In the old Cunar commandery," replied Kargen, "although I suppose it belongs to the Temple Knights of Saint Mathew now."

"I wonder how the Church feels about that?" said Natalia. "I can't imagine the Cunars are too happy with the loss of property."

"If they wanted to keep it," said Athgar, "they shouldn't have declared war on us. As far as I'm concerned, it's the spoils of war, and if we choose to gift it to the Mathewites, there's little they can say about it."

"My bondmate," said Natalia, with a chuckle. "Ever the diplomat."

"In any event," said Belgast, "the Temple Knights of Saint Mathew saw fit to accept our invitation to bring more knights here, necessitating the promotion of Brother Yaromir to captain."

"Temple Captain," corrected Natalia. "It's a subtle distinction, but an important one."

"He's also agreed to take on the responsibility of patrolling the city streets," said the Dwarf. "I'm told crime has gone down significantly in the last few months."

"See?" said Athgar. "The Petty Kingdoms can be civilized after all."

"Now the war is over," interrupted Kargen, "what is the next task awaiting our attention?"

"Good question," replied Athgar. "I suppose Master Rugg can continue building stone walls around the rest of the villages like he did in Runewald, and we'll make more warbows for the other tribes. Who knows, maybe we'll settle down and have a few more children? What do you think, Natalia?"

"I would like that," she replied. "I'm also looking forward to allowing Oswyn to grow up in peace and quiet."

Athgar knitted his brows. "I'm afraid that's not likely unless you believe the family gave up on her?"

Natalia sighed. "No, I suppose not. I wish I could go there and reason with them somehow, but I doubt that would work."

"It is what comes with being powerful," said Shaluhk. "They fear you, while at the same time they covet your power. As you said previously, the family spent years trying to produce a mage of your capabilities. You slipped from their grasp, and they are eager to get you back."

"Or Oswyn, and therein lies the problem. While the family is still out there, she'll never be safe."

"No one here will ever let anything happen to your daughter, sister-mine. She is of the Red Hand now, and nothing can change that."

"You're right, of course," said Natalia. "Yet here we are, still seeking legitimacy in the eyes of the Petty Kingdoms even as the family influences the courts of kings."

"It is an uphill battle, as your Athgar would say. A difficult journey, but not an impossible one, and a path we will travel together." They rounded a corner to find themselves facing their temporary lodgings. "Ah, here we are at last."

"Finally," said Kargen. "I am looking forward to what Skora has prepared."

They stepped inside to the scent of roasting meat. The great Orc chieftain's stomach gurgled, leading Oswyn to giggle hysterically. So intense was the laughter that the others felt compelled to join in.

"Come," said Athgar. "Let's find out what we have waiting for us, shall we?"

Skora soon appeared. "We cleared away the table in the dining hall. Better to eat, I think, in the Therengian style than that of the Petty Kingdoms, wouldn't you agree?"

They took seats on the floor in a rough circle. Skora directed several youths to pour wine and hand out the food. Serving at what passed for the court of the High Thane was considered a great honour, and many of them would soon be old enough to join the fyrd. How better to learn of the rulers of Therengia?

Athgar waited until everyone's cups were full before raising his on high. "Let us drink to absent friends," he said, "and to those who carry on in their absence." He paused. "To Artoch."

"And Uhdrig," added Shaluhk.

"And all the others who made this day possible," said Kargen. "May they now enjoy the fruits of their labours."

HOME

Spring 1108 SR

A gar pulled back on the bowstring, lining up his target.
"*Now let fly,*" said Laruhk.
The young Orc loosed his arrow, watching as it sailed forth to narrowly miss the tree. He stomped his foot in frustration.

"*I will never master this thing,*" the young Orc complained.

"*You must have patience. The bow is not a weapon that comes easily.*"

"*Yet it is the lifeblood of our tribe, and I am unable to wield it. I will disappoint my father.*"

"*You disappoint no one,*" said Laruhk. "*Your father, like you, did not take easily to the bow.*"

"*That surprises me. Was he not a great hunter?*"

"*He can use a bow when needed, but it is not his calling. Now, give him an axe, and there is none who can outfight him.*"

"*Did he use a bow as a youngling?*"

"*He did, or at least he tried to, but some Orcs develop later in life.*"

Agar stiffened. "*Are you saying he was weak?*"

"*Not at all, merely that his strengths lay elsewhere. Your father is a natural leader, and that is something quite rare. You likely do not remember, but he led us here, crossing a hostile kingdom and vicious mountains to bring the tribe to safety. Very few could have accomplished that feat. I have no doubt had it not been for your father, we all would have perished.*"

"*She spoke with the spirits of the Ancestors. I do not believe she expected to see ghosts.*"

"*What else would she think would happen?*"

Laruhk shrugged. "*Who can say? She was still a youngling—we both were. Can you say you were any different at that age?*"

"*No, I suppose not. Very well, what do we do about this?*"

"*About what?*"

"*About Agar's propensity for fire. Do we tell Kargen?*"

"*I think I shall tell Shaluhk first. I have known her longer.*"

"*Of course you have. She is your sister.*"

"*Yes, but as her older brother, I feel I owe it to her.*"

"*You are twins,*" said Ushog. "*You are the same age.*"

"*That is one way of looking at it, but I still came out first.*"

Ushog shook her head. "*Did you? I sometimes wonder.*"

Shaluhk spooned the porridge into Oswyn's mouth. "*There, there,*" she soothed, speaking in the Orcish tongue. The child stared back, her gaze firmly fixed on the shaman's face.

"She loves you," said Natalia. "How is it that you can get her to eat that, while I can't?"

"Maybe she prefers us to speak in our native tongue? Your Orc is getting better. You should give it a try."

"I believe I shall." She watched as her daughter swallowed, then giggled. "Thank you for doing this," Natalia continued. "I've been so worn out since our return from Ebenstadt."

"It is understandable, considering all you have been up to. Besides, Oswyn is no bother at all."

Skora appeared, bearing two wooden cups. "I thought you two might like something to drink."

"Yes, thank you," said Natalia.

The old woman set the drinks down and stared at Oswyn. "She has a very happy soul. I can't remember a child so full of life."

"Was Athgar like that?"

"Not with a younger sister to take care of, he wasn't. I've discovered, over the years, there is nothing more inclined to kill the joy of early life than having a younger sibling."

"That's a rather gloomy way of looking at things."

Skora shrugged. "It's merely an observation. I speak in generalities, of course."

"Have you known no siblings who got along?"

"A few, but it was the exception, not the rule. Not to say they would argue or anything, rather that the older child invariably becomes responsible for those younger. It matures a person quickly, too quickly, if you ask me. Parents should take more care not to steal their offspring's childhood."

Natalia turned to Shaluhk. "What about you? Would you agree with Skora's assessment?"

"It is rare amongst Orcs of our tribe to have more than one youngling."

"You have Laruhk."

"Yes, but we are twins, not separate births."

"Does Laruhk know that?"

Shaluhk laughed. "He always claims to be the oldest, yet somehow I became the responsible one."

"Perhaps he'll settle down now he's bonded."

"We can only hope."

Laruhk's voice echoed throughout the hut. "Shaluhk? Are you there?"

"In here," the shaman replied.

He entered, with Ushog following him in. They both looked uncomfortable as if they were hiding something.

"Well?" said Shaluhk. "Why are you just standing there? If you have something to get off your mind, then say it."

"I need to speak to you," said Laruhk, "about Agar."

"What about Agar? He has not been hurt, has he?"

"No, nothing of the sort." He looked around the hut, his eyes taking in the presence of Natalia. "Should I come back later?"

"No. You can speak freely. We are all family here."

Laruhk sat down, Ushog by his side, holding his hand.

"Well?" said Shaluhk. "Out with it."

"I am of the opinion Agar is… gifted."

"Gifted?"

"Yes, I believe he has it within him to become a master of flame."

Shaluhk laughed. "He is still a youngling, Brother."

"Yes, but he shows a remarkable capacity for making fire, and you know what they say about great suffering…" His voice trailed off as he read the pain in his sister's face. Natalia expected a quick rebuke, but the shaman turned to face her instead.

"What do you think, Nat-Alia? Could my brother be correct?"

"It's difficult to say. I started manifesting before I was six, which is considered rare for Humans. Admittedly, Agar is four, but he's more akin to an eight-year-old in Human terms. It's within the realm of possibility that what Laruhk suggests is true."

"And if it is, what do we do about it?"

"I would suggest Athgar talk with him. He must be apprised of the dangers."

"Dangers?" said Shaluhk.

"I had an affinity for water," explained Natalia, "but other than calming flowing rivers or calling fish, there was little I could affect. A future master of flame, however, is far more likely to inadvertently start a fire."

"You believe that likely?"

"At such a young age, there is little control, but Agar is bright. If we talk to him of what is transpiring, I'm sure he could easily learn to control his urges."

"Urges?"

"Yes. Sorry, aside from Athgar, my knowledge of Fire Magic is limited to what they taught us at the Volstrum. There, we learned practitioners of pyromancy are particularly prone to the power of fire. As one of the most destructive schools of magic to learn, without proper training, many students end up..." Natalia's voice trailed off.

"You are talking of self-immolation," said Shaluhk. "The concept is not unknown to me. Even Athgar almost succumbed to such a fate. Had you not been there that day, he would have perished."

"I still don't understand how I saved him," said Natalia, "nor can I bear to think of the ramifications had I failed."

"Amongst the Orcs, the tradition is different. A master of flame will take an apprentice as soon as one demonstrates the potential, but this is typically at a much older age than Agar is now."

"Artoch would know what to do. He showed Athgar how to harness his inner flame."

"Then I shall call for his spirit to guide me," said Shaluhk.

"Do you want me to talk to Athgar?"

"Do you think he would be amenable to the idea?"

Natalia smiled. "I think he would be thrilled."

"Then please do."

"When would you like to start?"

"How about right now? It appears Oswyn has drifted off to sleep." Shaluhk looked around the room. "Skora? Would you take her?"

"Of course," replied the old woman. "It would be my pleasure."

Agar stepped into the room to see the High Thane staring into the fire.

"Come in," said Athgar. "Take a seat opposite me."

"Mother said I was to speak to you," said the youngling, "although she did not say why. Am I in trouble?"

"Not in the least. How has your day gone so far?"

"As usual as any other?"

"Laruhk tells me you know how to create a fire. That's quite the accomplishment for an Orc of your years."

Agar shrugged, looking for a moment just like his uncle. "It is nothing."

"On the contrary," Athgar continued. "It's quite a significant feat. You should be proud of your accomplishments. Are there any other skills you have that you'd like to share?"

"Like what? That I speak the common tongue of Humans in addition to my own? Almost the entire tribe can do that."

"Tell me what you think of fire."

The youngling stared across at Athgar. "I do not understand. You ask me to speak of flames—they are hot. What else is there to know?"

"Do you fear them?"

"No. Why? Should I?"

"Fire is the most destructive element in the land. It can consume anything."

"You tell me that which I already know."

"Do you remember much of when you were younger?"

"No. Mother tells me a Fire Mage badly burned me, but I do not remember."

"It's true," said Athgar. "My own sister, Ethwyn, betrayed us and kidnapped Oswyn. When you tried to intervene, she unleashed a fire streak at you. If it hadn't been for your mother's healing, you would have died."

"I believe you, but that was in the past. We are now in the present."

"Have you heard of Artoch?"

"Yes. He was the master of flame who taught you how to harness your inner spark. Everyone knows that story. Why do you ask?"

"There are those of us who have come to think you might contain an inner spark of your own."

"Me? A master of flame? How? Neither of my parents is so gifted."

"Yes, but neither were mine. They say great suffering can unlock power of this nature. In my case, it was likely the destruction of my village that precipitated the release of my inner spark. I believe yours was when Ethwyn set you ablaze."

A mild look of panic crossed Agar's face. "Am I in danger?"

"No, at least not yet. I suspect it will be years before you are able to wield magic, but it would be wise to prepare sooner rather than later."

"Prepare, how?"

"If you are willing," said Athgar, "I should like to teach you more about Fire Magic and help you learn to meditate."

"Are you suggesting we walk around the village handing your ring out to everyone we meet?"

Natalia chuckled. "That would be a bit awkward, wouldn't it?" She placed the ring back on her own hand and watched as the gem turned almost black.

"Good to see you've still got your power," mused Athgar. "That reminds me, I spoke with Agar today."

"And?"

"I showed him how to meditate."

"And did he find his inner spark?"

"He says he did, but apparently, it was quite small."

"That's to be expected, considering his age. What you see as the inner spark is what the Volstrum called potential."

"Just how common is Water Magic?"

"Stanislav could tell you much better than I—he was the mage hunter."

"Then let me put it another way; how many students were at the Volstrum at any one time?"

"It varied. There were over half a dozen in my intake, and that's only girls."

"How many intakes are there a year?"

"Only one, but the numbers can vary from year to year. A student typically receives two years of casting training once they're unleashed. Still, you must remember they spend years before that learning the rudiments, not to mention both men and women are inducted into the family."

"Any way you look at it, that's a lot of spellcasters."

"Indeed. It's what allows them to command a presence at almost every court in the Petty Kingdoms."

"Except here," corrected Athgar.

"So you're not counting me, then?"

"I didn't think you still considered yourself a member of the family?"

"I don't, although now you mention it, the name has come in handy on occasion, at least when dealing with the Petty Kingdoms. Aside from that, I'm happy to be referred to simply as Natalia."

Athgar looked at her ring. "Where does magerite come from, precisely?"

"I've heard it's mined somewhere in Ruzhina, but as to where, I'm not sure. I do know, however, there are two types, red and blue, but I suppose there could be others."

"Does it have to be enchanted to glow like that?"

"No," she replied. "It does that in its natural state, although I imagine the raw gem would make it harder to see the colour." She held her hand out, admiring the ring. "Once cut, it really catches the light, wouldn't you say?"

"Not as much as your eyes," said Athgar.

"Why, High Thane, I do believe you're flirting with me. We should talk of such things more often."

"Whenever you like," he responded, moving closer.

They embraced, then shared a passionate kiss. It would have lasted longer had Oswyn not taken the opportunity to cry out.

"Sorry," said Natalia, breaking the hug. "It seems our daughter wants some attention."

"Agar," called out Oswyn.

Athgar couldn't help but smile. "Well, it's not us she wants after all."

"No," agreed Natalia. "She wants her brother."

"Funny how she accepts him as family."

"You accept Kargen as your brother."

He laughed. "I suppose I do, don't I? I never really thought about it, but Kargen and Laruhk are more like family than my own parents... or my sister." His mood darkened.

"Ethwyn was twisted by Korascajan," said Natalia. "You can't blame yourself for that. You and I know what happens when the family gets hold of someone. Do you believe one day she can be persuaded to come to her senses?"

"No. She kidnapped Oswyn and tried to burn Agar to death. I have no room in my heart to forgive her."

"And if you met her again?"

"Then I would do my best to kill her. It's the only way to keep Oswyn safe, and I have no doubt you'd do the same."

"You're right," said Natalia. "I hate to admit it, but I wouldn't even hesitate. Does that make me a bad person?"

"No, it makes you a mother."

"I imagine her skill will have improved considerably since we last saw her."

"Are you worried she might return?"

"To Therengia? I doubt it. We're safe here, and everyone in the village knows her by sight. She wouldn't be able to set one foot inside Runewald before an arrow found a home in her chest. That doesn't preclude the possibility she might plot with others to somehow take revenge."

"Well," said Athgar, "we never meet with outsiders without lots of people present, so if she sent someone in after us, they'd have a hard time getting anywhere."

"She's a Sartellian, and they're notorious for being powerful."

"You think their magic is a danger?"

"Not as much as it used to be. Since Rugg replaced our wooden palisade with a stone wall, there's less to worry about on that score. However, a concentrated effort could still do a great deal of damage, not necessarily to us, but to the village in general."

"Then we must remain vigilant." His gaze wandered to Oswyn, who was reaching out. "She really wants that ring."

Natalia handed it to their daughter, who then ran off with a shriek of delight, yelling for Agar.

"I hope you weren't expecting that back," said Athgar.

Agar, drawn by the noise, appeared at the door.

"Blue ring," said Oswyn, holding her trophy aloft. She placed it in his hands, and the colour quickly dissipated, leaving her with bitter disappointment. "Blue gone."

The Orc placed the ring back in her hand, watching her face light up as the gem changed colour once more. "There," he said. "The ring is mended. It is now the colour of a blueberry."

"Blueberry," said Oswyn, placing the gem into her mouth.

Agar reached out quickly. "No, Oswyn. Do not eat it."

She stopped, then let her mouth fall open, allowing him to fish out the ring.

"This goes on your hand," he said, "not in your mouth."

"Agar eat."

"A ring is not to be eaten."

"Agar eat."

"It is not food, Oswyn."

"Agar eat!" the young girl demanded.

The Orc sighed, then popped the ring into his mouth, pretending to munch away at it, even going so far as to rub his stomach to aid in the game.

Oswyn giggled uncontrollably, but then Agar went rigid.

"Agar?" called out Natalia. "What is it?"

He spat the ring out, letting it fall into his hand. "I am afraid I broke it."

His face turned a darker green, betraying his embarrassment. Natalia moved closer to take a look. The pale-blue magerite was, from the top, cut into an octagonal shape nestled in a setting of silver. Somehow, the gem became dislodged, twisting to the side, no longer aligned with its housing.

"This is strange," said Natalia. "It looks as though the magerite rotates." She took it, slipping it onto her finger and watched as it turned back to its familiar dark-blue. Soon it was almost black, which only accentuated that the setting and the gem were misaligned.

She used her fingers to twist the gem, holding it up before her to examine it. "Something has released the gem. It's popped up slightly." She rotated it farther to be rewarded by a slight sound.

"What was that?" asked Athgar, moving closer.

Natalia stared at the ring, not quite believing her eyes. "A small metal pin has popped out."

"A pin? Whatever for?"

"I have no idea. I've never seen its like before. The gem has also sunk back into its setting." She tried twisting the gem again, but to no avail."

"I am truly sorry," said Agar.

"There's nothing to be sorry for," said Natalia. "You did us a great favour. I've had this ring for years, but I never knew it could do this?"

"Whatever this is," added Athgar. "That pin is very small. Could it be a weapon?"

"Too small. How could it be a weapon?"

"Perhaps as a way of administering poison?"

"It's tiny," said Natalia, "and even if that were the case, I should think there's a much greater risk of injuring the person wearing it." She moved closer to a torch. "Just a moment," she said, then was rewarded with a very faint click. "The gem pulls up, then rotates." She twisted it again, this time in the other direction, and the small pin disappeared. The magerite, now having completed its movement, lowered back into the setting. "It seems to be spring-loaded."

"We should take this to Belgast," suggested Athgar. "He may know of such things."

"And we will, in time, but we only just got home. The last thing I want to do now is ride all the way back to Ebenstadt. Whatever this is, it's been a secret for years. A few more weeks won't make much of a difference."

"I do not understand," said Agar. "How did I activate it?"

"Your teeth must have forced the gem up when you pretended to chew it."

"Yes," added Athgar, "and then the gem rotated while in your mouth. If not for your little game, we would never have discovered this thing... whatever it is."

"Agreed," said Natalia. "Although I wouldn't recommend you go around eating rings in the future. I hate to think what this could have done to you had you swallowed it."

"Where did the ring come from?" asked the young Orc.

"It was given to me when I graduated from the Volstrum. Each graduate is given one, although it's a brooch or amulet rather than a ring in some cases. It's meant to display the magical power of a member of the family."

"How?"

Agar nodded sagely. "You are wise, Father."

"And you are far too serious for an Orc of your winters."

"We live in serious times."

Kargen looked at Shaluhk, who appeared resigned to her son's demeanour. "He is not wrong," she said. "For two years, we have been at war. He remembers little of peace."

"Then let us change that," suggested Kargen. He turned to Athgar. "What do you think?"

The High Thane knew what was coming. "A feast? Precisely my thought. I shall send word to all the villages, each to celebrate our great victory over Novarsk in their own way."

"And when is this great feast to take place?" asked Shaluhk. "It is one thing to announce such a thing, quite another to make all the preparations."

"Would a ten-day suffice? That would allow time for word to travel."

"That would be most acceptable."

"Then so be it," said Athgar.

Kargen wore a big grin. "And we must organize a hunt to provide food! I hear the deer have returned now the warmer weather is upon us, and my bow grows restless."

"As does mine," added Laruhk. "It longs to hunt meat instead of enemy warriors. When do we start?"

Natalia rose to her feet. "It's clear you have much to plan. Shaluhk and I will consult with Skora and make arrangements for the celebration itself while you see to the provisioning of meat." She glanced at the shaman. "Is that acceptable to you?"

Shaluhk rose. "Of course. I thought we might try something a little different. While we were in Ebenstadt, Belgast introduced us to something called pudding…" Their voices trailed off as they left the fire.

"It appears the decision has been made," said Kargen. "And here I thought I was the one in charge of such things."

Athgar laughed. "We are part of a greater thing, you and I, a family, and that comes with its own rewards."

ATTACK

Spring 1108 SR

Anatoli Stormwind crouched, looking out over the field at the distant walls of Runewald. "A difficult entrance, I think."

"Nonsense," replied Valaran Sartellian. "We shall be in amongst them before they even know we're here." He glanced behind to where half a dozen armed men waited. They were the finest warriors the family could muster, easily capable of taking on a bunch of barbarians. He returned his attention to the walls.

"The gate is the key," said Valaran. "Seize that, and we'll have everything we need."

"Getting in isn't the problem. It's escaping that bothers me."

"Once we reach the target, I shall cast ring of fire, taking us all to safety."

"And if we're attacked before you complete the spell?" asked Anatoli.

"Then I must rely on the rest of you to keep me safe until I'm done. I know it's difficult to believe, but I've done this sort of thing before."

"Kidnapping a child?"

"Not precisely," said the Fire Mage, "but I once infiltrated the castle of Grimfrost to extricate one of your brethren."

"Grimfrost? Never heard of it."

"Nor would I expect you to. It lies in the Southwest Region of the Petty Kingdoms."

"Is it Dwarven?" asked Anatoli.

"No, although its architecture was."

"I would feel better if they let me learn the spell of recall."

"Don't be absurd," said Valaran. "You're not powerful enough for such a spell. You must bide your time and wait until you grow into your magic."

"I am quite comfortable with my magic," replied the Water Mage, "but this insistence of working with Korascajan makes things difficult, to say the least."

"Do we not both serve the family?"

"Of course, but there seems to be a difference of opinion as to who is in charge of this task."

"I am the more powerful mage," insisted Valaran.

"Yes, I know you are, but the soldiers belong to the Volstrum."

"Come, you worry too much. Night will soon be upon us, and then we can make our move. Succeed in this, and there shall be plenty of accolades for us both."

They returned their attention to the distant walls. As the sun disappeared over the horizon, a soft glow emanated from the village.

"Looks like they're having a celebration," said Valaran. "If we're lucky, our target might be even easier to find."

"This is a fool's errand," replied Anatoli. "Natalia Stormwind is a powerful caster. She won't sit by and let us take her child."

"Come now. What is raw power when compared to years of experience? I am far more capable than her in the casting of spells."

"And the Orcs?"

"They are a savage race who will run at the first demonstration of my power."

"Clearly, you think a lot of yourself. Did you forget they managed to defeat the Holy Army? Not to mention that of Novarsk."

"Do you think an army honestly rivals the might of a mage unleashed? You give them too much credit."

"I do not agree with your assessment," said the Water Mage, "but we are committed to this enterprise, nonetheless. Let it not be said a Stormwind backs down. How shall we proceed?"

"The gate is the first priority," said Valaran. "Once that is done, we'll move quickly, sowing confusion. To that end, I brought along some help." He pointed to the large bag he'd tossed to their left.

"What is it?"

"Clothes. We shall dress as they do, making it difficult for them to identify us."

"You really think that will work?"

"Of course. To help, I'll conjure smoke. Between that irritating their eyes and our ruse, we should have little difficulty getting to our quarry. Just remember, if you're not within range when I cast my ring of fire, you'll be left behind."

"And if any of our foes are caught up in the spell?"

"We are recalling to the Volstrum, where guards will be expecting us. Don't worry, my friend; all is taken care of." After changing their attire, the Fire Mage returned his attention to the distant gate. "Come. It is dark and time for us to make our move."

Valaran led them through the field in a crouch, the better to avoid detection. They drew nearer to the gate, and he motioned for them to halt. Atop the entrance stood a pair of guards, and he pointed to them.

"You take the Orc," he whispered, "and I'll take the Therengian."

At a nod from Anatoli, he began casting. A few brief words of power were all that were needed, and then a tendril of flame shot out, flying across the distance to wrap itself around the guard's neck. A strangled cry escaped the man just before Valaran yanked his hands back with a jerk, pulling the man from his perch.

Anatoli, meanwhile, cast a spell of his own. Ice shards flew towards the Orc, splattering against the creature's back, knocking him from view.

"Now," called out Valaran. "Run!"

Their feet carried them swiftly, their own men keeping pace behind them. The gate, a modest affair, consisted of wooden doors hinged on either side, with a drop bar in place. However, the Fire Mage wasted little time, electing to throw his arms out in an under-the-arm motion. A ball of flame sprang from his hands, rolling across the ground, igniting the grass as it went. Flames exploded, leaping into the air as they struck the door.

Anatoli paused and began calling on his inner power to summon a creature of solid ice. The warriors split to either side, eager to give the thing space, for although they didn't understand what it was, they knew the lumbering brute was dangerous. The ice golem stepped forward and smashed the scorched gate with its fists. Wood splintered, weakened by fire, and then the doors flew open, revealing a mass of startled Humans and Orcs sitting around a great firepit.

Valaran, following in the creature's wake, tossed streams of fire left and right. He halted only long enough to throw a spell of smoke on the fire before continuing with his wild casting. One of his men took a hit from a mage within the village and froze solid before breaking into ice fragments.

A movement to his right caught his attention, and he thrust out his hand, conjuring forth a wall of fire to cut off any possible counterattack. He felt raw power flowing through him, the rush, as magic erupted from his fingers. He was Valaran Sartellian, a great Fire Mage—nothing could stop him.

Anatoli watched as smoke billowed forth, blinding the crowd. He'd located their target right before Valaran's spell went off, so he sent the golem towards her. Now, unable to see much in the smoke, he merely followed the colossus, secure he would be seen as less of a threat while his servant wandered the village.

The plan was progressing much better than he'd hoped. Villagers ran in all directions, eager to be away from the violence of battle. Those who remained took up arms, but the smoke blinded them, making resistance all but impossible.

The first sign of real trouble was when he saw ghostly forms approaching. Initially, they were indistinct, melding in with the smoke, making them nearly invisible. These figures, however, moved with purpose, unlike the villagers, ignoring the smoke and coming directly for him. They cut down one of his men, then moved closer, their spears reaching out towards him. He looked on in horror as they coalesced into Orcs only a moment before a tip of iron silenced his voice forever.

Valaran, hearing the screams of his victims, revelled in them. He absently shot off another streak of fire, igniting a hut before turning his attention to their target. As a Fire Mage, he'd learned long ago to ignore the irritation of smoke. Instead, he embraced it, feeling his way through its obstruction to get closer to his prey.

He finally spotted the young girl standing behind her mother, who was trying to take down the golem. Valaran rushed forward, eager to gain his prize, but an arrow hit him in the leg, causing him to stumble. Suddenly a young Orc appeared out of the smoke, another arrow nocked.

Up went the mage's hands, sending forth a spiral of flame to wrap around the youngster, whipping up the air and pinning him in place. Valaran laughed out loud at the child's helplessness, but it was short-lived as an axe took him in the back of the head. The Fire Mage tumbled forward, his spell forever broken.

Natalia poured everything she had into the golem, but ice did little damage against the great creature. She glimpsed Laruhk rushing forward, his axe taking a chunk out of the monster's leg, yet still, it kept advancing.

She risked a quick glance behind her to see Oswyn still standing there, complete terror filling her eyes. Athgar rushed up beside her, his arms thrown out in front, directing a stream of fire. The creature came closer, smashing aside Laruhk, who sailed through the air to land unconscious.

Natalia switched tactics, directing her spells towards the ground, ice forming around the creature's leg, slowing it until finally pinning it in place.

The Orcs, spurred on by this success, resumed the offensive, joined by Therengians who had returned with their weapons. Great chunks of ice were sliced off the golem before it teetered to one side, then crashed to the ground, its legs no longer able to bear its weight. Athgar rushed forward, pouring forth all the fire he could muster.

"Enough!" shouted Natalia, clutching his arm. "It is defeated."

He halted, turning his attention to dissipating the pall of smoke hanging over the village. Slowly, it cleared, revealing the devastation.

Kargen stood over a body, examining it closely. Agar stood by Oswyn, bow in hand, looking around for any danger that might still threaten. Shaluhk, meanwhile, was busy dismissing the spirit warriors she'd summoned.

"This was the family's doing," said Natalia. She moved to crouch by the dead Water Mage and looked at his ring. "A Stormwind, by the look of it."

"This one wears a brooch," said Kargen.

Natalia began shaking. "They came for Oswyn."

Athgar moved closer, holding her tight.

"Will there be no end to this?" she asked.

"It's all right," he soothed. "We defeated them."

"Have we?" she spat out. "How long until they strike again? Even when they're not here, we fear their return. We can't live like this. Something must be done."

"You're right," said Athgar. "The question is what?"

Natalia looked down to where her hands were clasped. She rubbed them together as if washing away dirt. Her eyes caught a glimmer from the fire. "This ring," she said. "Illiana wanted me to have it. Why do you think that was?"

"I haven't any idea. We don't even know what it signifies."

"No, but it must be important, else why give it up?"

"Then it's time we found out more about it. We'll leave for Ebenstadt in the morning and see what Belgast makes of it."

His eyes drifted over to Oswyn and Agar. The young Orc stooped by the Sartellian's body, examining the man's brooch. The magerite was colourless, evidence of the fellow's death, but it turned a crimson colour as the youngling took it in hand.

"I shall send out hunters," said Kargen. "If these men had any more accomplices nearby, we will soon find them."

Shaluhk shook her head. "They were incredibly bold."

"Or stupid," added Laruhk. The Orc hunter was sitting up now, rubbing the back of his head while Ushog comforted him.

"Back to your huts," called out Athgar. "The celebration is over. Rest up while you can. There will be much work needed tomorrow." He turned to Natalia. "How far away is Karslev?"

"If you're thinking of taking an army to defeat them, think again. There are hundreds of miles between them and us. Far too many to seriously consider something like that."

"We cannot let this go unpunished."

"Then we will take this fight to them," said Natalia.

"But how?" asked Athgar. "You just indicated it's too far."

"True, but I can no longer sit idly by while the family plots against our loved ones."

"Tell me of the family's home," called out Kargen. "Perhaps there is a way we can take retribution against them after all."

"What are you suggesting?"

"They invaded our home. The time has come to turn the bow in the other direction."

"I agree, but I'm not sure how we could do that?" said Natalia. "The family is powerful, far more so than us."

"It still has a home, does it not? What if we damaged the Volstrum?"

"I doubt that could be accomplished. The place is huge, but now that you've suggested it, there may be another way."

"Go on," urged Athgar.

"The Volstrum trains mages, but the real power is found at the head of the family's home."

"And where is that?"

"Stormwind Manor. It's been handed down through the line of grand mistresses over the years. I never saw it myself, but my understanding is it's nothing more than a large house and estate. Stanislav might know more though."

"It is likely to be heavily guarded," said Kargen. "How many should we take?"

"I'm afraid strength isn't the way," said Natalia. "And in any case, there are no Orcs in Karslev. You would raise too much suspicion. Better to proceed alone, I think."

"I'm coming," said Athgar. "Oswyn is my daughter too."

"You can't go. You're the High Thane."

In answer, the Therengian turned to his closest friend. "Kargen, would you consent to rule in my place until my return?"

"I am not sure the Council of Thanes would agree to that."

"They made me High Thane. That gives me the right to appoint whomever I want, as far as I'm concerned."

"Very well. I shall agree," said the Orc chieftain.

"Excellent," said Athgar. "We leave knowing our home is in good hands; however, I will take measures to ensure the thanes are aware of my decision before I leave."

"You can not take Oswyn," said Shaluhk. "It would be much too dangerous for her. We shall look after her, and you may rest assured that she will never be far from our sight."

Natalia moved closer to give the shaman a hug. "Thank you, Shaluhk. It means a great deal to us knowing she'll be safe."

"When will you leave?"

"I'll draft my letters tonight," said Athgar, "and send them off first thing in the morning, then we can be on our way."

"How long is the journey?"

"That's Natalia's area of knowledge." He looked at his bondmate.

"Don't look at me," she replied. "I fled Karslev in a hurry and never looked outside the carriage. All I know is it took weeks to get to Draybourne. Stanislav would know more as he's travelled extensively."

"Then we should start this trip by going to Ebenstadt and seeking his counsel."

"I shall ensure you have provisions," offered Kargen, "but I would advise you to take your bow, my friend. If the journey is as long as it sounds, you will need to replenish along the way. Where does Karslev lie?"

"To the north," said Natalia. "That much I know for sure."

"Then I would suggest you visit Gal-Drulan after you leave Ebenstadt. The Cloud Hunters came from the north. They can give you a much better idea of what lies in that direction, maybe even escort you partway."

"A good idea," said Athgar. "I've been meaning to visit them, but with all this fighting, there hasn't been much of an opportunity."

"A problem soon rectified. I shall have Shaluhk send word by casting spirit talk and conversing with Uruzuhk."

"A useful spell," noted Natalia. "And one I'm eager to incorporate into the Army of Therengia."

"You think it that useful?" asked Athgar.

"It allows us to talk in person to our captains, regardless of how far away they are, giving us a distinct advantage which the enemy knows nothing of. Combined with all the mages at our disposal, it makes us a force to be reckoned with."

"Good, because little else seems to work to convince the Petty Kingdoms. I tire of this constant warfare. Why can't they desire peace as much as us?"

"You forget," said Natalia, "that the Petty Kingdoms have been in an almost perpetual state of war since they were formed. Well, I suppose that's not entirely true; some kingdoms managed to avoid it, but there's always been conflict somewhere on the Continent."

"Not so surprising when you think of it," added Shaluhk. "Those very same kingdoms were born in war. They fought to divide up Therengia and then fought with each other over the scraps."

"Yes," agreed Athgar, "and now they seek to do the same to us."

"Ah," said Kargen, "but this time, they met their match. Nat-Alia is a fully-trained battle mage with more spellcasters than any other kingdom. Who else can claim such a force?"

"Ruzhina," said Natalia. "I know, in theory, the King of Ruzhina is not part of the family, but the Stormwinds hold sway over many of the Petty Kingdoms, perhaps Ruzhina the most. Do not, for one moment, believe they wouldn't hesitate to deploy mages of their own should the kingdom be threatened."

"Wise words," said Shaluhk, "and ones we should all bear in mind going forward."

EBENSTADT

Spring 1108 SR

With the defeat of Novarsk, trade with the Therengian villages had grown considerably, and now the eastern gatehouse of Ebenstadt was always busy. The influx of visitors created a backlog, meaning simply entering the city could take half the morning.

Athgar's gaze wandered over the crowd before them. They would likely not gain entrance until this afternoon, and it galled him to think of the delay that would have on their plans. Natalia, sensing his frustration, took his hand.

"There's no hurry," she soothed. "The family has existed for centuries. A few more days will make little difference."

"What if I told them who we are?" he said. "At least then we wouldn't have to wait."

"And draw attention to ourselves? I think not. Besides, you're the one who keeps saying you don't want special treatment."

"That's before I knew I'd spend half the day waiting in line. What's taking the guards so long?"

"Your orders, remember? You didn't want any agents of the family entering Ebenstadt. That means each and every person who passes through those gates has to be interrogated."

"Interrogated?" said Athgar. "You're not suggesting they're being tortured?"

"No," said Natalia. "Interrogated as in talked to. We don't use threats here, remember?"

"Oh yes. I must be thinking of the other Petty Kingdoms."

"When did you become so bitter?"

"I can't help it. We have Therengians flocking to us from all over the Continent, and they all tell the same stories of subjugation and mistreatment. It's enough to drive a person mad."

"Come now," she replied. "You mustn't let it get to you. They came here seeking a new life, and you're largely the one responsible for that."

"It wasn't just me," said Athgar. "Many others were involved. I only hope it hasn't all been for naught."

"Why would you even think that?"

"How long, do you suppose, until another crusade is organized against us?"

"The Petty Kingdoms would have a hard time organizing that, especially considering the Church's presence here in Ebenstadt. In any case, I believe they have more pressing business in the west."

"Oh?" said Athgar. "Like what?"

"Halvaria? Rumours are that the great empire is looking to expand its borders again, and that's got everyone in a tizzy."

Athgar laughed. "A tizzy? You'll have to remind me, is that more, or less intense than being upset?"

"I'd say it's halfway between upset and angry. I do like to be precise in my use of the term."

The crowd inched forward, bringing them slightly closer to the gate.

"Looks like we're finally making some progress," mused Athgar.

"Something's happening," said Natalia. "Soldiers are exiting."

They both watched as a dozen warriors left the city, their new blue surcoats bright in the morning sun.

"Somebody's finally decided to do something about this crowd," noted Athgar. Sure enough, the men spread out, the better to investigate more of the visitors. It didn't take long until a warrior approached the two of them.

"What is the purpose of your visit?" the young man asked.

"We are here to visit some friends," said Natalia.

"Oh yes, and what friends might those be?"

"Stanislav Voronsky and Belgast Ridgehand."

The guard stared back, clearly thinking this was some sort of joke. "Really? And who might you be?"

Athgar expected her to make up a name, but instead, she appeared irritated. "I am Natalia Stormwind, and this is Athgar, High Thane of Therengia."

"Sure you are, and I'm the King of Novarsk."

Her mouth fell open, and she struggled to respond. "It's true," was all she could manage to say.

The guard placed his hands on his hips, adopting the manner of a condescending parent. "If he's the High Thane, then where is the Thane Guard?"

Athgar stepped in. "I'm travelling within Therengia. Why would I need a guard?"

"Come now," the man continued. "Enough of this nonsense. Who are you two, honestly?"

"I told you," said Natalia. "I am Natalia Stormwind."

"Then prove it."

"I beg your pardon?"

"You heard me. Prove it."

"And how would you suggest I do that?"

The guard looked around the area, his gaze finally resting on a tree to which he pointed. "If you're such a great mage, use your magic on that."

She took a step, thrusting her hands out in front. The air buzzed with magical energy, and then a white beam shot from her, striking the tree and encasing it in ice.

The guard paled. "My apologies, Y—Y—Your Grace," he stammered. "Come. Let me escort you through the gates, the both of you."

They followed him. "Happy?" said Athgar. "You terrified the poor fellow."

"He had no cause to be rude, and I shall not apologize."

"Well, at least he'll have a story to tell his grandchildren one day."

They passed under the archway and into the city itself. Ebenstadt was busy with many merchants setting up stalls near the gate, the better to entice new customers. They left their guard and made their way farther in.

The thane's estate was nothing more than a large house previously used to house the Cunar regional commander. However, after that order abandoned the town, it fell into the possession of Therengia and now housed what passed for the ruling council of the city.

Athgar and Natalia were immediately recognized as they made their entrance. Moments later, a servant appeared to render what assistance she could.

"Can I help you, Your Graces?"

"Yes," said Natalia. "Is Stanislav here?"

"He is," the woman replied. "If you'll follow me, I'll take you to him." She led them through the building, heading towards the back, then paused at a door. "He is within," she announced. "Is there anything else I can get you?"

"No, thank you," said Athgar.

Natalia pushed open the door, revealing a table, around which various mismatched chairs were scattered. Upon two of these sat Stanislav and Belgast, deep in discussion over what appeared to be a map of the region. With their conversation now interrupted, they looked up.

"Natalia, Athgar," said Stanislav. "Good to see you both. What brings you to Ebenstadt?"

"You, actually," Natalia replied, "but it's good that Belgast is here. We would value his thoughts as well."

"That sounds a tad serious. Anything I should be worried about?"

"Plenty, but let's take a seat first, shall we? How have things been in Ebenstadt?"

"Quiet."

She eyed the table. "And what's this?"

"We were trying to settle an argument," replied the Dwarf.

"An argument about what?"

"We're attempting to place Gal-Drulan on this map we have, although admittedly, it's not the best representation of the area."

"Few maps are," noted Stanislav. "What we really need is a decent cartographer."

"I have a cousin who does just that," said Belgast. "Should I send him a letter?"

"That's the first sensible thing I've heard you say all day."

"Wait a moment. I'm the one who suggested the brandy."

"I concede the point. Then it's the second." Stanislav's attention turned once more to their visitors. "What, exactly, are you two doing here in the city?"

"There's been some trouble," said Athgar.

"What kind of trouble?"

"The family tried to take Oswyn again."

"I trust no one was hurt?"

"Not on our side," said Natalia. "At least no one Shaluhk couldn't heal. I can't say the same for the interlopers."

"And you believe they came through Ebenstadt?"

"No, but we decided we've had enough."

"Meaning?"

"We intend to go to Karslev and put an end to this once and for all. That's what we need you for."

"Me?" said Stanislav.

"Yes. You're far more familiar with the area than we are. I hoped you'd tell us the best route."

"I'll do better than that," the mage hunter replied. "I'll take you there myself."

"Aren't you needed here?"

"Not really. The city pretty much runs itself, and if there's any trouble, Brother Yaromir is more than capable of dealing with it."

"You mean Temple Captain Yaromir," corrected Belgast. "They promoted him, remember?" He turned his attention to Athgar and Natalia. "When do we leave?"

"We?" said Athgar.

"Of course. You can't expect me to miss out on an opportunity for adventure."

"Have you ever been to Karslev?"

"No, and therein lies my advantage."

"Which is?"

"You lot are all known to the family, but I have no such connection. And let's be honest, most of you Humans can't tell one Dwarf from another. That means I can move about freely—important when you need to gather information."

"What about your business here?"

"You mean my cousins?" said Belgast. "They don't need me. They've been smithing away for months all by themselves. Now, are we going by horse or by boat?"

"We haven't planned that out just yet. I suppose it largely depends on what Stanislav suggests."

The mage hunter cleared his throat. "I assume you want to enter the city unannounced?"

"Naturally," replied Natalia.

"Then we should avoid the regular roads. There's a river that forms the eastern border of Novarsk. I'm told it eventually leads to the Great Northern Sea."

"Have we any boats?"

"We don't," said Belgast, "but the Cloud Hunters do. I imagine they'd be more than willing to lend them to us."

"What kind of boats?" asked Athgar.

"They call them umaks. They're small, typically holding half a dozen people, along with their goods."

"And they sail these on the river?"

"Where else?" said the Dwarf. "And no, I suppose technically they're not sailing them but paddling them."

"So you want us to row all the way to the sea?"

"Not at all. It's downriver. Most of the time, you'll be coasting with the current."

"How do you know so much about the Cloud Hunters?" asked Natalia.

"It's purely business, I assure you. I offered them the services of my cousins."

"The smiths? But they're far too busy in Runewald."

The Dwarf dismissed the thought with a wave of his hand. "I'm not talking about Kieren and Targan. No, I'm talking about my cousin Harmetia Sternaxe and her daughter, Weylin."

"Just how many cousins do you have?"

"Yes," added Natalia, "and are they all moving to Therengia? Not that we have any objection, mind you."

Belgast laughed, the sound coming from deep in his belly. "It's clear you don't understand how Dwarven families work, but yes, my extended family is quite large. Most of them are members of the traders' guild, so they're always looking for new opportunities, and this land has them in abundance. Not only will they help build up Therengia, but they'll make a reasonable profit doing so. It's an arrangement benefiting all of us."

"So you're saying you've been to Gal-Drulan?"

"Isn't that what I said?"

"Not in so many words. How long does it take to get there?"

"About two days? We take the road to Finburg, then turn north. It lies within the Restless Hills."

"That sounds ominous," said Athgar.

"It does," agreed Belgast, "not that it matters. We'll be travelling down-river by boat, assuming Grazuhk has no objection." He turned to Stanislav. "How long a trip do you reckon this will be?"

"That's hard to answer. Ideally, we want to follow the river all the way to Carlingen, but if we're travelling with Orcs, we may need to disembark sooner." He looked upward, trying to remember what he knew of the area. "If memory serves, we'll skirt the border of Novarsk, then follow a tributary to the north. I imagine it'll be a few weeks at least, most of it through rough country."

Athgar was intrigued. "Rough, meaning?"

"Wilderness, primarily occupied with nothing more than animals native to the area."

"So mostly unexplored, then?"

"Yes, precisely. Of course, we should be safe if we're aboard boats, but I suggest we still stop to camp at night. I wouldn't recommend trying to navigate the river in the dark."

"Why not? It's not as if it'll take us anywhere we don't want to go."

"True," said Stanislav, "but there are other hazards that would be particularly dangerous in the dark."

"Such as?"

"Rapids, for one, or possibly even waterfalls. One must be careful when paddling in unknown waters. Hopefully, Natalia's mastery of Water Magic would be of benefit to us."

"I don't see how," she replied. "It's not as if I can raise the water level on the rapids."

"What about talking to the fish?"

"I can't talk to fish," said Natalia.

Athgar laughed. "Yes, what a ridiculous notion."

"I can only talk to water mammals."

Athgar's laughter died, leaving him open-mouthed. "You can what?"

"Well, maybe talk isn't quite the word I should use. I can communicate at a rudimentary level using a spell."

"To a water mammal?"

"Yes, something akin to an otter, for example. They often know the waterways and might be able to warn us if, for instance, there's a large predator in the area or if a waterfall is nearby."

"You never told me you could do that?"

She smiled. "It never came up before."

"You're just full of surprises. I'm glad you're on our side."

"Me too. Now, as much as I want to talk more of such things, there are arrangements to make. We'll need supplies if we are to carry on with this scheme of ours."

"Easily done," said Belgast. "I can have everything ready by morning. I would, however, like to know where we go after Carlingen?"

"Oh, that," said Stanislav. "Carlingen is a port on the Great Northern Sea. From there, we'll hire a ship to take us to Porovka. Then, it's a relatively straightforward trip to Karslev."

"And that would be overland?" asked Athgar.

"Yes, although I wouldn't recommend walking, far better to hire a coach."

"Why is that?"

"The way is populated by a series of roadside inns, but they're designed to be one day's ride apart. Go on foot, and you'll end up spending the bulk of your time in the countryside."

"Suits me," said Athgar.

"I know it does," said Natalia, "but it might attract unwelcome attention. Foot traffic is not common between the great cities of Ruzhina."

"I wonder why?"

"Only important people travel."

"I don't understand."

"It's simple," said Stanislav. "Ruzhina is ruled over by elite nobles who keep a firm grip on the populace. Chances are anyone on the road will be seen as a potential runaway and subject to arrest."

"Runaway?" said Athgar. "You mean, as in escaped slaves?"

"They're not slaves so much as indentured servants. Still, their presence outside of their place of work is considered ill-advised and highly unusual."

"Then a carriage it is."

"What about after we arrive in Karslev?" asked Belgast. "Is there an actual objective, or are we only there to cause mischief and mayhem?"

"That," said Natalia, "has yet to be determined. Naturally, we shall give it plenty of thought, but the overall idea is to hurt them somehow." She leaned on the table, then happened to look down at the map. The sight of the ring on her finger reminded her of the other reason they came to town. "That reminds me, Belgast. We have something to ask you about."

"Go on."

She removed her ring, showing them how to release the gem and expose the small metal pin. "What do you make of this?" She passed it to the Dwarf.

"This looks like a key," he replied.

"A key to what?"

"I can't say exactly, but such things are usually for some sort of secret compartment. Where did you get it?"

"It belonged to my grandmother, Illiana Stormwind. She gifted it to me on my graduation from the Volstrum."

"I doubt it was given lightly. It would take a master craftsman to make it, which would be costly. Clearly, she thought a lot of you."

"She did," said Natalia. "She also gave me a bag of gems, which I had Stanislav sell to finance my escape."

"She definitely wanted you to get away," said Athgar. "Else, why give them to you?"

"That's not all," suggested the Dwarf. "If she gave you that ring, she likely knew sooner or later you'd be bound to discover what it was. I'm guessing whatever that key opens holds something important."

"Enough to bring down the family?"

"Possibly, or at the very least, diminish their influence."

"Perhaps," said Athgar, "if we got a hold of whatever it unlocks, we could bargain with it in exchange for them leaving us alone?"

"I'd certainly be willing to give it a try," said Natalia, "but where would we start? It's one thing to have a key, quite another to know where it could be used."

"You say Illiana gave it to you after the graduation?" asked Stanislav.

"Yes. Well, on the day of the ceremony, to be exact. I saw it before the ceremony, but I had no idea she was actually going to have it presented to me. And from the looks of others, they were surprised as well."

"Could it be used at this Volstrum place?" asked Belgast. "Illiana used to work there, didn't she?"

"Yes, but not for some years. She'd become the head of the family and lived at Stormwind Manor, but I don't know where it's located."

"Hmmm, me neither," said Stanislav. "I've only been there once, and that was so long ago I couldn't possibly find my way back. Remember, it's the traditional home for the head of the line. As such, we can expect it to be heavily guarded."

"Guarded or not," said Natalia, "that's where we must look. Illiana's ring is the key to unlocking this mystery, possibly even ruining the family itself. We'd be fools to pass up an opportunity like this."

GAL-DRULAN

Spring 1108 SR

The thick mist created a foreboding atmosphere as they set out on their journey the next day. They talked little as they made their way up the Finburg road, each too engrossed in their own thoughts and fears to give voice to them.

They encountered little in the way of traffic, save for a group of soldiers marching back to Ebenstadt. There was no sign of recognition in the warriors' eyes as they passed, or from their captain, a severe-looking fellow, whose gaze Stanislav seemed to be avoiding.

It wasn't until after they were gone that Athgar brought up the matter. "Am I imagining things, or were you avoiding that captain?"

"I had no desire to create a scene," replied Stanislav, "but the fact is I owe the man some coins."

"How did that come about?"

"I may have had a little too much to drink and made an unwise decision."

"Which was?"

In reply, the mage hunter gave him a forlorn look. "Take my advice, Athgar, don't mix gambling and drink. Don't get me wrong—kept separate from each other, they're both entertaining, but they make a devastating combination."

"How much did you lose?"

"I can't quite recall, but more than I had on me at the time and not something I'm eager to discover the details of. Now, not to change the subject, but how much longer do we have to travel?"

"Some time yet," noted the Dwarf, "but we'll halt for a break once we pass that tree up yonder."

Athgar looked down the road. The indicated tree appeared miles away, no more than a speck in the distance, yet he knew it couldn't be all that much farther. He kept walking, but no matter how many times he glanced up, it never seemed to grow any closer. Added to that was the heat, for although it was still spring, the day was proving to be more like the middle of summer.

After finding a stream to slake their thirst, they halted, still shy of their target. Athgar collapsed on the ground, the sweat dripping off him. He closed his eyes against the sun, letting his breathing slow down, only to feel a shadow pass over him. He opened one eye to see Natalia standing above him.

"Are you all right?" she asked, her face a mask of concern.

"I'm fine. Why?"

"You look a little flushed."

"It's just this heat."

"Why don't you use your magic?"

"I can't banish the heat," said Athgar.

"No, but your spell of warmth can regulate temperature. I assume that means it can prevent you from overheating?"

He sat up. "Why didn't I think of that?"

She knelt beside him, her smile inviting. "That's what I'm here for."

Athgar stood, then gave her a kiss. "Thank you."

"For what?"

"For reminding me I'm a master of flame. Lately, I've spent so much time looking after the kingdom, I'd nearly forgotten." He began casting his spell, calling on his inner spark to draw forth his power. He released the magic, feeling it suffuse him and immediately regulating his body temperature. "Ah, that's much better. Can I offer you the same?"

She nodded.

"Hold still," he said.

Athgar repeated the spell and watched as Natalia grew more relaxed. "Would anyone else like a nice spell of warmth? Despite its name, it will keep you from overheating."

Stanislav and Belgast both took the offer, and within moments, they all felt refreshed. Invigorated by their new sense of comfort, they continued on their way, finally passing the tree, which for so long had mocked them by its distance.

. . .

Late that night, they set up camp, with Athgar using his magic to illuminate the area. Having made good progress, they soon fell asleep with little thought to putting someone on watch.

Athgar awoke to the sound of an animal rooting through someone's belongings. He quickly cast a spell, causing a green flame to spring to life in his hand. There, to his side, he spied a badger rooting around his pack, searching for something to eat, his claws leaving several holes in it in the process.

They stared at each other for a moment before the creature turned, lumbering off into the darkness. Athgar let his beating heart return to normal, then decided someone must remain on alert. Thus, he was standing watch as the others awoke.

The next day they made good time, and by early afternoon, the distant rooftops of Finburg came into view. However, the road turned north, so they bypassed the city, continuing on their way to Gal-Drulan.

The sky grew darker, threatening to release a torrent of rain. Athgar wondered if they might be better served to seek some form of shelter. He cast about, looking for a place which would be suitable for a camp, but his experience with the badger last night dampened his enthusiasm for such a move. He decided to press on, hoping to reach Gal-Drulan before nightfall. The hills soon came into view, and shortly after that, a trio of Orcs spotted them, moving to intercept.

"*Greetings,*" called out Athgar, using the Orcish tongue. "*We come seeking your chieftain, Grazuhk. I am Athgar, son of Rothgar, and these are my friends, Nat-Alia, Stanislav, and Belgast.*"

"*Welcome one and all,*" replied the largest Orc. "*I am Gamrag, sister-son to our chieftain. We have been expecting you, High Thane. Shaluhk sent word you would be coming. If you will come with me, I shall take you back to our village.*"

"*Lead on, and we shall follow.*"

The Orc hunter led them through the hills, and a short time later, the village appeared in the distance. Unlike the huts of the Red Hand, the Cloud Hunters elevated their dwellings on poles such that each floor was raised above Athgar's head, creating a far different sight than what he was used to at the other Orc villages. He wondered for a moment if the height was to keep animals at bay, say wolves, or maybe even badgers?

An Orc female walked briskly towards them. "*Gamrag, who have you there? Is that the High Thane?*"

"*It is, Mother.*" He turned his attention to Athgar. "*Allow me to introduce my mother, Uruzuhk, shamaness of our tribe.*"

"*Greetings,*" said Athgar. "*I understand you expected us?*"

"*Indeed. A hut has been prepared for your use, but if you come with me first, I shall introduce you to my sister, Grazuhk, who is also our chieftain.*"

She led them farther into the village to a tall structure, towering above the rest, with a ladder leading up to a balcony that surrounded the place. Once inside, they were greeted by Grazuhk.

"*It is an honour to meet you,*" said the Orc chieftain. "*Now, come. Sit, and we shall begin by feeding you. Once that is done, there is much to discuss.*"

Belgast let out a loud belch. "*Pardon me,*" he said in Orcish. The others laughed.

"*It is good to see you are comfortable in our presence,*" said Uruzuhk. "*Shaluhk tells me you and your companions are travelling north?*"

"*Yes, that's right,*" said Natalia. "*We hope to follow the river down to the sea. We seek a Human city called Carlingen that lies at its mouth.*"

"*That is a very long distance indeed. One that requires weeks of travel, much of it through dangerous lands.*"

"*Do you know the area well?*"

"*The region within a ten-day's travel is well known to us, but any farther away is not.*"

"*Our hunters have travelled through it, though,*" said Grazuhk, "*and we would be pleased to supply you with some boats and guide you.*"

"*That would be most appreciated,*" said Natalia.

"*My sister tells me you seek retribution against this family of which we have heard so much.*"

"*Yes. They threatened our daughter, Oswyn.*"

"*Then it is only right that you punish them for their transgression.*"

A tall Orc stepped into the hut, his robes hanging from a thin frame.

"*Ah, Rotuk,*" said the chieftain. "*Our master of air. We were just talking about the High Thane's journey to the north.*"

The newcomer moved farther into the room, bowing at the group of visitors. "*It seems I must apologize for my lateness. I was out in the hills when you arrived.*"

"Hunting?" asked Athgar.

"*No, communing with nature. I often find moments of solitude help me understand all that is around us.*"

"*Is that common for an Air Mage?*"

The Orc looked confused for a moment before understanding took

"Isn't he a little old for that?"

"Not at all. His affinity for magic came much later in life."

"Then he's like me," said Athgar. *"I didn't know I was gifted with Fire Magic till I suffered a great loss."*

"The same for Gamrag. He lost his twin when a river serpent attacked his umak."

"A river serpent? I don't much like the sound of that. How long ago was this?"

"Just last year, on our migration here."

"And where, precisely, did this tragedy occur?"

"On the very river we will be traversing."

Athgar stared at the master of air, trying to gauge his honesty. At first, he thought this was some type of joke, possibly even a ritual of sorts to see how determined their group was to continue. Unfortunately, it was not the way of Orcs to make such a jest, so he had to take the fellow at face value.

"How common are these river serpents?" Athgar asked.

"Not common at all," said Rotuk. *"They are primarily found in the deeper parts of the river. As such, there will be little possibility of encountering them in the first ten-day. They are also unlikely to threaten a trio of boats, preferring instead to go after solitary targets."*

"Why is that?"

"Their method of attack is not suitable for multiple opponents."

"And just how do they attack?"

"They tend to snake around the boat, crushing it in their coils. Those who are not crushed are then chased down before they reach shore. The river serpent's bite is deadly."

"Are they poisonous?" asked Athgar.

"No, but their jaws are powerful. It is said they can crush the skull of an Orc with little difficulty."

"That explains why the Petty Kingdoms didn't settle along the river's edge."

Rotuk shrugged. *"Perhaps. You are the first Humans I have met, so I am unable to speak for them."*

"I'm curious," said Natalia. *"I know Shaluhk invited you here, but where did you come from?"*

"The very region into which you now travel. For generations, we lived along the banks of the Windrush, where the water meets the river of stones. It was a peaceful land with plentiful game. Our hunters ranged far and wide with little danger, but then the Humans came. At first, only hunters, but then others, drawn by the tales of shadowbark."

"Shadowbark," said Athgar. *"I remember that. It's used for furniture, isn't it?"*

"Amongst other things," replied Natalia, *"but I'd no idea it could be found this*

far north. I can see why people pushed eastward; shadowbark trees would be worth a fortune."

"*Did they settle along the river?*" asked Athgar.

"*No,*" said Rotuk. "*Unlike other wood, shadowbark does not float, making it necessary to carry it overland. We tried to reason with the Humans, but they refused any peaceful overtures, bringing more warriors instead. Thus, the conflict began.*"

"*I'm sorry,*" said Athgar. "*The same happened in Ord-Kurgad. Humans came seeking something in the Orcs' territory, ready to force the Red Hand out at the point of a sword.*"

"*In spite of that, I am told you and your people live amongst the tribes in peace.*"

"*We do, but we are Therengians. There has always been peace between our people.*"

"*Nat-Alia is not of your race, is she?*"

"*No, but she is still considered a member of the tribe. Humans and Orcs can live together in peace, but it takes a lot of work on both sides.*"

Rotuk nodded his head. "*It is true. Some of my own people pushed for war, even as the Humans began to outnumber us. Only the wisdom of Grazuhk led us here. She had the determination and fortitude to see us through this time of strife. I do wonder, however, how long it will be before Humans once again try to claim our lands?*"

"*If they do, they shall be met by an army. We are kindred folk, Orcs and Therengians, and we will stand together to defend our homes, no matter who threatens.*"

THE JOURNEY BEGINS

Spring 1108 SR

The launching point for their trip downriver was a small pond around which the Orcs had constructed a series of huts to keep their umaks safe from the elements. They even went so far as to build a longhouse for the hunters while preparing for any trips they might consider.

Athgar was fascinated by the boats themselves, a flat-bottomed construction consisting of a wooden frame lashed together. Over this stretched an animal hide, heavily treated with something to make it waterproof. He was reminded of deerskin, yet the colour and rough texture indicated otherwise. Whatever the skin was, it made for a light boat, easily transported by a pair of hunters.

The Orcs carried three of these craft to the pond's edge, setting them down in the water before loading in the food and water. Shortly thereafter, they invited everyone to board.

Athgar settled into the middle of one such craft while Natalia, being a Water Mage, sat closer to the bow. Gamrag took up an oar, as did another hunter named Zarig, who sat between the pair of Humans.

Belgast and Stanislav sat in another of the umaks, along with two more Orcs, Azug and Morgash, the Dwarf looking particularly uncomfortable. The third such boat, crewed by Rotuk and Sholar and loaded with supplies, brought up the rear. Their passengers in place, the boats pushed out into the pond, following it to where a stream led westward. They proceeded in single file, a formation that proved necessary due to the relatively narrow waterway.

Despite the close confines, Athgar found the trip enjoyable. The boat proved stable, the progress swift, and the stream widened before long. The hills soon disappeared, replaced by grassy fields and the occasional clump of trees.

"This is marvellous," said Natalia, clearly enjoying the experience. "I forgot how much I like being on a boat." She cast her gaze back to where Athgar sat. "It's much smoother than sailing on the open sea, don't you think?"

"I do," he agreed. "Although I might remind you, the last time we were on a river, rygaurs attacked us."

"I remember." She smiled. "That's also the first time I saw you use your Fire Magic."

"Yes, and you accused me of working for the family. Still, I can't complain. The experience brought us closer together. However, I do hope there are no rygaurs in this area."

"I'm sure Rotuk would have mentioned it if there were."

That evening, they camped beside the stream, sleeping beneath the stars. The weather was warm but not unpleasant, so they felt refreshed by morning.

Their trek continued at first light. Halfway through the morning, the stream fed into the Windrush, the current picking up considerably. The Orcs only paddled when the riverbanks drew near, so fast did the water carry them.

Late afternoon found them slowing once again as the river widened. Now the hunters dug in with their paddles, the umaks proving equal to the task.

The banks here were lined with trees, principally pine. Every now and again, they spotted grasslands poking through with the occasional deer coming to drink by the river. It was a peaceful journey, with Athgar struggling to remain awake, but slumber finally claimed him as his head dropped to his chest.

Natalia, on the other hand, was enthralled by their progress. Rocks replaced the pine trees as the river entered a ravine, speeding up considerably. The boat jumped around as the current took hold, but the Orcs remained calm.

Athgar awoke to see walls of stone on either side of the river. "Where are we?" he called out, his mind struggling to make sense of his new surroundings.

"The river cut through some hills," said Natalia. "It's nothing to worry about."

"Easy for you to say; you're a Water Mage."

"I seem to recall you being able to swim, and the shore is not so distant."

"True. I can swim, but how would I scale those cliffs? I'd be imprisoned here forever."

"No, of course not," she replied. "You'd only need go upstream or down, and then you'd be free. For a man who fears little in battle, you appear uncomfortable around water."

"I was startled, that's all. I fell asleep and awoke to this." Athgar stretched his arms out to either side. "Although I must admit it's a pleasant enough sight."

He was about to say more when a roar echoed off the rock walls.

"*What was that?*" said Athgar, reverting to Orcish.

"*I do not know,*" replied Gamrag, "*and I am not sure I want to find out.*"

"*Do we need to get out of the river?*"

"*No. To do so would only put us in greater danger.*"

"*Look,*" called out Natalia. "*To the south!*"

Their heads swivelled to look at a distant shape up in the sky. Whatever it was flapped its wings, then coasted towards them.

Natalia already had her hands out, ready to cast a spell if needed. Athgar considered preparing one himself, but the range was too far for him to hit anything. As it drew closer, its outline grew more distinct—a snakelike head with horns, giving it the appearance of a dragon. Two lizard-like legs dangled from beneath it, but it mounted a set of leather-bound wings in place of forelegs. A long tail ending in a wicked stinger balanced it all out, leaving no doubt to its identity.

"*It's a wyvern*," called out Natalia as she let loose with a spell, sending a shard of ice flying towards it. The dexterous creature easily dodged to the side, then climbed higher, and for a moment, it looked as though it might leave them alone. The turning point came as it unexpectedly folded its wings and plummeted towards them.

Athgar cast a streak of flame, grazing the creature, but it continued its descent, leaving a trail of smoke behind it.

Natalia ducked as the creature pulled up and flew over top of them. Her head came up in time to see the thing's stinger smash into Zarig, knocking him to the bottom of the umak while leaving a rip across his chest. Black blood flowed freely, but even worse was the terrible wail he let out as his skin bubbled and boiled.

The wyvern made a sharp turn as it approached the cliff, then began climbing once more. Athgar moved closer to Zarig, desperate to stem the flow of blood. Natalia called out more words of power, her hands releasing another streak of ice, this time splattering across the creature's chest. It appeared to do little damage, and moments later, chunks of ice fell from the wyvern, dislodged from its scales by its constant motion.

"It's coming for us again," she called out. "Try your fire!"

Athgar quickly cast, letting his fire streak loose as the wyvern came in for another pass. He watched in silence as the flames struck its chest, but it showed no sign it even felt the attack as it flew over them, low to the water. Everyone ducked, hoping to avoid the great stinger.

A cry of anguish erupted from the supply boat, and then a splash as someone was knocked overboard by the force of the blow. Athgar looked down at Zarig, but the Orc hunter lay still, his life force having fled.

"My spell did nothing," he called out.

"It must have a natural resistance to magic. String your bow; it's the only chance we have."

He dug around the bottom of the umak, searching for his weapon while the second boat came up beside theirs. Stanislav crouched low in the bow, but Belgast stood, pickaxe in hand, daring the thing to turn on him.

Athgar, having found his bow, rushed to string it, a difficult proposition while having to watch for an impending attack.

The wyvern circled around, its tail poised for its next strike as it climbed slightly, then came sailing back up the river, skimming along the water's surface. Athgar noticed the ripples the beating of the creature's wings created on the river even as he pulled back on his bow.

Closer it came, opening its maw, ready to rip open anything that might oppose it. Athgar controlled his breathing as he waited for the perfect moment to strike. Natalia ducked once more, and as the wyvern passed over her head, Athgar let loose with his arrow. The wind from its wings knocked him from his feet as it let out a strange keening noise before continuing on upstream, gaining height. They could only watch as, off in the distance, the creature made a slow turn, preparing to make another pass. The real question was who would be its target. Natalia looked downstream, away from the thing, and began casting.

Athgar had no idea what she was doing but readied another arrow. His eyes locked on his target until he could make out his last arrow protruding from the wyvern's mouth. It had lodged in the gum, likely a painful reminder of the dangers of archery, yet still it approached, ready to repeat its attack. He let fly, watching the arrow close. Suddenly the boat came to a halt, throwing him off balance, and he fell.

The great shape flew over him as the wyvern's stinger whipped out, narrowly missing him to punch a hole in the umak's side. There was a colossal thud, and then something splashed into the water.

Athgar leaped to his feet. Judging the creature's approach, Natalia had frozen the river before throwing up an ice wall. Having swept towards them at such great speed, the wyvern, unable to gain enough height, had smashed into the magical barrier sending chunks of ice flying. It then plummeted onto the frozen river, where its weight worked against it, breaking through the surface.

Its shrieks of rage echoed off the cliff walls as it thrashed around in the water while Gamrag turned the boat around, trying to distance them from the creature. Athgar felt waves strike the umak, threatening to capsize them before they could get to safety. Another arrow flew from his bow, but the target was almost impossible to see. He briefly glimpsed a dark shadow beneath the boat as the current carried them downstream, but the creature rapidly fell behind as the Orcs paddled with all the strength they could muster. He watched it pulling itself ashore, and then the river took a turn, blocking the view.

He held his breath; they all did, but it soon became clear the wyvern would not return. The Orcs steered the boats to the bank, and then they disembarked, thankful to be on dry land once more.

"*We lost Zarig,*" said Gamrag, "*and Sholar as well. I saw her go overboard.*"

"*Do you think it will come back?*" asked Athgar.

"*No, it appears it has had enough. We are lucky you were with us, Nat-Alia, else nothing would have dissuaded its attack.*"

"*It is a pity we could not defeat it,*" added Rotuk. "*For the scales of such a crea-ture would make a fine set of clothes.*"

"*Two lives it took,*" said Gamrag, plainly upset. "*A high price indeed. Forget your fine set of clothes, Rotuk. I would prefer our hunters back.*"

"*As would I, yet now we have nothing to show for its defeat. Those lives are therefore not avenged.*"

"*Life is not about revenge,*" said Natalia.

"*Are you not travelling north for that very same reason?*"

She wanted to disagree, but the answer caught in her throat. Was she so blinded by the thought of revenge that she would put others in danger? The mere thought sobered her.

"*We must take care of the dead,*" said Athgar. "*What are the customs of the Cloud Hunters?*"

"*They joined the Ancestors,*" replied Gamrag. "*It only remains to destroy the mortal remains. Sholar, unfortunately, lies beneath the river, but the body of Zarig shall be burned once we clear this accursed area.*"

"*And how much farther do you think that would be?*"

In answer, the Orc gazed skyward, seeking the sun. "*We shall be free of it before nightfall, of that you can be sure. First, however, we must patch the umak. Only then can we proceed.*"

The repairs proved easy enough, allowing them to continue their journey after only the briefest of delays. By late afternoon, they cleared the cliffs, and the land opened up into an area thick with trees.

They waited until a suitable clearing presented itself before they pulled the boats up on shore. With the umaks secure, wood was gathered for a funeral pyre. Darkness descended by the time the bed of sticks was finished. They laid the body of Zarig upon it, and Rotuk said a few words in praise of the hunter's life. Athgar then called forth his inner spark, igniting the deathbed to form a funeral pyre.

The fire consumed what was left of Zarig as they stood and watched. No, Athgar corrected himself—it was not Zarig, merely dead flesh and bones. The Ancestors had claimed the hunter, and he now lived on in the spirit realm. At least that was the Orc belief.

He found himself mulling over his own mortality. Should he die, would he be remembered? Would future generations call upon his spirit to offer them guidance? The Orcs certainly believed that, and although he hadn't seen the evidence himself, he knew Natalia had witnessed Shaluhk commu-nicating with the dead. This was proof of an Orcish Afterlife, but did the same hold true for Humans? Did they turn into spirits, wandering the

Afterlife for all eternity? Or did they continue to serve their Gods in the hereafter?

The fire crackled and popped as the flames consumed the dead Orc's body. Athgar, his thoughts troubled, turned from the blaze to catch a glimpse of glowing eyes. He froze, afraid some vicious animal had come to wreak havoc amongst them, but then the creature moved, revealing the shape of a wolf.

He relaxed. Amongst his own people, such an appearance was considered a good omen. But then he paused, for he'd always been taught the Old Gods did not interfere in the world of the living. The very thought struck him as odd, for if that were the case, why would they believe in omens? Belgast interrupted his musings.

"That blasted thing almost killed us all," he fumed. "We must take better care in future."

"How?" said Athgar in response. "The thing was upon us quickly and resistant to our magic."

"I suppose that's true, but I would suggest you at least keep your bow strung in future."

"I can see you know little about bows."

"Why would you say that?"

"Keeping a bow strung for too long weakens it."

"Well, what do I know? I'm a merchant, not an archer. Still, there must be something we can do?"

"Stay more alert to the possibility of further attacks from the air, although I doubt there are many other flying predators around with a wyvern in the area."

"Say," said the Dwarf. "You don't suppose that thing will come after us, do you?"

"I certainly hope not, but just to be safe, I think tomorrow we'll put as much distance behind us as we can."

"Aye, but in the meantime, we should rest. We'll all need to take turns paddling now that we're down by two."

"I hadn't considered that. Tell me, Belgast, have you ever travelled by boat before?"

"Not like this, I haven't. Oh, I've been on riverboats before, but they were all those Human ones with masts and a solid deck, not these tiny things. I can't say I'm resting easy knowing a simple hide is all that separates me from a watery grave."

"You don't like the water?"

"Can you blame me? A Dwarf's idea of a perfect place is somewhere surrounded by stone, not some flimsy excuse for a boat."

"Hey now," said Natalia, drawn by the conversation. "The Orcs offered us what assistance they could. You must learn to be more thankful."

"Oh, I am," said Belgast. "Believe me, I truly am, but these deaths hit me hard. How many other dangers must we face as we head towards the sea?"

"You make a good point," said Athgar, "yet there's more to consider. Once we're done in the city, we must still return home."

"I suppose that's true, but hopefully, we won't take the same route. Maybe even return by way of Kragen-Tor? I'd love to show you my home."

"I thought Runewald was your home now?"

"Can't a Dwarf have more than one home?"

"Of course he can," said Natalia. "Now, it's getting late, and we've got a busy day ahead of us tomorrow."

"Someone should stay on watch," said Athgar.

"Yes," agreed Belgast. "They should be armed with ranged weapons and watch the sky."

"Oh yes?" said Natalia. "And tell me, how would you see anything in the dark?"

"Night vision. We Dwarves might not be as good at it as the Orcs, but we're still better than you Humans."

"Thankfully, that has been taken from our hands. The Orcs already set up a watch system, and neither of you is part of it."

"What about Stanislav?"

"What of him?" replied Natalia. "He's been asleep for some time now. I suggest you join him."

king about the baron's oppressive manners. Rest assured, I will do all I can to correct this issue."

She saw a look of hope spring to the fellow's face. He opened his mouth to speak, but she cut him off.

"If you do not tell me your name, sir, I will not need to lie about knowing your identity."

"Thank you," he mumbled. "And may the Saints guide you on your way."

"You say we should leave the river. May I ask how far until we must do so?"

"Not far. You'll know when you're close; there's a large oak tree with roots extending into the river. Just beyond is a turn where the rocks first appear."

"Thank you," said Natalia. "We will now take our leave of you."

They wandered back to the boats.

"Are you sure that was a good idea?" said Athgar.

"What? Offering help?"

"We're meant to be headed to Karslev, not stopping along the way to put pressure on a noble."

"I have an ulterior motive," said Natalia. "If we can gain favour with the king, he might allow us passage on one of his ships."

"You have a devious mind and a much better grasp of such things than I do."

"Well, I learned all about courts at the Volstrum. The least I can do is put some of that knowledge to work on our behalf."

"You're enjoying this far too much!"

"I must agree. It's truly frightening how easily I fall back into my old ways. You must promise to keep me on the straight and narrow."

"I shall do my best."

The boats pushed off and resumed the trip. The river here was wide but shallow, and Athgar swore he could see the bottom of the river several times.

The oak tree soon came into view, its gnarled roots protruding like a nasty wound from the riverbank. They pulled the umaks ashore, then made their way towards the expected rapids to gather a sense of the area before carrying their boats any farther.

They'd expected to see water swirling around a series of rocks. Instead, the river was so shallow you could easily walk across it, leading Athgar to wonder where it all was going. Natalia stepped into the river, sure-footed and feeling at home in the water.

"There's a pool at the base here," she noted, "which likely means there's an underground tunnel feeding the water through." She knelt in the river and began casting, words tumbling from her mouth in a soothing tone.

Athgar had never seen her quite like this. Typically, when she cast, the words of power carried weight, but these almost felt like a lullaby. The water splashed near her, and then a head appeared. At first, he took it for a gigantic rat, but then it swam towards her, revealing its flattened tail.

He'd heard of beavers but had never seen one. It was quite an odd-looking creature, yet it didn't look menacing despite its size and appearance. Natalia held out her hand, and it came towards her. She leaned forward, uttering more words, and the beaver chattered back excitedly.

Athgar was mesmerized. She had told him it was possible to communicate with river mammals, yet to actually see it was another experience altogether. He wanted the moment to last forever, to revel in the sight before him. This was true magic, not of death and destruction, but of friendship and trust. The beaver turned, splashing back into the deep water.

"I was right," she said. "There's a tunnel beneath that empties below."

"How far below?" asked Belgast.

"According to my new friend, we should be able to spot it from over there." She moved downriver, stepping carefully to avoid slipping in the shallow water. It took her but a moment to spot what she was looking for. "I see it," she announced. "There's a swirl of water where the tunnel comes up. Do you see it?"

Athgar stared but saw nothing. "I'll take your word for it."

"Beyond is plain water, but we must beware the water snake."

"Water snake?"

"Yes, Ash Biter's name for it."

"Ash Biter?"

Natalia chuckled. "That's what he calls himself. It's his favourite type of wood. Of course, that's a Human translation."

Belgast let out a snort. "And here I thought this was going to bite us in the ash."

"I don't believe I'm familiar with a water snake," said Stanislav, ignoring the Dwarf's comment. "Are they common in this region?"

"I believe he was talking about a river serpent," said Natalia, "judging from the size. He mentioned it was big enough to swallow him whole."

"I am suddenly overcome with a desire to walk."

"It can't be that bad," said Belgast. "If we can survive a wyvern, we can survive anything."

"Better we don't tempt it," said Natalia. "In any case, the northern side of the river looks like it's more traversable. We should collect the boats and keep moving."

They returned to the umaks to gather their things. The boats proved remarkably light, yet they were all sweating profusely by the time they reached the rocky shelf.

"This won't take too long," said Belgast.

"Easy for you to say," replied Stanislav. "You're not carrying a boat."

It was true. The Dwarf, with his shorter stature, couldn't carry one end of an umak, not for lack of trying, of course, but manoeuvring the boats through the underbrush was difficult at the best of times. It would have been almost impossible with one end lower than the other. In the end, they compromised. Athgar and Natalia carried one, Gamrag and Rotuk another, while Morgash and Azug, the final two Orc hunters, brought the third.

Over the course of the next mile or so, the river dropped close to one hundred feet, and they passed several waterfalls, the last one being the largest. At its base, they halted once more. Athgar and Gamrag scouted out the area while everyone else rested until they returned later in the day.

"Anything of interest?" asked Natalia.

"I'm afraid it's difficult terrain," said Athgar. "There's far too much vegetation to carry the boats. We must enter the water. How far down was this river serpent supposed to be?"

"In this very area, but I assume it will roam up and down the river looking for food."

"And how big is this thing?"

"Larger than one of our boats, I imagine."

"That doesn't exactly inspire confidence. Could you use your magic to talk to it?"

"I doubt it," said Natalia. "The spell assumes the creature involved would not be hostile. It must also be a warm-blooded, air-breathing animal, whereas a serpent would be closer to a giant snake."

"So that's a no, then?"

"Most definitely."

"Have you any spell that might keep it at bay?"

"I suppose I could calm the water."

"How would that help?"

"I imagine it would be attracted by movement or noise. If I make the river calm, there'll be fewer waves to rub up against the boats. And we'll need to paddle quietly."

"It's worth a try," said the Dwarf.

"We'll make camp," said Athgar. "There's no sense entering the river until morning. The last thing we want to do is find this thing in the dark." He paused, considering his words. "Say, they don't come out of the water, do they?"

"No," replied Natalia. "Serpents like to remain submerged whenever possible. That doesn't, however, preclude the possibility of them attacking anything close to the riverbank, so I would advise we keep well back from the water's edge."

"An excellent idea."

Morning came far too early. They struggled out of bed to a mist hiding the far bank of the river. After a brief meal of dried meat, they loaded the boats. The water was still, making the hair on Athgar's neck stand up on end. Therengians had a lot of superstitions regarding still waters, but he was determined to appear calm.

They pushed off, Athgar paddling in the back and steering the boat. With Azug in the front, Natalia, free of such a burden, watched their surroundings, lest one of her spells be needed. Behind them followed Gamrag, Morgash, and Belgast, while Stanislav and Rotuk brought up the rear.

Athgar risked a look over his shoulder; the mist already hid the third boat, and he fought down panic. Water was not his favourite domain at the best of times, and the thought of a river serpent lurking beneath set him on edge.

The boat bumped against something, and he froze while the umak kept gliding forward, carried by the last stroke of his paddle. A ripple caught his attention, and he saw a dark shape beneath the surface, moving roughly parallel to them. Natalia saw it, too, but remained calm.

They sat there silently for an agonizingly long time, and Athgar had to force himself to breathe. The boats slowed slightly, but the current had them, and they continued drifting downstream.

The ripple came closer, and then a crest sprouted from the river, reminding Athgar of a large dorsal fin. As it headed directly for them, he imagined a giant head rising from the water, mouth wide open and ready to engulf them.

A slapping sound near the shoreline caught his attention. The great river serpent altered its course while Athgar sought the source of the noise, only to spot Ash Biter rushing off into the trees.

Athgar paddled for all he was worth, eager to put as much distance between them as possible. The umak leaped forward, and he kept up his pace until the mist masked the shadow. His nerves calmed, but then a terrible roar echoed off the trees, sending shivers down his back. A quick glance over his shoulder told him the others had closed the distance, yet still, the thought of the great serpent drove them on.

CARLINGEN

Summer 1108 SR

Slop buckets emptied into the streets of Carlingen, the effluent running in rivers beside the dirt roads. Occasionally, wooden planks were put down to help avoid sinking into the muck and mire making up most of the town's thoroughfares. Belgast stepped in something vile and let out a curse.

"I thought you said people came here for anything and everything."

"I did," replied Stanislav. "Although perhaps it deserves some explanation. They don't come here because of any treasure; they come here because there are few laws governing how people behave." He glanced around at the townsfolk. "The streets, for example, are run by gangs, the docks by pirates, and the palace itself? Well, that's a whole other story."

"You're not making this sound very enticing."

"Nonsense. I've been here many times, and I've had very few problems. We're also in a group. That should help."

"Help what?"

"To keep us safe. Now, somewhere down here is the road that leads… ah, there it is. This way!"

Stanislav turned left onto a road a little drier than what they had so far seen. Individuals in well-made clothing walked up and down what looked like a well-to-do business area, while warriors wearing orange surcoats with puffed-up chests and shiny armour wandered around.

"Those are the king's men," noted Stanislav. "This entire area is his domain."

"I thought the whole kingdom was his domain?" said Athgar.

"It is if you want to get particular, but he rarely concerns himself with events outside of his immediate control."

"Why is that?"

"Who knows?"

"How far to the palace?" asked Natalia.

"It's just up here. Actually, you'll be able to see it as the road curves to the right."

Their small group continued along, drawing a lot of attention from the neatly dressed guards.

"What's the matter with you?" said Belgast, looking at one of the fellows who sneered as they passed. "Haven't you ever seen a Dwarf before?"

"Ignore them," said Stanislav. "If you attempt to engage them in conversation, it'll only get worse. Trust me, I've tried."

The road turned, and then the palace came into view—an impressive structure because of its size, but not at all ornate. In style, it was similar to the great fortress of Corassus, although these walls were shorter than those of the city-state.

The gates were open while a trio of guards stood watch, looking vigilant and well-armed. Upon their approach, the group was challenged.

"Who goes there," demanded the oldest of the three.

"Anastasia Stormwind," said Natalia, using the most haughty voice she could summon.

The guard clearly recognized the name. "My pardon, Your Grace. I assume these individuals are part of your entourage?"

"They are."

"Are you here to see His Majesty today?"

"That is not a matter to be discussed with a mere guard."

The man turned to his companions. "Don't just stand there," he barked out. "Move aside and let Her Grace pass!"

They entered the palace.

"That was impressive," whispered Athgar. "Does the Stormwind name always carry so much weight?"

"That's what they taught us."

"And who is this Anastasia Stormwind?"

"I made it up. I just liked the name."

"What now?"

"We try to find out the lay of the land, or in this case, the palace."

"This place is a wonder," said Belgast. "As in, I wonder how it's still standing—the stonework is atrocious."

"I think," said Stanislav, "that this is an example of form over function. No one ever accused the ruling family of Carlingen of having any sense of artistry when it comes to architecture."

"What's the king's name?" asked Natalia.

"King Maksim the Fourth. His family have ruled for more than two hundred years."

"And before that?" said Belgast.

"There was no 'before that'. This area was all wilderness."

"I have to admit the city is impressive for one that's only two hundred years old. Still, they could have done so much more had they spent some time planning things out a little."

"In this town, wealth talks"—Stanislav lowered his voice—"or the appearance of it. It's not only about flaunting your fortune; it's about acting like spending it is of little concern to you."

"And that works?"

"It's said Carlingen has been the fortune of many, although at what cost is unknown."

"I'm not sure I follow?"

"For every success story, there are a hundred failures. People are swallowed up by this city, never to be seen again."

"In that case," said the Dwarf, "I suggest we keep together as much as possible."

Natalia stopped short, almost causing the others to bump into her. She stared down the hallway, where a pair of women emerged from a doorway —one dressed in fine clothing, the other likely a servant.

"What's wrong?" said Athgar.

"I know her. We were at the Volstrum together."

Athgar looked around, desperate to find an escape route, but it was too late. The women were coming directly towards them.

"Greetings," called out the well-dressed one, who looked about to say something else, but then her demeanour slipped, and she let out a shriek of joy. "Natalia? Natalia Stormwind?"

"Svetlana? What are you doing here?"

"My goodness, it's been years. I haven't seen you since we graduated. How have you been?"

"Well," replied Natalia, struggling to hide her discomfort. "You?"

Svetlana's face fell slightly. "I've been here for the last five years. Not exactly my first choice, if I'm being blunt. Where did they send you?"

Thankfully, the woman had obviously heard nothing of Natalia's escape.

"I was in Draybourne," she lied, "down in the Duchy of Holstead. Are you familiar with it?"

"I can't say I am, but no matter, you're here now. What brings you to Carlingen?"

"We came here seeking a ship, in fact."

"Let me guess; you're returning to Karslev for your next assignment?"

"Something like that, yes."

"I wish I'd been recalled. It's ghastly being stuck here."

"What's the king like?"

"He's young," replied Svetlana, "and impressionable. He also has a weakness for a pretty face. I've managed to get him wrapped securely around my finger. Did you need to see him? I can arrange that if you like?"

"I would love to," said Natalia.

"And who are these people?"

"This is my entourage. It's not safe travelling unaccompanied these days."

Svetlana moved towards Athgar, looking him up and down. "This one's a fine-looking fellow. What's his name?"

"Why don't you ask him yourself?" said Natalia, the hint of a smile creasing her lips.

Svetlana gazed deep into Athgar's eyes—an unsettling experience. "Well? Who are you?"

"Rothgar," he replied.

"He's been with me for years," explained Natalia. "Tell me, did you ever end up breeding?"

"No. I was told I wasn't powerful enough to warrant that. A pity, as I looked forward to it. You, however, were the most powerful graduate in years. Surely they bred you?"

"They did. I had a daughter."

"Just the one?"

"That's all I could manage in the time they gave me."

"Might I ask who they chose for you?"

Natalia waved off the remark. "Oh, you know, the usual, a Fire Mage of great power." She winked at Athgar as her old school chum took in the rest of her party.

"An old man and a Dwarf. My goodness, Natalia, you've acquired quite an interesting group. Oh yes, I forgot. This is Olya."

The servant curtsied. "Pleased to meet you."

"Now," Svetlana continued, "you must come with me. We have much to catch up on."

"But I'm here to see the king," Natalia objected.

"There'll be plenty of time for that later. I'll introduce you myself." She took Natalia's arm and began leading her down the hall. "Now, tell me everything you've been up to these last few years."

Natalia collapsed into a chair. They'd found lodgings at the Warriors Rest, right across the street from a heavily fortified building of some sort. It was already dark when they arrived, and now that the rooms were sorted, they were all thoroughly exhausted.

"By the Saints, that woman can talk," said Natalia. "I don't remember her being so... verbose. Then again, she was always asking questions, so I shouldn't be so surprised."

"What did you talk about?" asked Athgar. "The last thing I heard was her wanting to know all about what you've been up to. I trust you didn't tell her the family was out to get you?"

"No, of course not. I simply told her what she wanted to hear."

"Which was?"

"All about the tempestuous affair I had with a king."

"A king?"

"Well," she said, smiling, "others might call him a king. I prefer the term 'High Thane'."

"So you told her about us?"

"Let's just say I used our relationship as a framework. The rest I made up. I spent more time turning the conversation around to talk about her. She seemed to enjoy that."

"How well did you know this woman?" asked Athgar.

"Svetlana was a fellow student, but I hesitate to use the term friend. She's a high-born, you see, and—"

"High-born?"

"Yes, someone born to the family. In other words, her parents were Stormwinds or Sartellians. Naturally, they selected her to become a battle mage with breeding like that. She treated me abysmally at first—they all did, simply because I wasn't one of them. That all changed when I won the competition. After that, everyone more or less accepted me. Well, maybe 'accepted is a little strong. More like respected my power; none of them were particularly friendly."

"And now?"

"She's realized she's lower on the pecking order. Did you notice her ring?"

"I can't say I did. Why?"

"It's blue magerite, but it's much paler than mine. That shows her relative power."

"So how powerful does that make her? And please, put it in terms I can understand."

"Powerful enough to graduate but not enough to breed. There's also the matter of her assignment to Carlingen. You can't get much more out of the way than this."

"So you're saying this isn't a prestigious assignment?"

"That's putting it mildly, but she does, at least, have the ear of the king here." She looked around the room, taking in their surroundings. "I see you didn't waste your time while we were busy chatting. Why did you pick this place?"

"I'm glad you asked," said Athgar, getting to his feet. He moved to the window, throwing the shutters wide open. Across the street sat the large fortified building. "Anything look familiar?"

"It looks like the Cunar commandery in Ebenstadt. Excuse me, I mean the Mathewite commandery."

"I'm told it's the same general layout, but this one is the training centre for the Temple Knights of Saint Agnes. Its presence here also makes it one of the city's safest areas."

"Are you suggesting they patrol the streets hereabouts?"

"They do, as a matter of fact. While you were off chatting about old times, Stanislav and I ran across one of their knights who recommended this place and told us about this section of the city."

Natalia rose, moving to the window to stand beside him. "I wonder how many Temple Knights it holds?"

"I don't know," said Athgar. "And to be honest, I don't really care, as long as they keep the peace. I'm far more interested in how you propose to broach the subject of a ship with the king."

"By invoking the name of the family. Svetlana tells me he's already under her control. It shocked me at first, but now that I look at all we've been through, I suppose it makes sense."

"What does?"

"Don't you see?" said Natalia. "The family doesn't just want a presence at each court; they want to control each court."

"And how do they do that?"

"A variety of ways if Svetlana is to be believed."

"Such as?"

"Intimidation, bribery, seduction—you name it."

"That's terrible," said Athgar. "Have they no morals?"

"You think a family who wanted to force me to bear children has morals?"

"No, I suppose not. I hadn't honestly thought about it. Does that mean you have an audience?"

"I do, and a private one at that. It seems the Saints heard our prayers."

"Or the Gods," added Athgar.

"Perhaps we're both wrong, and it's the Ancestors. It doesn't really matter, does it? What does matter is that I have a chance to speak directly with the king. I also planted a seed in Svetlana's head."

"Which was?"

"She knows she holds little value for the family. Here, however, she has the king's attention. Why not capitalize on that for her own advancement?"

"Meaning?"

"What if she married him?"

"But she's not a noble, is she?"

"No," said Natalia, "but imagine the influence she would gain for the family if she married into royalty, not to mention the rise in stature for him by marrying into a powerful line. Both sides would win."

"But that would make the family even stronger. I thought you wanted exactly the opposite."

"I do. I know that despite her protestations to the contrary, Svetlana is fed up with the family. This allows her to take a position that makes her virtually untouchable by the Stormwinds."

"Wouldn't they just kill her?"

"No, of course not; that would mean losing face. The family prides itself on its reputation as a force no one dares cross. They can't afford to go around killing the very nobles they hope to control. How would it look?"

"And will she do it, do you suppose?"

"I think she will. She claims to delight in controlling the man, but deep down, I believe she's fallen in love with him. She certainly talked about him in glowing terms when you lot weren't around. She seems happy, possibly for the first time in her life. In a sense, it's hard to believe she's the same Svetlana I knew back at the Volstrum."

"But the king here is ineffective. We saw that for ourselves."

"Yes, but think what he could do with her as his closest advisor. She is a battle mage, remember, and fully trained in the ways of politics. Who knows, maybe someday we'll be able to come and visit Carlingen as the Therengian delegation?"

"It WOULD be nice to have allies."

"Yes, and although the first step is small, at least it's in the right direction. Now, we must be off to bed. We have a busy day tomorrow—we're going to see the king."

"WE are?"

"Of course. You don't think I'd do it alone, do you?"

King Maksim the Fourth, had ruled Carlingen for the past two years, assuming the crown at the ripe old age of twenty-four, after his father succumbed to an unfortunate illness. His tenure as the king might have been brief, but he had grand ideas. Carlingen, at least in theory, commanded a large area, yet most of that was wilderness. Only the city itself was of any real value, but he hoped to change that. He'd suggested to his father that appointing barons would help expand the borders, but they had proven difficult to control once he claimed his kingship. Now, with the help of Svetlana Stormwind, he could usher in a stricter rule and regain the power his predecessors had whittled away.

The door opened, revealing Svetlana. He couldn't help but smile, for although she was a plain woman, he couldn't deny the attraction that existed between them.

"Your Majesty," she began. "I have someone I want you to meet. This is Natalia Stormwind, a mage of great power."

Natalia entered, making a deep curtsy. Behind her followed a trio of males, one of them a Dwarf.

"Greetings," said the king. "Any friend of Svetlana is welcome in my home."

"Thank you," said Natalia. "Svetlana spoke most highly of you. I see she did not exaggerate."

"So," the king continued, "what brings you to my city?"

"We are in need of your aid," she replied. "Aid which, while perhaps insignificant to you, could prove vital to the balance of power in the region."

The king sat up, his interest suddenly piqued. "Go on," he urged.

"We are on our way to Karslev, the capital of Ruzhina."

"I know where Karslev is. Might I ask the significance of this journey?"

"It's a matter that has far-reaching consequences for the Stormwinds," explained Natalia. "I imagine it could also greatly benefit your own rule."

"You intrigue me. What is this aid that you seek?"

"Merely a ship, Your Majesty, to take us to Porovka."

"And that is all?"

"That and perhaps a request that you pay more attention to your subjects."

The king stared back, unblinking. "What is it you are accusing me of?"

"You, personally? Nothing, Your Majesty, but it has come to our attention the Baron of Raketsk has been overtaxing his landholders."

"In what way?"

"He takes food in place of coins."

"A common enough practice," defended the king.

"Indeed, yet he leaves them with scant supplies to last the winter." Natalia briefly fell silent. "Were your other nobles to do likewise, you would soon have no people left to rule."

King Maksim looked around the room, taking in all the occupants. "What do you think, Svetlana?"

"I've known Natalia for many years," the woman replied, moving closer to stand before the king. "If what she claims is true, then it behooves you to take action. It may well prove to be the very thing that strengthens your rule." She reached forward, placing her hand upon his. In response, he grasped hers, holding it fondly.

"Then so be it," he said. "I will find a ship for Natalia Stormwind and have words with this baron of mine."

"Thank you," said Svetlana. She stared at him, continuing to hold his hand.

King Maksim spoke to the others. "You may leave us. I shall send word once we have further news of a ship. In the meantime, Svetlana and I have much to discuss…" He turned to her. "Wouldn't you agree?"

Her smile lit up the room. "Indeed, Your Majesty."

POROVKA

Summer 1108 SR

T he ship pitched violently, sending Athgar scrambling to grab hold of
the railing while Natalia stood calmly by the mast, her eyes scanning
the horizon. A light drizzle in the air was enough to obscure the immediate
area, yet the Water Mage appeared unfazed by it.

They'd left Carlingen on the early morning tide, sailing north along the
coast. In theory, the trip was easy enough, for the *Bergannon* only had to
follow the coastline. It soon became apparent the ship didn't so much sail as
wallow, with the deck pitching back and forth and tipping to the sides with
every wave.

Athgar thought Natalia's magic might help, but try as she might, her
spells could do little to correct the *Bergannon's* roll. She'd finally given up on
the idea, consigning them to a rough voyage.

To be sure, his own stomach was testy, but he felt positively fit
compared to Belgast. The poor Dwarf had spent the bulk of his time
perched at the railing, waiting for his breakfast to make its escape. As the
day wore on, Athgar became used to it, enough that he could wander the
deck without fear of releasing his stomach's contents.

Natalia not only endured, she thrived, and he saw the joy she had at the
sight of the Great Northern Sea. From his point of view, it was little other
than a grey-green mass of water, but she saw endless open seas teaming
with life.

They spotted a whale farther out to sea late in the afternoon, which Natalia said was a good omen. Athgar wondered if that meant the ship might stop rolling, but it proved not to be the case.

That night, they lay below deck, Natalia fast asleep while Athgar tried to relax. Every time he felt his eyes closing, the ship would roll, and then his body would do likewise. After the third such event, he gave up any pretence of trying to sleep and went up on deck. The dim moonlight reflected off the sea as the ship, anchored for the night, had its sails furled and only a single crewman on watch.

"Good evening," the man called out.

"It's a calm night," said Athgar.

"It is, although I daresay tomorrow won't be so. We're in for a storm, if you ask me."

"Why would you say that?"

"I can feel it in the air."

Athgar was about to ask if he was a mage of some sort but thought better of it. He wandered over to the starboard side, gazing at the distant tree-covered shoreline, and thought of his new home back in Runewald.

"I'm surprised there aren't more kingdoms along here," he called out. "The land looks quite inviting."

"That's Zaran," the crewman said. "They call it the Lost Kingdom."

"Lost? It doesn't seem to have gone anywhere."

"A fellow calling himself King Karzik claimed it. He left Carlingen with a fleet of six ships and landed up the coast, not too far from here, as a matter of fact."

"How long ago was this?"

"Nigh on a century."

"What happened to them?"

"That's just it—no one knows," said the crewman. "They found the ships' wreckage and evidence that the survivors went inland, but naught was found of them. To this day, it's still a mystery."

"And so Zaran remains a wilderness?"

"Aye, but both Ruzhina and Carlingen recognize it as a kingdom."

"I would hazard a guess that has more to do with politics," said Athgar. "I imagine Ruzhina enjoys having a safe border."

"It has no army, that much is true, but I'd hardly call it safe. Over the years, we've heard rumours of terrible things living there. Even now, the occasional hardy adventurer enters that foreboding land, seeking out its treasures."

"And do any of them return?"

"Only those who give in to their fears."

"King Karzik," said Athgar, mulling over the name. "It's an unusual name."

"You'll get no argument from me."

The wind picked up, sending a shiver down the Therengian's neck. "I think I shall return below. This weather is a tad cool to my liking."

"Suit yourself," said the crewman. "And sleep well. You'll need your strength tomorrow."

Natalia awoke with a start to find the ship rocking violently. Obviously, a storm had been unleashed, for she heard rain crashing down on the deck above. To make matters worse, the ship's caulking needed repairs, resulting in a near-constant dripping below decks.

She decided to let Athgar sleep, intending to make her way above decks. As soon as she threw open the hatch, however, water sluiced down, drenching her in its icy grip and taking her breath away. Rethinking her plan, she moved back to her husband and crouched beside him. A gentle touch was all that was needed, and then he was staring up at her.

"Something wrong?" he asked.

"I need to go up on deck and help out," she explained, "but the water is absolutely frigid. I hoped you might cast a spell of warmth on me."

"That won't keep you dry."

"No, but at least I won't freeze."

"Very well," he said, getting to his feet. The ship suddenly pitched, and he staggered to the side. Only Natalia's hand stopped him from hitting his head on the deck beam above. "This is going to be more difficult than I thought." He braced himself before he began calling on his inner spark. Moments later, Natalia felt a comforting warmth envelop her body.

"Shall I come up with you?" asked Athgar.

"No, remain here and stay dry. I shan't be long."

She returned to the stairs and climbed up, grasping the hatch and steeling herself for the inevitable sluice of water. She felt a reassuring touch on her ankle and looked down to see Athgar.

"As if I'd let you go up there alone," he said.

"Don't say I didn't warn you."

She pushed open the hatch, and a flood of water cascaded down, drenching them both. Natalia made her way up, then moved closer to the mainmast. At some point, someone had tied a length of rope around its girth, and she took hold of it, steadying herself. Athgar soon joined her, squinting against the blast of rain.

"I can calm the waters," said Natalia, "but I'll need both hands."

"I understand." He gripped the rope with one hand and then stood behind her, his other arm wrapped around her waist. With the howling wind and the press of water, he could hear little but soon recognized the buzzing in the air as her spell built. It didn't take long before there was a marked reduction in the pitching of the deck.

"There," said Natalia. "That's much better. Now, I'll call on the currents to give us some forward mobility. That should steady us even further."

Again, magic words tumbled from her mouth, releasing the spell, and then water swirled around either side of the hull. The *Bergannon* began moving, its deck stabilizing as it sliced through the water. Natalia turned, facing Athgar, his arm still around her.

"That should do it," she called out, her voice faint against the backdrop of the storm.

"I'm guessing we need to remain on deck?"

"Yes, just in case we near any rocks, then my magic will be needed."

"Well," he said, pulling her closer, "at least we'll be warm."

She laughed. "Of course we will. You cast your spell of warmth."

He grinned. "That's not quite what I meant."

The storm raged for most of the morning, but when the clouds finally broke, it revealed a far calmer sea than either of them had hoped for. Natalia renewed her spells from time to time, and the *Bergannon* continued steadily northward.

They kept the coast in sight, for the captain feared the deep waters for some reason. Athgar had a hard time understanding why until Natalia informed him of some of the creatures that lived out at sea.

Whales and seals he was familiar with, but her description of a large tentacled thing made him swear off ships altogether. With memories of the river serpent still fresh in his mind, he had no desire to see the seaborne equivalent or any other creature of similar size.

Thankfully, the rest of the trip proved uneventful, and within a fortnight, they spotted Porovka. Unlike Carlingen, this great city was fortified with a sea wall to protect the harbour. The *Bergannon* finally sailed into the port and dropped anchor.

The four of them took their leave of the captain and were rowed ashore. The Dwarf's first action upon landing was to drop to his knees and kiss the ground.

"I assume you won't be sailing again any time soon?" said Stanislav.

"Not if I can help it," Belgast replied. "That was, quite possibly, the worst experience of my life. It'll likely take weeks for my stomach to recover." He stood for a moment before spotting a nearby tavern. "Then again, maybe not. Shall we partake of an ale?"

"Shouldn't we be heading inland?" asked Natalia.

"I believe he's onto something," said Stanislav. "It might give us a chance to get the lay of the land."

"I thought you were from Ruzhina?" said Athgar.

"I am, but I've been away for quite some time. It would be prudent to bring myself up to date on recent events before we proceed."

"Come along, then," said Belgast, his stomach's unease having vanished at the thought of a drink.

The Laughing Dog was a modest affair boasting little other than a single room and a motley collection of mismatched chairs and tables. Upon being seated, they were given an extremely pale ale. Athgar was a little leery of the stuff, but Belgast drained his tankard in one gulp. As the Dwarf set down his cup, he let out a belch that echoed off the walls.

"Not bad," he said. "I'll have another, if you please."

The barman, happy to oblige, took Belgast's coins and set another tankard before him.

"Tell me," said Belgast, "what's new in these parts?"

"Nothing much," the man responded. "Things have been quiet of late."

"No rumours to speak of?"

"A Church ship was spotted off the coast a week ago, but it never entered the harbour."

"A Church ship? I didn't know they had a Holy Fleet up here in the north."

"They say it harbours to the west," explained the barman. "In a chain of islands called the Five Sisters. Has done for some years now."

"And it sails off the coast of Ruzhina?"

"Their ships sail all over the Great Northern Sea, constantly on the lookout for raiders and pirates."

"And has that proven successful?" asked Natalia.

"Such attacks are rare now, not that I know from personal experience, but you know how patrons talk."

"It's a frightening thought," said Athgar.

"What is? A Church ship?" asked the Dwarf.

"Naturally. I can't say I welcome the thought of a bunch of Cunars breathing down our necks. We haven't had the best of relations with them in the past."

"Their ships aren't run by the Cunars," noted the barman.

"If not the Temple Knights of Saint Cunar, then who?" asked Athgar.

"Saint Agnes."

"Well, that's a development I hadn't expected," said Natalia. "How long has that been around?"

"We first heard of them some ten years ago. Since then, their presence has increased substantially."

"I wonder what that portends," mused Athgar.

"It's the empire," said Natalia. "War is coming, and the Church is trying to prepare for it."

"You mean the Halvarians? I thought they'd been quiet of late."

"They were likely lulling everyone into a false sense of security."

"Maybe they only want to be left to themselves?"

"No," said Natalia. "They claim it's their destiny to rule over the entire Continent. I can't see them just sitting back and letting us live in peace."

"Well," said Athgar, "it's not as if they threaten us here. This part of the Continent is about as far away from them as one can be."

"That's true for the moment, but the more they grow, the stronger they get."

"I'm not sure what you're trying to insinuate."

"The Petty Kingdoms must hold them off now, while there's still a chance."

"And do you think they can do that?"

Natalia looked down, apparently not pleased with her own thoughts. "I'm afraid not. They spend all their time bickering with one another. It would take a powerful leader to unite them long enough to defeat the empire, if that were even possible."

"Every army has its weakness."

"True, but Halvaria is immense."

"So was the Old Kingdom, and that still fell."

"True, but Halvaria must be twice the size Therengia was when it was destroyed."

Athgar smiled. "That means it'll make more noise on the way down."

"How can you be so flippant about something so dire?"

"I have no control over the Petty Kingdoms' politics, and I'm pretty sure the nobles of the Continent would take little advice from the likes of me."

"You might be surprised," said Natalia. "One person, in the right place at the right time, can make all the difference."

"Well," he replied. "I, for one, am pleased to be right here with you at this exact time."

Stanislav rose, downing the rest of his drink. "You lot wait here. I'm going to arrange a carriage."

"I thought we were walking?" said Belgast.

"It's a lot of steps to get to Karslev. I don't know about you, but I prefer not to wear out my boots."

"Sounds reasonable. You find us a carriage, and I'll stay here and keep this ale warm."

"Be careful," warned Natalia. "We're in Ruzhina now. The family holds a good deal of sway here."

"I will," said the mage hunter. "I promise."

By the time Stanislav returned, Belgast was well into his cups. Athgar had seen the Dwarf consume vast quantities of alcohol in the past, but always to little effect. Here, it wasn't so much that he was drunk as overly talkative. He began regaling the patrons with tales of great heroes and mighty deeds. The Therengian feared he might tell of more recent exploits, thus revealing their true identities.

Thankfully, the mage hunter returned before the Dwarf could finish his tale of the Dragon of Eastholding. With the help of Stanislav, they dragged Belgast from the tavern and convinced him to enter the carriage. The driver snapped out his whip, and they began moving, Belgast soon falling asleep.

"That was close," said Athgar.

"Yes," agreed Stanislav. "Was that the Dragon of Eastholding he was talking about?"

"Yes, why? Have you heard it?"

"You might say that."

"Meaning?" prompted Natalia.

"The story has no end. At least that's been my experience."

"What do you mean, 'no end'?"

"He goes on about it forever. I spent an entire evening listening to him rambling on, and he never got to the end. Personally, I don't believe there is one."

"How can that be?"

"I think he makes up the thing every time he starts. I must have heard it half a dozen times, each one different, yet all called the Dragon of East-holding."

Athgar chuckled. "Perhaps that's our secret weapon, boring stories to lull the family into a false sense of security?"

"At this point, I'd take anything," said Natalia. "The closer we get to Karslev, the more unease I feel. We're almost there, and we still don't have a plan. It's beginning to feel like a fool's errand."

"We'll find a way. We just need some time.

"At least there's some good news," said Stanislav.

"Which is?" asked Natalia.

"Word of your troubles with the family seems to be largely confined to those in charge. I'm guessing they would be too embarrassed to admit you escaped them."

"How does that help us?"

"It means," said Athgar, "we can go about our business in Karslev with little chance of discovery."

"As long as you avoid the Volstrum," added Stanislav. "I'm sure Marakhova Stormwind would not be so quick to forget you."

"Agreed," said Natalia, "and we have no idea who's in her inner circle. We must be extra careful."

"That's not as difficult as you might imagine. The people who run the Volstrum seldom travel outside its walls. That does give us a certain amount of freedom."

"Are you sure?" asked Athgar.

"Positive. I lived in Karslev most of my life, and I could probably count on one hand the number of times I ran into any member of the Volstrum within the city itself."

The Therengian peered out the window as the carriage passed through the streets of Porovka, but he could see the city walls fast approaching. They would soon be in the countryside and on their way. He turned to his travelling companions.

"What can we expect in Karslev? I mean, as far as the city is concerned, is it much like this place?"

"Not quite," replied Natalia. "In fact, it's the most singular city I've ever seen."

"I would agree," added Stanislav. "Karslev was carefully planned right from the beginning. It has wide streets, far wider than anything else I've seen on the Continent, and I've travelled quite a bit. Also, many of the buildings are made of stone."

"They don't use wood?"

"They do on the outskirts, but Karslev is very old. Most of the buildings date back centuries, and stone and brick replaced wooden walls over the years."

"The other thing you should be aware of," said Natalia, "is the social structure. In Ruzhina, nobles own the peasants."

"You mean as slaves?" asked Athgar.

"In a manner of speaking. They're actually indentured servants. In theory, they can buy their freedom by working off their contracts, but that seldom happens."

"Truly?"

"Oh yes," said Stanislav. "I was once one myself. I only escaped because war came to Ruzhina. I used the bounty from joining the army to pay off my debt. Had it not been for that, I would be there still, assuming, of course, I wasn't dead by now."

Athgar let it all sink in. "I don't think I'm going to enjoy Karslev very much."

ARRIVAL

Summer 1108 SR

By any standard, Karslev was an immense city. Less impressive was the fact that it boasted no walls to defend itself or even a tower to hold back any potential attackers. For all practical purposes, the city was utterly undefended if one ignored the presence of the Volstrum.

The magical academy's reputation was what, in truth, protected the city, for who in their right mind would seek to take on the most powerful line of spellcasters to ever live? Through selective breeding, they'd created a veritable army of incredibly gifted Water Mages, who stood head and shoulders above any others who might seek to challenge them for supremacy.

Despite the apparent lack of defences, Athgar found the city intimidating. He'd seen stone buildings before; even Ebenstadt had a few, but what he hadn't expected was their overall height. He had never seen ones of more than two floors, yet here, in the capital of Ruzhina, three or more appeared to be the norm.

The carriage dropped them in front of a house before continuing on its way. Stanislav waited until the sound of the horses' hooves dissipated before speaking.

"This house belongs to an old associate of mine. I haven't seen them in some time, so it's best you let me go and talk before I introduce everyone."

"And what are we to do in the meantime?" asked Athgar.

"Just wait here. I shouldn't be long."

"Don't you think that might draw unwanted attention?"

"We are surrounded by houses. I doubt anyone will even notice."

Natalia looked around them. "It's not a wealthy section of the city. I wouldn't think any Stormwinds live here."

"Thank Gundar for that," said the Dwarf. He stepped off the road and sat down on the grass, stretching out his legs. "I'm going to take a nap. Let me know when something interesting happens." He promptly lay down on his back and closed his eyes.

Stanislav went and knocked on the door. He spoke with the person who answered, his tones too low for anyone else to hear.

Athgar moved to stand beside Natalia. "Who do you think that is?" he asked in a whisper.

"I have no idea. I really don't know much about his past outside of his role as a mage hunter. I do trust him, however. After all, he helped me escape the Volstrum."

"It's not him I distrust."

"What are you suggesting?"

"Merely that he's been gone from Karslev for a few years. That's plenty of time for the family to get hold of his associates."

"And do what?" asked Natalia. "Set up a trap? They'd need to know we intended to return to do that, and we didn't even know ourselves until the day before we left. You must strive to be more trusting."

"Natalia," Stanislav called out. "There's someone here I'd like you to meet."

She moved closer to see an older woman, more akin to the mage hunter's age, standing in the doorway.

"This is Laisa Voronsky."

"Radetsky," the woman corrected. "I gave up using your name years ago."

Natalia's eyebrows shot up.

"We were once married," explained Stanislav. "In any case, she's agreed to take us in temporarily."

"How temporary?"

"Until we conclude our business here in Karslev."

"You must come in," said Laisa. "We can't have you all hanging around here like some common labourers." She led them into a large room with a plain, wooden floor and an assortment of chairs. "Have a seat," she added, "and I'll fetch you something to drink. Have you eaten at all?"

"No," said Stanislav. "We only just arrived by coach."

"Well then, it appears I shall need to spend some time in the kitchen."

"Shall I help you?"

She gave him a look that brooked no interference. "And since when have I ever needed YOUR help?"

Duly chastised, the mage hunter joined the others and took a seat.

"Is that truly your wife?" asked Natalia. "I thought she died?"

"She might as well have. I came back from a trip abroad to find she'd taken up with someone else. Not that I can blame her, mind you. I was gone an exceptionally long time."

"Let me guess, someone named Radetsky?"

"Yes, he died about five years ago, right before I helped you escape. This was his house."

"He seems to have provided for her future. What did he do?"

"A merchant—wine merchant, to be exact."

"Really? Did he make his own wine?"

"No, but he specialized in buying and selling it. I shall miss him if only for the fine wine he imported from Reinwick."

"You knew him?"

"Naturally. Otherwise, I never would have agreed to Laisa's remarriage."

"Hold on a moment," said Athgar. "Are you saying you unmarried her? I didn't even know that was possible." He glanced at Natalia and blushed. "Not that I would ever consider that myself, of course."

"The custom in Ruzhina," explained Stanislav, "is a husband and wife may call off their marriage provided he finds someone else to support her."

"I thought you said you came back to find her living with him."

"I did, but they weren't married!"

Athgar shook his head. "What strange customs you people have."

"Hey now," said Natalia. "They're my customs, too, not that I have any interest in using them. I'm happy with the way things are between us."

"Me too."

Laisa stepped back into the room, carrying a wooden tray filled with cups. "Here we are," she said. "A nice light wine to help drive the thirst away."

They each took one, drinking sparingly, even the Dwarf.

"A marvellous taste, that," said Belgast. "Might I ask what it's made from?"

"Apples, although there are a few herbs thrown in to give it additional flavour. I make it myself."

"Have you ever thought of selling it? I daresay you could make a fortune off it."

"I'm afraid my days of running a business are at an end. I'm content to live out my life in peace and relaxation."

"A pity," said Belgast.

"Are you familiar with the family?" asked Natalia.

"Naturally," the woman replied. "One can hardly live in Karslev and not know of them. What is it, in particular, you want to know?"

"We know all about the Volstrum, for I was a student there, but we're looking for the home of Illiana Stormwind."

"If you're looking for her, you're too late. She died some time ago. Marakhova Stormwind rules the family now, or so I'm told."

"That's not good news," said Stanislav. "She never did like me."

"She wasn't fond of me either," said Natalia. "That's going to make things a little more difficult."

Athgar was intrigued. "This Marakhova, you say she's the head of the family. Does she live in an immense house?"

"Yes, Stormwind Manor. It's the ancestral home of the head of the family and has been for generations."

"And where might we find this manor?"

"It lies to the east of the city, surrounded by a large estate. But if you're going there, you'll need to take care."

"Who says we're going there?"

Laisa gave Athgar a look that said he wasn't fooling anyone.

"Maybe we just have an interest in politics?" he countered.

"Come now, I know Stanislav. He wouldn't be here for no reason. Add to that your little enquiry about Stormwind Manor, and I can easily see it's more than just a convenient topic of conversation."

"I like her," said Belgast. "She's very plain-spoken."

"All right," said Stanislav. "It's time for the truth."

"Are you sure we can trust her?" asked Natalia.

"If I didn't feel that way, we wouldn't be here."

Laisa crossed her arms. "Go on, then," she urged. "Time to tell me what you're all up to."

Stanislav sipped his wine, taking a moment to gather his thoughts. "This," he said, raising his glass to indicate Natalia, "is Natalia Stormwind, who graduated from the Volstrum back in the summer of oh-three. From the moment she finished her training, they began grooming her for greater things."

"Greater things, meaning?"

"They wanted to breed me," said Natalia. "Not that I had any say in the matter."

"Let me guess," said Laisa, turning to Stanislav. "You helped her escape."

"I did."

"That explains why you haven't been around these last few years, but what I don't understand is why you're back here now?"

"It's definitely worth a try," said Athgar. "How would we find out about something like that? Is there a festival around here we don't know about?"

"No," said Laisa. "At least not anything the Stormwinds would celebrate. They're not the type to take part in such things."

"Do they have no gatherings at all?"

"Most assuredly, but only family members are usually invited, and only the most influential ones at that. You'd have a hard time trying to pass yourself off as one of them. In any case, aren't those the very same people who are looking for you?"

"They are," said Natalia.

"Then you have your answer," said Laisa. "You'd be walking straight into a trap. You might as well surrender now and resign yourself to imprisonment, or worse."

"What could be worse?" said Athgar. "Death?"

"No," replied Natalia. "She's referring to forced breeding." She shuddered. "I won't submit to that, not under any circumstances."

"There must be a better way to approach this," suggested the Dwarf. "What are our strengths?"

"That's easy," said Athgar. "Natalia. She's likely the most powerful caster in these parts."

"Powerful in terms of raw ability, possibly, but not necessarily the most effective."

"What do you mean?"

"Simple," continued Belgast. "We already know the Stormwinds are capable of more spells than Natalia."

"That's true," she agreed. "Graduates are armed with the most basic battle spells. Only those with more experience are given access to the Inner Sanctum."

"What's that?"

"A great repository of advanced magic. It's where the masters all go to learn new spells."

"Where is this repository?" asked Athgar. "And more importantly, how could we gain access to it?"

"To what end?"

"It's full of spells. It's literally the equivalent of sneaking into a castle and finding the armoury."

"Not quite," said Natalia. "Spells take time to learn, not to mention plenty of practice. You can't just grab them and leave—magic doesn't work that way. In any case, it's out of our reach. The Inner Sanctum lies within the Volstrum, and that, my friends, is the most heavily guarded building in Karslev."

"All right," said Belgast. "That's another idea we can't pursue. What else have we got? Athgar's a Fire Mage, pardon me, a 'master of flame'. Could he burn down the manor?"

"I could definitely give it a try," said Athgar, "but then we lose whatever that ring unlocks. We need to get inside the place, not destroy it, at least not until we get what we're after."

"The problem," said Natalia, "is we don't even know what we're looking for. How, then, do we go about searching for it, even if we CAN get inside?"

"It's a puzzle, to be sure," said Athgar. "The one thing we do know is we lack sufficient knowledge at the moment to do much of anything."

Stanislav snapped his fingers. "Then that's where we'll start."

"I'm not sure I follow?"

"We'll concentrate for now on finding out as much about our adversary as possible."

"In regards to what?"

"Anything and everything. We need to know who stays at the manor, how many guards they have, how often do they leave, all sorts of things."

"And how do you propose we discover all this—just walk up to the guards and ask?"

The mage hunter smiled. "We observe. Find out the taverns they frequent, and buy lots of drinks. Above all, we keep our ears open. When people drink, they often complain about their lives. We should be the sympathetic ears that take all this information in."

"So we do what?" asked Athgar. "Listen to gossip?"

"If need be, yes. The more information we gather, the bigger the picture we'll see. Even seemingly insignificant things can reveal more important parts of the whole. Take, for example, a guard who complains about the food."

"How would that help us?"

"By itself, it likely doesn't, but what if he mentions who supplies the food? Now we have another person we can talk with, hopefully finding out even more."

Athgar grinned. "I see now. The real difficulty will lie not in collecting all this information but making sense of it."

"I can help with that," said Laisa. "I've been dealing with gossip all my life."

NEWS

Summer 1108 SR

Akim Zhukov rested his elbow on the table in an attempt to steady his hand. He was eager to partake of the full tankard he held, but his companion, a thin fellow, named Sergei, kept rambling on about all manner of things. Akim didn't want to appear rude, so he held his drink, even as his taste buds were desperate to experience the golden-hued mead.

"Like I was saying," continued Sergei, "the captain wasn't having any of it. Why, if he hadn't spoken up, I'd be out there still, freezing my arse off in the middle of the field."

"It's the middle of summer," said Akim. "Hardly the type of weather in which one would freeze."

"Well, maybe not, but I'd certainly die of boredom. The captain was so apologetic, he gave me a week off."

Akim laughed. "Lucky you. You'll be back just in time to be bored to tears."

"What makes you say that?"

"Surely you remember what's in two weeks?"

Sergei screwed up his eyes and looked at the ceiling, a mannerism often mocked. "Can't say I do."

"The Volstrum is having its graduation. That means you'll be run off your feet as they all leave, then have nothing to do till well after dark."

"Not necessarily. I might be chosen as one of the guards who accompany the mistress."

"I highly doubt Marakhova Stormwind would be interested in having you as a bodyguard."

"Why not? Am I not a competent warrior?"

Akim laughed again. "Is that what you think she likes? Someone who's merely competent? Look around you, man. Half the people in this place could beat you in a fight, some with one hand behind their back."

"All right, I'm not claiming to be anything special, but you don't need to be so nasty. What's the matter? Did somebody upset your mother?"

"Leave my mother out of this. The last thing I want right now is another family argument."

"Speaking of Mother," said Sergei, "how has she been of late? She was taken ill, wasn't she?"

"She was, but she seems to have made a full recovery."

The discussion continued, but not for the man at the door. He stood, tossing some coins onto the table before he left without saying a word.

"I have it," announced Stanislav. He had just returned from a trip to one of the local taverns, but the smile on his face told everyone they had finally discovered something useful.

"Well?" said Laisa. "Don't just stand there like a dog with a bone, out with it."

"There's a graduation coming up in a few days. Everyone of import will be at the Volstrum, including some guards from Stormwind Manor. Although it's never left unguarded, the fact remains there'll be fewer guards around to give us grief."

"It couldn't be a trap, could it?" said Belgast.

"I would presume that highly unlikely," said Natalia. "For one thing, they've no idea we're even here."

"What time of year do students usually graduate?"

"It varies from year to year. My own ceremony was held in the autumn, but it's not unheard of for a summer graduation. I believe it has more to do with the number of students who have completed their training and less with the calendar." She looked at Stanislav. "How long do you reckon we have?"

"Two weeks. Plenty of time to prepare. I would suggest we get out there as soon as possible. We talked about getting the lay of the land, but we haven't even seen the place yet. We need to know how many entrances it has and whether there's a window that might serve our purposes."

"A good point," said Athgar. "And the guards will not be very alert."

"What makes you say that?" asked Stanislav.

"I would imagine Marakhova will insist on taking the best guards with her. That means leaving the less capable men behind to stand watch."

"That's still people we have to get past," said Belgast.

"That doesn't worry me. I'm a hunter, and the estate is outdoors—the perfect place for me to practice my craft."

"They could still give the alarm."

"Yes, they could," said Athgar. "That's why we'll dispatch them as we go in."

"You mean kill them?" said the Dwarf.

"That's precisely what I mean. Better to do so upon entering rather than leaving. The last thing we want is our escape route blocked."

"A good point," said Stanislav. "So, once the guards are taken care of, how do we proceed?"

"WE don't," said Athgar. "Only Natalia and I will enter. We'll need you two outside to warn us if others approach, not to mention keeping an escape route open."

"Why you two, specifically?"

"I'm the sneaky one, remember? And Natalia will have a better idea of what to look for than any of us. What time do these graduations typically start?"

"Late in the afternoon," said Natalia, "at least mine was. The ceremony itself isn't overly long, but then everyone sits down for a meal. I don't imagine it'll be finished till well after dark."

"And how long would it take for a carriage to get from the Volstrum to Stormwind Manor?"

"Can't say I know for sure, but based on what Laisa has told us, it would probably be pretty late, perhaps even midnight, before anyone returned." She took a breath, thinking things through. "We must be careful not to underestimate the guards. The Stormwinds insist on employing only the best."

Athgar considered her words carefully. An alert guard was their biggest threat, for even one could quickly spoil their plans. "We'll go in just after dark. That should still give us ample opportunity to search the place."

"Are you sure?" said Belgast. "The compartment could be anywhere."

"True," said Natalia, "but we can't search everywhere without leaving some trace of our presence. If it's not somewhere near at hand, I'm afraid we have little chance of finding it."

"Where would you like to start?" asked Stanislav.

"My first inclination would be an office. You can't run something as big as the family without lots of correspondence, which means there's liable to be a room dedicated to such a pursuit. Illiana would have spent a lot of time there, and I can think of no better place to conceal something personal, can you?"

"I would think her bedroom, more likely, but you make a valid point. Do we know where either of those would be located?"

"It shouldn't be too hard to find," chimed in Laisa. "You're looking for a room with a desk or table in it, along with ink and quills. Also, if you can't recognize a bedroom when you see it, you have far worse problems. In any event, I doubt they'd be hidden, especially if they're used frequently."

"In that case," said Athgar, "I believe it's time we head out there and see it for ourselves, don't you?"

"I would suggest we rent a carriage and at least ride by," said Stanislav. "We'll get a much better feel for the place in daylight."

"Agreed," said Belgast. "Though we'd best not linger; it might draw attention. Tell me, other than the manor, where does the road lead?"

"Eastward," replied Laisa. "Towards the mines."

"Mines?" said the Dwarf. "That sounds interesting. Do they extract metals or minerals?"

"I don't know. I've never seen them myself, but they're supposed to be right on the eastern border of Ruzhina. They say nothing lies beyond that but harsh wilderness."

"My kind of land," said Athgar.

"Let's not get distracted," said Natalia. "We should concentrate on finding out as much about Stormwind Manor as we can. We shall ride by the estate, get a quick overview, and then return at dusk for a more in-depth exploration. Now, remember, we're not going into the place quite yet, but we need to identify where the guards are, how many and, if we get close enough, where the doors are."

"And all that under cover of darkness?" said Stanislav. "I don't envy the task."

"I wouldn't worry so much," said the Dwarf. "The guards are all Human, aren't they?"

"As far as we know. Why?"

"Your race has no night vision. That means they'll cluster around light sources, and as for the doors, they'll be lit up so people can see them. Remember, this is an estate, not some commoner's home."

"An excellent point," said Natalia. "Now, we'd best get going if we hope to be there before dark."

. . .

The carriage rattled down the road, jostling the occupants from side to side. It hit a huge rut, sending them all crashing to the left side of the tiny cabin.

"We should have brought horses," said Athgar.

"Nonsense," replied Stanislav. "This way, we can conserve our strength for when it's needed."

"Yes, but what about the coachman? Won't he wonder why we're going out here, to the middle of nowhere?"

"Don't worry. I've known Ivan for years."

"And you're sure you can trust him?"

"He's the same man who got Natalia out when she fled Karslev all those years ago. I trusted him then, and I have no reason to doubt his loyalty now."

The carriage slowed as a large manor house came into view.

"An impressive sight," said Belgast. "I shouldn't like to think how many men it would take to guard that place."

In terms of style, it was somewhat lacking in overall appeal, for it was a two-storied structure forming little more than a rectangle. However, its size spoke volumes about the family's wealth.

"By the Saints," said Natalia. "It's almost as large as the commandery back in Ebenstadt."

"Not quite," said Stanislav. "It's as tall, no doubt about it, but it's only about half the length. Still, an impressive building nonetheless."

A side road led up to the front of the place, but Ivan wisely chose not to use it. Instead, he remained on the main road as it veered off to the left, allowing them a decent view of the end of Stormwind Manor.

"I see a side entrance," noted Athgar.

"Yes," agreed Stanislav, "and it looks like there's a garden out back, likely for entertaining. I imagine there'll be a door there as well."

"That's probably the best entrance. All those trees in the back will provide good cover. How many guards have you seen?"

"Seven, so far," said Belgast. "Three in front, two at the side entrance, and two in back, although there's probably more."

"Those windows," said Natalia. "The ones up on the second floor. Might we use them to effect an entry?"

"Indeed, but how would you get up there without alerting the guards?"

"Could you draw them away?"

"Even if we try," said the Dwarf, "we'd be alerting them to our presence, in which case you might as well stroll in the front door."

They continued on, the view soon blocked by a thick forest. The coachman cracked the whip, and the carriage sped up.

"Where to now?" asked Athgar.

"Ivan will take us down the road about half a mile or so. According to Laisa, there's an old, abandoned manor down a side road."

"Who abandons a manor house?"

"The Stormwinds, or so it would appear. It lies within their lands."

"Are you sure it's not guarded?"

"Yes. It hasn't been used in over two hundred years. It was the original Stormwind Manor, although perhaps manor is a little bit of an over-statement."

They sat in silence until the carriage slowed once more. When it finally came to a halt, they all hopped out.

The original manor had been built with defences in mind, for it was a stone construction, complete with crenellations and small, one-man towers jutting out from the walls. The place had obviously been neglected for years, as two of the towers had collapsed, while a third was missing a signif-icant number of bricks. The front door had also succumbed to nature's torment and now lay on the ground, warped and broken.

Stanislav entered, his footsteps echoing out from within. "There's no one here," he called out, "save for some roosting birds, but a thorough search might just prove beneficial."

"You suspect someone could be hiding here?" asked Athgar.

"Someone or something. There ARE lots of animals in the region, and I wouldn't put it past one or two to take up residence here."

The rest of the party entered and began systematically searching the place, but little was found, aside from mice and birds.

"It must have been nice in its day," said Natalia. "The floor alone looks like it cost a small fortune."

"The floor?" said Belgast.

"Yes. Beneath all this dust and leaves are coloured tiles."

The Dwarf knelt, sweeping away the dirt with his hands. "So there is."

Their task complete, they gathered in the entranceway. "How far away is Stormwind Manor?" asked Athgar.

"I would guess no more than a mile," said Stanislav. "It lies due west of us, if I've got my bearings correct."

"Closer to one and a half," said Belgast. Upon seeing all eyes on him, he continued. "Us Dwarves have a keen sense of distance. It comes in useful when mining."

"Shall we have a look?"

"By all means," said Natalia. "Lead on."

They made their way westward. Belgast's assessment proved accurate, and after a mile and a half, they found themselves looking out from the cover of trees.

"How many guards do you see?" asked Athgar.

"Two," replied Natalia. "This looks like the short end of the house."

"When we come back," said Belgast, "you might find that door locked."

"What makes you say that?" asked Athgar.

"Simple. It won't be needed. With the matriarch away, she'll want the place kept safe, and that side door doesn't look like it sees much use. Better, I think, to lock it and use the guards elsewhere."

"You make a compelling case."

"Curious," said Natalia. "I don't see a stables, or a carriage house, for that matter."

"They must be on the far side," said Stanislav. "We should work our way over there."

Athgar looked skyward. "We've some time yet before it gets dark, but let's not linger. Belgast might be able to see in the dark, but the rest of us are only Human."

They skirted the forest's edge, giving them a view of the ornate gardens sitting out back. Eventually, they spied the stables and carriage house, separate buildings accessible by travelling up a short trail. Soon, they were crouched in amongst the trees, looking at the west end of the manor house.

"No third entrance," noted Stanislav. "What do you think, Natalia?"

Her eyes drifted up to the windows on the second floor. "I imagine those are guest rooms, and the servants' quarters are on the ground floor, close to the kitchen."

"What makes you say that?"

She pointed. "The chimney there is large, probably fed by the kitchen."

"But there are chimneys on the east side too," said Athgar.

"Yes, but they're much smaller and likely there to heat the place in winter."

"Does it get cold in these parts?"

"Very much so," said Natalia. "The Volstrum has thick walls, but even there, the halls were chilly come wintertime."

"We have a good view of the back from here," mused the Dwarf. "Do you still think the upper floor is your best choice, Natalia?"

"I believe it the only choice if we are to enter unnoticed. The problem will be getting close enough to climb those vines that crawl all over it."

"Will they support your weight?" asked Stanislav.

"They'll have to," she replied. "The real question is how we can draw the guards away without raising the alarm."

"I thought the plan was to eliminate them?" said Belgast.

"It occurred to me that wouldn't work."

"Why not?"

"We have no idea how often the guards are replaced. I don't imagine one of them finding a body would be to our advantage, do you?"

"No, I suppose not. Do you have a spell that might suffice?"

"I might," said Athgar. "Artoch taught me one called scintillating flame that could help."

"How does that work?" asked the Dwarf.

"It creates a faint light that floats around in the air. It's meant to keep animals at bay long enough to outrun them."

"Will it work on guards?"

"I'm not sure. We'd have to try it out."

"Not here, surely?" said Belgast. "I shouldn't like to alert them of our presence at this precise moment."

"You can try it back in Karslev," said Stanislav. "In the meantime, we need to get back to the carriage."

Athgar led them, sticking close to the edge of the forest. The return trip seemed to take much longer, and for the last few hundred yards, he was forced to conjure a small flame lest they stumble over the underbrush. Eventually, they spotted the old building where Ivan waited for them.

"Informative trip?" asked the coachman.

"Yes," said Stanislav. "Very productive, but we're ready to return to Karslev now. I hope travelling in the dark won't be too difficult?"

"Not at all," the man replied. He climbed up to his perch, then waited as the others got inside the carriage. They lurched forward, making a wide circle, and were soon back on the main road, heading towards the distant spires of Karslev.

"That was most interesting," said Belgast. "I expected far more guards."

"The extras are probably inside," said Natalia, "but don't forget, many of those will be with Marakhova when she attends the graduation ceremony."

"Let's hope so, or we may all find ourselves down a mineshaft without a ladder."

He stepped back from the wall, then ran three steps towards her, launching himself up as high as he could before clutching her arm and pulling himself up. Natalia edged farther along while he followed along behind.

The tiny platform was only wide enough for him to scuttle along on his hands and knees. Ahead of him, Natalia held on to the windowsill, using it to steady herself as she got to her feet before carefully opening it.

Athgar reached her position just as she climbed inside a modest room containing a series of bookshelves along one wall. Against the other side sat a couple of chairs, along with an unlit lamp. Athgar entered the room, closing the window behind him. A minor spell was all that was needed to conjure forth a small flame to illuminate the area.

"This is unused," said Natalia. "There's a thick layer of dust everywhere." She had the feeling of being watched and cast her gaze over to the chairs. On the wall behind them were two paintings, each depicting someone wearing the formal robes of a battle mage. She moved closer to take a more detailed examination before waving Athgar over with his flame.

"Something interesting?" he asked.

"These two are Stormwinds," she replied. "At least according to the nameplates."

"Why would they put them here?"

"They're likely all over the house. It's a large family."

"We haven't got time to go over the family tree. We need to find whatever that key unlocks."

They both made a cursory examination of the bookshelves, but it soon became apparent there was no sign of a lock. Athgar moved to the door, pressing his ear against it. Natalia held her breath, her heart pounding. Moments later, he nodded, then slowly opened it to reveal a hallway beyond, running left and right, turning at either end.

"Pretty standard layout," noted Natalia. "Go left. I expect Illiana's room will overlook the manor's entranceway."

Out they went, Athgar leading, his small green flame illuminating the hall. They halted at two different doors, taking the time to open them and peek within, but they appeared to be nothing more than guest rooms.

They reached the corner where the hallway turned to parallel the front of the house. More doors came into view as they went, leading to even more guest rooms. The flame's light flickered off the walls, giving the place an eerie feeling. Athgar suddenly halted, causing Natalia to bump into him.

"What is it?" she whispered.

"This ends at a balcony. I think it opens up into the entranceway." They moved closer to see a wooden railing and the end of the hallway. Natalia crept up to a door that stood to the left, trying the handle.

"In here," she said.

They stepped in, closing the door behind them. An immense wooden desk, coloured so darkly as to appear almost black, dominated the room.

"Shadowbark," said Natalia. "There can be little doubt this was once Illiana's office."

"How can you be sure?"

"This desk alone is worth thousands. No one would go to the expense of buying it only to have it sit idle."

Athgar moved to the window, drawing the thick curtains closed. A few moments later, he uttered words of magic as he pointed at a candlestick sitting on the desk. It jumped to life, illuminating everything with a pale yellow light.

Natalia searched the drawers while Athgar cast his gaze around the room. Rolls of parchment littered the shelves here, along with three thick books. He selected one of the tomes, placing it on the desk.

"What do you suppose this is?" he asked.

"I have no idea. Have a look while I check for secret compartments." She began tapping on various parts of the desk but to no avail.

Athgar opened up the book, flipping through a few pages. "It looks like some sort of family tree."

"Any names we might recognize?"

"Lots of Stormwinds and Sartellians, but I'm not familiar with any of these first names."

"Go to the last page and see what's there."

He did so to be rewarded with a half-filled page. From there, he flipped backwards. "These are breeding notes," he said. "There's even a mention of potential matches for you."

"For me? Are you sure?"

"Unless you know another Natalia Stormwind?"

She stopped what she was doing to come closer and look for herself.

"That's me, all right."

"Who's this fellow, Vasili Sartellian?"

Natalia thought back. "I believe him one of the three candidates they wanted me to breed with. Look here, there are two other names, both crossed out. Either they died, or the family decided they weren't suitable for some reason. In any case, it matters little; I chose you. Now, close that thing up. We haven't much time, and we still need to keep searching."

Athgar replaced the book and then noticed another painting on the wall

—a portrait of a stern-looking individual with a youthful face and fine clothes.

"Antonov Sartellian," he read aloud.

Natalia stopped what she was doing. "That was my father, at least according to Stanislav."

"How would he know?"

"Illiana told him."

"I can see the family resemblance," said Athgar. "You look a lot like him. If he was a Sartellian, does that mean he was a Fire Mage?"

"I suppose so. Why?"

"Wouldn't that mean your mother was a Water Mage?"

"Or the descendant of one. We know magic often skips a generation or two."

He shook his head. "This life," he said. "Had you made other choices, all this could have been yours."

"I never wanted any of this, and to be honest, it wasn't only the thought of breeding that turned me off the family."

"Then what was it?"

"They spent years at the Volstrum teaching us to obey the family and follow the rules. Graduation would inevitably lead to a life of serving the family with no thought to my own wishes or desires."

He turned to her, smiling. "Well, I, for one, am glad of the choices you made, even if it proved dangerous at times."

"As am I," she said.

A footstep echoed outside the room, and they both froze. Athgar waved his hand, using his magic to extinguish the candle. The footsteps lingered a moment before receding.

"We should get out of here," Natalia whispered. "Whatever we're looking for doesn't appear to be here."

"Agreed. We need to find Illiana's bedroom."

He pressed his ear to the door, listening carefully. "I think it's safe. We'll double back down the hall and make our way around back."

"Agreed."

Athgar opened it and looked outside. All appeared well, although admittedly, it was pretty dark. He stepped out, then conjured a small flame that he carried in the palm of his hand.

Natalia followed, retracing their path to where they'd entered. They paused to get their bearings before proceeding towards the rear of the manor. Here, the corridor turned again, much as it did in the front.

They had proceeded past the turn and were heading for the centre of the manor when Athgar first heard the footsteps. He doused his flame and moved to stand against the wall, indicating Natalia should do likewise.

The steps drew nearer, and then lantern light flooded the hallway, held aloft by a man bearing a sword. As soon as he came into view, Natalia cast a spell, sending shards of ice flying towards him. They struck him in the chest, knocking him backwards, the lantern tumbling from his hand.

Expecting more men at any moment, Athgar readied a spell of his own, then noticed the oil from the lamp leaking out onto the floor. He targeted it instead, sending a small flame to ignite the oil. Fire billowed up to the ceiling, sucking the air from the immediate area. Athgar backed down the hall as thick, black smoke rolled towards them.

Natalia was already turning the corner, heading back the way they'd come while Athgar kept his front to the enemy, expecting a rush. There was a great noise as if an enormous bird had flown by, and then the fire went out. He knew what it meant—a Fire Mage more powerful than him had snuffed out the flames.

"We're in trouble," he said. "There's a Sartellian coming."

Natalia rushed to his side, sending a spell down the corridor, but in her rush to loose it, she misjudged the distance. The shards struck the wall, ice fragments exploding everywhere.

Soldiers rushed forth, crowding into the hallway. Athgar and Natalia turned and ran and were almost back to where they entered when a wall of flame shot up, blocking their way. They turned to see a trio of mages coming towards them.

"Marakhova!" shouted Natalia. "You were supposed to be at the graduation."

"You fool. There's no graduation. You played right into our hands, Natalia. Now surrender before we are forced to take extreme measures."

"Never!"

Natalia called forth words of power, but a crossbow bolt pierced her shoulder before she finished casting. She staggered back, pain lancing down her arm as she called out to Athgar, but he had dropped to his knees, a bolt protruding from his chest.

She pointed her hand, willing the magic to come. Ice frosted the hallway, the cold creeping towards the enemy like a north sea tide. The foremost warrior looked down in fear as the frost passed his position, freezing his legs to the floor. He screamed out in agony.

Another bolt sailed towards them, taking Natalia in the leg this time. She felt its impact, felt the bone snap with the force of the quarrel, and then her leg gave out beneath her, sending her crashing to the floor. Her spell, no longer under her control, dissipated, and the frozen guard fell heavily, his legs useless. Marakhova ignored him, stepping past the poor fellow to kneel by Athgar, placing a slender blade at his motionless neck.

"Surrender, Natalia, or Athgar dies." She saw Natalia's confusion. "He's not dead, at least not yet, but it's your choice whether he lives or dies. Surrender yourself, and I shall have Sorentis, our Life Mage, save him."

"You lie," Natalia screamed back.

"Now, why would I do that? We want you back in the family, my dear, not dead. You're far too valuable to kill. Of course, we will kill you if you refuse my offer, but not before you watch your husband put to the knife. Make your choice."

Natalia felt fear growing inside her. Athgar was down, and without help, would surely die. She had only one option. "I surrender."

Marakhova stood, waving a pair of guards forward, then turned to one of her robed companions. "Bind his hands and then drag him downstairs and have Sorentis stand by. We don't want him to die, but he'll be more compliant if he remains wounded."

The guards seized Natalia's arms, twisting them behind her back and tying them together. Marakhova moved closer, then reached out and tore the bolt from her leg.

Pain shot through Natalia as flesh ripped, blood flowing freely. She gritted her teeth, trying to remain awake as the grand mistress of the family tore the second one from her shoulder. Another jolt of excruciating pain coursed through Natalia, and dizziness threatened to overwhelm her. One of the guards grabbed her hair, pulling her head back while the other poured liquid down her throat.

"We brewed that magebane especially for you, my dear. A dose that concentrated would kill another caster, but you? Well, you're the exception, aren't you?"

"How?" Natalia managed to spit out. "How did you know we were coming here?"

"I told them." A voice echoed out from farther down the hall, but there was no doubt as to the owner.

"Laisa? Why?"

The woman moved closer, standing over the Water Mage. "Coins, why do you think? The family pays well for information like this."

Marakhova turned to her third companion. "You may pay her now."

A purse was handed over, and then Laisa skulked away.

"You see? We reward those who faithfully serve the family."

The guards dragged Natalia to her feet. Her head swam, for the magebane had already started having a soporific effect on her. She'd been given the stuff many times over the years but never this strong. Natalia fought to stay awake, to see what happened to Athgar. The thought made her look down, but all she saw was a red smear where he'd been dragged away.

"Let's take her downstairs, shall we?" said Marakhova. "Then we can reunite her with her husband, if only for a moment."

They half carried her down the hallway, her legs refusing to work correctly. The room spun as she struggled to remain conscious. At the top of the stairs, she felt a rush of vertigo and quickly closed her eyes, but it didn't help. Her head flopped to the side, and then she felt like she was going to vomit, but nothing came of it.

Her arms were grabbed even tighter, and then she was lifted, the movement sending fresh waves of pain through her body. The entire room swam as she descended. She felt as if she were in a waking nightmare.

Athgar knelt at the base of the stairs, his wound still bleeding, but at least the bolt had been removed. A bar had been passed behind his elbows, with his arms wrapped around it and chained in front. Behind him stood a guard, sword held at the back of Athgar's neck, ready to plunge it down should the command be given.

"As you can see," said Marakhova, "he is alive and shall remain as such provided you cooperate."

"Let him go," demanded Natalia. "He has nothing to do with any of this."

"Oh, but he does. He is the instrument by which we tame you, Natalia. As long as you cooperate, he lives, but one false move, and I'll order his throat slit." Marakhova smiled. "And don't for a moment think he has any chance of escape. We've dosed him with magebane, although not as concentrated as that which surges through your system."

Natalia felt despair envelope her. It was over. Her plan to hold the family accountable had failed, and now both she and Athgar were at their mercy. There would be no happy ending for them. As she succumbed to the magebane, her final thoughts were of how she would spend the rest of her life in servitude to Marakhova Stormwind, never to see Athgar or Oswyn again.

CAPTURED

Summer 1108 SR

Athgar opened his eyes to utter darkness, yet the ground beneath him shifted, causing him to roll from side to side. He attempted to move, only to find his wrists bound by metal rings with a solid bar of iron connecting them to keep his hands apart. It was an effective way to prevent casting, and the thought sent him into a panic. He closed his eyes, willing his heart to slow. Such displays would do little to help him in his current circumstances.

He sat up, reaching out in the darkness to better understand his surroundings. It didn't take long to find metal bars, and before long, he concluded he was in a cage of sorts.

His ears picked up a whinnying, and he felt the wood beneath him shift once more. Not just a cage, then, but one within a wagon; that much was now clear. He moved slightly, feeling pain in his chest. Remembering the bolt, he reached up, touching the wound. Blood encrusted his shirt, but some time had passed, for it was dry.

The next thought to hit him was of Natalia. Was she safe? He vaguely remembered them threatening her, and then the pieces fell into place. He was being held hostage to ensure her behaviour. The thought of it made his blood boil. He struck out, his hand feeling a sharp pain as it struck the iron bars.

Where was she, and what would they make her do? Would they force her to return to Runewald and bring back Oswyn? He shook his head. Their daughter was safe with Kargen and Shaluhk, and if Natalia showed up, he had no doubt she would inform them of her situation.

Athgar knew he was only useful if he survived. Were he to die, the family would have no hold over her. Perhaps the best thing to do would be to kill himself? He quickly dismissed the thought. He was alive, and while he lived, there was always hope. He must take stock of his situation, biding his time, waiting for the moment to act.

Closing his eyes, he called upon his inner spark, only to find it deep inside but impossible to embrace. It was as if each time he tried to touch it, his hand would fumble, missing it entirely. Athgar had never been given magebane but knew of its effects from all Natalia had said. His mind raced, trying to recall anything and everything about the strange concoction. Brewed from exotic plants, it must be ingested to have an effect, but everything else was pure conjecture. Natalia once told him students at the Volstrum were dosed with magebane twice a day until they learned to cast their first spell. It, therefore, was logical to assume a dose would only last half a day.

He began running his hands over himself, looking for any additional wounds. Everything appeared intact, although his head pounded. His chest was healed, but he suspected only enough to close the skin, for the inside still pained him if he moved suddenly.

How long had it been? His last meal had been before they headed out to Stormwind Manor. At the moment, he was not hungry, far from it, in fact, for everything ached, but that likely had more to do with the magebane than the need for food. With no indication of any light leaking through the wagon, he concluded it was still night.

Time dragged on, and he wondered if he wasn't trapped in some strange place between the world of the living and the Afterlife. Eventually, a small amount of light permeated his surroundings. What appeared to be a wooden cover was above, and the cracks where the planks met allowed enough light for him to make out other details.

His first thought was to see what could be made of the cage. It had a wooden base with four walls and a top of solid iron bars. It looked as though entry was gained from above, for he could make out hinges on one side and a large padlock and hasp on the other. He tried reaching through the bars, but his hand restraints made such action impossible.

He could do little more than wait, and as he sat, he gave more thought to his predicament. They'd dosed him with magebane, but when? Just after he was captured was the most probable time, for they wouldn't wish him to use his magic to attempt escape. That meant they needed to repeat the process half a day later.

He wracked his brain, trying to put together a timetable. They entered the building after dark, and their search of the premises hadn't taken overly long. By his reckoning, they were captured well before midnight, which meant he could expect a visitor sometime before noon. Of course, he had no guarantee of that. There was always the possibility that they'd double dosed him or somehow administered more while he was unconscious. The truth was he lacked sufficient knowledge to know for sure.

The sound of feet and of other horses drifted to his ears as the wagon slowed. He had the impression he'd arrived somewhere, although he had no idea if this was his final destination.

The noises increased, and then the wagon finally halted. He heard the distinct sound of the coachman jumping down from his perch, then voices came from the other direction. Someone near the back rattled a key against a lock, then the door opened, flooding the place with light, forcing Athgar to shield his eyes.

"What have we got here?" came a gruff voice.

"Another slave for the mines," replied a woman.

"We'll put him in with the others."

"Take care. This one is not to be killed out of hand. He has some value to us."

The gruff voice barked out a laugh. "Then why send him here?"

"He's leverage."

"Oh, I see. Well, in that case, let's get him out here, shall we?"

Athgar, now accustomed to the light, watched as the fellow entered the back of the wagon. He loomed close, peering in at the prisoner.

"He's a Therengian," the man remarked.

"What of it?" said the woman.

"I've never seen his like before, not here in Zurkutsk."

"Don't be fooled by his eyes. He's a Human, just like the others."

"Fair enough." He turned, bellowing for help.

More men joined him, and they started pulling the cage back towards the rear of the wagon. Athgar considered striking out at their hands, but it would do little save for enraging them, so he decided to bide his time. They dragged the cage to the edge before they toppled it, laughing as it fell to the ground. Athgar, his head striking the bars, felt pain lancing through him.

"Careful," came the woman's voice. "Remember, we want him kept alive."

"How alive?"

"I don't care how he's treated, if that's what you mean, provided he still breathes."

Three men moved closer, righted the cage, and then stood back while the gruff-voiced man unlocked the cage. "Now, don't go making any trouble," he warned, "and we'll get along famously." He lifted the top off, then directed two men to come forward.

Athgar's arms were seized, then they lifted him from the cage. He took in his surroundings. The road beneath him was a muddy affair, while the smell of pine hung heavy in the air. Groups of individuals walked past, connected together by belts and chains while at their side, keeping an ever-watchful eye on them, were a pair of guards, each carrying a club. These were used to occasionally strike at those they considered lagging, although, in truth, Athgar could see little difference in the prisoners' gaits. He tried to see where they were going, but the wagon blocked his view.

The gruff-voiced one pushed him while the other two brandished their clubs. Athgar staggered forward, his head still pounding as the mud beneath him sucked at his boots. Below him, in a shallow valley, he saw a series of crude huts encircled by a palisade. Outside this defence were even more huts. He suddenly realized the wall was not to keep invaders out but prisoners in. One building stood taller than the rest in the outer ring, and he struggled to make out its purpose. Behind it, teams of horses were harnessed to some sort of yolk, yet he could see no sign of a wagon to which it might be attached.

A yell came from his right, and then a club struck him on the side. He moved left as a wagon rode by, filled with what looked like rocks and stones.

"Keep your eyes to the front, slave," bellowed Gruff.

They descended into the valley, keeping to the edge of the road. More wagons passed them, some loaded with stone, others returning with nothing. They were obviously digging for something, but Athgar saw no signs of anything other than plain old stone. Even that was reasonable had it been cut into blocks, but this was little more than rubble. Whatever they were after clearly required a lot of digging.

He was suddenly struck by the thought that this wasn't a mine at all but simply some form of prison. If that were the case, someone had gone to extraordinary efforts to build it.

"This way." His guard pointed with the club, indicating a nearby building. Athgar altered course and was led inside to come face to face with a man of average build, roughly the same height as himself, but his white hair and beard singled him out. His gaze bore into Athgar's soul.

"I assume you are the Therengian, Athgar?"

"I am."

"And I am Corderis Stormwind, Master of Zurkutsk. Do you know why you're here?"

"I am a hostage to ensure the cooperation of Natalia Stormwind."

"Good. That will make this much easier." He turned to the guards. "Remove his binders."

"My lord? Are you sure that's wise?"

"Do as I say," he snapped.

Athgar waited as they undid the manacles.

"There, that's better," said Corderis. "Now, let's have a discussion, shall we? You've been sentenced to imprisonment and hard labour. If you behave yourself, you'll live. If, however, you choose to be uncooperative, then you will pay the price."

"Which is?"

The Master of Zurkutsk chuckled. "Ultimately, death, but there's much we can do before that. Personally, I'm rather fond of removing fingers, although I've been known, on occasion, to cut out someone's tongue." He saw Athgar's look of disgust. "Shocking, isn't it, but then again, I wouldn't be required to resort to such barbaric acts if people behaved. There's more to consider in your case since word of your death could negatively affect Natalia's cooperation. Should that occur, you shall both find yourselves removed from the land of the living."

"Death doesn't frighten me."

"Yes, that's right, you believe in the Afterlife, don't you? I hear it's common amongst your kind."

"Don't the Saints preach about it?"

"They do," said Corderis, "but whatever gave you the impression WE do?"

Athgar felt a lump form in the pit of his stomach.

"Ah," his captor continued. "I see that has taken you by surprise. Never mind, you'll get used to it. Now, as to rules, they are simple. During the day, you'll be sent below, where you'll work with picks and shovels. You're looking for magerite—are you familiar with it?"

"I am, although I must admit I've never seen it in its natural form."

"Don't worry, it's relatively easy to distinguish from the surrounding rock. You'll work each shift until your team uncovers their quota of the stuff. In other words, you are expected to find some each and every day."

"You need that much?"

Corderis chuckled. "I will excuse your ignorance. Magerite comes in various shapes and sizes, much of which is essentially unusable. Less than one in twenty samples is suitable for our purposes. That's why we mine so much. Now, where was I?"

"Oh yes," he continued. "When your shift is complete, you are brought to the surface and fed. From this point forward, your life consists of eating, sleeping, and mining, and of those three, you should consider mining the most important. Find lots of magerite, and your life shall be much less exhausting. Fail to find any, and you may find yourself starving to death."

"You spoke of a team?"

"Yes, you'll be put into a group for each shift. Typically, this will be about a dozen individuals, but the groups tend to whittle down significantly as losses occur. Occasionally, we will combine one or two groups to make them more efficient, but you'll have no control over that. I like to keep things as simple as possible—work hard, and you'll survive. Fail, and you'll find your time here short. Do we understand each other?"

"We do."

Corderis leaned in close, lowering his voice. "Do not cross me, Therengian, or I shall release my wrath upon you."

"Understood," replied Athgar.

"Take him away, and see he is put with the others."

"Yes, my lord," said the guard.

Athgar was taken to one of the huts he had spied earlier, not too different in layout than those back home. But whereas Runewald's buildings were made of wattle and daub, there was nothing but wood on these walls, allowing the chilly outside air to permeate the place.

"This is your new home," the guard announced. "You'll start work on the next shift. Until then, you'll wait here."

Athgar watched the man leave. It seemed odd, being a prisoner without shackles or chains. He had the freedom to move around; that much was clear, but where would he go? If he put his mind to it, escape would not be difficult, for he could survive in the wilderness easy enough, but the thought of Natalia being punished for his actions sobered him. He must behave himself, if only for her safety.

He picked a spot and lay down, exhaustion overwhelming him. Yelling interrupted his slumber, and then the door opened, admitting dozens of individuals. Men and women entered the hut, each waiting at the doorway as chains were removed. Most collapsed to the floor, too weary to do much of anything, but at least one woman noticed his presence and came towards him, with two others accompanying her.

"Who are you?" she asked.

"Athgar of Athelwald," he replied, not deigning to name his current home. "Who are you?"

She ignored his question, instead staring at him. "Strange name that, and look at those eyes. You're one of those Therengians, aren't you?"

"I am."

"You're clearly not from the Volstrum. Why are you here?"

"Why would I be from the Volstrum?"

His question surprised her. "You don't know?" She looked at her companions, but they simply shook their heads. Her attention returned to Athgar. "We are the Disgraced."

"Meaning?"

"Each of us, for some reason or another, was unable to complete our training."

He could almost taste the bitterness in her voice.

"Some were removed shortly after our arrival," she continued, "while others were lucky enough to learn the rudiments of spellcasting. Of course, that matters little here. You, however, don't look like a typical Water Mage."

"I'm not. I'm a master of flame."

"A Sartellian? Here in Zurkutsk?"

"No, Artoch taught me."

"Who's that?"

"An Orc of the Red Hand."

Her blonde companion was clearly disgusted by the thought, for she recoiled in horror. "Such a thing cannot be!"

"Hush now, Anushka. If there's one thing I've learned, it's that we shouldn't judge people for the circumstances of their birth." She returned her attention to Athgar. "Tell me, how is it you came to be here?"

"I was captured while breaking into Stormwind Manor."

His interrogator stared down at him, a slight smile threatening to escape the corners of her mouth. "Stormwind Manor? How interesting. And what, may I ask, persuaded you to undertake that endeavour?"

Athgar was torn. Was it wise to reveal all to these people? He stared at the woman, trying to ascertain her character.

"Well?" demanded the woman. "What have you to say for yourself?"

Athgar shrugged, then decided to come clean. "My wife and I broke into Stormwind Manor to save our child." He saw the looks of confusion. "My wife's a graduate of the Volstrum. Have you heard of her—Natalia Stormwind?"

His interrogator crouched, staring at him. "Who did you say?"

"Natalia Stormwind. You know her?"

"Indeed I do, or rather, I did. She's your wife?"

"Yes, and we have a daughter, Oswyn."

She held out her hand. "Welcome to Zurkutsk, Athgar of Athelwald. My name is Katrin Stormwind."

TRAPPED

Summer 1108 SR

Natalia stared down at the exquisite meal set before her. The finest chef in Ruzhina had prepared it, yet she sat there, longing for Skora's simpler fare.

At the head of the table sat Marakhova Stormwind, her stern countenance keeping the others in check. They were joined by Tatiana Stormwind, whom she remembered from her time at the Volstrum, along with two other men she'd never met before. All wore the blue magerite denoting them as Water Mages. The colour of their rings left no doubt their respective power levels, for both were dark blue.

"Now, Graxion," said Marakhova. "You must tell us how things are going in Zowenbruch. I understand there have been some gains there of late."

The red-haired fellow sat up straighter. "They have, indeed, Matriarch. They made overtures to the Duke of Erlingen at our behest. It's hoped an alliance might convince them to take collective action against Ulrichen."

"Is that desirable?" asked Natalia.

Graxion shot her a look of irritation. "Not that I would expect one of your age to understand, but yes, it is. For too long, Ulrichen has been a pain in our backsides."

"And what is it they did that has vexed you so?"

"They refused our offer of a court mage," explained Marakhova. "We can't very well have that going on. It might cause others to join in, and then chaos would reign." She saw Graxion's eyebrows shoot up. "Oh yes, I forgot to introduce you. This is Natalia Stormwind, one of our brightest graduates." She turned to Natalia. "Meet Graxion Stormwind, the former court representative to Zowenbruch, and Veris Stormwind, an advisor to the family on matters of a military nature. Of course, Tatiana you already know —she's the new Grand Mistress of the Volstrum."

Graxion's companion stood, offering up a bow. "I am pleased to meet you, madam." His accent was unusual, and Natalia found it impossible to pin down. Definitely not from Ruzhina, yet he still bore the family name.

"Greetings, gentlemen," she said, "and congratulations to you, Grand Mistress."

Marakhova turned her attention to Veris. "What is your assessment of their military prowess?"

"You mean Ulrichen? They have the numbers but lack experience. Unfortunately, the road system is underdeveloped, making any potential invasion more difficult. Of course, that's not necessarily our only option there."

"Meaning?"

"The king is unpopular, and several potential rivals have been identified should we need them."

"Excellent. Then I shall consider the problem taken care of."

"I have heard some other disturbing news, however, concerning Novarsk."

Natalia's ears pricked up.

"Go on," urged the matriarch.

"It seems their army was defeated by another claiming to represent Therengia."

"I had hoped the Old Kingdom would have remained dead and buried, but it appears someone has come along and seized the opportunity to resurrect it."

"So it would seem. Unfortunately, we have no first-hand accounts since our last court mage to King Vastavanitch died some years ago. The king was, I believe, succeeded by a daughter named Rada."

Marakhova's scrutiny turned to Natalia. "What do you know of this?"

"It's true," Natalia replied. "Their army was defeated, and Rada imprisoned. Novarsk is temporarily under the rule of Therengia."

"Is this your doing?"

"Not directly. After the end of the Holy War, many flocked east, determined to set things right. Thinking Therengia weakened by these attacks, Queen Rada attempted a full-scale invasion but was unsuccessful. In fact, quite the reverse—it was an utter disaster."

"Who leads this 'Therengia'?" asked Veris.

"The High Thane, their version of a king."

"You are remarkably forthcoming," said Marakhova, "especially considering your current circumstances."

"I have nothing to hide," said Natalia.

"We need to get someone into this High Thane's court," noted Veris. "Graxion, would you consider it?"

His companion nodded. "I would certainly welcome the chance."

"I doubt it would work," said Natalia. "They seem to have an aversion to members of the family."

"Something easily remedied," said Graxion. "In my experience, few kings can resist gifts of wealth or power."

"He is no ordinary king."

"Ah, a challenge. This makes it even more interesting. Tell me, Matriarch, would you allow me this singular honour?"

"I will consider it," said Marakhova, "but there are other factors of which you should be made aware."

"Such as?" asked Graxion.

"While we don't know a lot about the place, we do know this kingdom has a large number of Orcs amongst them. In addition, their Human population is largely of Therengian heritage, which is not too surprising given its name. It does mean, however, they have their own ideas about how things should be done."

"So they were of interest to us in the past?"

"They only came to our attention when we sought Natalia."

"What do you mean 'sought'?"

"She fled the Volstrum," said the matriarch, "attempting to hide out in the wilds of the Continent. We sent agents to snatch her back, but they discovered she'd taken refuge in this new kingdom. Unfortunately, our attempts to bring her here were less than successful, until now, that is."

"And so the wayward daughter returns?"

"More or less. I found it's better not to dwell on the details."

Veris turned to Natalia. "And how long, might I ask, will you be amongst us? Some time I hope?"

"At least for the foreseeable future."

"Then I toast to your health." Veris raised his glass. The others soon joined in, the matriarch with a sly smile. Natalia raised her own, then took a tiny sip of one of the finest vintages she'd ever had. Back at the Volstrum, she would have felt honoured just to taste it, but now all she wished for was the simple mead of her adopted people.

"Why am I here?" asked Natalia.

"You are part of the family," replied Marakhova. "It is my intention that you take up the duties of a Stormwind. However, we can't send you to a foreign court, so I brought Tatiana here to make you another offer." She turned to the grand mistress. "Would you care to explain the details?"

"Certainly, Matriarch. Natalia, we feel your exceptional talent needs to be shared. To that end, I have conferred with the matriarch, and we agreed the best use of your skills would be to teach at the Volstrum."

"So I am to have my magic restored?"

"Not immediately. To begin with, you would teach theory to the new initiates. As you yourself have experienced, it is a crucial time in the development of a mage, and we are eager to identify potential battle mages as early in the process as possible."

"Yes," agreed Marakhova. "When you are not teaching, you would remain here, at Stormwind Manor. Each morning you shall be taken, under guard, to the Volstrum to carry out your duties, returning in the evening."

"And if I refuse?" asked Natalia.

"My dear, must I remind you who we hold at our mercy? Your actions have consequences. Cross us, and it will go ill for him."

"And you expect me to put up with this for the rest of my life?"

"I expect, in time, you will come around to our way of thinking. I don't WANT you to be a prisoner, Natalia. Prove to me your loyalty can be counted on, and you shall have anything you wish."

"Even my husband?"

"Behave, and I might see my way clear to allow you to visit him eventually."

"Her husband?" said Graxion. "You haven't imprisoned a Sartellian, have you?"

"No. Natalia decided to forgo the normal selection process and bed an outsider."

The look of revulsion was plain to see. "What a waste," he mused.

"On the bright side, he is a Fire Mage, and I hate to admit it, but a rather accomplished one too."

"Have they any progeny?"

"They do, in fact. A daughter, though I doubt she will exhibit Natalia's potential."

"That's what comes from breeding with outsiders," noted Graxion. "Still, she looks young enough to continue breeding. You should contact Korasca-jan. I'm sure they could recommend an appropriate sire."

"Let's get her settled in first, shall we? There's plenty of time for that."

Natalia bristled. "Am I to have no say in this?"

"Don't worry, we shall give you choices."

"Yes," added Graxion. "This one or that one." He burst out laughing but sobered up as soon as he saw the matriarch's look of disdain. "It's not as bad as it sounds. My own coupling was pleasant, and it's not as if you're expected to raise the child yourself unless you wanted to, of course."

If it had been within her power, she would have sent ice shards into him, but all she could do was stare daggers. The room fell into an uncomfortable silence until Tatiana spoke up.

"Tell me, Natalia, how has your casting progressed? You were quite the spellcaster when you graduated. Have you seen fit to expand your repertoire?"

"I have."

"Natalia won a competition for us back in the day. She's always had tremendous potential in that regard. I seem to recall the old matriarch Illiana taking an interest in you. She even gave you her ring, if I recall."

"She did." Natalia held it up.

Veris's jaw dropped. "Is that magerite? I've never seen one so dark. You must be powerful indeed."

Graxion wore a troubled expression. "I thought magebane suppressed such powers?"

"And so it does," said Marakhova. "Magerite ignores such things, measuring innate ability rather than current power. She is no threat to anyone at present."

"The more remarkable fact is her parentage," said Tatiana. "Her mother was a simple peasant woman with no magic whatsoever."

"And her father?" asked Veris.

"Alas, we have no idea, although we suspect he was a Stormwind."

"That would put a Fire Mage on her mother's side, then, wouldn't it? After all, it's the combination of the two that creates such power in the first place."

"That would definitely explain a lot. They say magic can often skip a generation or two, and we know next to nothing of her mother's history."

"Not entirely true," offered Marakhova. "She worked on the estate of Baron Rozinsky. We looked into her history years ago, trying to find out more, but the baron was very lax in his record keeping. The truth is we have no idea how long she worked there. For all we know, she was born on his estate. At the time of her death, she was an indentured servant. We have no theory of how she came into those circumstances, particularly when her predecessors were likely members of the family. I'm afraid it shall forever remain a mystery."

Natalia picked away at her food as talk at the table fell to more mundane topics. They spoke of the theatre, making her think of when she and Athgar dressed up in costume to infiltrate a ball. Later, the conversation turned to ships for some reason, and all she could envision were her desperate attempts to save Athgar from drowning down near Corassus. Her life before meeting him had been dull and depressing—now she dreaded her future without him.

There was no denying the opulence in which the family lived. To them, she would always be a Stormwind—they had made her so. Her future children would be high-born, the very thing she had learned to despise at the Volstrum. Natalia longed to see Oswyn, if only one more time. Despair threatened to overwhelm her, and she clamped down on it. Oswyn was safe; her tribe would see to it. Natalia was filled with a new sense of purpose. If she remained a prisoner here for the rest of her days, she would at least have the satisfaction of knowing their daughter would grow up free to make her own decisions.

With the ending of the meal, the dishes were taken away. Servants brought in wine, and the group moved to a more informal setting. Stormwind Manor held several rooms that boasted cushioned chairs and fireplaces to keep the chill at bay. Marakhova led them to one such room on the eastern side of the building, just below the same room Natalia and Athgar first entered. Natalia took a seat while most of the others gathered around the fire. Tatiana, however, chose to move a chair closer to her, then sat.

"I know this is not ideal for you," she said quietly. "I heard you ran away, but no one said why? Was it the thought of breeding?"

"That was what pushed me over the edge. Since my graduation, I'd been having doubts about the family's role in things."

"What kind of doubts?"

"Illiana Stormwind visited to warn me that people in the family might target me."

"Your grandmother was a wise woman."

Natalia looked up in surprise. "You knew she was my grandmother?"

"Indeed," Tatiana said, her voice kept low. "I was one of the few entrusted with such knowledge. The others here don't know, especially Marakhova, and if I were you, I would strive to keep it that way."

"I know so little of Illiana."

Tatiana stood. "Then come, and I shall tell you of her."

Natalia rose, the action noted by the matriarch.

"And where do you think you're going?" said Marakhova.

"It's my fault," said Tatiana. "I thought we might stretch our legs and talk of the Volstrum. Much has changed since her graduation."

"Very well, but don't go outside. The guards have instructions to prevent Natalia from leaving."

"Understood, Matriarch."

Tatiana led Natalia into the hallway. "The Stormwinds trace their lineage back more than five hundred years. Within the confines of Stormwind Manor are paintings of most of them, at least the more recent ones. I used to come here often, back in the day."

"Back in the day?" said Natalia.

"Yes, when Marakhova first took over the Volstrum. Illiana was the grand mistress, of course, but once chosen as the matriarch, there was no going back."

"You were Illiana's spy?"

Tatiana smiled. "You might say that. Illiana was concerned the Volstrum might become corrupted."

"What do you mean?"

"There have always been those who struggle to attain power, and they can be quite ruthless. Illiana was told her son died by self-immolation, not too rare an occurrence amongst Fire Mages, but over the years, she began to have doubts and became obsessed with finding the person responsible."

"And did she?"

"If she did, she never told me. It did lead her to you, however, or I should say it led her to believe you were her granddaughter."

"She didn't know when I first arrived?"

"No, not at all," said Tatiana. "That realization didn't dawn on her till many years later."

"You say you spied for her. She didn't trust Marakhova?"

"Not in the least. She wouldn't have supported her for the position of Grand Mistress of the Volstrum if it hadn't been for pressure. Think of it as a compromise to ascend to the head of the family."

"She'd grown disenchanted with the family."

"How did you know that?" asked Tatiana.

"She pretty much told me so herself. In her words, she hung on by a thread. I wouldn't have been able to escape if she hadn't given me the precious gems."

"She aided your escape?"

"Not only that, she sent Stanislav Voronsky to find me and keep me safe."

"Voronsky? The mage hunter?"

"Yes. My only friend from my days at the Volstrum."

"Not the only one," said Tatiana. "Look, I know you don't want to be here."

"But…?"

"Bide your time. You are a powerful mage, Natalia, but you lack knowledge of the most formidable spells. I can help you elevate your magic to a whole new level."

"Why would you do that?"

"Because I believe in Illiana's vision for the future of the family. She wanted to expunge the more forceful members of the line."

"Like Marakhova?"

"Yes, she was always in your grandmother's shadow, coveting what she couldn't have."

"Do you believe Marakhova is responsible for Antonov's death?"

"Unlikely. That happened long ago, the same year you were born."

Tatiana paused, considering her next words carefully.

"You should know Illiana was always going to become the matriarch. She was the only person all sides could agree on."

"I had no idea."

"Nor were you supposed to. She didn't want to burden you with any of this."

"You were horrid to me," said Natalia. "Why the change of heart now?"

"I was stern with you because I had to be. Had I softened my approach, it would have been brought to the attention of Marakhova. The truth is my sole purpose for being at the Volstrum in the first place was to keep an eye on you and make sure nothing untoward happened. I'm sorry if that offended you, but it did keep you safe."

"My only desire is to escape this place and return home."

"And I shall do all I can to help, but now is not the time, and here is not the place. Come to the Volstrum, play the part of the dutiful instructor, and I'll have you back to casting in short order."

"And then?"

"Then I can give you access to something that will increase your knowledge of magic by leaps and bounds. There will come a day when your power will be tested, Natalia. Let me help you destroy your enemies once and for all."

THE MINES

Summer 1108 SR

The line moved forward when the whip cracked overhead. Like the others, Athgar wore a leather belt connecting him to his fellow miners by a length of chain. On either side of the line walked two guards who used their clubs liberally.

In the early morning hours, the guards had roused them from their sleep, forcing them to line up in the cold air outside. Now they trudged through the mud towards the tallest building, leaving him to wonder what lay within. The other members of his group were obviously used to this routine, for they offered no resistance and remained silent.

They halted as the group in front was led into the building. Shortly thereafter, he struggled to identify an unusual sound drifting forth until it finally stopped. He looked around but saw no signs of panic or distress in the others. This must be an ordinary occurrence in this place, so he closed his eyes, trying to calm his nerves.

They remained there for so long he nearly fell asleep standing up. Then the strange noise began anew, lasting for a shorter period before the door opened. They were prodded forward into what looked like a large wooden crate. Athgar glanced up to see a series of ropes and pulleys above them as the door closed. Someone barked out a command, a horse whinnied, and then the crate moved up slightly. Two men rushed forward to remove large timbers, then he detected a slight sway. Evidently, they hung in place, for a moment later, that same noise came from above as he felt himself descending.

Athgar was familiar with the concept of a mine, although he'd never seen one himself. He briefly wondered what Belgast might make of this contraption they were using, but then he dismissed the thought. The Dwarf was safe, or at least he believed him to be—that was some consolation.

The air grew foul, and he noticed several of his companions taking shallower breaths. The platform finally came to a rest, then someone opened one side to reveal a rough-cut tunnel.

"You lot, down that way," ordered a guard.

"Are we to dig with our hands?" asked Athgar.

"No," said Katrin. "Picks and shovels are farther along, but first we must get these chains removed."

Strange-looking lanterns lit the way, and something about them seemed different. "The lights," he said. "They don't flicker."

"That's because they're not lit by flames, rather magic. Have you never heard of a ball of light?"

"Can't say that I have, although I must admit they're brighter than I would have thought."

"Quiet down there!" yelled a guard.

They proceeded in silence. The tunnel went for some distance, and Athgar wondered if there was actually an end to it. Eventually, they emerged into a large chamber where a group of guards waited. Two of them moved forward and removed the chain binding them together.

Katrin then led them to an opening, where a stack of tools stood. Their group was small, only eight individuals, but they knew their business. Five of them selected picks while the two largest individuals took shovels, along with some heavy canvas sacks.

"What should I take?" asked Athgar.

"A pick. Our job will be to cut through the stone until we find the magerite. Alfie and Felix here will carry away the rock we dislodge."

"And how will I know magerite when I see it?"

"In its uncut state, it looks much like a large block of salt, except it will have a light hue—blue magerite will glow slightly since we all have innate Water Magic. The red is a little harder to find. Then again, we've never had a Fire Mage down here before. I'm curious to see if it glows in your presence."

"Where do we dig?"

"Pretty much wherever we like. The best place to start is usually the end of a tunnel, but some groups have had success widening them out."

Katrin led them down a series of twisting tunnels. They passed by two other groups, each intent on digging out the sides of the corridor. Eventually, they came upon a wall of sheer rock.

"We'll start here," she announced. "We dig two at a time while the rest take a break."

"Wouldn't it be more efficient for all of us to mine?"

"Don't worry, you'll get plenty of time for that. You must pace yourself. We work in short spurts. As one person gets tired, another steps in to take their place. If someone finds something, they'll sing out."

Athgar observed while the digging began. As bits of rock fell, they were scooped up by the shovels and dumped into the sacks. Every so often, they would fill one, then Alfie and Felix would drag it farther up the tunnel, returning some time later with an empty sack.

He finally got his chance to dig. The rock was very hard, requiring every ounce of strength he could muster. He dug in with all he had.

"Conserve your strength," warned Katrin. "We'll be here most of the day."

To Athgar, this was an endless chore. To break up the monotony, he took turns hauling away the rubble, but he soon lost track of time. Occasionally, other prisoners would come by bearing water skins, and they would all slake their thirst. Hunger, however, was their constant companion.

Athgar found himself on a break, pondering his bleak existence. He sat down, his back against the wall, and closed his eyes. Someone sat down beside him, and he looked to see Katrin.

"You never told me how you met Natalia," she said.

He laughed. "She tried to kill me."

"Why would she do that?"

"A case of mistaken identity. We were in Draybourne. Are you familiar with it?"

"Can't say that I am. Is it close by?"

"Not in the least," said Athgar. "It lies south, beyond a mountain range, in the Duchy of Holstead. In any case, I was in the city and saw what I took to be a woman in distress. A group of men followed her, and I thought their intentions less than honourable. I went after them, the idea being to stop them and help her escape. What I didn't plan on was the fact she was willing to make a stand."

"What happened?"

"She used her magic to defeat them but mistook me for one of them. A bolt of ice knocked me unconscious, and when I awoke, I was in a room at an inn. She ended up nursing me back to health, and the rest is, as they say, history."

"And now you're married and have a child!"

"Yes, a daughter, Oswyn."

"It's hard to believe," said Katrin. "Then again, so is this place."

"Tell me, why send you here? Wouldn't labourers be better at digging?"

"It's the magerite, you see. It's tough to tell it from quartz. All the Disgraced have the capacity for Water Magic, which makes the blue magerite glow when we're near."

"And the red magerite?"

"Usually, that's found by happenstance, but the Stormwinds aren't much interested in it. They'll still take it if only to trade with the Sartellians, but it's not something they encourage."

"And how much of this stuff must we find each day?"

"A fist-sized chunk is enough to win us a meal."

"That much?"

"Bear in mind that's the raw size. After cutting and shaping, they'd be lucky to make two or three rings from it."

"All this effort just for a stone that glows."

"It's much more than that," said Katrin. "A decent-sized one can be empowered—imbued with magic if you will. My understanding is it's the only gem that holds a spell. Mind you, not many spellcasters will go to the trouble."

"Why is that?"

"The act of imbuing an item with magic weakens the caster. It's like they surrender part of themselves when they create it."

"So there are very few enchanted rings."

"Not enchanted," corrected Katrin, "empowered."

"What's the difference?"

"Enchantments are a specific school of magic, but empowering can be done by anyone with sufficient magical ability."

"Even me?"

"Yes, although not when you're dosed up with magebane."

"Am I still dosed?" asked Athgar. "I haven't eaten for at least a day."

"They spike the water, so yes, you're still under the influence. If you don't believe me, try using your magic."

He closed his eyes, digging deep to find his inner spark. It lay there still, ready to spring up at his command, but all attempts to call on it failed. He shifted slightly, only to see it flare up, however briefly.

"What's this?" he said.

"What's what?" said Katrin.

"My inner spark, it flared."

"Your what?"

"My inner spark. The Orcs taught me how to harness it. That's how magic works."

"No, it doesn't," she replied. "Magic is called from the body."

"Fed by the spark. It's the very foundation of my Fire Magic."

"And you can see this spark?"

"Yes, but it flared for a moment."

"What were you doing?"

"Just shifting my arse; it was getting sore. Wait—that gives me an idea." He stood, then closed his eyes, concentrating. With the spark coming to mind, he moved around slightly, noticing it flare again as he got closer to the wall.

"Here," he said. "Dig here."

"I beg your pardon."

"There's something here," Athgar explained. "I don't know how I know, but it's close."

Someone passed him the pickaxe, and he began digging away at the rock. After several swings, a large piece slewed away, revealing a red glow.

"Red magerite," said Katrin, her face full of wonder. "How did you do that?"

"Who knows? Orc training, I suppose." He attacked the wall with renewed vigour, revealing their target, a chunk of glowing red crystal roughly half the size of his fist.

"Will this feed us?" he asked.

"No," said Katrin, "but if you can teach us to pull off that trick, it would save us a lot of time."

"Then sit down," said Athgar. "There's no time like the present."

Of all their group, only Katrin appeared to have the mental discipline to call on her inner spark, although the term didn't quite fit what she saw. She described it more as a light, blue in colour, but the effect was the same. In any case, it took what Athgar could only assume was the greater part of the morning for her to master the technique.

Several guards passed them by, assuming, no doubt, they were simply taking a rest. Discipline here was nowhere near as severe as it was on the surface, for those who chose not to produce would not eat. It mattered little to those in charge if someone preferred to starve to death.

Finally, confident in her new-found technique, they returned to the end of the tunnel, where she put it to use.

"It's no good," she said. "I can't see any change."

"Perhaps it's the location," offered Anushka. "There might not be any magerite here for us to find. Athgar was pretty close when he discovered the red."

They moved back up the tunnel, going slowly and guiding Katrin, whose eyes remained closed. They passed by the two groups they saw earlier, then emerged into the large chamber where they'd acquired their tools.

"We'll try another tunnel," said Katrin. "There's got to be some around here somewhere."

Athgar picked one at random and led the group no more than fifty paces when Katrin suddenly halted.

"Here," she said. "It flared." She moved around, homing in on her target, her hand finally pointing at a section of wall. "This spot," she announced.

They attacked the wall with the picks and were soon rewarded with a chunk of blue magerite. It was a strange sight, for as each worker drew closer, it would glow, then dim as the pick wielder backed up slightly to swing anew. It gave the effect of a pulsating light, something Athgar found particularly amusing.

The crystal finally fell to the ground, and Katrin scooped it up. It was large, fully half the size of her head, and judging from the other's reaction, a rare find indeed.

"Our day is done," said Katrin, relief flooding her face. "Your little exercise in meditation has proven most beneficial."

"Agreed," said Athgar, lowering his voice. "But I would suggest we keep that from becoming common knowledge. If everyone learned how to do that, the people in charge of this place would seek to exploit it, then we'd all be doing more work."

Katrin led them back into the main chamber, where they dropped off their tools and turned in their finds.

"Impressive," said the overseer. "We haven't found one this big for months." He used a jeweller's scale to weigh it, after which he made a careful notation in a journal. Satisfied with his entry, he unlocked a strongbox and withdrew eight wooden disks, passing one to each of them.

"We exchange these for food," she explained, "but be warned, there are some who might seek to take it from you by force."

As it turned out, her warning was unnecessary, at least for today. They made their way back to the lift, then as they waited for the next group to descend, they were once more chained together. Once the new workers exited the platform, they moved forward, and the crate began lifting.

"What a strange contraption," said Athgar. "I've never seen its like."

"I've heard it claimed it's a Dwarven design," said Katrin, "but then again, the Dwarves get credit for anything of a mechanical nature." She turned to Athgar. "Have you ever met a Dwarf?"

"I have, as a matter of fact. I count one as one of my closest friends."

"You must tell us more. We know so little of the mountain folk."

"I'm not sure what there is to tell. They're slightly shorter than us, but each is an individual. You might as well ask what Humans are like."

"Is it true that they're stubborn?" asked Anushka.

"Not really. I always found Belgast pragmatic. I suppose they have a reputation for not running from a fight, but then again, with shorter legs, what choice do they have?"

"What about Elves?" asked Felix. "Ever meet one of those?"

"Can't say that I have, but I spent most of my life amongst the Petty Kingdoms, or at least in their lands."

"I used to dream of travelling," said Katrin, "but then I started having trouble with my spellcasting before failing several of my courses. It takes years to become a battle mage, and I couldn't even learn to properly target a spell. Tell me, how long did it take you to master Fire Magic?"

"Just over a year, but the Orcs do things differently from the Volstrum. Natalia told me you spend years learning theory?"

"We do. All of us did, but only two made it past the unleashing."

"That's when you learn spells," noted Alfie.

"Yes, Natalia mentioned that. You said two of you made it past?"

"Yes," replied Katrin. "Anushka learned the basic spells but was dropped before she got to battle magic."

"And you?"

"I progressed a little further in the program."

"So you were taught together?"

"Not at all. Anushka is slightly younger. She was in the year behind me."

"Is this how they deal with all the failures?" asked Athgar. "Not that I mean to imply anything."

"The family doesn't believe in wasting resources."

"Yes," added Anushka. "We must all live to serve the family."

"I understand your bitterness," said Athgar, "but we must deal with the present, not dwell on the past."

Their movement ceased, and the door opened, revealing the mid-afternoon sun. Katrin stepped out into the light of day, revelling in it.

"It's been some time since I was able to do this," she remarked. "Now, come on, it's time to eat."

She led them to what he first took to be another living hut. Inside, however, sat a series of empty tables. A large pot hung over a fire at the other end of the room, tended to by a fearsome-looking woman with black hair and a filthy apron. Each of them took their turn picking up a wooden bowl and spoon, then watched as the cook ladled out a thick porridge.

"This doesn't look too bad," said Athgar. "It reminds me of the porridge

Shaluhk makes." He shovelled some into his mouth then choked, spitting it back out. "I stand corrected. This is nothing like Shaluhk's."

"Who's Shaluhk?" asked Katrin.

"An Orc. The shaman of the Red Hand, to be more precise."

"And she makes you porridge regularly, does she?"

"She and her bondmate, Kargen, are our closest friends. We often eat at each other's huts."

"The Orcs are disgusting," said Anushka. "They feast on Human flesh."

"No," said Athgar, "they don't. Truth is, they eat much the same things as we do, although a little more meat than we might consume. Most in the Petty Kingdoms believe them savages, but in my experience, they are far more civilized than many Humans." He looked around the room, but the cook was busy stirring the pot. "For one thing, the Orcs don't believe in slaves."

THE BAROSHKA

Summer 1108 SR

Natalia entered the room, causing all within to fall silent. Their youthful faces looked at her expectantly, an act she found slightly unnerving. Two long tables ran the length of the room, with students sitting on either side, while at the end was an immense lectern upon which she placed her book.

"Good morning, students."

"Good morning, Mistress," they all chimed in.

"I am Mistress Natalia, and I shall be teaching you the history of magic. Now, I understand you were taught the basics, so who can tell me where magic originated?"

Several students raised their hands. They were all thirteen to fifteen years old, the typical age at which training would commence. Many could already read and write when they came to the Volstrum, but a select few had needed to be taught such skills, thus making them the older students amongst her group.

"You," said Natalia, pointing.

"The first magic was performed by the woodland folk, then taught to early Humans. Their magic was crude, and it took Humans to develop it into the art it is today."

"A nice quote. I see you read the *Historica Magicae*. Now answer me this: how much of it is true?"

She saw the look of confusion and well understood it. Finally, a blonde-haired girl raised her hand.

"Go ahead," said Natalia.

"It was written by the founders of the Volstrum."

"That it was. Now, where did they get their information from? Are you suggesting they were old enough to be there when Elves passed on that knowledge?"

The class all laughed, leading the individual to blush. "No, Mistress."

"Quiet, class," said Natalia, consulting her notes. "Ludiya has given us her best answer. Has anyone else something to add?"

Another raised her hand.

"Yes, Serafina?"

"It's passed-down knowledge from the days of our ancestors."

"Excellent answer. It's part of our written history that we learned magic from the Elves, but what if I told you it wasn't true? What if we learned it from someone else? Someone with a tradition of magic that predates even the woodland race?"

"Like who?"

"The Orcs."

They broke into laughter again, Ludiya joining in this time.

"I'm serious." The room went quiet. "What do you know of the Orcs?"

"They are primitive savages," piped in Serafina.

"How do you know that?"

"Everyone knows that, Mistress."

"You only know what you were told. No doubt, when you were young, you were taught faeries stole the souls of babies. Do you still believe that?"

"No."

"And why not?"

"Because we know better," said Ludiya. "And you can't compare fairies with Orcs."

"Why not?" asked Natalia.

"Everyone knows fairies aren't real. And in any event, Orcs can't read. How could they ever learn magic?"

"It seems you are under the impression literacy is an important part of spellcasting. While that's our tradition, it is far from the only one."

"You're making this up," said Ludiya. "Is this some sort of test?"

"Not at all. The truth is I have spent time amongst the Orcs." She saw their looks of shock. They were surprised and yet eager to hear more.

A hand went up at the back.

"Yes, Yeva?"

"What kind of magic did they use?"

"The tribe I spent the most time with utilized Fire Magic."

"I bet they weren't as good as the Sartellians."

"On the contrary. Their current master of flame is one of the most powerful Pyromancers I've ever seen."

"Are they a threat to us?"

"Not at all," said Natalia. "Why would you even think such a thing?"

"Only a disciplined mind can control the element of fire."

"And you think the Orcs lack that discipline? I have witnessed their training methods, and while different from ours, they still have merit. You would be wise to pay attention to other races. We can still learn a lot from them."

"Like what? Other than magic, I mean."

"They value family, much as we do." She thought it over for a moment. Considering the family's approach to children, perhaps that wasn't quite true. "Let me rephrase that: they care about the members of the tribe, as we care about other members of the family. In essence, the tribe IS their family."

Ludiya raised her hand once again.

"Yes?"

"How do you know the Orcs taught us magic?"

"Because, unlike the other races, the Orcs can talk to the spirits of their Ancestors. In this way, they have a direct link to their forebearers."

"I don't believe it."

"That's entirely within your rights, but answer me this: you clearly know little of Orcs—what do you know of Elves?"

She saw the blank look. "As I thought. I could just as easily tell you magic was found under a rock, and who's to say I'm not correct? The point I'm trying to make is just because something is written in a book doesn't make it the truth. The *Historica Magicae*, interesting as it is, was written from the perspective of a member of the family. Thus, it results from a rather singular point of view."

"How important to us is this knowledge?" asked Serafina.

"To be honest, not at all."

"Then why teach it?"

"That's a good question. We learn history to avoid making the mistakes of our ancestors. Who here has ever burned themselves?"

No one answered, not surprising considering most had an army of servants to look after them growing up.

"You know not to grab something hot because of someone else's experience. The same thing can be said for magic. None of you are casters yet, but Saints willing, you'll all pass your unleashing and become Stormwinds one day. When that happens, you'll learn how to use the power currently lying dormant within you. The Volstrum prepares you for that day by teaching you all the basics of magic. Yes, some of it is boring"—everyone chuckled —"and yes, some of it is quite exciting, but the family is not investing all this time and effort in your development to have you accidentally freeze your fingers off."

Their faces quickly turned serious.

"Now, let us turn our attention to more recent history—the founding of the Volstrum."

"How was your first class?"

Natalia looked up to see Tatiana. "Lively. I had to field no end of questions."

"Interesting. I remember the history of magic as being a terribly dull affair. How did you keep them engaged?"

"I can't give away all my secrets."

"Speaking of secrets, come with me. I have something to show you."

Intrigued by the offer, Natalia followed her old instructor into the hallway. "Where are we going?"

"To a place most don't even know exists."

They threaded their way through a maze of hallways to a staircase. Natalia expected to be taken to the second floor, but instead, Tatiana moved beneath the set of stairs.

"It's in here somewhere," she muttered. "I always have a hard time—ah, there it is." A clicking noise accompanied her words, and then she swung a section of the wall aside, revealing another set of stairs heading downward.

She took a lantern from a shelf within, uttering words of power to activate its magic. A bright light sprang forth, illuminating the area.

"Come," she said. "Let me introduce you to the Baroshka."

"Baroshka? I thought you were taking me to the Inner Sanctum."

"That is for any battle mage who has completed their training. This, on the other hand, is a place of creativity where a select few can learn to unlock the most powerful of spells."

The stairs ended in a large room, with grand columns supporting a vaulted ceiling. Beautiful murals decorated the walls, but the white marble floor grabbed her attention. The inscribed magical runes were easy to read on the circle of gold and silver.

"A magic circle," said Natalia. "I didn't know the Volstrum possessed such a thing."

"It dates back centuries," explained Tatiana, "yet its secret is known to only a few."

"How few?"

"Less than half a dozen, and that list does not include our matriarch."

"It's an impressive work of art but of little use to me."

"For now," said Tatiana, "but bide your time, and eventually, you'll be permitted to use your magic. This circle will magnify your power, Natalia, allowing you to perform magic undreamed of." She moved to the far end of the room, where ornate pillars framed a door. "In there are the most powerful spells known to us. Many have sat for generations, untapped."

"Why? Wouldn't the family want to learn them?"

"I'm sure they would, but in the hands of the wrong people, they would be too destructive. As you are well aware, Fire Mages can lose their minds, but the same can be said for our own school of magic."

"If they are so dangerous, why tell me about them?"

"Because you have the potential to learn them all! You alone have the discipline and the power to unlock these ancient secrets. Use them to destroy your enemies!"

"I can't."

"Not yet you can't, but if you are patient, in due course, you'll be able to learn them."

"I don't have time. Every day I serve is another day Athgar is held as a slave."

"What if I told you that all of this"—she waved her hands around the room—"could save him?"

"How?"

"Come. I have more to show you." Tatiana led her through the door into the Baroshka's arcane library. It was not much to look at, mostly a collection of old tomes and parchments, but at the centre stood a table with a trio of chairs. "Help me push these out of the way," she said. "I need some space for this demonstration."

"Demonstration of what?"

Her old instructor smiled. "Wait and see."

They pushed the furniture aside, then Tatiana moved to the centre of the room. "Come and stand beside me," she said, "and watch as I perform a ritual."

"A ritual? We learned about those at the Volstrum, but we were never taught any."

"I know. I was one of your instructors, remember?"

Natalia took up her position and watched as Tatiana closed her eyes. Her arms moved, tracing intricate patterns as words of magic tumbled from her mouth. The air grew chilly, her breath frosting as the hair on the back of her neck stood on end, and then something began materializing before her. At first, it looked like two ice columns, but as the spell progressed, they became joined at the top, forming an arch. Tatiana called out a final word of command, and the centre of the arch changed suddenly, revealing the room beyond.

"What do you think?"

"It's amazing," said Natalia. She moved around it, examining it from both sides, but no matter where she stood, the archway revealed the other room.

"It's called a frozen arch. Come," she said, reaching out with her hand."

"There's more?"

Tatiana chuckled. "There most certainly is." She took Natalia's hand in her own and stepped through the arch. Natalia found they were now in the room with the magic circle. She looked behind her, seeing the archway, or at least a duplicate of it. Between the pillars was the Baroshka's arcane library. She moved around it, opening the door to see the original arch beyond.

"It works both ways," explained Tatiana. "Although it won't last much longer. I can also dismiss it at will." She waved her hand, and both arches vanished.

"How far can you travel using such a spell?"

"It depends on an individual's power. An accomplished mage might manage a thousand miles or more, but there is a limitation."

"Which is?"

"The destination must always be a circle of power, and you must have committed it to memory."

"I'm not sure what that means," said Natalia. "Are you suggesting I memorize the layout of the circle?"

"Yes, and the good news is it has nothing to do with your ability to cast. In other words, you can do so even under the influence of magebane."

"How do I study it?"

"I shall show you that eventually, but not today. We must get you back upstairs in time for your next class."

"How long have you known about this?"

"Years. It's how I communicated with Illiana after she left the Volstrum."

The full import of her words ran through Natalia's mind. "That means there has to be a magic circle somewhere in Stormwind Manor."

"There is," said Tatiana, "although I suspect by now Marakhova knows all about that one. It means, once your magic is restored, you'll be able to travel freely back and forth between here and there, providing you manage to find the time to commit the two sites to memory."

Natalia hugged her old instructor. "Thank you, Tatiana, for all this."

"Don't thank me yet. We have much more to do if we are to honour your grandmother's legacy."

The most pressing thing on Natalia's mind was time. Each day meant another day of Athgar's suffering, another day denied the chance to hold Oswyn. Days became weeks, and before she knew it, a new class started. She quickly became the new students' favourite and worried her teaching only made the family stronger. She countered that fear by introducing discussions on various topics, encouraging the students to think for themselves and question rules passed from on high.

There came a day, midsummer, when she sat eating her lunch, and Tatiana entered the room, making a show of speaking with each occupant in turn. As she approached Natalia, she gave her a withering look.

"What's this?" she asked, her voice stern. "Your attire is unsuitable, Natalia. See that you change it." In a much lower voice, she whispered, "Go to the interview rooms. I'll meet you there."

Natalia knew the place well. When a potential candidate first arrived at the Volstrum, they would be taken to a plain room holding only a table and two chairs. Here, they would be assessed by a senior member of the Volstrum's staff to determine if they possessed the potential to make decent family material.

She looked down, acting the part of the chastised instructor as she waited for Tatiana to finish her charade by having a few choice words for other staff members. Once she left, Natalia rose, exiting the room in a hurry.

The interview rooms were near the back of the Volstrum, not too far from the stables. The place reminded her of her own arrival at the Volstrum all those years ago and her initial terror at her new surroundings. She found the hallway easy enough and soon located Tatiana.

"Come in," the grand mistress bid, "and close the door."

"What are we doing?"

"I'm taking you to the circle so you can begin committing it to memory."

Tatiana cast the spell, the room soon growing chilly, the walls frosty, and when the archway finally appeared, they stepped through. Tatiana then dismissed the spell.

A voice drifted out from the arcane library. "Tatiana, is that you?"

Natalia froze. Footsteps drew closer, and then a familiar face entered. There, standing before her, was Galina Stormwind.

"Ah," said Tatiana. "I believe you know each other?"

"What's she doing here?" asked Natalia.

"I was about to ask the same thing," replied Galina.

"I have taken her into my confidence," said Tatiana, "much as I did you."

They stood in awkward silence until Natalia spoke. "How have you been, Galina?"

"Well enough, thank you. I managed to secure a position here at the Volstrum. And you?"

"Oh, I ran off, got married, and had a daughter. Other than that, not much."

"You have a daughter?" Galina smiled. "I wish I'd been so lucky."

"Whatever do you mean?"

"The family saw fit not to breed me. They said I wasn't powerful enough."

"The same thing happened to Svetlana—you remember her?"

"Of course." Galina moved closer, clearly unsure of how to react. "I'm sorry for all I put you through. I could blame it on my upbringing, but the truth is I desperately wanted to belong, and mocking you made me more acceptable to the others."

"I accept your apology," said Natalia. "If there's one thing I've learned of late, it's that the family can be quite ruthless when it wants something. You obviously know about the circle here. I assume that means you're working with Tatiana?"

"I am. She recruited me right after being appointed grand mistress."

"I needed someone I could trust," said Tatiana, "and Galina proved quite valuable after her graduation."

"In what way?" asked Natalia.

"I was waiting to be selected for a court assignment," explained Galina, "but when they assessed my power, they declined to offer me anything. As a result, I was stuck here with nothing to do."

"She ended up helping me," said Tatiana. "A sort of assistant, if you will. More and more of Marakhova's time was taken up with politics, and it fell to me, as her designated successor, to pick up the slack."

"So she knows everything?"

"Not exactly. She can use the circle here and certainly knows one exists at Stormwind Manor but has never actually seen it, let alone committed it to memory. As to your own circumstances, she knows little, other than the fact you left the Volstrum under less than ideal circumstances. If you wish to tell her your tale, feel free. She is completely trustworthy. However, you don't have the time at this precise moment."

"I don't? Why not?"

"Because I'm going to show you how to memorize this circle, of course!"

THE DISGRACED

Autumn 1108 SR

"This is ridiculous," said Anushka. "Here we are, loaded up with our daily haul of magerite, and we just sit down here, waiting."

"Be patient," said Katrin. "If we tell them our secret, they'll only push for more. This way, we at least have time to think."

"I don't need more time to ponder my miserable existence."

"Then ponder this," said Athgar. "How can we escape?"

"That's easy," said Anushka. "We don't. Did you forget our guards control the box that lifts us from the mines? What would you have us do, escape their custody to be forever entombed in stone?"

"I know the situation is bleak, but it won't always be so."

"What are you getting at?" asked Katrin. "You're not suggesting that one day they'll let us all go?"

"No, of course not, but people make mistakes, and that includes our captors. We must be mindful of our surroundings and learn all we can."

"Why?"

"To be prepared, should an opportunity present itself. At the very least, it will give us something to do."

"I still don't understand," said Anushka.

"Think on this for a moment," said Athgar. "Suppose you decided to take that pick and sink it into the head of one of those guards. What do you imagine would be the result?"

"Death, most likely."

"Clearly, but I'm talking about the immediate effect. Here you are, standing over the body of a dead guard. What happens next?"

"I'm not stupid enough to kill a guard."

"You're missing the point," said Athgar. "The idea is to try to reason out what the enemy would do in those circumstances. It might not be you who kills him; maybe some other prisoner goes berserk and does it."

"In that case," said Anushka, "we need some additional details."

"Such as?"

"Does the guard cry out as he dies?"

"Let's assume he does."

"Then that's easy. Guards will come running from all directions. They'd probably beat the attacker senseless."

"Agreed," said Athgar. "Now, what happens in the rest of the mine as the guards all swarm him?"

He saw the realization dawning on her.

"They would leave it unguarded."

"Precisely."

"Are you suggesting we have someone attack a guard?"

"No, at least not yet. This is merely a way of taking stock of our situation. If we are to ever escape this place, we'll need to know what our options are."

"I see what you mean," said Katrin. "Attacking a guard might make a distraction, but it doesn't get us out of here."

"Correct," said Athgar. "So the question is this: what would precipitate an evacuation of the mine?"

"Uncovering a golem?" offered Felix.

"Or some other type of monster," added Alfie.

"I doubt that's a possibility," said Athgar.

"Why would you say that?"

"How long has this mine been in operation?"

"More than a century."

"And in that time, how many creatures has it unleashed?"

Alfie's face fell. "None."

"So then, what else is a possibility?"

Ulyana shuffled forward. She was the quietest of the group and seldom said much of anything. "A cave-in?"

"Now you're on the right track." He was about to say more but then heard a guard approaching.

The fellow paused to look at them. "You won't find much standing around here."

"We're just resting," said Katrin.

The guard shrugged his shoulders. "If you want to starve to death, that's your business." He continued on his way.

Anushka spat on the ground. "I hate them," she said. "I'd kill them all if I had a chance."

"We all would," added Katrin.

Athgar returned his attention to the task at hand. "Has there ever been a cave-in?"

"Yes," said Alfie. The others looked at him in surprise. "What? I've been here the longest. I've seen one myself."

"What happened? Did they evacuate the mine?"

"No, they sent down more guards to keep the place safe, and then the rest of us dug out the bodies. Not a pleasant experience."

"And this is?" chimed in Felix.

"What about the time those workers collapsed?" suggested Alfie.

"Oh yes," said Katrin. "An entire group of workers were digging down one of the side tunnels, and they all fell unconscious. They said some kind of vapour was released."

"Vapour?" said Athgar. "What do you mean?"

"They were searching for magerite and found an iron deposit. News of their discovery was taken to those in charge, and they decided it might be worth investigating further. They began digging out the ore but passed out when a terrible smell was released. Out of twelve miners, ten died."

"Yes," added Ulyana, "and two guards died trying to save them, all from a shortage of breath."

Athgar was intrigued. "What about the survivors?"

"They were sick for days."

"Sick, how?"

"They had difficulty breathing and were dizzy."

"And they had terrible headaches," added Felix.

"So what happened to that section of the mine?"

Katrin laughed. "That's a story in and of itself. They decided whatever it was could be burned out."

"I presume that was unsuccessful?"

"Oh no, it burned, far more so than they expected. I didn't see it myself, but I heard the fireball was worse than that of the strongest Fire Mage. I remember the rest of the tunnels were smoky for weeks. It was so bad they suspended mining."

"Did they evacuate?"

"Not until after the fire."

"Say," interrupted Felix, "you're not suggesting we look for more vapours?"

"No," replied Athgar. "That would be too dangerous, but at this stage, even the rumour of something like that might be enough to upset the applecart."

"What applecart?" said Alfie.

"Never mind him," said Ulyana. "He'll figure it out, eventually."

Katrin chuckled. "Alfie can be challenging at times, but he's a good friend. Now, let's get back to this whole idea of escaping, shall we? What would be the next step?"

"A good general knows his enemy," said Athgar.

"Are you saying you've led warriors?"

"Let's just say I've seen a battle or two. Now, as I was saying, we need to know everything we can about our captors."

"Such as?" asked Katrin.

"Well, for one thing, how many of them are down here in the mine, as opposed to being up on the surface?"

"Anything else?"

"Yes," continued Athgar. "What is their quality? Are they trained warriors, or merely thugs?"

"What does that matter?" asked Ulyana. "They still have weapons, and we don't."

"It matters a great deal. A trained warrior will run to a battle, ready to fight by himself, if need be, but a thug will avoid one unless he has numbers on his side. It sounds as if there are more prisoners here than guards, but how badly do we outnumber them?"

"How should we know?"

"That's just it," said Athgar, "we don't, but we can find out."

"How?"

"By observing them."

"That would take forever," said Anushka.

"Have you something better to do with your time? You were the one complaining about having nothing to do. Well, now's your chance to rectify that."

"How do we count them?" asked Felix. "They're constantly moving around."

"Guards are individuals, just like us."

"They're nothing like us," spat out Anushka.

"They're still individuals. Pay more attention to their appearance. Look for anything that might identify them, like a scar or skin blemish. Even something they wear sets them apart from the other guards. If you see them this way, you'll become more familiar with their patterns."

"Patterns?" said Katrin.

"Yes," said Athgar. "Everybody has their own habits. Think back to your time at the Volstrum. Do you remember your instructors?"

"Of course."

"And what makes them memorable? Was it their appearance or their behaviour?"

"A little of both, I suppose," admitted Anushka.

"Then that's what you're looking for. The point is, if I describe the guard who's tall and blond, you should know exactly who I mean."

"We have a blond guard?" said Alfie.

"It's only an example," explained Felix, before returning his attention to Athgar. "What else do we need to do?"

"It would help immensely if we could somehow remove the magebane from the water."

"Not much chance of that," said Katrin. "This place is full of would-be mages. They're hardly going to make a slip-up like that, and we can't go without water."

"Could we maybe find an alternate source?"

"Like what?"

"I don't know. Are there sometimes pockets of water amongst the rocks?"

"Not that I'm aware of."

"It's too bad we're dosed up," noted Anushka. "Creating water is a spell I've mastered."

"I wonder…" said Athgar, his voice trailing off.

"Go on," urged Katrin. "What is it you're thinking?"

"It's only the beginning of an idea. How long does it take magebane to wear off?"

"Half a day, at least, but you'd have a hard time going without water in this place."

"But what if you didn't dig?"

"Then you wouldn't eat."

"True," said Athgar, "but if, for example, Anushka went without water, eventually she'd be able to produce her own, then we could all drink fresh, untainted water."

"She'd need a container to hold it. Otherwise, it would absorb into the floor. The other problem I see is the rest of the group would still be dosed with magebane."

"Not if they're down here long enough. You said it yourself: we're stuck down here until we find more blue magerite. It would be easy enough to draw it out until our powers returned. As to a container, I admit that poses a bit of a challenge, but I doubt it's an insurmountable one."

"That still leaves us trapped in the mine," said Katrin.

"Yes, but at least we have another piece of the puzzle."

"So I don't drink anymore?" asked Anushka.

"No, drink normally for now. All of this will do us no good without the rest figured out. We'll keep going on as we are, but observe everything we can. Even small details could spell the difference between escape or disaster."

Athgar sat up with a start, an image of Natalia still fresh in his thoughts. For weeks he'd been tormented by this vision, yet nothing could clear it from his mind. In his dream, he struggled to reach her, but no matter how fast he ran, she faded into the distance.

The sweat poured off him, and for a moment, he wondered if he hadn't fallen ill. To make matters worse, there was a distinct chill in the air, making him worry about how he would keep from freezing to death once winter arrived.

He lay back down, pulling the threadbare blanket over him once more, but despite how hard he tried, he couldn't calm his fears. Deep down, he knew the family wanted Natalia to have more children. How far would they go to satisfy that desire? The thought made him shudder. His mind wouldn't rest, so he rose, making his way to the window, and pushed the shutter open a bit, taking a deep breath of the cold night air.

Guards wandered around, wrapped in warm cloaks, carrying lanterns to light their way. Unlike in the mines, there were no worries about vapours above ground, so they used whale oil to fuel their light sources. It left a distinct smell of fish in its wake, which only added to the oppression of the place.

Beyond the palisade, he could see the tops of trees, their wild nature mocking his inability to be under the canopy of green. All his life, he'd lived amongst the forests. The mine and the buildings above it marked the land he loved like some savage scar. The vision before him brought only more despair, the feeling of hopelessness growing within him, but he could do little to suppress it.

He thought of Oswyn and smiled. The chance of seeing her again was slim, especially in his current mood, but at least he had the satisfaction of knowing she was safe. He'd once dreamed of her running through the forest as a young woman, the Orcs following her. Was that a prophetic vision or only a wish for her to enjoy a future free of strife? He struggled to remember the details. No, there'd been the sounds of battle. It appeared even in his dreams, she lived in a world of conflict.

The thought sobered him. He was the High Thane of Therengia. That kingdom, his home, would not submit to the ever-present threat of the Petty Kingdoms, not while he still lived!

He felt anger building within and fed it. Better to die trying to live free than be a slave the rest of his life. Another guard wandered by, his lantern bobbing as he walked. Athgar looked around at the other huts. They were poorly made, with gaps in the walls that let the cold in, yet they had one thing in common—they would all burn nicely, and what better way to feed a fire than with whale oil?

He turned from the window, securing the shutters, not that they made much difference from the icy wind outside. His eyes took in the prisoners crammed into this particular hut. There must've been close to thirty of them. He was saddened by the thought of how many might die before they could taste the air of freedom.

The next day he was unusually quiet as they descended once more into the mines. His companions, sensing his mood, chose not to engage in conversation. It wasn't until they picked up their tools that he finally snapped out of his aloofness.

"I've been thinking," he said at last. "We've discussed several things over the last few weeks but never committed to taking any action, aside from observing, that is."

Katrin took an immediate interest. "What are you proposing?"

"It's time we took stock of what we've learned. Where are we on counting guards?"

They all turned to Anushka, who'd been put in charge of gathering everyone's observations.

"Our best estimate puts the number at thirty," she announced. "That's for down here in the mine, of course. The full complement of the place is a little harder to estimate as we don't have a clear view of what goes on outside the palisade. The best guess would be at least a hundred."

"And the worst guess?" asked Athgar.

"More like two hundred." She shrugged. "As I said, we have little to go on concerning above ground."

"Anything else we should know about?"

"Yes. A number of the guards form a faction of sorts."

"Meaning?"

"They watch each other's back and take retribution on those prisoners they see as causing the most problems."

"How many in this faction?"

"Five," said Anushka. "We refer to them as Scar Face, Left Limp, Patchy Beard, Tall Man, and Sneer."

"Sneer?"

"Yes. He has a disfigured lip, probably from a wound at some point. It gives him a mocking expression."

"That's a pretty small gang."

"Agreed, yet they seem to have a lot of influence over the rest of the guards."

"In what way?" asked Athgar.

"They're all afraid of these five individuals."

"Interesting."

"Interesting, good?" said Katrin. "Or interesting, bad?"

"A little of both, if I'm being honest. On the one hand, they're liable to help each other quite readily."

"And on the other?"

"If we target all five," said Athgar, "there's a good chance the others won't intervene."

"And how do we do that?"

"I'm still working on it, but it's another piece of the bow."

"The bow?" said Alfie.

"Yes, a bow has many parts, all of which must work together."

"What parts does a bow have?"

Athgar smiled. "It has limbs, a grip, a nock at either end, and, of course, the string. You also need an arrow if you're to make it useful."

"You know a lot about bows."

"That's because I used to craft them."

"That's all well and good," said Katrin, "but much of what we came up with is simply conjecture."

"Then it's time we took some steps to test things out."

"Where do we start?"

"Anushka," said Athgar, "tonight, when we eat dinner, I don't want you to drink anything. Can you do that?"

The woman smiled. "So we're finally going to see if the magebane can wear off?"

"Yes, but only as a trial. Bear in mind it might not work."

"Why wouldn't it?" Anushka asked.

"Well, for one thing, they might be lacing our food, not just our water. There's also the problem of thirst. If Anushka doesn't drink, her mouth may become parched, especially down in the mine, where dust and dirt are everywhere. Having her magic back will be useless if she can't intone her spell."

"What about a container?"

"Could we smuggle a cup from our meal?" suggested Felix.

"I doubt it," said Katrin.

"Then," said Athgar, "we'll dig out a temporary hole in the rock, just to try things out. The idea here is to determine if the magebane wears off. Once we confirm that, she can go back to drinking the water they provide, which then allows us to carry on to the next stage."

"Which is?"

He smiled. "How much heat do you suppose would be required to set fire to whale oil?"

THE VOLSTRUM

Autumn 1108 SR

The ring mocked Natalia as she stared at it. Despite all her hours mulling it over, she still had no idea what it unlocked. And time worked against her, for with every day that passed, the prospect of a Sartellian showing up grew. Marakhova had sent word that Natalia was once again in their hands, and it wouldn't be long now before they tried to force her to bear them a child.

The thought sent her into a panic. It would be different if she could access her magic, but they still forced her to take a heavy dose of magebane twice a day, even after nearly two months.

Tatiana assured her the restriction would end in due course, but as the days grew shorter heading into winter, her life remained the same. She rose early, dined at Stormwind Manor before being escorted, under guard, to the Volstrum. Only within those halls was she allowed any freedom to move around. It made perfect sense, of course, for it was one of the most closely guarded buildings in all of Karslev. The original designers of the place knew young students might be tempted by the offer of outside distractions, so they'd restricted the number of exits.

As a student, Natalia had little free time to consider such things, but now, blessed with an overabundance of the same, she found it galling. Following Tatiana's suggestion, she'd thrown herself into her new work. The students responded with a fierce devotion, many of them speaking highly of her. They weren't bad. Natalia even liked them, but the thought that she was training them to follow in the footsteps of Marakhova was infuriating.

She gazed at the ring again, looking for inspiration. More than likely, it unlocked something in Stormwind Manor, but travelling around the place unwatched was nigh on impossible. Her thoughts drifted to the magic circle in the Baroshka. She had, under Tatiana's supervision, committed it to memory. Should she eventually regain her magic, her first step would be learning the frozen arch spell so she could then use it to search the manor.

She told herself that wouldn't work. She still needed to find the circle within the house, for one thing. For another, Marakhova never seemed to leave, seeing it as a place to welcome visitors as if she were a queen holding court.

It looked more and more like coming to Karslev was the worst mistake of her life. Natalia felt tears welling up inside and fought them down. The only way out was to play along, continuing this subterfuge until... and that was the question. How long must she keep this up? Where was Athgar, and was he even still alive? Should she demand to see him? It was a tempting idea, but she soon dismissed it, for the request would only play into the enemy's hands. They knew the only reason she cooperated was in exchange for his continued life. All her efforts over the past two months would be wasted, and then she would need to start building trust all over again.

Natalia stared at the book before her, chastising herself for her thoughts. She should be preparing for a lecture, not regretting past actions. She flipped open the book, a treatise on warfare, and perused its pages. A chapter on Dwarven tactics caught her attention, and reading the brief summary made her think of Belgast. She suddenly remembered she knew nothing of the Dwarf's fate or Stanislav, for that matter. Laisa betrayed them, but was she still carrying on her ruse, or had she turned on everyone? Natalia suddenly realized they might have been imprisoned or even killed. Their lives would be useless as threats—did that mean they were already dead?

The scraping of a chair across the floor interrupted her thoughts.

"What's that?" Galina asked.

"I'm giving a lecture on battles," Natalia replied.

"You're talking to students who can actually cast spells now. I suppose that means you're moving up in the world."

"I'm still not allowed to use my magic."

"True, but look at the bright side of things. It's costing them a fortune in magebane." She glanced at the open page. "Dwarves?"

"Yes. It reminds me of a friend of mine who was nearby when we were captured. Say, you don't think you could make some discreet enquiries, do you?"

"What kind of enquiries?"

"I need to find out if he's been arrested."

"I'm not sure I would know where to start."

"I have an address," said Natalia. "You could start there."

"All right. I won't make any promises, but I'll see what I can do. What name am I looking for?"

"Belgast Ridgehand, he's a Dwarf. Oh, and there's also Stanislav Voronsky."

"The mage hunter?"

"The same. Do you know him?"

"I've seen him before. When we were students here, he was responsible for almost a quarter of all the new prospects. Whatever happened to him?"

"He helped me escape the Volstrum, so they imprisoned him."

"But you said he accompanied you here? How did he manage that?"

"Illiana released him," explained Natalia, "and sent him to find me."

"To bring you back?"

"No, to ensure I was safe."

"Well," said Galina, "that didn't end well for him. Give me the address, and I'll see what I can do."

"Very well," said Natalia, "but be careful. When we first arrived here, we stayed at his former wife's house. She's the one who told Marakhova about us."

"And so the plot thickens. I will have to be very careful. Anything else I should know about?"

"You know my husband is being held hostage?"

"I do," said Galina. "Tatiana told me."

"I need to know where he was taken."

"Why? So you can rescue him? You have no power, Natalia, or any resources here in Ruzhina."

"I won't be a prisoner forever, and when I do get free of this place, I shall go and rescue him."

"Providing you find him."

"Exactly," said Natalia.

"Discovering the location of your husband will prove daunting, but actually seeing him will be next to impossible."

"Meaning?"

"Do you know what happens when a student fails the Volstrum?"

"No, I don't. I know Katrin failed, and she disappeared."

"Precisely," said Galina. "They're called the Disgraced, and their names are removed from each and every reference."

"Where do they go?"

"That's the big question. I've known students to disappear in the middle of the night. There's never a fuss about it, of course. They wouldn't want to alarm anyone, but they always go when others aren't around or asleep in their beds."

"Someone here must be aware of where they're sent?"

"You would think so, wouldn't you, but even Tatiana has no idea, and she's the grand mistress."

"Then who takes them?"

"Members of the family," said Galina. "I suspect this is all Marakhova's doing."

"And you assume Athgar was sent to the same place?"

"It would make sense, wouldn't it? Did they tell you anything about it when you were captured?"

"No, more's the pity. If Marakhova had gloated about it, at least then I'd have some idea as to his fate."

"I'll consult with Tatiana and see what I can find out. Several students left us in the last few months. Perhaps we can identify who took them?"

"Thank you."

"And as for your friends, I'm assuming neither is a mage?"

"Correct."

"Then they're likely locked up somewhere in Karslev. My first guess would be the *Carcarem Mortis*."

"The dungeon of death?"

"Despite its name," said Galina, "it's really nothing special. Ruzhina imprisons anyone who's perceived as a threat to its sovereignty. It wouldn't take much for the family to have someone incarcerated there."

"And how do we find them?"

"Easy. I visit the place. Believe it or not, they offset the cost of feeding the prisoners by encouraging people to pay for a tour. I'm told it's a popular pastime amongst the wealthy."

"So that's it?" said Natalia. "You just walk in and look for them?"

"I doubt it would be too hard to find a Dwarf, and I'm sure I'd recognize Stanislav if I saw him. He hasn't changed that much since we were students, has he?"

"Not really. His hair's a little greyer and a bit thinner as well, but he still looks the same."

"In that case, I'll find out if Tatiana can send me into the city on an administrative matter."

· · ·

The water dripped from the ceiling, the sound echoing off the slimy walls as it landed in the small pool.

"This is disgusting," said Belgast.

"So you've said," replied Stanislav, "on many occasions, I might add."

"Even a Dwarf wouldn't subject a prisoner to this kind of treatment."

"And what treatment is that? Do they not feed us? Do we not have water to drink? Perhaps you want someone to come and give you a nice fresh blanket?"

The Dwarf stomped across the room, rattling the iron grate that made up the door to the place. "And this is another thing. Look at the state of this iron? It's a downright poor excuse for workmanship."

"Come now," said the mage hunter. "It serves its purpose. It's bad enough being imprisoned, but must you complain about everything?"

"I would have thought you, of all people, would be more incensed."

"This is not my first time in prison, although I daresay it may well be my last."

"What's that supposed to mean?"

"I'm an old man, my friend, and these damp conditions are doing nothing for my health. I shall likely die before the year is out."

"Oh great!" said the Dwarf. "You get to die and get out of here. Me? Oh no, I'm a Dwarf. A life sentence for me is hundreds of years. Hundreds, Stanislav. That's like your entire life lived out two or three times!" He rattled the bars again to emphasize his point.

The mage hunter rose and crossed the room, careful to avoid the drip. "You say the iron is poor?"

"Aye, terrible work it is. Whatever smith fashioned these should be thrown out of the guild."

"And what guild would that be?"

"Why, the smith's guild, of course."

"There's no smith's guild in Karslev or anywhere in Ruzhina, for that matter."

The Dwarf eyed him suspiciously. "Why would you think that?"

"I don't think it—I know it. The King of Ruzhina outlawed them more than a hundred years ago."

"Why did he do that?"

"Because, by and large, the ruling family has always been convinced that people plot against them."

"And do they? Plot against them, I mean."

"There've been attempts over the years," said Stanislav, "but most of them never get past the planning phase."

"And how do you know this?"

"The Royal Household, like the family, has an extensive network of informers."

"You mean like Laisa?"

Stanislav winced. "Yes, sorry about that. Had I realized where her loyalties lay—"

"Forget it," interrupted Belgast. "There was no way you could have known."

"I must say you're taking this surprisingly well, complaining aside."

"That's because I already started planning our escape."

"Do tell."

"Every time I rattle this door, it weakens the mortar."

"Ah, now we're talking. How long before you break it?"

"By my estimation, about five years, but I'm in no hurry."

"How does that help me?"

The Dwarf shuffled his feet. "Yes, well, there is that, I suppose. Let me see if I can come up with something else." He wandered around the room. "No windows, so I suppose that's not an option."

"You suppose?"

"Well, if you put it that way, it's definitely not on the anvil." He paused, looking at the ceiling for inspiration. "How long do you reckon we've been here?"

In answer, the mage hunter looked at the wall. "Sixty-seven days."

Belgast turned towards him in surprise. "That's remarkable. I had no idea you possessed such a precise sense of time."

"I don't. I mark the wall every time they bring us food."

Footsteps echoed in the hallway outside, and a moment later, a well-dressed couple appeared.

The woman smiled. "Oh look, Ivan, a Dwarf. They're so… gnarly."

"Gnarly!" yelled Belgast. "I'll give you gnarly!" He rushed towards the door, causing the pair to back up, terror in their eyes.

"Well, I never!" exclaimed the man.

"Then you should get out more," yelled the Dwarf.

The visitors fled the hall, leaving Belgast and Stanislav once more in peace.

"Yelling at visitors will do you no good," said the mage hunter. "You should learn not to take it personally."

"Not take it personally? I'm locked away in a dungeon to rot away for the rest of my life. I don't know how much more personal it can get."

More footsteps echoed down the hall.

"Here comes another one," grumbled the Dwarf.

This time, a woman appeared, although she stood well back from the door.

Belgast eyed her suspiciously. "What do you want?"

"I assume you are Belgast Ridgehand?" Her eyes flicked to his companion. "And you must be the mage hunter, Stanislav Voronsky."

"Have we met?" asked Belgast.

"No, although I recognize your friend here. My name is Galina Stormwind."

"You're wasting our time," said Belgast. "Your lot put us here."

The woman moved closer to the door. "There are a great many Stormwinds in Karslev, and not all of them are adherents of Marakhova's policies."

"Meaning?"

"A friend sent me."

"A friend of a Stormwind is no friend of ours."

"Hold on a moment," said Stanislav. "I've seen you before, at the Volstrum, but that was years ago. You were a contemporary of Natalia, weren't you?"

"I was. As a matter of fact, we were in the same class. It is for her that I'm here."

"I'm not sure I understand?"

Galina pressed closer to the bars, lowering her voice. "I work with Natalia. There are those who wish to see Marakhova's tenure as head of the family come to an end."

"How does that help us?" asked Belgast.

"You're allies of Natalia. That puts us on the same side."

"It's not as if we can do much in here."

"At the moment, no, but be assured there are those outside who seek your release. In the meantime, I'll use our influence to help you."

"How?" asked Stanislav.

"The king keeps all his political prisoners here, but they don't all live in squalor. Those with the funds are permitted nicer cells."

"Just when I was getting used to all this splendour," said the Dwarf.

"I can also arrange proper beds and decent food."

"And what is the price of these favours?" asked Stanislav.

"Merely that you help Natalia when the time comes."

"Help her do what? Where is she?"

"She teaches at the Volstrum now," said Galina. "I work with her there."

"Why would she do that?" asked Belgast.

"Because her husband, Athgar, is being held hostage to guarantee her cooperation."

"I'm at a loss to see how we might help, especially considering our current circumstances."

"Getting you out of here is a simple matter of using a spell. The problem, however, is there's no place to hide you at present. There will come a day when we learn of Athgar's location. On that occasion, I'll free you from your incarceration, provided you help save him."

"How can I be certain you're telling the truth?"

"You can't," said Galina, "and I certainly wouldn't expect you to trust the word of a Stormwind. Give me a question to ask Natalia, something only she would know. I shall speak to her and return with her answer. Would that satisfy you?"

"It would," said Belgast, his face a mask of confusion. "Yet I can think of nothing to ask."

"I can," said Stanislav, "but it matters little. You wouldn't make the offer if you couldn't follow through."

"So we just trust her?"

"It seems we have little choice. Unless you prefer to rot away down here?"

"It's not so bad," replied the Dwarf, then turned to Galina. "You said you could get us better food?"

"I can."

"That's awfully tempting."

"Then you'll trust me?"

"I have a hard time trusting anyone who stands on the other side of a barred door, but I suppose I'll make an exception in your case."

"Good, you won't regret it. A few coins should ensure your humane treatment until I return."

"And then?"

"Then I shall pay the jailer to make sure your conditions improve."

"And you can't do that now?"

"I lack sufficient funds at the moment. My allies, on the other hand, have more than is needed to deal with the matter."

"Then I thank you for your help," said Stanislav, "and I'm sure my associate feels the same. Isn't that right, Belgast?"

The Dwarf grumbled. "Aye, I suppose so."

"Good, then I'll be on my way." She was about to leave, then turned to face them a final time. "Have you any message for Natalia?"

"Yes," said Stanislav. "Tell her we're well."

"And that we're here for her," added Belgast. "Whenever she needs us."

Galina smiled. "I shall be pleased to do so. Now I bid you a good day, gentlemen, and trust you will speak of this to no one."

The Dwarf looked at his companion. "Who would we tell?"

She left them, her footsteps echoing off into the distance.

"Well, that was certainly interesting," said Stanislav. "It appears our fortunes are about to improve."

"Oh, I don't know. I believe we were doing all right without help."

"Why do you say that?"

In answer, Belgast rattled the door. "Five years, Stanislav— that's all it would have taken."

MAGIC

Autumn 1108 SR

"Well?" said Athgar. "Feel any different?"

Anushka closed her eyes. Moments later, she began uttering an incantation. They'd picked one of the more out-of-the-way tunnels, the better to be far from prying eyes. Hollowing out a slight depression in the rock had been relatively easy. Now, they all held their breath as Anushka attempted her first spell in years.

The air tingled, a sure sign that magical power was about to be unleashed. She placed her hand over the depression, and a cloud of mist formed before solidifying into water. It wasn't much, but to the assembled witnesses, it was as if a miracle had just been performed.

Anushka looked at the small pool a moment before scooping up the water with her hands and drinking deeply. If the rest expected jubilation, they were surprised, for she soon spat it out.

"What's wrong?" asked Katrin.

"That water tastes terrible."

"Likely from the rock," said Athgar.

"What would you know of such things? You're a Pyromancer, not a Water Mage."

"That may well be, but I've seen my wife summon water on an occasion or two. The water is pure, as it should be if it's being summoned from the air, but all this dust we breathe in likely tainted it. Either that or the stone itself." He placed his finger into the small pool, feeling the depression in the rock before lifting it to his nose. "It does have a strange smell to it."

"Then we'll need to find something else to hold the water," said Katrin. "At the very least, we now know we can regain our magic."

"We also know the food isn't tainted, else Anushka would still be unable to cast. That's one more step on the road to our freedom."

"Freedom?" said Ulyana. "I'd hardly call it that."

Katrin snapped her head around, staring at the woman as if she'd been slapped. "Why would you say that?"

"What's the point of being free if we are to be hunted down by wild animals or slaughtered by soldiers?"

"What in the Saints' name are you talking about?"

"Wildlands surround this place," said Ulyana. "Who knows what creatures prowl the forest, looking for escaped prisoners to feast on? It might not be paradise in here, but at least we're alive."

"I can assure you the wilderness is nothing like that," soothed Athgar. "Especially so close to civilization."

"And how would you know?"

"I call that forest home, or at least a forest similar to it. Listen, I understand your hesitancy. After all, you spent nearly your entire youth at the Volstrum. I, on the other hand, spent my time learning how to hunt, make fire, and generally survive in that exact same terrain."

"Good for you," continued Ulyana, "but can you look after all of us?"

"Of course. Better yet, I can teach you the skills you need to survive out there."

"And how will you deal with a pack of wolves, or a bear, for that matter? We possess no weapons."

"You forget," said Athgar, "we have magic. And even if we didn't, we could fashion weapons."

"What type of life would that be?"

"We'd be alive," said Katrin. "And more importantly, we'd be free."

"Free to live a life of solitude and loneliness amongst the trees!"

"No one is saying we need to remain there," said Athgar.

"And what of your wife?" asked Ulyana. "Don't you want to see her again?"

"Of course."

"Then how does that fit in with this idea of wilderness survival?"

"I would make sure you're able to care for yourselves first." He immediately saw the problem. With word of his escape, there would be nothing to hold Natalia in check. She was a powerful mage, and without him as a method of controlling her, they would consider more extreme measures, possibly even sending her here, to the very mine they plotted to escape from.

The other alternative was almost too much to bear even thinking about. They wanted to breed more powerful mages. If they forced her to give birth to another child, would they even need to keep her alive afterwards?

He knew, in his heart, that as soon as he was free, he would seek her out. It was the only way to ensure her safety. How long would it take, he wondered, before word of his escape reached Stormwind Manor? Could he even find the place? The trip to Zurkutsk was carried out in darkness, yet it had been no more than half a day from his point of capture. If he could get back to Karslev, he was sure he could find someone to take him to the manor.

"Well?" pressed Ulyana, interrupting his thoughts.

"Well, what?" he replied. "I'm sorry. I was deep in thought."

Ulyana folded her arms. "Ugh! This is so frustrating."

Katrin was quick to keep the peace. "We don't have all the answers at present, but with further discussion, we'll find a way to make things work. We had tremendous success today, and regaining control over our magic will help immensely in the coming months."

"Months?" said Felix. "That long?"

"Naturally. We shouldn't rush things."

"Why not? I should think we'd want to act sooner rather than later."

"Katrin is right," said Athgar. "If we act too soon, we'll fail, and then things will become that much tougher for us."

"So we are to stay here forever," said Felix. "Plotting rather than acting?"

"No, a time will come."

"Yes, but when?"

"Soon," soothed Athgar. "Before winter at the latest."

"Why?"

"Escaping in the snow will make it too easy for them to find us, not to mention making hunting more difficult." He looked around the group. "I don't suppose any of you have ever dressed a carcass?"

Alfie was the first to speak. "Why would we put clothes on a dead body?"

"He means cutting up a deer," explained Felix. "Or any other animal he's killed."

"Why didn't he just say that?"

His companion rolled his eyes.

"What about the soldiers?" asked Anushka.

"What soldiers?" replied Athgar.

"I heard there's a camp not too far from here. The king maintains a company to guard the frontier."

"Why would he do that? It's not as if the wolves would invade the country and threaten the crown."

"He's more concerned with the undead."

Athgar felt the hairs on his neck stand up. "What undead?"

"Haven't you heard the stories?"

"You mean about the self-proclaimed King of Zaran? But that border is too distant to be a threat here, surely?"

"She's not talking of Zaran," explained Katrin, "but something far worse."

"Which is?"

"The Kingdom of Shadows."

"That's nothing but fairy tales," said Felix. "Told at night to frighten small children."

"Yet even those have some basis in fact," said Katrin. "We learned about it at the Volstrum."

"We did," agreed Anushka. "Although I remember little of it. Wasn't it blamed on an Enchanter?"

"It was. A woman by the name of Vicavia. The story goes, she lost a child. Grief-stricken, she delved into all sorts of nefarious magic in an attempt to create life."

Athgar was repulsed. "Are you saying she attempted to resurrect her child?"

"No, but she tried to create a new child through horrible experiments."

"And she stole children to use as subjects," said Anushka. "The spectre of Vicavia is said to walk the streets, looking for children who are out late at night. At least that's the legend."

"That part's not true," said Katrin. "But the king did hear of her work and sent warriors after her."

"Let me guess," said Athgar. "She fled eastward, into the wilderness?"

"Yes, and every so often, strange creatures emerge from the lands to the east to strike fear into everyone."

"What kinds of creatures?"

"The stuff of nightmares, to be honest. We read an account of a creature killed not too far from here. He was—how did the author put it? Oh yes, covered in scales, with rows of teeth as sharp as the finest sword."

"There are many strange things in the land of Eiddenwerthe," said Athgar, "but I would hardly call that unusual. What you described sounds an awful lot like what the Orcs call the First Race."

"First Race? You must tell us more."

"According to their Ancestors, the First Race lived all across the Continent, long before the Gods placed the Elder Races."

"Which are?" asked Alfie.

"The Elves, Orcs, and Dwarves. Humanity didn't come along until thousands of years later."

"Typical drivel," said Felix. "Everyone knows Eiddenwerthe was bequeathed to us Humans. The Saints even say so."

"They do nothing of the sort," said Athgar. "I've had this discussion with Natalia many times. You might not agree with worshipping the Old Gods, but the Saints were mortal Humans. How, then, would they have the ability to bequeath to us that which they don't control?"

"Let's not get into a theological debate," said Katrin. "I believe what Athgar is suggesting is this… abomination that wandered out of the wilderness was the remnant of a lost civilization. Isn't that right?"

"Yes, at least based on what you described. I can't be completely sure, you understand. For one thing, I've never seen one of the First Race myself, but I'm told that far to the west, they've re-emerged after centuries of remaining hidden from us. Shaluhk tells me they call themselves Saurians."

"She's the Orc shaman you've spoken of before, isn't she?" asked Anushka. "How would she know this?"

He was about to answer, then thought better of it. It was not his place to explain the Orcs' ability to communicate over great distances, although it did give him an idea.

"Let's just put it down to magic, shall we? Now, on another matter, I wondered if you could tell me something, Katrin?"

"If I can."

"Are there any Orc tribes in Ruzhina?"

"Not that I'm aware of. In ages past, maybe, but history tells us the first king conquered all who stood in his way. There are still debates as to what that means, precisely, but the early accounts are lacking in details. Why do you ask?"

"Just speculating." Athgar felt crushed. Had there been tribes in the area, he could have gotten word back to Kargen and Shaluhk, perhaps even arrange for a group of hunters to come and guide them home.

"Home," he said aloud, mulling over the word.

"We have no home," said Katrin, "not anymore. The family took our past and forbade anyone to even mention our names. All records of us are stricken from the books, and even our own flesh and blood can no longer acknowledge our existence."

"What if I could give you a home, all of you? A place where you could settle down amongst new friends and be at peace."

"Sounds nice," noted Ulyana, "but the reach of the family is extensive. No one in the Petty Kingdoms would help a group of escaped prisoners from Ruzhina. They'd see to that."

"Ah, but Therengia is not part of the Petty Kingdoms, and there's no family there. Well, there is, but it's Natalia, so I'm not sure that counts."

"Are you sure we'd be welcome?"

"Most definitely. Let's just say I possess some influence with the person in charge."

"A real home?" said Ulyana. "I'm in." She looked around the group to see everyone else nodding their heads in agreement.

"All well and good," said Katrin, "but there's still the small matter of getting out of this place. Have we made any progress on that front?"

"No," replied Athgar, "but now that we know we can reclaim our magic, things may become a little easier."

"Don't get too carried away. You might be able to cast spells, but out of the rest of us, only Anushka and I ever succeeded. I should also remind you we both failed out of the Volstrum, so we're hardly what you'd call full Water Mages."

"A valid point. We should take stock of what spells you can cast. We know Anushka can create water. What else can she do?"

All eyes turned to their blonde-haired companion.

"I can freeze water as well, but that's about it."

"So no ice shards, then?"

"I'm afraid not."

"How about you, Katrin?"

"Like Anushka, I'm able to create or freeze water, or calm waves, for that matter. I did learn how to cast bolts and call a fog, but I'm afraid casting isn't the problem—it's the targeting. I failed the Volstrum because I couldn't consistently hit what I aimed for."

"From what you described, calling forth the magic itself is simple enough. It's your ranged magic that needs work. We must keep that in mind going forward."

"Natalia tutored me in those last few weeks, and I showed some improvement, but not fast enough for them to reconsider my fate."

"All of you possess the potential to be mages," said Athgar. "You have to, or else the family wouldn't have taken you under their wing in the first place. Once we're back in Therengia, we can complete your training." He held up his hand to prevent any arguing. "Only if you want to, of course, and definitely not in the same style as the Volstrum. The secret to magic is learning at your own speed, something your precious 'family' seems to have forgotten over the centuries."

"And what would be the price of all of this?" asked Ulyana.

"Merely that you would help out around the villages of Therengia."

"Doing what?"

"Purifying water, helping to find new wells, essentially in any way you can. You would, of course, be compensated for your work. In essence, you'd be part of the fyrd, although we need a new name to describe you."

"What is a fyrd?"

"The men and women of the villages band together in times of trouble."

"You mean war?"

"Yes, or some sort of natural disaster, like a flood, or to recover from a bad storm. Natalia, for example, sometimes goes to the river and calls the fish for people to gather. We also discovered she can create ice and snow to preserve meat."

He took a breath, seeing the sense of expectation in their eyes. "Look, I'm not saying Therengia is perfect. We are an ancient people; that much is true, but the realm is young, and we're still discovering new ways of doing things. One thing I can tell you, however, is that we are not anything like the Petty Kingdoms."

"You keep speaking of Therengia," said Ulyana, "but that kingdom was destroyed centuries ago."

"It has been reborn," said Athgar.

"Using that name was not their best decision. The rise of the Old Kingdom has always been feared, so much so that kings and princes alike will unite to see it destroyed."

"We have defeated all who came to destroy us, including the Temple Knights of Saint Cunar."

"You jest," said Felix. "They are undefeated."

"Not so," corrected Athgar. "The truth is they lost twice. In fact, at their first loss, at Ord-Kurgad, Temple Knights fought on both sides."

"Now you're not making sense. Everyone knows the Cunars are the true might of the Church."

"But not the only Temple Knights. Those of Saint Agnes fought with us, and even now, Mathewites reside in Ebenstadt, the largest city in Therengia."

"Are you suggesting," said Felix, "that the Church is at odds with itself? I find that very distressing."

"Yet not unexpected," said Katrin.

She had Athgar's full attention. "Why would you suggest that?"

"The biggest threat to the Petty Kingdoms isn't Therengia—it's the Halvarian Empire. They've swallowed up kingdoms by the dozens and show no sign of stopping anytime soon. They'd like nothing better than for the Temple Orders to fall into civil war."

"I'd hardly call it a war, more like the rogue actions of a few power-mad individuals."

"The effect is the same. You say you defeated the Cunars. How many, I wonder, were lost?"

"Hundreds. So many, in fact, that they abandoned their claim over Ebenstadt entirely."

"Still," said Felix, "they number in the thousands."

"True," said Katrin, "but those are scattered across dozens of Petty Kingdoms."

"I see your point," said Athgar, "but I can assure you no Halvarians were involved in either of those battles."

"While this discussion is fascinating," said Ulyana, "I might remind you we're still prisoners, and as such, are still expected to make our daily quota."

"You're right, of course. We best get back to work. Where do we dig, Katrin?"

She pointed right beside them. "Right here. I've been sensing it for some time."

They dug in with renewed energy, and moments later, Athgar's pickaxe sank deep into the rock. "I appear to have found something."

He pulled back the pick to reveal a hole in the wall. He pressed his face against it, but it was too dark to see much of anything. "I think we found a cavern of some sort. I don't smell any vapours, so I believe we're safe in terms of digging."

"Stand back," ordered Katrin, "and we'll open it up and see what's inside."

A few more swings was all it took to collapse the rest of the wall. Beyond lay a rough-looking cave, complete with rocky protrusions on the ground and ceiling. Ulyana pushed her arm through the opening, allowing their lantern to light the interior. She stepped through, the others joining her moments later.

It wasn't so much the sight that caught everyone's attention, but a sound, for somewhere, water dripped.

"It appears," said Athgar, "that we discovered an underground pool."

Katrin took the lantern and moved farther into the cavern. A small stream trickled from the wall, falling from about waist height to a pool around ten paces in diameter. She reached out, cupping one hand and gathering a sample that she quickly tasted. Everyone held their breath, and then the woman turned to the rest.

"It's clean," she announced.

STORMWIND MANOR

Autumn 1108 SR

Iliana's portrait hung, not in the great hall, but in one of the lesser corridors of Stormwind Manor, the final insult to the once-great matriarch.

Natalia had only met her on a few occasions, but whoever painted it really captured her essence. She had been a strong-willed woman and, as she now knew, her grandmother. Part of her wished she'd gotten to know her better. Her only meaningful interaction with the woman was right before her graduation, and even that was little more than the briefest of words, hardly a conversation at all.

"I hate to admit it," interrupted Marakhova, "but it's quite a good likeness. I shall have to see if the same artist is available when my own is mounted in a place of honour."

"She was a great matriarch," said Natalia. "Why did you relegate her to such an ignominious location?"

"You mean here, close to the servants' quarters? The truth is she was weak and unfit to wear the mantle of matriarch."

"Why do you hold such animosity for her? Even in death, you feel the need to denigrate her memory."

"This family has taken centuries to build its reputation. The courts of the Petty Kingdoms send delegates here, all just to beg us to send mages to their courts. Do you understand the work and perseverance required to make that happen?"

Natalia stared back, unwilling to argue.

"She would have thrown it all away," the matriarch continued. "As I said, she was weak."

"I saw no sign of that."

"You never saw her try to interact with other members of the family! They are a ruthless bunch, requiring nerves of steel, yet all Illiana could do was compromise, compromise, compromise. I swear the woman never made a hard decision in her entire life."

"She was selected as matriarch."

"She was the only one they could agree on. Like many kingdoms, there are factions within the family, each fighting for its own methods to be invoked to accomplish our objectives."

"And what objectives would those be?"

A smile crept to Marakhova's lips. "I see what you're doing, Natalia, but it matters little. Even if you did ascertain the true motives of the family, there's nothing you could do about it."

Natalia found the threat intriguing. She'd always believed it was about influencing the courts of the Petty Kingdoms, but the matriarch's words gave her the impression there was something else more sinister at play here.

"Then why not tell me?" she prodded.

Marakhova took a moment to think things over, then shrugged. "I might as well. Let's hope when you realize the true scope of our power, you'll come to understand just how dangerous it is to cross us."

Little chance of that, Natalia thought. You tried to kill me and abduct my child. How much more dangerous could you be? She bit back her feelings, instead waiting for the matriarch to continue.

"As you know, the family has strived for generations to produce the most powerful mages in all of Eiddenwerthe."

"The most powerful Water Mages," corrected Natalia. "Although I suppose we should include Fire Mages as well."

Marakhova waved away the objection. "They are the most basic elements, and let's face it, the other schools are pretty useless when it comes to battle. In any case, after centuries of refining our breeding program, we managed to produce the most powerful mages of this generation. You, of all people, are a shining example of that. Admittedly, your birth escaped the knowledge of our experts, but obviously, two mages of exceptional capacity sired you."

"My mother was a peasant," said Natalia, "and your claims of being most powerful mages are spurious at best." She thought of Shaluhk. "There are other powerful mages out there. The family is no more powerful than they."

"You're upset. It's only natural considering your current circumstances."

Natalia couldn't help herself. "How many members of the family have you sent after me? And how many came back? Sartellians and Stormwinds don't seem to last long around me."

Marakhova's eyes turned cold. "They were defeated more by their inept plans than by the force of magic."

"I'm sorry," said Natalia.

"For what?"

"That you believe that. I killed Nezerov Sartellian myself. Would you like to know how?" She continued, not waiting for a response. "I froze him, then he shattered into thousands of pieces. Have you ever witnessed anything of that nature? I have, and I can tell you it was quite horrific. There was no master plan, merely an accidental encounter that led to a duel of arcane powers, and in the end, he failed you."

Natalia watched the matriarch pale, and then she understood. "You've never been in a fight, have you? For years, you've ruled over the Volstrum, telling people how to conduct themselves in a battle, and yet, you"—she pointed her finger to emphasize her words—"never in your life have you cast a spell under those conditions."

Marakhova visibly straightened. "I might not have seen battle, but I am still the head of this family, so I suggest you keep your opinions to yourself."

"Why am I here?" asked Natalia.

"As I said before, you're a member of the family."

"No, I mean, why am I here today, in Stormwind Manor, during the day, instead of at the Volstrum?"

"You are here to meet some important people," the woman replied, her voice steely. "People who will have a tremendous effect on your future. It is therefore imperative that you are on your best behaviour."

"And if I'm not?"

"I shouldn't need to remind you that your husband is still our prisoner. Then again, perhaps I do. What if my people sent you an ear? Would that convince you of the folly of your rude behaviour?"

"No," said Natalia, feeling her heart jump into her throat. "I'll behave. I promise." She cursed herself inside, for she'd been trying to ingratiate herself with the head of the family, not upset her. "Might I ask further of these guests?"

Marakhova held out her hand. "Come. We shall go and greet them directly."

The matriarch led Natalia through the manor, emerging at the entrance hall in time to welcome their new guests. A gaunt man with a pockmarked face bowed at their approach.

"Matriarch, we are honoured."

"Gallus Sartellian, how nice to see you again. I trust your trip was uneventful?"

"It was, Your Grace. Allow me to introduce my travelling companions. This is Diomedes Sartellian." He nodded at the tall, red-haired youth. "He's only recently completed his studies at Korascajan. And this"—he nodded at the second man, a fit-looking fellow with an immaculately trimmed beard and moustache—"is one of our junior instructors, Balmund Sartellian. He is also a three-time champion."

"Of what?" asked Natalia.

"Each year, Korascajan holds a competition amongst the students to identify those who have benefited the most from their time there."

"So you're basically saying you just gave him a prize for being a student."

Gallus bowed his head, the smirk on his face plain. "I can see I am no match for your companion, Matriarch. Is this Natalia Stormwind?"

"It is," replied Marakhova. "I will admit she cleans up nicely, but the same cannot be said of her manners, and for that, I ask your forgiveness in advance."

"There's nothing to forgive, Your Grace." He cast his gaze at Natalia, letting his eyes devour her. "I look forward to getting to know her better."

"I'm right here," said Natalia. "Or are you so feared of women you must address them through others?"

"Ignore her," said the matriarch, "and let us sit down for a meal. I don't know about you, but I'm famished." She led the group into the adjoining room, where a meal awaited them.

Marakhova sat at the head of the table, with Natalia immediately to her left. Gallus took a seat beside Natalia, while across from her sat the other two, each spending far too much time staring at her. Servants soon appeared, bringing food and drink aplenty, and then the eating began.

Natalia, used to the camaraderie of Runewald, was surprised when everyone ate in silence. It was not unwelcome, though, for it allowed her some peace of mind, however temporary, while she partook of her meal.

Once the food was done, more wine was brought out. The plates were carted away, and then the conversation began, starting with Gallus.

"The matriarch tells me you're quite powerful," he said, this time talking directly to Natalia. "Might I see it?"

"See what?" she replied.

"Why, the ring, of course. How else am I to judge your potential?"

She held out Illiana's ring. Gallus had been expecting a light shade of blue, but the near-black gem left him speechless.

"Incredible," said Diomedes. "I've never seen its like."

"It's a trick," added Balmund. "Marakhova is having fun at our expense."

"I can assure you this is no trick," said Natalia. She removed the ring and placed it on the table.

Balmund, not one to miss an opportunity, snatched it up, examining its pale colour. "Definitely blue magerite."

"Let me see," demanded Diomedes. He took the ring, holding it close to his eyes the better to see it. "He's right," he admitted, passing the ring, in turn, to Gallus.

The pockmarked mage set the ring before Natalia, who then donned it. The stone grew darker almost instantly.

"Impressive," he said, then placed his hand flat on the table, revealing the deep scarlet of his own ring.

"Now, now," said Balmund. "Let's not show off here. We were all chosen for our strong potential, but there's more to this than simple power."

"There is?" said Gallus. "And what, pray tell, would that be?"

"Discipline and mastery."

"Nonsense. Only raw power counts in this regard. That's what is meant by breeding. It has nothing to do with who your parents are and everything to do with potential." He turned to Marakhova, who'd been listening to the entire conversation. "Wouldn't you agree, Your Grace?"

In answer, she sipped her wine, taking her time while she enjoyed watching her guests squirm in their seats.

"I should think," she finally said, "that there are several things to consider. Yes, power is certainly one of those, maybe even the most important of all. Still, we must also examine the ability of each to father children in the first place. Balmund, I believe you are an only child, while Diomedes comes from a large family. Unfortunately, of all your siblings, none proved capable of using Water Magic."

She paused, taking another sip and savouring it before continuing. "At least Gallus has a sister who became a Stormwind, although it would have been better for you had you been twins."

Natalia took it all in. She knew this was coming, knew what the family wanted her to do. Her past history with the Volstrum had let her come to grips with the family's wishes in this regard. However, watching Marakhova be so merciless with these men was somehow satisfying.

"Have you made a decision?" asked Gallus.

In answer, the matriarch turned to her charge. "What do you think, Natalia?"

Obviously, Marakhova already knew the answer. "None of them are suitable," Natalia said, a little relieved, if only for now.

"Quite right," Marakhova agreed. "She is a gifted asset, Gallus, and cannot be wasted away on someone undeserving."

"Undeserving?" he shot back. "How dare you! You may be the matriarch, but you can't treat me this way. My family traces its heritage back to the founding members of this family."

"Spare me your righteous indignation. This family exists for the sole purpose of breeding more powerful mages. Your ancestors have very little to do with your ability to procreate other than to have created you in the first place. Now, be quiet, or the guards will be ordered to escort you from the building."

"You wouldn't dare!"

"Wouldn't I?" Her voice was calm, but her look could cut through the heaviest armour.

Gallus stared back, his face now bright red. At a loss for words, he fought to make a statement of some sort that would allow him to recover his dignity.

"Tell me of your family history," said Natalia, trying to defuse the situation.

"As you are no doubt aware, Alexi Sartellian was the first member of the family to propose the selective pairing of mages to produce offspring with more potential. He was not the founder of the family, mind you, but was instrumental in its development into the family as it exists today."

"And was he your ancestor?"

"No, but my ancestor was his brother, born and raised by the same parents, so as close to a direct descendant as you can find."

"All true," quipped Balmund, "but hardly unique. Half the Sartellians alive today can trace their ancestry back to Alexi. After all, that selective breeding process has led to the establishment of the most influential lines."

Gallus ignored the fellow. "What of your family, Natalia? They must be powerful indeed if that ring is to be believed."

"My mother was a peasant," said Natalia, enjoying the revulsion on the mage's face.

"And your father?" asked Balmund.

"I never knew my father. For all I know, he could have been a peasant as well."

"Yet here you are, possibly the most gifted mage I've ever seen. How do you account for that?"

"Simple," she replied. "I don't. And furthermore, I feel this entire concept of breeding is both repulsive and far-fetched."

"Why would you say that? You must admit the family consists of the most powerful mages in all the known lands."

"Not at all. Unlike you, I've spent time amongst the Orcs, learning they are just as adept as the family at using magic. I'm willing to acknowledge that the family is the most influential in the courts of the Petty Kingdoms, but that has more to do with the fact you kidnapped or even downright murdered any mage the family couldn't control. It's not so hard to be the most powerful when the only ones competing are from amongst your adopted relatives."

Balmund was about to say something, but Natalia cut him off. "Can you honestly sit here and tell me your ancestors weren't as powerful as you?"

"No, of course not, but—"

"And did they have access to the same spells?"

"I would imagine so, but—"

"But nothing. I'm sure if you dug deep enough into the Volstrum's records, you could read all about your glorious ancestors and their accomplishments. Still, I doubt any of it would prove they were weaker or more powerful than any other. You may make aspersions as to their potential, that hidden energy that powers magic, but there is no actual way to measure it, short of a ring like this." She held up her hand to illustrate the point. "Have you any idea what I've been doing here since my return to Karslev?"

Once more, his mouth opened, only to be cut off, this time before even a word escaped.

"I've been teaching history, specifically the history regarding the family's rise to prominence. It may surprise you to know some hundred years after the death of your precious Alexi Sartellian, another ancestor discovered magerite. That particular gemstone did more for the Stormwind's lineage than any selective breeding. It allowed a person to gauge the untapped potential of a candidate."

"Thus proving my point," Balmund managed to squeak out.

"Quite the reverse, actually. Many people born to powerful mages fail out of the Volstrum, either because they can't handle the intense training or because they possess little in the way of power. Your breeding doesn't work, and those failures are the proof of it."

"Do not mention the Disgraced," warned Marakhova.

"Why? Because they've been stricken from history? Is that your answer to everything, simply forgetting about them and banning any mention of their names? Because it doesn't work. Failing to acknowledge their weakness doesn't make it disappear, even though you like to think it does."

"Do not speak of things you don't understand. Even the Disgraced have their uses."

Shocked, Natalia thought back to when Katrin, her only friend in the Volstrum, was removed from her classes due to poor grades. Even Stanislav had been unable to determine her fate. Could it be she somehow survived?

"Are you suggesting they still live?" she finally asked.

"Why would you think otherwise? We don't go around killing members of the family, Natalia. That would be a complete waste of resources."

"Then what do you do with them?" She held her breath, praying to the Saints that the matriarch would reveal something, anything, to put her mind at ease.

"They serve in other ways," was all Marakhova said. "Now, I believe this discussion has reached its conclusion, don't you?" She didn't wait for an answer, instead ringing the small bell used to call servants. They dutifully swarmed the table, carrying away glasses and pulling out chairs.

"Thank you, everyone, for coming," the matriarch said, addressing her visitors. "I am truly sorry you journeyed so far to hear this news, but I assure you I summoned you here only with the purest of intentions. A carriage will return you to the city, and from there, you may use the magic circle to return to Korascajan."

Natalia caught her breath, unaware the matriarch even knew of the circle in the Baroshka, let alone the place itself.

Gallus bowed respectfully. "As you wish, Your Grace."

Everyone rose, then the men made their way out to the entrance hallway.

"You'll like the circle," noted Gallus, clearly talking to one of his companions. "It gives one an incredible view of the city."

"Why is that?" asked Diomedes.

"It's high up in a tower, with a window overlooking much of Karslev."

Natalia let out a sigh of relief. It appeared the Baroshka was still secure.

CONTACT

Autumn 1108 SR

T he ancient text was difficult to read, primarily because of the flowery hand of whoever had scribed it. Even so, Natalia struggled through, for it detailed the discovery of magerite and the subsequent development of what would become the mine called Zurkutsk. A particularly long and challenging paragraph caught her attention, as it revealed that, of all the mines in Ruzhina, this was the only location that held the arcane crystal.

She sat back, letting the words sink in. The entire social hierarchy of the family was based on magerite; this discovery must have been of tremendous value to the line. She read on, hoping to learn more, and the next statement was the revelation she was looking for. According to the author, the raw form of blue magerite will glow when near any person with the capacity to wield Water Magic. It was therefore decided to use failed candidates to mine for it.

This simple statement brought things into sharp focus. Was this the ultimate fate of Katrin and the other missing students? Years ago, she'd asked Stanislav to find her old friend, but nothing had come of it. Could this be the reason why?

Further reading revealed the resulting mine was kept under the family's control rather than the King of Ruzhina. More than anything else she'd read today, this statement gave her hope that this was where they'd imprisoned Athgar. The real question, of course, was how to confirm it.

She sought out Galina, for she'd been the one who knew the most about the Disgraced. Indeed, she'd even speculated Athgar's fate was intertwined with theirs. Now, with evidence in hand that they were at Zurkutsk, Natalia felt her pulse quicken.

"I think I found him," she blurted out.

Galina looked up from where she sat, perusing some handwritten notes. "You mean Athgar?"

"Yes, and the Disgraced. What do you know of a place called Zurkutsk?"

"I've heard the name, although I can't recall where. It's a mine of some sort, isn't it?"

"Yes. It's the only known source of magerite."

"I fail to see how that connects to your husband?"

Natalia calmed herself, for spilling out her thoughts too quickly would make her sound mad. "You once told me you had no idea where the Disgraced were taken, but I believe it's to this very mine."

"Why would you think that?"

"According to an old account, the raw form of magerite will glow in the close proximity of any who possess the corresponding magical potential. Who better than failed students to mine such crystals?"

"Crystals? Don't you mean gems?"

"There seems to be a difference of opinion about what magerite is," explained Natalia. "But regardless of that, it would explain a great many things."

"I don't see how? Couldn't any labourer mine for the stuff?"

"No. By all accounts, it looks very similar to quartz. The entire deposit was found by happenstance. Had a Water Mage not accompanied them, they would have ignored the area altogether."

"It's a compelling argument, but hardly proof, and why would they send Athgar there? Wouldn't he be more useful locked up somewhere close by?"

"He's a Fire Mage. Presumably, that means he could detect red magerite. And why keep him local when there's already a secure mine in which to hold him?"

"I have my doubts," said Galina, "but it certainly bears further investigation."

"And how do we do that?"

"Simple. We send someone to visit the place."

"Yes, but who? I definitely can't go, and it might look suspicious to have someone from the Volstrum going there."

"What about your friends, the old man and the Dwarf? Would they be up to it?"

"They're in prison, remember?"

"Yes," said Galina, "but I can visit them, and I know how to cast the frozen arch. I could bring them back here, to the Volstrum."

"Wouldn't their disappearance be noticed?"

"Most assuredly, but whom would they seek to blame?"

"You."

Galina chuckled. "That might be an issue if I'd used my real name, but I'm far too clever for that."

"Still, we can't keep them here. Stanislav might get away with being in the Volstrum, but Belgast is a Dwarf."

"An easy enough problem to solve. I'll use my magic to bring them here, to begin with. Then you can fill them in on what you know and make some plans to send them to Zurkutsk."

"And then?"

"The frozen arch works both ways," said Galina. "I'll find a safe place within the city, then open a gate to the circle, and they can step through from this end."

"Placing them outside of the Volstrum," finished Natalia. "I like it, but how do we get them into Zurkutsk?"

"That's for you to discuss with your friends. I can provide them with funds, but I can't protect them without exposing everything, and the last thing I need is for Marakhova to learn about all of this." She waved her hands around, indicating the room.

"Agreed. When do you propose we start?"

"Give me a day or two to find out more about Zurkutsk. We don't want to send these fellows in blind. How about we plan this for the end of the week?"

"Very well, although truth be told, it'll be the longest three days of my life."

"In the meantime, I suggest you dig up everything you can about the place in those books you found. Even minor details may prove important in the long run."

"I shall," said Natalia, "and I'll start giving some thought as to how Stanislav and Belgast might gain entrance to the mine."

"Yes, as long as they don't intend to act like new prisoners. After all, we want to be able to get them out again once they're done there. Do you think they will try to rescue Athgar, or is their trip only to gather information?"

"That largely depends on what they find."

"Well," said Stanislav, laying his head on the pillow. "This is definitely better than that last place."

Belgast paced the room, his boots echoing on the wooden floor. "I don't like it," he said. "Not enough stone. What is it with you Humans and using wood for everything?"

"It's easier to work with."

"Yes, but it doesn't last half as long."

"You forget," said the mage hunter. "We Humans are lucky to live much past fifty. Wood lasts long enough for our uses."

"I suppose I never looked at it that way." The Dwarf paused in his pacing as he detected the sound of footsteps. "Someone's coming."

"Our benefactor?"

"We shall soon see."

Galina appeared, although her journey didn't end there, as she produced a ring of keys, then unlocked the door.

"You have keys?" said Belgast. "How quaint. Are we then to simply walk out the front door?"

"Not quite," she replied. "The owner of this key ring will soon discover its absence."

"Then why are you here, and more importantly, what has this to do with us?"

"Give me some room, and you shall soon see." She waited for the Dwarf to back up and then began casting. The ritual took longer than any spell Stanislav had ever seen. He started questioning if the woman was calling on a deeper level of magic or was merely incompetent. Soon, however, the air took on a chill right before a frozen arch appeared before them, its centre displaying a completely different room from the cell they were in.

"Step through," said Galina, "but be quick about it. I shall then follow and dismiss the spell, thus erasing any sign of how you escaped." Even as Stanislav and Belgast examined the arch, she tossed the keys to the floor.

"After you," said Stanislav.

"Oh sure," said Belgast. "Send the Dwarf in first. Is that all I am to you? A bird?"

The mage hunter screwed up his face. "What in the Saints are you talking about?"

"We use birds to detect unknown gasses in mines."

"Fine. If that's how you feel, I'll go first."

"And make me look like a coward? I don't think so!" Belgast stepped through the archway.

Stanislav now saw him standing on the other side, yet as he peered around the outside of the arch, all he could see was the empty cell.

"Hurry up, for goodness' sake," urged Galina. "I can't hold this open forever."

He hurried through to emerge into a subterranean hall of some type.

"Stanislav!" Natalia approached and gave him a big hug.

"Good to see you," he said gruffly.

Galina followed, dismissing her spell.

Belgast, meanwhile, examined the floor. "This is fine work," he noted. "Did a Dwarf build it?"

"I have no idea," said Natalia, "but it's good to see you both hale and hearty."

"What is this place?"

"You're beneath the Volstrum. I realize it's a lot to absorb, but I can assure you we're safe, at least for the moment."

"And Athgar?"

"That's why I brought you here," Natalia said. "I believe I know where he is, but we don't know for sure."

"Well, spit it out," said the Dwarf. "Where is it you think they've got him?"

"In a place called Zurkutsk. It's a mine."

Belgast rubbed his hands. "A mine, you say? Tell me more."

"We believe it's where they dig up magerite. Stanislav, you remember Katrin?"

"Your friend from the Volstrum? Of course, but all attempts to find her came to a dead end."

"Not anymore. It seems likely that all those who disappeared were taken to Zurkutsk."

"Then let's go there and find them."

"It's not that simple. The family runs the mine, and I'm too closely guarded."

"Guarded?" said Belgast. "I see no guards here?"

"I am free to wander within the Volstrum, but the guards will not allow me to exit. In addition, at the end of each day, a carriage comes to take me back to Stormwind Manor, along with a detachment of guards. My absence would quickly be noticed."

"Then we'll go," said Stanislav. "Although I have no idea how we'd get in."

"I do," said the Dwarf.

"You do?"

"Yes. I just said so, didn't I?"

The mage hunter rolled his eyes. "Would you care to explain, or shall we wait until we all die of old age?"

"Everyone knows Dwarves are experts when it comes to mining."

"And?" prompted Natalia.

"And that's the key, don't you see? I'll gain entrance by telling them the family hired me to look at their mining efforts to see if we can make any improvements in the way they do things."

"Improvements?"

"Yes, ways to increase their production of magerite."

"But you don't know anything about magerite," said Stanislav.

"True, but I'm a fast learner with an excellent memory. Fill me in on what you know, and I'll do my best to impress them. Don't worry. I may not be an expert about mining this magerite stuff, but I can throw around some Dwarven terms and confuse them."

"Very well," said Natalia. "Come with me, and I'll show you what I discovered. Can you read the common tongue of Humans?"

"If I must."

Later that afternoon, they sat around the table, open books staring back at them.

"Well?" said Natalia. "Had your fill?"

"This is all fascinating stuff," said the Dwarf. "According to these notes, magerite is only found in one place? I find that hard to believe. I think it more likely they didn't look elsewhere."

"Where else would they look?"

"They'd need to check similar areas in terms of rock formations and such. Based on this, it would also be handy to have a mage present."

"Wouldn't that only work if the magerite was nearby?" asked Stanislav.

"You were paying attention?" said Belgast.

"Of course. What else am I to do while waiting for you?"

"You could help read through all these books."

"My strength lies in reading people, not the written word."

"An important skill," said Natalia. "Particularly now that you're about to travel to Zurkutsk. The real question is how to convince the guards the family sent you."

"Would they use written orders?" asked Stanislav.

"Not likely," she said. "The family doesn't like leaving a trail, and this place is one of their most closely guarded secrets."

"Then we'll use that against them."

"I'm not sure I follow."

"Well, it's simple, really," said Stanislav. "If the place is such a secret, only the most trusted members of the family would know of its existence."

"Wouldn't the king know about it?" asked Belgast.

"He likely knows it's a mine," suggested Galina, "but I doubt he knows its true purpose. Nor would he bother to ask, providing it generates revenue for him."

"Ah. My kind of king—corruptible."

"You like a dishonest king?" said Natalia.

"Not generally, no, but in this case, it suits our purpose. I've seen enough royal courts in my time to be at home in them, and that's another thing we can bring to bear."

"So you're going to throw around the king's name now?"

"Not unless I have to. In my experience, it's better to hint at such things and let everyone make assumptions."

"What about you, Stanislav? Any ideas?"

"I'm more of a make-it-up-on-the-spot type of person. Once I get a grasp of the people in charge, I'm confident I'll know what to do. I am curious, however, about what this mine looks like."

"I have no idea," said Natalia. "You, Belgast?"

The Dwarf thought it over before answering. "Mines come in all shapes and sizes. Us Dwarves tend to mine in the mountains, so ours almost always consist of tunnels and caves, but you Humans practice all sorts of strange customs."

"Like?"

"Like open-pit mines, where you scrape away all the dirt and expose the minerals beneath. In this case, however, I'd hazard a guess they dug down deep into the ground to retrieve it."

"What makes you think that?"

"Some of these references we read refer to how deep they went and this"—he dug through the pile of books—"this talks of a mechanical contraption to raise and lower people to the depths."

Stanislav read through the notes. "Is that a Dwarven invention?"

"As far as I know. We've used something similar for centuries. We call it a lift because it lifts people out of the shafts, but I've heard it called other things."

"What do they use to control it—pulleys?"

"Yes, or, in our case, gears." He saw the blank looks. "I suspect here pulleys are much more likely. Depending on how many people they're sending down at a time, they'd need significant strength to work it."

"Like a team of horses?"

"Aye, either on a windlass of some kind or connected to a set of ropes. Both methods have their strengths and weaknesses. Now I think of it, that might be our way in."

"In what way?"

"I can draw up some plans for a series of gears—think of them as toothed wheels. I'll say the family is considering replacing the horses with them on account of wearing out the beasts."

"And you think they'll believe you?"

"Certainly. Why wouldn't they?"

"What about horses?" said Stanislav. "We can't very well arrive in Zurkutsk on foot. It'll attract far too much attention, and hiring on a carriage would mean letting a coach driver in on our plans. Not exactly something I'm comfortable with after the example of Laisa's betrayal."

"Horses, I can do."

"Now, how do we get out of here?"

Galina rose. "That's on me. I found a reasonably safe place for you to hide. I'll go there directly and create the frozen arch, then all you'll need to do is step through."

"We could use one of them back in Ebenstadt," said Belgast. "It would definitely make travelling back and forth to Runewald easier."

Natalia chuckled. "If I return in one piece, I'll see what I can do about that. No guarantees though. We'd be required to create a magic circle, and that, my friends, is no simple task."

"I'll be on my way, then," added Galina. "Watch for the spell. It's draining to cast, and I can't hold it open forever."

"Will do," said Stanislav. He waited until she ascended the steps and heard the door close before continuing. "Can we trust her?"

"Of course," said Natalia.

"How can you be sure?"

"She works with Tatiana, the new grand mistress, and she, in turn, was a close confidant of Illiana."

"Did I ever tell you about the last time I saw Illiana?"

"Yes. She told you I was her granddaughter."

"There was more," said Stanislav. "She worried her enemies would try to use you against her and wanted you free from such things."

"I wish I had the chance to know her better. I can't help but feel she was murdered for trying to bring changes to the family, although what those changes were is beyond me."

"Based on what she told me, I'd have to agree. She took an enormous risk letting me come after you."

"Why would you say that?"

"Marakhova arrested me after I helped you escape. I don't imagine the new matriarch was too pleased to find out Illiana let me go."

BLUFF

Autumn 1108 SR

A light rain began, and with it, a wind whipped up. By the time
Stanislav and Belgast were closing on Zurkutsk, they were thoroughly soaked and shivering from the cold. To make matters worse, it was
far later in the day than either of them would have liked. It's not that their
directions were faulty, for there was but a single road going nowhere else,
but the distances involved had been vastly underestimated.

"How are you at starting a fire?" asked Belgast.

"In this weather? You must be mad," replied the mage hunter. "It might
be easier if it wasn't for all this rain."

"There are plenty of trees hereabouts. I suggest we take shelter under
one."

"It's as good an idea as any," said Stanislav. They proceeded up the road,
keeping an eye out for any suitable cover.

The Dwarf was the first to spot it—a cluster of three pine trees conve-
niently arranged in a triangle. Soon, they were beneath its boughs, and
Belgast began retrieving what sticks he could. Stanislav picked out a spot,
then cleared away the forest debris, giving them open ground to sit on.

Belgast finally returned bearing an armful of wood for the fire. These he
stacked before placing some moss and smaller twigs beneath to act as
kindling. He then picked out two of the driest sticks and began twirling one
against the other, trying to light the fire.

It took a while to see a wisp of smoke, but finally, the Dwarf managed to bring forth a flame. The heat was welcoming, far more so than the rain, and Stanislav moved closer, warming his hands at last.

"We'll camp here tonight," he said, "and approach the mine first thing in the morning. That should give us plenty of time to look around while daylight holds."

"Do you really believe they have Athgar?"

"It's as good a place as any to keep him. Tomorrow, we'll see for ourselves. If there are no prisoners here, then we'll simply return to Karslev."

"Fair enough," agreed the Dwarf. They settled in for the night, but Belgast, not one to prefer the wilderness, kept hearing the rustle of the trees and feared they would soon be under attack. As a result, he slept little, and as dawn finally broke, he was still tired.

They retrieved their horses and carried on towards Zurkutsk. From their vantage point on the road, they saw the mine below, set into a shallow valley surrounded by more pine trees. Here they halted, getting off their horses to take in the view.

"There," said Belgast, pointing. "That will be the lift mechanism in that tall building."

"I see," said Stanislav. "It appears you were right about the horses. What do you make of those long buildings within the palisade?"

"They're crudely constructed. My guess would be that they are for prisoners."

They stayed there, watching for half the morning. Groups of up to a dozen individuals came out, each chained to the other through loops on large leather belts worn by all.

"That presents a problem," said Belgast. "If we're to rescue Athgar, we'll need to get those chains off."

"Might it be easier to remove the belts?"

"That's a good idea. I'll bear that in mind. How many guards do you see?"

"Lots."

"That's not very descriptive. Can you be more precise?"

"More than enough to deal with the likes of us," said Stanislav. "We're not going to be able to fight our way out of this. We must use subterfuge."

"Getting in is easy enough, and even out, at least for the two of us, but I'm having a hard time figuring out how to rescue Athgar without drawing attention."

"We need a diversion."

"What do you have in mind?"

"An uprising would be ideal," said Stanislav, "but I'm not sure how we'd accommodate that."

Belgast urged on his pony. "We don't even know if Athgar is here. Come. Let's get inside and look around first. Then we can worry about making plans."

They trotted down the road and into the mining camp. There was little in the way of actual defences here. The prisoners were kept in dingy huts within the palisade while the guards lived in the nicer quarters surrounding it.

"State your business here," one of the guards called out as they brought their horses to a halt.

"We are here at the behest of the Stormwind family," said Stanislav, the lie coming easily to his lips. "This Dwarf here is Bagran Ironwhistle. Perhaps you've heard of him?"

"Can't say that I have."

"He's an expert in mining."

"Yes," added Belgast. "I was sent here to take stock of this mining operation and assess areas of possible improvement, with the intention of making the entire thing more efficient."

The guard eyed them suspiciously. "On whose authority, precisely?"

"Come now," said Stanislav. "Who do you think?"

"Not the matriarch, surely?"

The mage hunter shrugged. "It surprised me, too, but you know how she can be."

"I do," the guard agreed. "Very well. Over there, you'll see a dozen horses penned in. Drop your mounts off there and head into the adjacent building. You're looking for Corderis—he's in charge."

"Thank you. You've been most helpful. I'll be sure to mention you in our report."

The guard smiled, forgetting he'd never given his name to the two visitors. They rode to the indicated location, where two men took their horses. A third one came out of the building, spurred on, no doubt, by the sounds of their arrival.

He was about to say something when his eyes beheld Belgast. Clearly, the presence of a Dwarf took him by surprise, for he gaped, unable to frame a suitable greeting.

"You must be Corderis," called out Stanislav.

The fellow blinked back. "I am," he replied. "Who are you?"

"Merely a humble servant of the family, but this fine Dwarf is Bagran Ironwhistle."

"Please pardon my ignorance, but I have no idea who that is."

"Nor would I expect you to. He's an expert in mining who the family sent to see if there are any recommendations he can make to improve the efficiency of the place."

"I'll have you know we do quite well here. We don't need the advice of outsiders."

"Then let me do my job," said Belgast. He moved closer so he wouldn't need to yell. "Look, I'm sure you do a wonderful job here, and I'm not about to upturn any baskets. Show me around, and I'll write a glowing report about what you do here. Who knows, you might even find yourself rewarded for your fine work."

"Very well," Corderis begrudgingly grumbled. "I'll show you around. Where would you like to start?"

"That tall building—I assume it's used to carry the miners into the ground?"

"It is," said Corderis proudly, "and quite something to see in action. Come, I'll explain how it works."

Prodded with a club, Athgar awoke.

"Get up," roared the guard. "You're needed below."

"Why?" asked Katrin. "What's happened?"

"There was a cave-in. You're to dig out the bodies."

"But we just returned from our shift."

"Tell that to somebody who cares."

They rose, then waited as the guard threaded the chain through their belts. Moments later, they were ushered outside, where they shivered in the cool air.

"This way," barked another guard, and they set off at a steady pace towards the main shaft. They were getting ready to enter the cage when Athgar heard a familiar voice.

"And I suppose these ropes are attached to counterweights?"

"You know your stuff," replied the voice of Corderis, the man in charge of Zurkutsk.

"Yes, well, I studied under the great Karzan Stonebelly. No doubt you've heard of him?"

Athgar realized it was Belgast, and that could only mean one thing—he'd come here to rescue Athgar. He cast his eyes around, looking for anything that might alert the Dwarf to his presence. He settled on pushing Alfie, who walked in front of him. The fellow stumbled forward, then Athgar purposefully tripped him up, sending him sprawling to the ground. So tightly were they tied together that his fall dragged Athgar down with him, the pair of them creating a chain reaction causing almost the entire group to lose their footing.

"Watch where you're going!" yelled Athgar, his voice as loud as he could make it. Alfie tried to protest, but his fellow miner was having none of it. "You almost broke my leg!" Athgar shouted.

Behind him, others complained, causing the guards to break up the argument by the liberal application of their clubs. Athgar changed tactics, waiting until one was close and then reached out, as if he were slipping, and dragged the guard to the ground.

The man's comrades moved in quickly, grabbing the Therengian by the arms and holding him tight while the other fellow regained his feet. Moments later, he thrust the end of his club into Athgar's stomach, winding him.

Belgast's voice boomed out. "What's this now? Don't tell me you beat the miners?"

"Only those who give us trouble," replied Corderis.

Athgar saw the Dwarf's wink before he looked down. "Sorry," he said. "I slipped trying to get up." They pushed him into the cage, along with his companions and the door closed.

"That was unwise," their guard announced. "You made Corderis look like a fool in front of guests. He won't soon forget it."

"Who's the Dwarf?" asked Katrin.

"Some visitor the family sent. That's all I know."

They rode down in silence. A cloud of dust caked their throats as the door opened at the bottom, where another guard waited for them.

"Get that chain off and take them down the west tunnel."

"Will they be digging?" asked their escort.

"No. Hauling away the rock the others dig out. Although at the rate they're going, there may be a body or two to carry out by now."

Once the chains were removed, they were pushed farther along the tunnel, where other miners carried out sacks of small rocks as the sound of digging soon reached their ears.

The tunnel section that had collapsed was close to where they found the hidden cave, and Athgar wondered if the collapse might be related to its presence. Their escort was soon lost in the throng of workers. Athgar pulled Katrin aside.

"It's now or never," he said.

Her eyes went wide. "Why? What's happened?"

"Did you see those people up top?"

"You mean the visitors? Yes. Why?"

"That Dwarf is a friend of mine, and he likely hasn't come alone."

"How do we proceed?"

"Gather the others. We'll meet in the cave we found. Do you remember where it is?"

"I do—it's down a side tunnel we passed on the way here."

"Good. All this confusion over the collapse is just what we needed. Have them go there one or two at a time. The last thing we want is for them to see a large group of miners going in the wrong direction."

"That still doesn't get us out of here."

"No, but if we can seize the cage when it's ready to return to the surface, we might be able to take them by surprise."

Belgast watched as the horses began straining against the ropes. Someone removed a long wooden pin, and then their handler began leading them closer to the tower and, in turn, lowering the lift. A clever design, yet the Dwarf could see all sorts of inefficiencies.

"Your horses look blown," he remarked. "Do you always work them so hard?"

"Not at all, but we had a small collapse this morning necessitating more trips than usual."

"Do you not possess another team of horses?"

"I'm afraid not," said Corderis.

"I'll mention that to my client," said Belgast. "I'm sure she'll see the wisdom of sending you replacements."

"That would be most appreciated. Thank you."

"Not at all. After all, we're all here for the same reason."

"Might I go down on the next trip?" asked Stanislav. "I'd love to see what it's like from the inside."

"As long as you stay out of the way," replied Corderis.

"Are these collapses common?"

"They happen from time to time. It's not so much the loss of life that's frustrating, it's the time we waste having to restore the tunnels back to working condition."

"I assume you have lots of miners?"

"More than enough for our purposes, yes. The Volstrum has been most generous in that respect."

The horses halted, and the rope went slack, indicating the lift had hit bottom. The team was disconnected from the lines, then turned around, where a second rope was attached.

Belgast watched it all. "How do you know when they're ready to come back up again?"

"There's a rope at the bottom attached to a bell up yonder." He pointed halfway up the tower. "When that rings, the horses will be walked forward once more, raising the cage."

They stood for some time, and Belgast wondered if the thing hadn't broken. He was about to suggest something to that effect when the bell finally rang. The handler urged the horses forward, and the rope went taut as it began lifting the cage.

Stanislav wandered around to where the front of the cage would be, then he struck a relaxed pose, his hand coming to rest on the hilt of his sword. Corderis had not bothered to disarm either him or Belgast, something the mage hunter found unusual when around prisoners. Then again, they'd passed themselves off as agents of the family. He waited, listening to the creaking sound as the pulleys did their work, until they finally ground to a halt. A guard opened the tower door, revealing the cage that would take Stanislav down.

"Go ahead," called out Corderis. "When you get to the bottom, seek out Grastad—he can show you around."

"Thank you, I will." He stepped inside, nodding his head in greeting to the guard, who then closed the door, cutting off most of the light.

Stanislav looked around, but there was not much to see. The cage itself was of little interest. He closed his eyes and counted to ten before opening them again, letting them adjust to the dim light.

He felt a jarring, and then the cage swayed slightly. Obviously, the stops had been pulled, and he now hung from the rope. A groan from above demanded his attention, and he looked up to spot part of a massive wheel turning. This, in turn, lowered a rope and his descent began.

The deepest that Stanislav had ever gone below the surface was the odd cellar or two, but this shaft appeared to stretch on forever. He felt the walls closing in on him and, for a brief moment, feared the shaft itself was in danger of collapsing, but then reason took hold, and he relaxed.

He marvelled at the construction of it all. The shaft was, in essence, nothing more than a large chimney, yet just beyond the cage's sides, it looked like a secondary shaft had been sunk. He would feel a breeze every so often, and then he understood that air was somehow pumped down into the depths.

Stanislav was no expert in such things, but he'd heard breathing so far under the ground was quite difficult. It was a relief to realize that no such problems awaited him here.

He thought back to the scuffle above. Athgar had obviously seen Belgast, but how about Stanislav? The last thing the mage hunter wanted was to surprise the Therengian, especially since that might give away the fact they knew each other. How, then, would he approach the fellow? He felt the bump as the cage halted at the bottom, and one side opened up, revealing a guard.

"Are you Grastad?" Stanislav asked.

"I am," the man replied. "And who might you be?"

"A representative of the family, here to investigate matters. Can you give me some idea of how things are going down here?"

"It's chaotic, I'll grant you that, but we're making progress."

"How many miners work here at present?"

"All told, close to two hundred. Most of those are forming a line to pull out the debris while a team of about a dozen take turns digging away at the collapsed stone with pickaxes. Would you care to take a look?"

"By all means, lead on."

They passed by a long line of workers moving bags of stone back towards the lift. The site of the collapse was easy to spot, for the line of people led right to it, but Grastad stopped suddenly.

"Something wrong?" asked Stanislav.

"Someone's missing."

"What do you mean 'missing'? Surely you can't keep track of everyone?"

"Not everyone, no, but there's a rather fetching woman I've had my eye on for some time, and I don't see her."

"Could she still be on the surface?"

"No, I saw her come down myself." Grastad kept looking back and forth at the workers, trying to pin her down. "She's got to be here somewhere." He wandered back up towards the lift, pausing at a side tunnel.

"Did you find her?" asked Stanislav.

"No, but I believe I know where she went." He unhooked his club from his belt and entered the smaller tunnel. Stanislav followed him, drawing his sword.

ESCAPE

Autumn 1108 SR

"What now?" asked Katrin.

They'd gathered in the cave to sort out their plan. Alfie and Felix were the last to arrive, their picks still in hand.

"First, we arm ourselves," said Athgar. "Then we head for the cage. With any luck, we'll overpower the guards and send the signal to lift us up to the surface."

"And then?"

"Then we must improvise. My hope is that we can cause a general uprising, sowing chaos and confusion. The ultimate objective will be to get as far into the forest as possible."

"I think not!" The words echoed throughout the cave. Two men stood at the cave entrance, the one in the lead hefting his club like he meant to use it. Behind stood his companion, ready with a sword, most of his body hidden in the shadows like some creature of the night.

"Stand aside, Grastad," said Athgar. "We have no quarrel with you."

"Not entirely true," said Alfie, hefting his pick. "There's still the matter of that beating you gave me two weeks ago."

Grastad grinned. "You deserved that. You're nothing but a filthy castoff, fit for naught but digging rock and stone."

Athgar placed his hand on Alfie's forearm. "Hold, my friend. He seeks only to enrage you." He took a step forward, his eyes locked on those of the guard. "There's only two of you and eight of us. Do you really think you intimidate us?"

"Two?" said the darkened figure. "I believe you've sorely miscalculated." Athgar immediately recognized the voice but hid his surprise.

Grastad, misinterpreting Stanislav's remark, smiled. "The two of us are more than sufficient to deal with the likes of a filthy Therengian."

He stepped forward, raising the club to strike, but the mage hunter's sword stabbed into his back. The guard fell to the ground, then looked up in shock as Stanislav loomed over him.

"He's not a filthy Therengian. I'll have you know he bathes regularly."

"Traitorous cur!" shouted Grastad. A swift kick sent the club flying. "You'll pay for this," yelled the guard.

"I think you forget who holds the sword." Stanislav plunged the tip down, killing the man instantly. "Ah well. He wasn't much of a conversationalist, anyway."

Athgar ran forward, embracing the man. "By the Gods, it's good to see you, my friend."

"And you." Stanislav held his companion at arm's length. "You look reasonably fit, although that guard had the right of it."

"Meaning?"

"You are badly in want of a wash."

"Never mind that. Where's Belgast?"

"Up above, watching over the mechanism that raises and lowers the lift."

"Lift?"

"Yes, it's a Dwarven term. It's the strange cage that brings you down here and lifts you back up. Now, much as I'd love to catch up on things, I doubt we have the time. We must act quickly if we are to be successful. Have you a plan?"

"To make for the cage. Can you get us to the surface?"

"I think so," said Stanislav, "but might I propose a slight change to your plan?"

"By all means."

"We attack the guards down here first. With them out of the way, we'll have weapons with which to arm you."

"You lead," said Katrin, "and we'll follow you as if you're in charge."

"And you are?"

"Katrin."

"Katrin Stormwind? Sorry, I suppose most of you are Stormwinds. You have no idea how long I've been searching for you."

"For me?"

"Yes," said Stanislav. "Natalia asked me to look for you when you were removed from the Volstrum. I even visited your father, although I must admit that was not the most productive of encounters."

"You can catch up later," said Athgar. "We must act decisively before word gets out of our absence."

"Come this way." The mage hunter led them back into the side corridor, then up to where the rescue operation was underway.

The guards, too engrossed in overseeing their work, failed to notice their approach, the mistake costing them dearly. Alfie drove a pick into the back of one, while a fellow prisoner, seeing his chance, sent the end of his shovel into his own captor's stomach.

The corridor descended into chaos as prisoners turned against their oppressors. It wasn't only the guards who suffered, for as soon as they were eliminated from the fight, others turned on their fellow inmates. Captivity is a harsh taskmaster, and there are often those who feed off the weak. Now, free to use their picks and shovels as weapons, the victims became the masters, venting their pain and oppression against those who once sought to dominate them. So grisly was the retribution that Athgar turned away from the sight.

"Come," said Katrin. "We must get to the lift before someone else takes news of the uprising to the surface."

She rushed off, forcing Athgar and the rest to catch up only to find her crouched by a corner in the main cavern, peering around to where other guards stood watch over the lift. Thankfully, the uprising had not yet reached this location, giving them a few brief moments to decide on a course of action.

"Allow me," said Stanislav. He stepped out, trying to look as nonchalant as possible. "Excuse me," he called out. "I wonder if I might have a word?" He drew closer, then began engaging in idle chit-chat.

Athgar watched the man in action. As a mage hunter, Stanislav spent years interviewing people and knew how to keep them engaged. He subtly moved towards the lift as he talked, causing both guards to place their backs to Athgar's group.

The Therengian moved forward, his years of hunting serving him well. He gripped his club, the prize taken from the grasp of a dead guard.

Stanislav reached into a pocket and attempted to retrieve some coins. He had the full attention of his audience now, so he fumbled, letting the coins fall to the ground and then backed up, complaining about his clumsiness.

It had the desired effect. The guards, eager to retrieve the coins, were still bent over when Athgar struck, his club smashing into one's head even as Stanislav drew his sword and stabbed the other.

Katrin and the rest were soon beside them, divesting the bodies of their weapons. A moment later, they opened the door to the cage, Stanislav seeking the rope that signalled those above that the lift was ready to ascend.

"Get in," he urged, "and I'll give the rope a pull."

A sound echoed from down the tunnel as a swarm of miners flooded towards them.

"Come," shouted Athgar, frantically beckoning them into the cage. "Freedom awaits, but we'll need to fight for it."

The mage hunter pulled the rope and then forced his way into the lift, closing the door behind him. With all the extra miners, it was a tight fit. Time stood still until he finally felt the floor below swing slightly as they rose. The great wheel far above groaned in protest, and even the ropes seemed to complain. Athgar stared upwards, fearing the strain would be too much and the rope would snap, sending them crashing to their deaths. He closed his eyes, trying to picture the daylight above.

It took forever to ascend, yet he knew only the anticipation of the battle to come caused the feeling. He opened his eyes and looked around, noticing the gaze of the others on him.

"When we get to the surface," he began, "you should spread out as much as possible. It'll make it much harder for them to counter our attack." He saw their looks of determination tinged with fear. He reminded himself these people were by no means warriors. Instead, they were intellectuals gifted not with strength and endurance but the potential for magic. How many would win freedom, and how many would die, or worse yet, be recaptured? He shuddered, for he could well imagine what form the family's wrath might take on those who failed to escape.

The cage finally slowed, swaying slightly before a noticeable bump that indicated the wooden blocks were put in place to secure the lift. He gripped his club tightly and found himself holding his breath.

The outer door to the tower opened, flooding the space with light. The guards stepped forward in their usual manner and unlatched the door that functioned as one side of the cage.

Ordinarily, they would swing it out, but as soon as the latch was sprung, those within pushed forward, forcing the door wide open and sending the guard sprawling. Athgar hung back, allowing the others to rush forth. He spied Alfie and Felix, pushing their way to the front and then lost sight of them.

"Come," shouted Stanislav. "We haven't much time."

They charged out to witness the prisoners already swarming over the grounds of the camp. The guards, caught entirely unawares, scrambled to find shelter, rushing into buildings in a vain attempt to reach safety.

The mage hunter led them around the tower to where Belgast held the team of horses. Nearby lay the body of a guard, and the Dwarf shrugged. "He panicked when he heard you lot coming off the lift."

"What are you doing?" said Stanislav. "Leave the horses. It's time to go."

"Not until I bring up another load. We can't abandon them down there."

"I must find the others," said Athgar, his eyes searching the scattered prisoners. He spotted Katrin with Anushka, trying to break down the door to one of the barracks while others egged them on.

Ulyana, meanwhile, had taken down a guard who'd been escorting some chained prisoners, and she was now in the process of releasing them using the guard's keys. He reached Ulyana first, pulling her away as she completed her task.

"Get back to the tower," he yelled. "Seek out the Dwarf in back, where the horses are." He moved on to the barracks.

Whoever was inside had barricaded the door, trying to protect themselves, but it proved to be their death trap. Even as Katrin and Anushka tried to force it, someone threw an oil lamp, striking the side of the structure, and soaking it. Moments later, the fire took hold, racing up the wall and quickly reaching the thatched roof.

Athgar pulled Katrin back as fire spread across the roof. "Come. We must leave now," he shouted.

They turned and ran, their speed fuelled by fear. He kept his eyes out for Alfie and Felix, but they were nowhere to be found. Belgast led the horses around again, pulling the lift back up to the surface.

"Last one," he said, "then we best be on our way."

"Where's Stanislav?"

"Getting our horses."

The Dwarf halted, then moved to the back of the tower and pulled the lever that set the stops in place. "There, that ought to do it."

A crossbow bolt whizzed past, and Athgar looked to see a group of guards coming from the north. They'd organized themselves into a solid line and now advanced, not with clubs, but with swords drawn, while those on either flank sent bolts flying towards the fleeing prisoners.

"Come on," yelled Athgar. He ran around the tower, using its bulk to shield them from the deadly missiles. "We need to get out of here." His eyes befell the palisade wall. Those within would still be prisoners, yet there was little he could do to free them. Even now, the guards counterattacked, and it wouldn't be long before the tide of battle turned in their favour.

He spied Stanislav, who had rounded up a trio of horses and rode directly for them, but then a mob of escaped prisoners spotted him as well. Athgar had a brief view of his comrade being pulled from the saddle, and then he disappeared from sight, lost amongst the horde's wrath and terror.

"No!" the Therengian cried out. He rushed forward, heedless of the danger and soon reached the throng, pushing his way through to find the stricken mage hunter. The fellow lay on the ground, curled up into a ball as they beat him. Athgar tried in vain to stop his attackers, but their blood was up, and vengeance was in their hearts.

Athgar felt a blow to his back and realized, with a shock, they were now attacking him. The fools were like animals, desperate to feed off the life of their victims.

He felt something wet splatter his face and looked up to see the tip of a crossbow bolt protruding from someone's eye. A dull thud announced the arrival of another. The crowd turned on their new attackers with wild abandon.

Athgar grabbed Stanislav by the arms and began dragging him to safety. Belgast soon joined, and between them, they managed to lift the mage hunter to his feet. He was in a lot of pain but appeared to be more or less intact.

"We can't stay here," shouted the Dwarf, casting his gaze around. "What's the fastest way out?"

"That way," said Katrin, pointing to the west. "Into the forest."

Belgast peered over his shoulder to where the guards cut the mob to pieces. It wouldn't take them long to resume their advance. "We'll never make it. Take Stanislav. I'll hold them off."

"No," said Athgar. "You're better suited to take him. I'll take care of this." He left no time for argument, running back towards the guards.

Athgar closed the distance, watching for any weakness he might exploit. The prisoners, their vengeance driving them mad, charged straight in, some of them cut down without a second thought. Their numbers, however, proved too much for their oppressors, who now fell back, desperately trying to maintain their good order.

Athgar saw his chance when a guard went down in the middle of the line, and his attacker, wielding a pickaxe, stumbled forward into the gap. Athgar ran for all he was worth. With a prayer to the Gods, he leaped, launching himself off the prisoner's back directly into the enemy's ranks. He felt the impact, and then he fell, taking at least two warriors with him. Emboldened by his recklessness, other prisoners renewed their efforts, splitting the line in two.

Athgar, lying in the mud, spotted a sword nearby and crawled towards it on his hands and knees. Pain lanced through his right side as something hit him, knocking him face-first into the ground. His left hand instinctively reached around, and he felt blood soaking his tunic. Looking up, he saw his attacker preparing for another blow, but so focused was the guard on this one target, he neglected to consider anyone else. A club smashed down on the fellow's head, glancing off his helmet, but the blow was enough to throw him off balance.

Athgar used the momentary respite to throw himself to the side while grasping the sword and swinging out in a wide arc, desperately attempting to save his skin. The blade sliced across the man's thigh, and already off balance, his attacker fell forward, surprising Athgar. Then he saw the blood running from the guard's head. It appeared the man's previous injury was much worse than Athgar had surmised.

He got to his feet and thrust the sword out as another guard charged towards him, hitting the man's chest, but armour halted the blow before any actual damage was done. The warrior struck out, and Athgar stepped back, attempting to parry with the unfamiliar weapon. He knew he was outmatched but did what he could to fend off the blows.

His opponent was an immense man, fully a head taller than Athgar. With shoulders rivalling those of the Orcs, he presented a formidable opponent with his sword raised on high. The Therengian desperately rushed forward, discarding the sword and tackling the brute, driving him to the ground. Athgar quickly grabbed the knife the fellow wore on his belt, drew it forth, and stabbed out in a fury of blows.

He heaved a sigh of relief as the body went still. Looking up, he saw that the fighting around him was now dispersing, no longer a battle against a formed line so much as a collection of individual struggles for survival.

He stood, scanning the carnage. Spotting an axe, still held in a dead man's hand, Athgar retrieved it, the weight of it reassuring.

Knowing that Belgast and the others had headed westward, he looked in that direction, hoping to spot them, but they were nowhere to be seen. Gods willing, they were already within the forest that would prove to be their salvation.

He called out, trying to get other prisoners to join him, but those around him chose to ignore his pleas for reason and escape. Off to the north, he heard horses and then noticed a group of riders leaving Zurkutsk. It appeared the guards were going for help. He suspected it wouldn't take long for them to reach a local garrison, and then the might of the Army of Ruzhina would return and crush the uprising.

Giving up on any chance of organizing the remaining prisoners, Athgar turned and sprinted towards the thick pine forest. As he reached the edge of the woods, he halted and turned to take one last look at the mine. Smoke billowed up from several buildings, and bodies, both guards and prisoners alike, were scattered over the grounds. Individual escapees wandered around the place, finishing off those guards who remained amongst the living. Athgar had seen his fair share of battles, but the brutality of the scene turned his stomach.

WILDERNESS

Autumn 1108 SR

A twig snapped, causing Athgar to pause in his tracks. He was deep in the woods, searching for any sign of his comrades, yet so far, his quest had yielded nothing. The sound of the twig changed all that. Somewhere out there, someone was moving through the trees. The real question was who, or perhaps he should say what?

Katrin had told him the story of Vicavia, but he'd thought little of it, chalking it up to a fairy tale meant to frighten children. Now, in the thick forests of Western Ruzhina, he wondered if there wasn't some truth in it after all.

He gripped the axe and slowed his breathing, the better to stop his heart from thumping. Again, the sound. He moved towards it as stealthily as he could.

A curse echoed through the trees, and Athgar relaxed. "Belgast?" he called out. "Is that you?"

"Athgar? By Gundar's forge, how did you ever find us?"

"It was easy enough," he lied with a smile. "All I needed to do was follow the cursing."

In amongst the trees, he finally spotted the rest of them. Stanislav staggered along with Katrin on one arm and Anushka on the other. Behind them came Ulyana, while Belgast had evidently chosen to take the lead. At

the sight of their comrade, they all halted. The mage hunter took the opportunity to lower himself to the forest floor.

"I'm glad you're safe," said the Dwarf, "and you arrived just in time."

"Just in time for what?"

"Why, to lead us to safety, of course. I can't make head or tail of these
woods. It's like being in a maze. The last thing I want to do is lead us back
to Zurkutsk."

Athgar moved to Stanislav's side. "How are you?" he asked, looking
down at the man's pale features.

"I've been better."

"He's badly bruised," added Katrin, "but I don't believe anything is
broken."

"We can't keep moving him," said Belgast. "He needs to rest. Have you
any idea how far we've come since we escaped?"

"I would guess no more than a mile or two?" said Athgar.

"That's a little close for comfort, don't you think?"

"I do, but we must deal with things as they are."

"You know your way around the woods, Athgar," said Katrin. "What's
our next step?"

"Our first priority will be finding shelter."

"Not water?" asked Belgast.

"No. By my reckoning, it won't be long now until Anushka can use her
magic, then we'll have all the water we can drink."

"And what, pray tell, do we drink it from? You didn't happen to bring
any mugs with you by any chance, did you?"

"No," admitted Athgar, "but we can improvise. Before we start worrying
about that, though, let's take stock of our resources, shall we?"

"I have a knife," said Belgast, "although not my pick."

"Did you lose it?"

"It's safe. I just didn't bring it with me. It would be hard to explain the
presence of a pick when I'm supposed to be an advisor, don't you think?"

"Yes, I suppose it would. I've got a knife I took off a guard and an axe as
well. That'll come in handy."

"I've got a club," added Katrin, "and Anushka and Ulyana both managed
to acquire knives. Unfortunately, no food, though."

"There should be plenty hereabouts," said Athgar, "but we'll need to put
some distance behind us before we worry about that. Aside from Stanislav,
is anyone else injured?"

They had little to report other than minor cuts and scrapes. Athgar
turned his attention to Belgast.

"How did you happen to visit during a collapse?" he asked.

"That was merely a lucky coincidence. I think your Gods were looking down on you."

"Where's Natalia? Is she well?"

"She was the last time we spoke to her."

"When was this?"

"A few days ago," explained the Dwarf. "They've got her working at the Volstrum."

He stared back a moment, trying to understand. "Why would she do that?"

"Marakhova used the threat of your death to bend her to their will."

"I seem to remember something to that effect, but my memory is a bit fuzzy. Does that mean she has access to her magic?"

"Not at the moment," said Belgast, "but she has made some allies. The new Grand Mistress of the Volstrum, Tatiana, is helping her, along with a fellow mage named Galina. She's the one who sprang us from the dungeons."

"How did you find me?"

"I didn't. Galina discovered the whereabouts of Zurkutsk, but until we laid eyes on you, it was all a bit of a gamble."

"Did you have an actual plan for what comes next?"

"I've given that quite a lot of thought over the last few days," said Belgast. "We can't take you back to Karslev; there'll be too many people watching for you, but there's another option."

"Which is?"

"How long can you survive in this wilderness?"

Athgar smiled. "As long as I need to. What is it you're thinking?"

"Stanislav is clearly not capable of being moved right now, at least not any great distance. I recommend you and the others set yourselves up in a camp somewhere and wait things out."

"For how long? And what about Natalia?"

"That's the second part of my plan. I'll return to the Volstrum and get word to Natalia that you're safe. With the threat of your death no longer held over her, she'll be eager to get out of there as quickly as possible."

"Yes, but how? She's as much a prisoner as I was."

"That's the easy part. Galina and Tatiana both have access to magic that could accomplish that."

"You must hurry," insisted Katrin. "Once word of Athgar's escape reaches Marakhova, she might lock Natalia up."

"I doubt they'd do that," said Athgar. "The threat of harm to me is what they think is keeping her in check. I believe they'll keep up that ruse as long as they can."

"Why would you say that?"

"Think about it. I've been locked up for months now and never had a single visitor. They've prevented Natalia from knowing my whereabouts, so why should now be any different? After all, they know I can't just stroll into the Volstrum and announce myself."

"You make a good point," said Belgast, "but I wouldn't want to push it. I believe it best I return to Karslev as soon as possible. I will, however, need some way of finding you when the time comes to return."

"Let's look for water first," said Athgar. "If we can find a stream or, better yet, a river, you can use that as a guide."

"I hardly see how that helps."

"Simple. When you return, follow the river to its source. I'll take care of the rest."

The Dwarf grinned. "In other words, you lot will watch the waterways."

"Exactly. Of course, I can't guarantee that'll work. It all depends on how our enemies react. If they send warriors in any great numbers, we'll need to retreat farther into the wilderness."

Ulyana shuddered. "What about Vicavia? Aren't you worried about her minions?"

"No," said Athgar. "Although, now that you mention it, that might work to our advantage."

"How so?"

"Katrin, you were the first to mention the legend. How widely known is the tale?"

"Every child in Ruzhina knows the story of Vicavia," the woman replied. "Why?"

"I thought we might give any possible pursuers cause to believe she's in the area."

"How would we do that?"

"Once I start hunting, we'll have plenty of bones. By combining those from different animals, I can create their worst nightmares."

"That's a fine idea, but aren't you forgetting something? How are you going to hunt when all we have is an axe and some knives?"

"You're forgetting, I'm a bowyer. Once we find shelter, I'll fashion a bow, then we'll have no end of food."

"How can you be so sure?"

"I've already seen tracks aplenty," said Athgar. "Not to mention all the plants we can eat. It may not be the fare you're used to, but it'll fill your bellies."

"Anything's better than the gruel they gave us back at the mine."

He looked down at Stanislav. "How are you doing? Do you believe you can carry on?"

In answer, the mage hunter stood, albeit a little unsteadily. "Ready as I'll ever be."

"Very well, then. I'll take the lead."

"Hold it," said Belgast. "How do you know which way to go?"

"That's easy," replied Athgar. "We go downhill. If we're going to find a stream, that's the most likely direction."

"How do you know that won't lead us back to the mine?"

"Simple, we've been descending since we escaped. The only way back is to travel uphill."

"So we're entering a valley?"

"Either that or the land is lower in this direction. In any event, water runs downhill, so sooner or later, we should find some, even if it's only a trickle."

They set off, taking their time and picking their route carefully, lest a steep incline prove too difficult for Stanislav.

They found their water source by late afternoon—a small stream running from the southeast to the north. Doubtless, it would eventually run to the sea or possibly join into some larger river, but for now, it was a godsend. They slaked their thirst, conserving Anushka's power. Moving upstream proved relatively painless, and before night fell, they'd covered a significant distance.

When they sat down to rest, Athgar surprised them all, for he'd gathered wood for a fire, then, pleased the magebane had finally worn off, used his magic to start it. As the heat warmed them, he searched around the immediate area, returning with several plants as well as some nuts and berries.

"This is a bountiful area," he said, "teaming with all sorts of food. At first light, I'll find some suitable wood and get working on carving a bow."

"How will you string it?" asked Katrin.

"Plant fibres, for now, hemp if I'm able to find it. I can always replace that with sinew once I catch us some meat."

"And how long to carve a bow?"

"That depends on the wood hereabouts. Were I back home, I'd typically take a couple of days, but this is a matter of survival, so I shan't worry too much about making it look nice."

"But how long?" echoed Belgast.

"I'll have it ready to use by late tomorrow afternoon, I should think. While I'm doing that, you lot can search for suitable wood for making arrows. Now, who wants to learn more about what plants we can eat?"

They settled in for the evening, not quite with full bellies, but at least with enough in them that it kept the pangs of hunger at bay.

The next morning, Belgast headed out. His plan was relatively simple: head west until he encountered a road or some other sign of civilization. As for the rest, they began gathering what wood they could find without resorting to chopping down trees, fearful the sound might carry. Athgar, for his part, managed to find a branch suitable for his bow on the forest floor. As luck would have it, the trees here were a mix of pine and other evergreens, including yews, making the perfect material for crafting a bow.

He got to work and soon had the bark stripped. Finding material for the bowstring proved a little more difficult. By late afternoon, he'd resolved to abandon the search, concentrating instead on whittling down some arrows. These would be crude affairs, made entirely of wood and lacking any real arrowhead or fletchings, but they would suffice for the moment.

Meanwhile, the others constructed some crude survival shelters using gathered pine boughs to keep the elements at bay. They consisted of an angled roof overtop a small area into which one or two people could fit. These they built around the fire, forming a circular camp.

By nightfall, they had a well-burning fire, shelter from wind and rain, should it come, and more food with which to fill their bellies.

The next day, Athgar completed his bow and went out in search of prey. First, he set some primitive snares in the hopes of catching smaller animals, then spent most of his morning along the stream. As the sole water source in the area, naturally, animals would seek it out. Thus it was he came across a young doe, slaking its thirst. The first arrow missed its target, but the second, loosed after the thing bolted, found its mark, and the creature faltered as it tried to flee deeper into the woods. Athgar used his knife to finish the animal off, then cut up the body.

His return to the camp was met with much enthusiasm. That night, they ate meat for the first time in months, and in some cases, even years. Athgar set about curing the hide as well as cleaning the bones and drying out some of the meat.

Over the next few days, Athgar fashioned spears along with more arrows, and the group became more comfortable with their surroundings. In his heart, he worried that something might have befallen Belgast, but he kept such things to himself. They were free of Zurkutsk, living off the land and surviving, if not thriving. The day would come when they would leave this temporary home, but for the moment, at least, he would keep them fed and ready to fight should the need arise.

. . .

Belgast stumbled out of the forest and onto a road, although perhaps road was a bit of an overstatement. Carriages had traversed the trail, for two deep ruts marked the ground, but the mud still sucked at his boots, making his progress slow.

A horseman appeared late in the afternoon, and although he refused to give the Dwarf a ride, he promised to report his presence to a nearby village.

As it turned out, Belgast was heading in the right direction. Early the following day, he came across a hunter supplementing his crops by setting up snares in the woods. The fellow proved friendly, escorting the Dwarf back to the village, where further transportation could be arranged.

The very next day, he was on his way, riding back towards Karslev in the company of a farmer taking goods to the city. By week's end, once again in the capital of Ruzhina, he took lodgings at a small inn near the city gates and began exploring the city.

His initial intention had been to call on Galina, but when he went to her home, he noticed the presence of others watching the place. Alarmed at this unexpected development, he was forced to consider other options.

If Galina was being watched, there was a good chance Marakhova suspected her of working against the matriarch's wishes. That likely meant anyone spending time in her company might be seen as a potential threat as well.

He navigated his way through the city streets, ending up within sight of the Volstrum but decided not to enter the place for fear of drawing undue attention. Instead, he chose to watch, looking for some way of entry that wouldn't arouse suspicion.

The day wore on, but still, he pondered his problem, for he had only a limited view of the massive building at present. He resolved to circumnavigate it, but it would likely take him the better part of the afternoon, for he could not afford to draw unwanted attention.

He made his way down the side of the Volstrum, staying across the street, keeping a lookout for any who might take undue note of his presence. He spotted a wagon at the end of the street, turning not away but towards the rear of the Volstrum.

Intrigued, he continued along to the corner, only to come up short at the sight of the back of the building, where there was a series of doors, each big enough to admit a wagon. Indeed, one of them was even open, and he could easily see a group of men unloading a cart.

It struck Belgast that this might be his avenue of entry. He knew, as a

Dwarf, his presence would generate a lot of interest. How, then, could he manage to enter without drawing too much suspicion? He thought of trying another bluff, but he'd already been captured by Marakhova's guards once, so the risk of being recognized was too high. He spent the afternoon watching crates and barrels being delivered, and briefly considered hiding inside of one. As soon as he thought it through, he dismissed it, for the chance of finding Galina or, better yet, Natalia, were slim, especially at night.

It was a most perplexing conundrum until he noticed a supervisor write a note and hand it to the wagoner. He quickly returned to the inn to compose a letter. It would need to be carefully worded, but he was convinced a few coins would ensure its delivery. It only remained to find someone he could trust to carry it.

In the early morning light, Belgast stood watching the back of the Volstrum as a pale-red wagon made its way through the doors and into that great structure. He hoped his letter would soon be delivered into the grand mistress's hands, either that or he would find himself set upon by guards. Only time would tell which fate he'd chosen for himself.

HIDDEN

Autumn 1108 SR

Natalia felt the carriage slide to one side as the wheels hit a rut. Taking little notice of the rough ride, her guards simply sat there, their eyes glued to her. It was a bit unnerving, to say the least, and she was glad when the Volstrum finally came into view.

The early morning mist still clung to the cobblestones as they came to a halt. Her guards watched her every move as she exited, then the Volstrum's own warriors took over the task of preventing her from escaping.

The carriage trundled off as she walked through the back of the building, cognizant that all eyes were still on her. Wagons were unloaded while other, more important dignitaries passed their horses to the stable hands. She entered the corridor leading to the interior, only to come face to face with Tatiana.

"Sorry, Grand Mistress," she said. "I didn't expect to see you here."

"Maybe not," the woman replied, "but the reverse is not true. Come. We have much to discuss, you and I."

"Is something wrong?"

"These are things best not talked of in public."

She turned and strode off, leaving Natalia rushing to catch up. As they turned a corner, Tatiana led them into an interview room, making sure to close the door behind them. The grand mistress immediately began casting, and Natalia waited as the frozen arch appeared.

"Go through," she ordered. "Galina will tell you all you need to know."

Natalia stepped through, appearing in the middle of the casting circle to see Galina waiting for her.

"Come," the woman said. "We have much to discuss."

"The grand mistress just used the exact same expression. What's happened?"

They walked into the arcane library. "We received word from Belgast. It appears they located your husband, but there were complications."

Natalia felt her heart skip a beat. "Is he still alive?"

"Near as we can tell, he is hale, hearty, and free."

"He's escaped?"

"He has," said Galina, "but as I said, there's been some complications. It appears Marakhova might be onto us."

"What makes you say that?"

"Your friend noticed my house was being watched. Unfortunate for us as we were to make contact there."

"Then how did he get word of Athgar to you?"

"He sent a note by way of a merchant. He's clever, this Dwarf of yours."

"He's a valued friend," said Natalia. "Did he say where Athgar was?"

"Living out in the wilderness, although he didn't give a precise location."

"So what's our next step?"

"That largely depends on you. How long ago did you eat?"

"Right before sunup."

"And I assume you drank your magebane like a good girl?"

Natalia bristled. "I'm hardly a girl anymore, but yes, I drank it. I had little choice, what with the guards standing watch over me. Why?"

"Circumstances are forcing our hand. Do you have a testy stomach?"

"No. Why?"

"A pity. Still, we might be lucky." She lifted a cup containing a foul-smelling brew. "Here, drink this."

"What is it?"

"Best you don't know. The idea is to empty the contents of your stomach."

"And that removes the magebane's effects?"

"Remove, no, but lessen, quite possibly. We know you are largely resistant to its effects, which means you are given a dose that far exceeds what any normal mage could endure. With any luck, this will remove enough of it so that your magic will return, although I doubt the effect would be immediate."

"And once my magic returns?"

"Then we have some work to do."

"Would you care to be more specific?"

"The plan is to get you out of here," said Galina, "but that might involve a fight, and you must be prepared."

"What about you and Tatiana?"

A wry smile crossed Galina's lips. "It's too late for us. If Marakhova's watching my house, it won't be long before she makes her move." She hefted a large book off a nearby shelf and deposited it on the table. "Drink up, Natalia, and once you purged the contents of your stomach, read through this."

"What is it?"

"A tome of spells, quite powerful ones, to be exact, many of them rituals thought lost to history."

"But couldn't you use them yourself?"

"No. Although I've studied them diligently, I've come to accept I lack the power to cast them. It is for you to carry on the tradition. My task is to remain here and buy you time to escape."

"Come with us," pleaded Natalia. "You would be welcome back in Runewald."

"It's a nice thought, but without us to hold off Marakhova and her lackeys, how would you escape?"

"There must be a better way?"

"If there is, I don't see it. Now come, drink up. We haven't any time to waste."

Natalia lifted the cup, a foul smell invading her senses. She fought back her reluctance and downed it in one go. Her throat constricted, and then her belly protested the vile brew.

"Over there," said Galina. "I've provided a bucket." She backed up, avoiding the smell as Natalia vomited. It took some time for her stomach to void its contents, and even then, her body was thrown into spasms as it tried to continue.

Eventually, even that subsided, and then Galina moved closer, placing her hand gently on Natalia's back. "There, there," she soothed. "It's all over now."

"That was horrid stuff. What did you say it was?"

"I didn't, and trust me, knowing will hardly help. Now, you must get to work on those spells."

"Won't I need to be able to cast them?"

"Not at all. You already know how to use magic. The only difference here is the actual incantation itself. Well, that and the hand movements, but those are nothing new."

· · ·

Natalia's eyes bored into the page. Galina was right—these spells were extremely powerful. Likely the most potent Water Magic ever created, yet only a select few had ever had the raw energy to power such incantations. It made her wonder who'd conceived these in the first place.

She closed her eyes and dug deep. Athgar taught her to seek her inner magic, and now she could feel it waiting to be unleashed, thanks to his techniques.

As an experiment, she pointed at a spot on the wall and called forth a word of power. A streak of magic shot out, striking the target and sending bits of ice everywhere. She smiled, for her power had begun to return. It wouldn't be long before she could try out some of the arcane lore locked within this very tome. Time passed quickly, so quickly that before she knew it, Galina returned.

"You missed your class," she said, sending shivers up Natalia's spine. "Don't worry, I took care of it. I told them you were indisposed and taught them myself. How goes the studying?"

"Well. I've even regained some of my power."

"How much?"

"Let's give it a try and find out, shall we?" Natalia moved to the centre of the room and closed her eyes. She called forth the image of the magic circle before beginning the ritual that would bring her there. It took but a moment to feel the familiar rhythm of her magic, then it poured forth as a frozen arch appeared. She immediately stepped through to find herself in the next room.

"It worked," she said, relief in her voice.

"So it did. Congratulations. Now, we must see about getting you out of here."

"Not quite yet," said Natalia. "I have a favour to ask."

"This is hardly the time for such things."

"Come. We are safe down here, and Marakhova has yet to send guards to arrest us."

"What is it you want?"

"Take me to Stormwind Manor." She saw the look of reluctance. "I know you've been there. You told me you were familiar with the magic circle there."

"That was Tatiana, not me."

"Then find her. Before I leave, I must go to Stormwind Manor, if only to commit the circle there to memory."

"That could prove very dangerous," warned Galina. "Marakhova has lived there for some time and will know of its existence."

"Yes, but I doubt she posts guards within the room that houses it. All I need is the time to memorize it."

"If you truly wish, I shall seek out the grand mistress. In the meantime, conserve your strength. You may soon have need of it."

Natalia sensed her magic growing stronger even as the words on the pages reached out to her. Her mind felt as though it were expanding, with more and more thoughts racing through it. She thought of Shaluhk and her encounter with Khurlig. That ancient shaman had invaded the Orc's mind, taken over her body, yet when finally vanquished, she left behind remnants of her knowledge. That same feeling pervaded Natalia's entire body now as if she were but an empty vessel filling with forgotten lore. It made her giddy, and she forced herself to take a break.

She now understood why this book was hidden away, for it could spell disaster in the wrong hands. The Volstrum, nay the entire family, always insisted on casting spells by releasing the maximum power one could muster. But from her readings, a controlled approach would be more appropriate. Fortunately, her time amongst the Orcs had taught her well, and she thanked the Ancestors for the revelation.

Tatiana looked flustered as she entered the room.

"Is all well?" asked Natalia.

"No, not in the least. I received word that Marakhova is on her way here, to the Volstrum. I suspect it's not a social call. The good news is it means the circle at Stormwind Manor is unattended. I shall take you there directly, but it will be up to you to return using your own spell."

"Understood," said Natalia. "Will you cast from here?"

"Not from this room, but from the magic circle. It will boost the power of my spell."

"Is it that much of a drain?"

"No," said Tatiana, "but I'll need to conserve my energy if I am to face Marakhova." She led Natalia through the door, then placed herself in the direct centre of the casting circle.

Natalia watched as the grand mistress began her spell and was immediately struck by the poetry of her movements. It was not so much casting as a graceful dance, a harmony of power and subtlety. Every mage had their own methods; some were nothing more than raw power pouring out of a mage like a bucket of water. Others, like Athgar and Shaluhk, appeared to be at one with nature, their energy flowing like a river with a gentle current. Tatiana's, however, was graceful, something Natalia had not expected.

The air grew chilly, and the spell's true artistry manifested itself when the arch appeared, for this was not the plain arch Galina had summoned. Instead, it was richly decorated with images of fish and kelp.

"It is done," announced Tatiana.

"The arch, it looks so different."

"It is the circle's effect. Each is unique, and this one was fashioned by a master of water."

"You make him sound like an Orc."

"I beg your pardon?"

"I meant nothing untoward," said Natalia. "It was merely your choice of words."

"You must step through. The longer this arch remains, the more power I must expend."

Natalia moved to the archway, peering through. Beyond lay a dimly lit room, its only source of light the glowing runes making up the circle. She turned briefly to the grand mistress. "Thank you."

"Do not thank me yet. You're far from safe. Now, go before I am forced to dismiss the spell."

Natalia stepped through. The first time she'd experienced this spell, she'd travelled only a few paces, with little in the way of discomfort. This time, however, the effect was more pronounced. She felt as though her whole body was being stretched, with lights flying past at impossible speeds. It only lasted a moment, yet it also seemed to take forever.

She appeared in the casting room below Stormwind Manor. The arch behind her vanished, and then the glowing runes on the floor dimmed, plunging her into darkness.

She stood in the silence, listening for any sounds alerting her of danger. Gradually, as her eyes adjusted, she could make out details. On a table, to one side, sat a small sphere glowing with a dim light. She moved towards it to get a better view.

It appeared to be made of crystal, but as she drew closer, it glowed, immediately revealing its true nature. It was, in fact, glass, with tiny, blue-glowing crystals embedded into its surface. It took only a moment for her to make sense of it.

"Magerite," she said, her voice echoing in the room. "How clever." She picked it up to feel the weight, and the light grew even brighter. It was definitely not something a person would want to carry around for any length of time, but it illuminated things nicely.

With the sphere in hand, she looked down at the circle, which consisted of two solid silver rings embedded in the floor, one within the other. Between these were runes made of poured gold, symbols that held the magic, ready to amplify it when spells were cast. The circle's interior was decorated with all manner of gold and silver inlays, weaving intricate water patterns and the creatures that dwelt within it.

Natalia looked away from the circle, as the last thing she needed was to be surprised by an intruder. Her attention shifted to the room itself, with its highly polished wooden walls yet no windows. The vaulted ceiling above used the same wood, with stone pillars rising from the floor to support it.

Only a single door graced the room. She quickly made her way over to it and placed her ear against the wood. Hearing nothing, she knew she was safe for the moment. Her attention returned to the circle, and she began the laborious task of committing it to memory.

The magical power was so strong here, Natalia felt as if a massive sea lay beneath the stone floor. So intense was this feeling that she wondered if it was truly the case? With her thoughts interrupting her study, she sat down to ponder her discovery.

She closed her eyes and began meditating. Athgar was the one who had taught her to harness her inner spark. She smiled at the memory, for in her case, it hadn't been a spark, but a pool of water, enfolding her in its calming embrace. However, this time, she felt no end to the water in which she found herself.

Her eyes snapped open when she realized just how powerful this magic circle was. She'd read about them, of course, and experienced the one back in the Baroshka. They went by many names: magic circles, circles of power, water circles, and that's not even touching the names used by the other disciplines. As a Water Mage, she could, in theory, make use of standing stones, earth rings, even life circles. In fact, the only one unavailable to her was a ring of fire, for it was the one type of magic that would act as a dampener on the element of water.

Her mind raced as she considered the repercussions. With this circle committed to memory, she could return here any time, at least in theory. The real limitation would be how far she would need to travel to get here. Tatiana told her there were limits to the distance the spell could carry someone, yet Natalia suspected she would have more than enough power to cross the Continent, if need be. The possibility gave her strength.

She stood there, clearing her mind of such thoughts. It would do no good to speculate on such things if she were caught here, unable to escape, and so she resumed studying the ancient runes.

. . .

Sometime later, she found herself outside the circle, her study complete. It would be foolish to take her memorization of it for granted, so she cast the frozen arch, calling upon her magic to connect to the very circle she was adjacent to. Closing her eyes to concentrate, she recalled the image in her mind, and then the arch took shape. She couldn't see it, of course, but the appearance of the frost brought a cold chill to the room. When her eyes finally opened, two arches stood before her: one to her front, the other placed directly in the centre of the circle.

Natalia stepped through, then dismissed the spell. Now ready to be free of the manor, she placed the glowing orb back where she'd found it before casting once more. The words of power came easily, and this time she pictured her new destination, the image clear in her mind. The arch appeared, and she stepped through to find herself back in the Volstrum's basement.

THE PORTRAIT

Autumn 1108 SR

Galina had left a letter on the table inside the Baroshka, awaiting Natalia's return. In a hurried hand, she'd explained Marakhova had indeed arrived and removed Tatiana from her position as grand mistress. Galina had escaped notice, for now, but would flee at the first opportunity and find somewhere safe to open a gate to get Natalia free of the Volstrum. Until then, she must remain safely hidden.

Natalia felt trapped. How long, she wondered, until the presence of this place was revealed? Could they somehow compel Tatiana to give up the secret of its existence? And how long could Natalia remain cooped up here? Her eyes wandered the room searching for answers, but none were forthcoming. She decided her time was best spent studying, so she opened the great book that held the ancient rites of magic.

The spells listed therein were of incredible power. Ordinarily, she would have devoured them all, but her present circumstances wore on her, and she worried she'd never again see Athgar or Oswyn. It came to mind that her greatest chance of escape might be to use the frozen arch to travel back to Stormwind Manor, then dismissed the idea. Galina had promised to open an arch to let her escape. She must give the woman time to find safety.

The day dragged on, and Natalia's stomach complained of its emptiness. Her resolve slowly crumbled until she finally felt the familiar tingle of magic as if a swarm of bees were nearby.

She exited the Baroshka in time to see a frozen arch appear on the magic circle. She could see naught but an empty room between its pillars, so she moved to its far side and looked through. Sure enough, Galina stood there, holding the portal open.

Natalia stepped through, and Galina immediately dismissed the spell. They were in a large wooden building, surrounded by boxes and crates, obviously a storeroom of some type, maybe even a warehouse.

"Natalia!" came the voice of Belgast. "By the anvil, it's good to see you safe."

She couldn't help but smile. The Dwarf, overcome with emotion, wept openly as he moved forward and embraced her.

"Touching," said Galina, "but we have work to do."

"Yes," agreed Belgast. "I acquired some ponies for us. It's time we go and find Athgar and leave all this behind."

"You don't have to tell me twice," said Natalia.

Outside waited the promised mounts, and soon they were in the saddle and heading eastward, leaving the city of Karslev behind.

Athgar pulled back on the string. The movement was uneven, with half the bow bending more than the other, revealing that additional work needed to be done. He set the bow down, saving it for another day.

"Problem?" asked Stanislav.

"Nothing that can't be fixed with time."

"Why are you even bothering with a second bow? It's not as if any of this lot can use one."

"In time, anyone can learn," said Athgar. "And it gives me something to concentrate on."

"You're missing Natalia."

"I am. I'm worried for her safety. By now, word would have gotten out about my escape. It could go ill for her."

"Nonsense. They won't kill her," said Stanislav. "She's too valuable to them."

Athgar stared at the ground. "It's all my fault. I should have dissuaded her from coming here."

"They came for Oswyn. What else could you do?"

"But what was accomplished here? We never unlocked the secret of that ring, nor did we do anything to dissuade the family from coming after us in the future. This trip has been a complete waste of time."

"Not quite. You managed to discover what happened to these people."

"And how does that help? Most of them either died in the uprising or were recaptured by the Army of Ruzhina."

"You don't know that," cautioned Stanislav. "And, in any case, at least you saved a handful of them."

"And what will they do now? Live in the wilderness for the rest of their lives?"

"Stop feeling sorry for yourself, Athgar. Natalia's a smart woman. She'll find a way to escape. We already know she's found new allies. You must have faith in her."

"Sorry," replied Athgar. "My faith isn't what it used to be."

"That's only natural, considering our present circumstances."

"You're the last person I expected to talk about faith."

"Why would you say that?"

"I suppose I never saw you as particularly devout."

"Because I don't preach the Saints' teachings to everyone I meet? Religion is meant to give an individual strength, not used to bludgeon others."

"Isn't that the very thing the Church does?"

"Not so," said Stanislav. "Although, admittedly, there are some who take it too far."

"Like the Temple Knights of Saint Cunar?"

"They didn't attack us due to their religious zeal."

"They didn't?"

"No. If you remember, they were infiltrated by the family."

"True," agreed Athgar, "but we still don't know why."

The mage hunter shrugged. "We can speculate all we like, but I doubt we'll ever know the real reason."

A clopping sound echoed off the trees.

"Did you hear that?" said Stanislav.

"I did. It sounds like horses coming from the west." He called out, "Arm yourselves."

The others crawled out of their shelters, crude spears in hand, ready to face whatever might come their way.

"I'll go and investigate," said Athgar. "The rest of you stay here."

"And if it's soldiers?" asked Stanislav.

"Then I'll let off a signal."

"What type of signal?"

"Well, let's put it this way—if you see trees catching fire, you'll know it's bad."

Athgar fetched his bow, along with a handful of arrows, then began weaving his way through the trees, occasionally stopping to listen for the horses.

It didn't take long for him to locate them. A trio of riders made their way down the side of a hill, and the moment he saw them, he broke out into a grin. He ran forward, yelling as he approached.

"Natalia!"

"Athgar!" she cried out. Not a moment later, she was afoot and rushing into his arms. They crushed each other in a tight embrace and held on, ignoring everything and everyone around them.

"Good to see you too," said Belgast. "By the way, this is Galina. She helped us get your wife out of the Volstrum."

Athgar finally released Natalia, although he kept hold of her hand. "Thank you," he said to Galina. "You have no idea how much this means to me."

"I can imagine well enough," replied Galina.

"That reminds me," Athgar continued, "I have a surprise for you, unless, of course, Belgast has spoiled it?"

"Don't look at me," said the Dwarf. "I didn't tell her anything. Well, hardly anything. Obviously, I had to explain where you were."

"What's this surprise?" asked Natalia.

"I found Katrin."

"Katrin? Really? I thought she'd be dead by now."

"Not in the least. Now, come, and I'll take you back to our camp."

The group walked, leading their horses through the thick forest. Having finally arrived at their destination, introductions were made, and Natalia found herself at a loss for words. Instead of talking, she embraced her old friend, holding on to her as though she would vanish at any moment. With reunions out of the way, they settled down around the fire.

"The question now," said Stanislav, "is where do we go from here? The safe course of action would be to travel south, through the wilderness, until we reach friendly territory."

"That's definitely an option," said Athgar, "but I feel as though that would be admitting defeat."

"We're free of the family's clutches," said Belgast. "I would count that as a victory."

"True, yet we failed to do what we came here for. I wish there were some way to punish them."

"Perhaps there is," said Natalia.

"What are you suggesting?"

"My recent sojourn at the Volstrum has allowed me to add some spells to my repertoire."

"Such as?"

"Well, for one thing, I can transport us there at any time, not to mention return to Stormwind Manor."

"Yes," said Belgast, "but the Volstrum is a veritable fortress. And what would be the point of transporting us to the manor?"

In answer, Natalia held out her ring. "There's still the matter of this."

"But we don't know how to use it?"

"Don't we?" She smiled.

"You discovered something," said Athgar. "I know that look."

"Well, let's just say I have my suspicions."

"We searched the manor, remember? It didn't go well."

"On the contrary. We had the answer before us the whole time."

"We did? When?"

"When we searched Illiana's office."

"But we didn't find anything."

"Oh, but we did," said Natalia. "We just didn't realize it at the time. I think it's hidden in the portrait of Antonov."

"What makes you say that?"

"It's obvious Marakhova knew nothing of the key, or else why would she leave it in my possession?"

"But wouldn't Laisa have told her?"

"I imagine she kept its existence to herself, perhaps to use in the future as some sort of bargaining tool?"

"That makes sense," said Athgar. "But of all the paintings in the manor, why that one in particular—"

"Because it's her son," interrupted Stanislav. "It all makes perfect sense to me now."

"What does?"

"Well, the ring, for one. Illiana made it a point to give Natalia her own ring. She must have intended for you to discover the key."

"Yes," said Natalia, "but whoever thought I'd return?"

"Obviously, she did, else why give it to you?"

"To make sure someone else didn't get a hold of it?"

"In that case, why not destroy it?"

"He makes a good point," said Athgar. "The real question, however, isn't where this secret is hidden, but what it holds."

"Information," said Natalia.

"How do you know that?"

"What else could you hide in a painting? Although I suspect it's not so much the portrait as the frame."

Athgar was skeptical. "Just how much information do you think is there?"

"Oh, I don't know," said Belgast. "I imagine several sheets of vellum could easily be concealed. It depends more on the style of frame than anything else."

"It was thick," said Natalia. "And whoever crafted such a compartment had to be trusted to keep the secret."

"But why hide anything at all? She was the family's matriarch. There's no one more powerful than that."

"Actually, the matriarch is not as powerful as you might expect. Tatiana showed me that."

"She did?" said Athgar. "How?"

"She spied on Marakhova, even after Illiana's death. She told me there are factions at work inside the family. In that regard, it's no better than the Petty Kingdoms."

"Well, if you think about it, it is a type of kingdom. Granted, it may not have borders, but their influence is likely stronger than any single country on the Continent, with the possible exception of the Halvarian Empire."

"She wanted me safe from the family. Deep down, I believe she regretted everything they'd done. This was likely her way of sabotaging them."

"How did Antonov die?" asked Athgar.

"He self-immolated," replied Stanislav, "a fate often found amongst Fire Mages."

"Could there be some secret about his death somewhere in that portrait?" asked Athgar.

"Like what?" asked Natalia.

"Could he have been murdered?"

"I suppose anything's possible, but why? He died years ago, long before Illiana was anyone of import. No, it must be something else, something that could hurt the family if it got out."

"Like what?"

"I don't know, but we should find out."

"What are you suggesting?"

"That we return to Stormwind Manor," said Natalia. "All of us."

"I'm in," said Katrin.

"As am I," added Anushka. "It's time the family paid for what they did to us."

Athgar turned to the last member of their group. "What about you, Ulyana? What do you think we should do?"

"I agree with the rest of you, but with one condition."

"Which is?"

"That Natalia show me how to use my magic."

Athgar looked at his wife. "Have we the time for that?"

"I don't see why not," she replied. "Things will need to calm down a bit before we take on the manor. Right now, Marakhova is on the defensive. She'll be expecting resistance as she consolidates her power. A week or two will make little difference. In fact, it might lull her into a false sense of security. The real question is how easily Ulyana takes to it."

"How long does it take for your magic to transport us to Stormwind Manor?"

"About the same length of time it takes to walk from here to that tree over yonder."

"I'm jealous," said Athgar. "I wish I had a spell that would allow us to travel such distances."

"There is one—it's called ring of fire. Unfortunately, I don't have access to it, nor, I suspect, does the Baroshka."

"The what?"

"The Baroshka. It's a treasury of knowledge that lies hidden beneath the Volstrum."

"A pity we can't go there."

"Oh, but we can," said Natalia. "I can open a portal to it at any time."

"How would we return?"

"That's simple," added Galina. "She keeps it open, and I step through to retrieve whatever we want."

"And what do we want?" said Athgar.

"Well," mused Natalia, "there's the ancient book of knowledge I was studying, for a start, not to mention any other books we might find useful." She looked at Galina. "Are you thinking what I am?"

"That we raid the place? It's a good idea, but I'd warn against taking too much. After all, eventually, we'll need to flee Ruzhina, and that's a little hard to do with dozens of books to carry."

"Still, we could start by getting that tome for now."

"I'm ready whenever you are."

Natalia turned towards her husband. "What do you think, my love?"

"We should be cautious. There's always a chance Marakhova may have discovered this hidden room of yours. I'd hate for Galina to step through and be overpowered by guards."

Stanislav stood, surprising the others. "Then I'll go with her."

"As will I," added Belgast. "I assume your spell will allow that?"

"It will," admitted Natalia.

"I should go too," said Athgar. "If there are any mages present, my fire spells may come in handy. Even if it's only guards, my axe will prove useful."

"Then it's settled," said Galina. "Prepare yourself, Natalia, and let's see if we can get that book for you."

. . .

It would hardly help if a wild animal attacked Natalia while the portal was open, so Ulyana and Anushka stood guard as the rest prepared to pass through the arch of frost.

Natalia began the ritual, the air in the vicinity growing chilly. From Athgar's point of view, his wife looked like she was wrapped in white light as the frost swirled around her before it crystallized into an archway. He felt a snap, and then the space between the arches revealed a room.

Galina immediately stepped through, appearing on the other side and waving back at them. Belgast soon repeated her steps followed shortly thereafter by Stanislav and Athgar.

The room was nothing like Athgar expected. Admittedly, the description had been sparse, but the thought of a subterranean cellar conjured forth images of bare rock and stone. Instead, he now stood in a room of splendour.

Galina disappeared through a doorway, and he followed her to discover a large room full of parchments and books. She hefted a larger tome and edged past him, returning to the arch.

Athgar simply stared at the room, finding it difficult to absorb the full impact of everything. A tug on his arm brought him back to his senses.

"Come," said Belgast. "It's a lot to take in, but we must return before Natalia uses up all her magic. I know you'd like to explore this place. I imagine there are untold treasures here, from a mage's point of view, but look on the bright side."

"Which is?"

The Dwarf grinned. "With Natalia's power, we can return at any time."

"There is that," the Therengian agreed. "All right, let us return to camp, but I promise you, one day, we'll come back here and pick the place clean."

"Oh, we can do more than that."

"We can?"

"Of course. We're beneath the Volstrum, Athgar. The very place that represents the power of the family."

"You're forgetting Korascajan."

"Yes, good point," said the Dwarf. "Let's call it half the power of the family, then. Now, imagine what you could accomplish if you burned it to the ground?"

"It's too massive for that, surely?"

"If there's one thing I've learned over the years, it's that everything burns, but you're the master of flame. I'll let you work out the details. In the meantime, let's get out of here, shall we?"

Belgast stepped through the portal, following Galina. Stanislav waited, one hand on a pillar of frost.

"Coming, Athgar?"

The Therengian took one last look at the room before stepping through the frozen arch.

RETURN TO STORMWIND MANOR

Autumn 1108 SR

Stormwind Manor

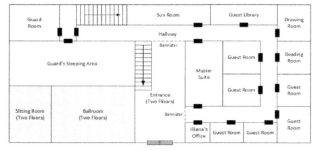

Upper Floor

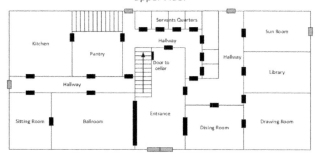

Ground Floor

Ulyana released the spell, and the ice shard struck the tree, sending bits of bark flying in all directions.

"Not bad," said Natalia. "Although I would prefer if you had hit the actual target."

"This is useless," replied Ulyana. "I guess I should have expected no less. Even you can't turn a failed candidate into a competent caster."

"Actually, you've made remarkable progress. You have no problem pulling the magic from within, only targeting it, and that will come in time."

"What if she tried something a little closer?" mused Athgar. "Artoch always said it was better to master one skill than two."

Ulyana knitted her brows. "Two?"

"Yes. What you're attempting is quite complex. You're calling forth your power, yet at the same time trying to estimate distance, calculate angles, and even account for wind, if the target is far enough away. The targeting alone is as complicated as using a bow."

"I can't exactly use an ice shard by touch."

"No," said Natalia, "but Athgar makes a good point. We should attempt a different spell. We could, for example, have you freeze water."

"That's hardly going to help when we enter Stormwind Manor. I might just as well carry a stick."

"How about creating ice?" said Athgar. "She could use that to freeze doors shut, couldn't she?"

"Yes," agreed Natalia. "That was one of Illiana's favourites."

Ulyana slumped to the forest floor. "Except we have no doors to practice on. We're in the middle of nowhere, remember?"

Katrin entered the discussion. "What about mist?"

Galina chuckled. "That was one of Nina's favourites, do you remember?" She turned her attention to Ulyana. "Come now, don't look so morose. Mist is a quick one, consisting of only three words of power."

"She has a good point," said Natalia. "Let's give it a try, shall we?" She led Ulyana away from the others, the better to concentrate on teaching her new student.

"This isn't going well," said Katrin. "I don't think she's cut out to be a battle mage."

"Nonsense," replied Galina. "It just takes some people longer to learn magic. We can't all be like Natalia and master things on our first attempt. What about you, Athgar? Did you have trouble learning magic?"

"I'm not sure I'd say trouble, but it required a lot of patience. Harnessing that kind of power is hardly natural. I'd liken it to herding deer."

"Deer?"

"I believe he means sheep," said Katrin, "but I see what he's getting at. There are so many things to worry about when casting. Not only do you have to remember the spell, but you need to form the images in your mind, as well as adopt a proper stance, particularly for a ranged spell."

"Yes," replied Galina. "I've fallen once or twice when casting. The blow-back from ice shards can be quite pronounced if you're not properly prepared."

"Blowback?" said Athgar.

"Yes, don't you get that with your fire streak?"

"Not at all."

"You do with ice shards," said Galina. "It pushes back as you release. It has something to do with the weight of the ice. I imagine Natalia has quite the time with it."

"Now that you mention it, she does often brace herself." He was about to say more when a thick mist enveloped them. All he could hear was a muffled curse. "I'm guessing she missed her target."

"This is useless!" called out Ulyana. "I'm never going to be a mage."

"But you already are," came the voice of Natalia. "Now, let me dismiss this, and we'll try again, shall we?"

Athgar waited, but the mist remained. "Is there a problem?" he shouted.

"Just a moment." The mist finally vanished. "Well, that was odd."

"Why? What happened?"

"I failed to dismiss the spell."

"That hasn't happened since when you were pregnant."

She laughed. "I'm not pregnant. I was merely being lazy."

"Meaning?"

"I thought I'd be able to do it by channelling only a portion of my power, but it appears Ulyana has more potential than we thought."

"How much more? You can't be suggesting she's as powerful as you are?"

"Not at the moment, but she's far more powerful than I would have expected for someone who failed the Volstrum."

"Meaning?"

"She has the potential to be a great battle mage, providing she can learn to control it."

"And for now?"

"We'll avoid picking distant targets."

That evening, they sat around the fire, discussing their options. Not that they weren't eager to begin the raid on Stormwind Manor, but they struggled to decide how to proceed once they arrived. Added to that was the stiff wind blowing in from the north, reminding them winter was on its way.

"I say we leave now," said Galina. "We're as ready as we'll ever be."

"Agreed," said Katrin, "but what time of day do we strike? If we go in too early, we'll stand a good chance of running across Marakhova"—she looked over at Natalia—"unless that's your intention?"

"Much as I'd like to see her at the receiving end of a spell, that's not our true objective."

"Then what is?"

In answer, Natalia removed her ring, rotating the magerite to reveal the key mechanism. "Illiana Stormwind herself gave me this ring. Somewhere in that manor house is a lock or secret compartment that holds something important."

"Like what?"

"I'm not sure, but she definitely didn't want Marakhova getting her hands on it. I think Illiana had a lot of regrets about whatever it is the family is up to."

"You mean sending mages to the courts of the Petty Kingdoms?"

"I believe it's something far more sinister."

"Such as?" piped up Ulyana.

"Galina might have more of an idea than me."

Everyone's gaze swivelled to the Volstrum instructor.

"I have no idea," the woman replied. "I know Illiana kept secrets. Saints know, the Volstrum is full of them, but only the most powerful of mages is privy to that sort of information."

"She makes a good argument," said Stanislav. "Could it have something to do with the Church?"

"Possibly," said Athgar. "We know a Sartellian infiltrated the Temple Knights of Saint Cunar and was successful enough to become a regional master of the order."

"No," said Natalia. "I don't think that's it. Don't get me wrong, it's disturbing, but there's more going on here that we're not seeing."

Athgar turned to the others. "As we said before, we believe the information is concealed in a portrait of Antonov Sartellian, Illiana's son."

"How do you hide information in a painting?" asked Ulyana.

"In the frame."

"Well," said Stanislav, "I wouldn't expect to hide much in a frame. Whatever it is must be concise and to the point."

"That's very much in keeping with Illiana's personality," said Galina. "Tatiana told me she was plain-spoken."

"Yet sophisticated enough to aid and abet your escape from the Volstrum."

"All this is well and good," noted Ulyana, "but the fact still remains we've got to get into Stormwind Manor. You told us you can use your magic to go there, Natalia, but how do we escape? Will your spell allow us to return here, to the wilderness?"

"No. The only way to do that would be to hold the arch open the entire time we're there, and even I don't possess that kind of power."

"That means we're fighting our way out," said Athgar. "Just in case any of you thought otherwise."

"And we'll have to go soon," offered Belgast. "Winter is coming, and the last thing we need to do is to escape and leave a nice trail in the snow for our enemies to follow."

"We'll go tomorrow," said Natalia. "Right after sunset."

"And if Marakhova is there?"

"Then we'll deal with her. I know it's not ideal, but as you said, the weather is turning against us."

"How do you suggest we proceed?" asked Galina.

"We'll begin by taking the arch to the manor's magic circle. Athgar and I will proceed up to Illiana's old office while the rest of you remain below. If things go badly, Galina will use another arch to take you to the Volstrum. At least there you can hide out until other arrangements can be made."

"Assuming you find whatever it is that's hidden, what's the next step?"

"Simple," said Athgar. "We return to the circle."

"We can't, remember? The spell can only target another magic circle."

"Then we'll rendezvous and leave by a more traditional route."

"What about pursuit?"

"I shouldn't worry too much about that," the Therengian replied. "They'll be far too worried about dousing the flames."

"What flames?"

"Didn't I mention it? I'm going to burn Stormwind Manor to the ground."

"You most certainly did not," said Stanislav. "Are you sure that's a wise idea?"

"They threatened my family. If you think I'll let them get away with that, you're sorely mistaken."

"From there, we head west," said Natalia. "If we can keep ahead of them, we'll hire a ship in Porovka."

"To sail back to Carlingen?"

"No, Svetlana is there. She might not harbour much love for the family, but she won't cross them, and once we've struck, they'll notify every court in the Petty Kingdoms to keep their eyes open for us. We'll sail west instead and land under assumed names, preferably somewhere that isn't under their influence."

"Is there such a place?" asked Galina. "Never mind, I don't want to think about it at present. We'd best get some rest. It's going to be a busy day tomorrow."

They assembled in a small clearing as darkness fell. Galina cast a spell, calling forth an orb of light to illuminate their surroundings. Each carried their meagre belongings, for never would they see their wilderness camp again.

Natalia began the spell, calling on her Water Magic to manifest the frozen arch. The familiar buzzing filled the air, and then the centre of the arch turned dark. Galina didn't hesitate, stepping through into the darkened chamber, letting her orb reveal its contents. One by one, they followed her lead until only Natalia and Athgar remained.

"Ready?" he said.

She nodded her head, then took his hand, squeezing it slightly. Together, they stepped through the arch into the chamber beneath Stormwind Manor. Galina's spell cast a soft glow, but that was soon joined by the magerite-imbued sphere Natalia had discovered on her last visit.

Stanislav had already moved to the door and was listening while the rest examined the room in silence. Natalia motioned for the other Water Mages to join her.

"Commit this circle to memory," she urged, "for we may require it in future."

"I'll show them how," said Galina, her voice hushed.

Athgar joined Stanislav. "Is it locked?"

"Let's find out, shall we?" Stanislav turned the handle, and the door swung towards him a hands-breadth. He peered outside to see a cellar, its walls lined with shelves and a set of stone stairs leading upwards.

Belgast pushed past them, his pick in hand. The Dwarf only went a few paces, enough to give him a better view of the stairs, before he turned and waved them out.

Athgar stepped into the room. They appeared to be in a storage cellar, although it took a moment for him to realize what exactly was stored here. He'd expected food but was surprised to see furniture of various sizes, along with a wide shelf stacked with picture frames. It made him wonder how unimportant a member of the family would be to be relegated to this pile of discarded portraits.

Natalia soon joined them. "Let's go," she said. "The rest will remain here to safeguard the circle."

"And if they're discovered?"

"Then they'll take what action they deem necessary to escape. In the meantime, we've got a painting to locate. You best go first; you're the stealthy one."

Athgar ascended the steps, axe in hand, ready to strike out should the need arise. At the top, he found a small landing with a door on one side similar to those above.

He pulled it open just far enough to take a quick peek before he quietly closed it and returned to Natalia's side, urging her down a few steps so they could converse.

"We appear to be coming up beneath the stairs in the main entranceway."

"That's good," she replied. "It means we can head straight to the upper floor."

"I'm afraid that's not all. I heard voices. Sounds like Marakhova is entertaining guests."

"Did you see them?"

"No, I don't think they're in the entrance hall, but off to one side or the other. Do you remember the layout?"

"Of course. I have been living here for the last few months."

"What's to the west?"

"A large ballroom. If Marakhova is having a get-together, that's the most likely place to do it. Either that or the dining hall. Did you hear the sounds of eating?"

"How would I hear eating?"

"The clinking of knives on plates. Someone talking with food in their mouth. Anything of that nature?"

"No."

"Then it's likely the ballroom. We can still get upstairs if we're careful. You remember the way to Illiana's office?"

"I think so. Up the stairs, then right, into the eastern side of the building. Continue on to the end, then loop around and take the other hallway overlooking the entrance hall at its end."

She smiled. "You have an excellent memory. Why don't you lead?"

"Watch your step. It's not well lit."

They returned to the landing. Athgar opened the door, leading Natalia out into the entrance hall, then alongside the stairs until they were almost at the bottom landing.

They would need to move in sight of the ballroom to go upstairs. Athgar waited, peering around the corner of the banister until sure none were looking.

He waved Natalia forward and then quickly followed her up. The top floor was dark, but enough light filtered up to find the hallway. Once they were heading east, Athgar conjured a small, green flame to light the way.

The floors creaked, so much so that they halted several times, fearing they would be overheard. They passed by the room they'd used to gain entry on their first visit, then the corridor turned westward. A dim light at the end marked where the hallway overlooked the entranceway. As they drew closer, Athgar extinguished the flame.

From their new vantage point, they could easily see into the ballroom, and for a moment, Natalia felt a wave of panic. Athgar gripped her hand, and she looked at him only to realize he was almost invisible in the dark. She calmed herself before she opened the door to Illiana's office. Athgar followed her in, closing it behind them before once more bringing the magical flame to life. Natalia stared at the portrait. Antonov Sartellian was a handsome enough man, but the frame was what interested her the most.

"Bring the light over here," she asked as her fingers felt around the edges of the portrait. Athgar stood at her side and lifted his hand, the flame floating above his palm, bathing the painting's edge in an eerie green light.

Natalia noticed what looked like a chip in the wood. She removed her ring, rotating the magerite to expose the key. With the gem pressed against the frame, the protrusion sat in a slight hollow. She now turned the ring and felt only the barest amount of resistance. Unsure of how to proceed, she looked at her husband, who simply nodded.

Applying a little pressure, she repeated the gesture. This time it rotated a full quarter turn before she noticed the portrait had popped out of the frame in one corner. She stared at it, hoping for inspiration before she concluded the portrait hadn't moved—the frame had. The bottom right corner had loosened from the front and now hung behind the picture. Natalia knelt and noticed that the bottom of the frame looked hollow.

Athgar moved his hand down, giving her more light to reveal what appeared to be a rolled-up parchment. "Looks like we found something."

"Yes," she agreed, "but what is it?"

"There's only one way to find out."

Natalia reached up, deftly grabbing the end of the parchment and pulling it until she could get a better grip. It easily slid out of its concealed location, revealing a tightly wound roll almost as long as her forearm. Having retrieved the document, she grasped hold of the frame and pulled it forward, feeling a satisfying click as it returned to its former position. Eager to peruse its contents, she moved to the desk and unrolled it.

Athgar held the flame off to one side to avoid igniting it. "Well? What does it say?"

She said nothing, so intense was her scrutiny, but her face went pale as she reached the bottom.

"How bad is it?" he asked.

Her eyes drifted up to her husband. "About as bad as it can get."

DISCOVERY

Autumn 1108 SR

A thgar held his breath. He could think of many things the family could do that would be considered 'bad', but Natalia's pale features had been entirely unexpected. Her hesitation to tell him of her discovery only made the situation worse.

"Go on," he finally urged.

"The family is in league with Halvaria."

"That's absurd. Why would they do that?"

"Because they ARE Halvaria."

"I don't understand."

Natalia sat down, too overcome with emotion to remain standing. "I should have realized," she said to herself. Athgar's look of confusion led her to work through her reasoning. "I knew the Volstrum trained a lot of mages, far more than would be needed for all the courts in the Petty Kingdoms."

"So they're sending mages to Halvaria?"

"Not only that. Think back to the history of Therengia."

"You mean about outside mages causing strife? We already suspected the family of that."

"Yes, but after the fall of the Old Kingdom, they learned what they did wrong. The next time they infiltrated a kingdom, they chose the court of Halvaria, only they didn't fail. It's the family who now controls it."

"But I thought they had their own emperor?"

"They do, but he's likely just a figurehead. I doubt he has any real power."

"Then why send mages to the courts of the Petty Kingdoms?"

"To make sure they never unite against the empire. Their job is to keep them fighting each other, weakening them all against the inevitable invasion."

"Wouldn't it be safer to train mages in Halvaria?"

"Not if they want the Petty Kingdoms to welcome them. As it stands, all the courts of the Continent fight over gaining a member of the family. It's seen as prestigious."

"So what do we do now? Expose them?"

"I don't know that it would do any good. Who's going to believe us when the only proof is a single letter?"

"But we can't let them get away with it!"

"I'm open to suggestions."

"What if we sent our own emissaries to each kingdom? After all, we now represent Therengia. That alone brings us plenty of attention."

"That's an excellent idea, but one I fear may be too late to save the Continent."

"Still, we must do what we can."

She cast her eyes down at the paper, a lone tear coming to her eye. "We can't go home, at least not yet."

"What are you proposing?"

"We have to break this hold the family has over the noble houses of the Petty Kingdoms. We ourselves must start the process. Only then will our emissaries be taken seriously."

He felt a sadness in his heart. She had the right of it, yet it meant they would not be able to return home to Oswyn. Then a thought struck him. "We must seek out other tribes of Orcs, so we can use their shamans to get word to Shaluhk."

"Agreed, but where do we start?"

"First, we get back to the others, and then we get free of this place."

"Very well." She carefully rolled up the paper and tucked it into her belt. "Help me move this desk."

"Whatever for?"

"So I have room to cast the frozen arch, unless, of course, you prefer to sneak back down those stairs?"

"No, no, it's fine. Here, let me help you."

They pushed it aside, clearing space for the frozen arch. Natalia began casting a long spell: a ritual, to be exact, and Athgar worried they might be discovered while she was in the middle of it. Much to his relief, the arch appeared, although it barely fit within the confines of the room.

She didn't wait for him to say anything. Rather, she took hold of his hand and pulled him through, emerging into the magic circle below.

"Did you find it?" asked Galina.

"We did," said Natalia, holding up the rolled parchment for everyone to see. "But now it's time to get out of here."

"On that note," said Athgar, "there's a slight complication."

"Which is?" asked Ulyana.

"It seems Marakhova has chosen this evening to invite guests over, and unfortunately for us, the only way out takes us right past them."

"What do we do now?"

"We fight," said Anushka. "What other choice have we?"

"There must be a better way?" said Stanislav. "Admittedly, Natalia is powerful, but as a group, we're hardly a match for the type of people Marakhova's likely to be entertaining."

"How about a diversion?" asked Belgast.

"Such as?"

"I don't know—a fire, perhaps?" He looked at Athgar.

"It would need to draw them away," said the Therengian.

"How about upstairs? That would at least clear them out of the lower floor."

"It's worth a try," said Natalia. "We should have remained in Illiana's office while we had the chance."

"Too late for that now," said Athgar. "I'll sneak upstairs and start a fire while you all wait here."

"No, I'll go with you. That way, we can use the arch to return here when we're done."

He wanted to say no but knew it would do no good. The rest stared at him expectantly. He nodded. "Very well, let's get to it."

Natalia and Athgar exited the room, again climbing the stairs up from the cellar. "Ever have the feeling we've done this before?"

Once again, they entered the front hallway, watching for any sign of discovery. Athgar led, taking the steps as quickly as possible once the opportunity presented itself. They were past being sighted by anyone in the ballroom and almost at the top step when disaster struck.

A shadowy figure on the upper floor came towards them from the east, and as it emerged into the light of the entrance hall, there was no mistaking the brown hair and grey eyes. When their gazes met, he knew there was no escape.

"Ethwyn!" hissed Athgar. His sister halted, clearly taken aback by the unexpected encounter.

"What are you doing here?" Her eyes moved slightly, taking in the form of Natalia. "I should have expected it."

"Listen to me," said Athgar. He opened his mouth to say more, to say anything that would prevent her from raising the alarm, but she was already casting. Athgar was pushed to the floor as Natalia threw herself at him, Ethwyn's streak of fire shooting over the stairs to strike the wall, sending flames rolling up to the ceiling.

"You filthy skrolling!" screamed Ethwyn, her hands already moving to focus her magical energies yet again. Natalia struck first, her hand thrusting out to fill the area with a thick mist. Athgar got to his feet, intending to descend the stairs, but from the commotion below, the guests evidently heard the altercation. A wave of heat came towards them as Ethwyn tried using fire to burn off the mist.

"This way," he shouted as he ran, making his way into the western end of the building. He turned around, fearing Natalia had been left behind, but she soon appeared through the mist, looking even more washed out than usual. The hallway ended in a door leading him to try the handle.

"We're trapped," she said, even as he discovered the door was locked.

He kicked out, but whoever built Stormwind Manor had spared no expense, and the door, made of shadowbark, resisted his efforts. The mist finally burned off, revealing a wall of fire crawling towards them. Athgar threw up his arms, extinguishing the flames.

A screech told of Ethwyn's frustration, and then more words of power began issuing from her mouth. Athgar reacted instinctively, sending a streak of flame down the hallway. His sister, too intent on her own casting, took the hit in the centre of her chest and fell backwards, screaming, although whether in rage or pain was unknown.

He followed his attack by rushing towards her. Not to be outdone, Natalia followed, pausing only long enough to quickly send ice shards down the stairs, with little to no time spent picking a target, but it did its job, giving pause to those below who were intent on climbing up after them.

Athgar ran past Ethwyn, then ducked as something flew at him from below. Ice struck the wall to his left, and then he was no longer on the top landing but in the eastern hallway. Natalia ran across the opening as a fire streak hit the ceiling, and then she, too, was in the hallway. Rather than follow her husband, however, she turned and cast, causing a wall of ice to block off any pursuit, at least for the present.

Belgast, waiting at the cellar door, listening for any signs of trouble, heard the commotion from upstairs. Although he failed to recognize the voice of Ethwyn, it was soon obvious things had not gone according to plan. He looked down the stone steps, but the disturbance had been loud enough to inform the entire group that something had gone horribly wrong. The Dwarf hefted his pick, testing its weight even as Stanislav came up the steps to join him.

"Ah well," said the old mage hunter. "Who wants to live forever, anyway?"

Galina, Katrin, Ulyana, and Anushka followed, discarding their weapons in favour of using spells. They all gathered at the top of the stairs and looked at Belgast, who held fast on to the door's latch. At a nod from Stanislav, the door flew open, and everyone raced through.

Galina was the first out. Having visited the manor before, she quickly took stock of the situation. She called up her magic, sending shards flying in the general direction of what enemies she could see. A Sartellian who had just fired off a blast of flame took a shard in the armpit and staggered back with a curse.

Anushka came second, sprinting for the front door. In her rush to escape, she failed to notice their opponents and stumbled into a woman in a bright-green dress. They tumbled to the floor, adding to the confusion.

Katrin and Ulyana squeezed through the door at almost the same time. Ulyana filled the area with a thick mist as Katrin threw up a circle of ice. The ice mirror appeared in time to deflect an attack, sending more ice splattering against the wall.

Galina smelled smoke. A Sartellian had been a little too free with their magic, and now a fire raged, although its precise location was difficult to determine in the mist.

The air suddenly cleared, and there could be no doubt why. Even as their eyes met, Marakhova cast anew. Galina threw up a wall of ice, desperate to stop the ageing matriarch. It sealed them in but prevented them from feeling the full force of the expected attack.

Anushka, the only one left out in the open, looked up to see a man staring down at her, a Fire Mage, if the scars on his face were any indication. He was twirling his hands around, conjuring his magic when she struck, kicking out with her leg and taking him in the shin. It did little damage but had the desired effect of interrupting his spell.

The floors groaned, and then came the sound of breaking wood. Even through the wall of ice, Galina saw something massive approaching, its head towering over everyone. It smashed into her spell, causing huge cracks to appear. One more hit was all it took, for the wall gave way, sending chunks of ice flying everywhere.

The creature standing before them was a massive humanoid, with distinct arms, legs, and even a head, but that's where the similarity ended, for its face was featureless, and instead of hands, it had large spikes that smashed the ice wall.

Galina had read of ice golems before but had never seen one in person. The creature loomed over her, and all she wanted to do was cower in fear.

Belgast pushed past her, driving his pick into what passed for the monster's foot. Chunks of ice slewed off, but the creature kept coming, forcing him to back up. It struck out with one arm, a sweeping gesture that lifted Galina from her feet and sent her smashing into the wall, where she slid to the floor, going motionless.

Belgast, fearless in the face of danger, struck out again, this time shattering the foot entirely. The golem struggled to remain upright, slowing its attack for the moment.

Katrin threw her efforts into another spell, encasing the golem's remaining foot in ice, and had she been able to continue, there could be no doubt her plan would have worked.

A Sartellian, spotting her efforts, had sent sparks flying to land beside her. Moments later, a fiery snake appeared, spitting flames and disrupting her concentration.

Stanislav ran forward to help Belgast but slipped on the ice and crashed into the golem. Anushka cast again, bringing up more mist and just in time, too, as more spells went off, ice and flames striking the walls on either side of her.

Belgast swung again, driving the pick down with all the strength he could muster. Into the other foot it went, and with the creature's base now shattered, it toppled to one side, crashing through the wall into another room. The Dwarf struggled to pick out his next target, but in the thick mist, all he could do was listen and keep low, the better to avoid incoming magic. Stanislav loomed out of the mist, shaking his head.

"This way," said Belgast, grabbing the mage hunter's arm. "We have to get out of here."

Smoke rolled down the hallway and seeped up from between the floorboards. Natalia's wall of ice held, but it was melting quickly as a shadowy figure on the other side poured magical fire into it.

"Come," said Athgar. "We'll circle around to Illiana's office."

"What good will that do?"

"The end of the hallway overlooks the entrance, remember?"

Even as he spoke, an enormous crash reverberated throughout the manor.

"What in the Gods' name was that?"

"Unless I'm mistaken," said Natalia, "that's an ice golem. Marakhova must have summoned it."

Athgar paled. Back at the Battle of Ord-Kurgad, Natalia had conjured just such a creature. Many Temple Knights of Saint Cunar had fallen attempting to kill the thing. What hope did a bunch of misfits have of defeating it?

Natalia grabbed his hand and ran, dragging him along with her. As they drew closer to the end of the hall, the scene in the entranceway grew most peculiar. Frost lined one wall while flames licked at the other, evidence of the magic being unleashed.

They skidded to a halt, taking stock of the fight below. A thick mist had filled the area, but thanks to all the Fire Magic, much of it had dissipated, making the entire scene look like the combatants waded through a waist-deep cloud. Beneath them, something rumbled, and Athgar could make out a gigantic frozen limb thrashing around as a streak of flame shot past them.

"They spotted us," called out Athgar. In response, he pointed a hand, sending a similar spell back at his opponent.

"We'll have to jump," said Natalia.

"Into that mess?"

She began casting. A cry from behind them caused Athgar to turn. Ethwyn rounded the far corner of the hall, with additional footfalls following her. Time was running out. He flicked his fingers, uttering words of power and was rewarded by three tiny sparks that flew down the hall and sank into the carpet.

Ethwyn ran forward, and as she reached the first spark, it erupted, sending a streak of fire upward, narrowly missing her. It did, however, make her pause. One of her allies rounded the corner and ran past, straight over another spark. This time the flame shot up, igniting the fellow's clothing. He let out a scream of pain just before he collapsed to the floor, rolling around, the agony of his cries echoing down the hall.

Natalia finished her spell, and the air, already abuzz with all the magic going off, hummed even louder. Athgar returned his attention to what she was doing. Before them, a ramp of ice descended to the main floor.

"How did you do that?" he asked.

"Never mind," she said. "Jump!"

He leaped over the railing and hit the ramp. His feet, unable to find purchase, slid out from under him, and he quickly accelerated as he descended. Someone stood at the bottom, a mage of some sort, preparing to cast a spell. Athgar smashed into him, sending the man sprawling. Moments later, Natalia came sliding down, and they both crashed into the legs of a table, grinding to a halt.

Behind them, the ramp effectively cut the enemy in two. Belgast and Stanislav came towards them, the Dwarf readying his pick for a strike. Athgar struggled to make sense of what was happening, but then the pick smashed into a nearby window.

"Let's get out of here," yelled Stanislav.

Athgar felt a sharp pain and looked down at a shard of ice sticking out of his leg. He cast his gaze around, looking for the mage responsible, just in time to witness Natalia unleash her fury. A streak of blue screamed across the room, and his attacker suddenly went stiff as their flesh froze. Hands dragged him up from the floor, and then Stanislav pushed him towards the broken window. Behind them, all was chaos.

Natalia spotted Katrin floating in the air, enveloped in a whirlwind of flames. Marakhova moved in for the kill even as a Sartellian encased the young woman in the tomb of fire.

In the end, Ulyana saved her. Ignored by those around her, she'd lain still, playing dead. Witnessing Katrin's imprisonment, she rose and seized a nearby candlestick, smashing it into the Sartellian's head. He crumpled to the ground, releasing his prisoner.

Again came the mist, but this time under Natalia's direction, cutting off everyone's view. She yelled out for her compatriots as she climbed through the window.

Athgar hobbled across the front lawn, an arm draped around Stanislav's shoulder. They paused long enough to look back at the manor. Flames were visible on the roof, and it wouldn't be long before the entire building was consumed.

Covered in blood and burns, Anushka staggered out the main door and, spotting the rest of the group, she started stumbling towards them. Before she had gone more than ten feet, she collapsed to the ground where she lay, unmoving. Natalia turned, ready to run over and help her, but Athgar held her back.

"No, she's dead, or soon will be. Look, the guards are coming from all over the estate."

Even as he spoke, one rushed up to the fallen woman, driving the tip of his sword into her back.

"Come," soothed Athgar, taking her arm. The group headed for the nearest group of trees, Belgast in the lead.

FLIGHT

Autumn 1108 SR

Ice shattered against the wall, sending shards flying everywhere. One clipped Galina's face, cutting her skin and causing blood to flow freely down her cheek. She cast another spell, conjuring forth a wall of ice, but with so much fire being thrown around, it wouldn't last long. When she spotted Katrin retreating towards her, she realized the battle was lost.

"Back to the cellar," Galina shouted. "It's our only hope."

She ran through the door and down the stone steps. Katrin followed, but as she passed through the doorway, an ice shard pierced her leg, sending her sprawling. Galina quickly reacted, rushing back up to drag her friend to the top of the stairs, slamming the door shut behind them before summoning ice to hold it secure.

Katrin staggered to her feet, blood running down her leg to pool on the floor. Galina took her arm and helped her down the steps. From above came the sounds of someone pounding on wood. The enemy quickly realized what she'd done, for the next sound was a rush of wind, and then flames licked at the bottom of the door.

They ran through the cellar and into the casting chamber as fast as possible. Katrin closed the door behind them, throwing her back against it to give it added strength. "We haven't much time," she said.

"I'll take us back to the Volstrum," said Galina.

"We'll be trapped there."

"Better there than here, and in any case, we'll be able to exit the Volstrum before they realize what's going on here at the manor." She began casting her spell to summon the frozen arch.

Everything appeared to be going well until Katrin felt the door shudder as someone threw their weight against it. Her eyes quickly went to Galina, but the spell was still in progress. She wanted to cry out, for they were so close to escaping, yet it would only take a moment more for the enemy to break down the door.

She hobbled forward, taking up a position within the circle before she turned to face the doorway. She heard a kick, and the door moved slightly. Another bang and the latch sprang free, allowing the door to fly open.

Katrin acted out of instinct, thrusting out her hands and casting the fastest spell she could think of. Ice appeared on the floor, quickly spreading to the walls. A mage rushed in, eager to get at his prey, but as his foot hit the ice, he lost his balance and fell, crashing to his knees. Behind him came a woman who cast a spark that sailed into the room and struck the floor. Moments later, a small serpent-like creature erupted, its body composed entirely of fire.

Small flames flew across the room when it spit, hissing as they hit the stone floor. Katrin crossed her arms and held on to her biceps, conjuring forth arcane power to protect her. Ice armour encased her just in time to save her life from the streak of flame sent to immolate her. Instead, it melted the armour on her right shoulder, the rest remaining intact.

The kneeling mage directed his attention to Galina, but as he thrust out his hand, frost engulfed it, slowing the limb and disrupting his casting.

A yell caught Katrin's attention, and she turned around to see her ally rushing through the completed arch. She tried to follow, but as she stepped, her leg gave way, and she flopped to the floor, the wind knocked from her.

More fire spit out, this time striking her leg. She heard the hiss as her ice armour melted away from another spot. Katrin dragged herself forward, desperately trying to reach the portal that lay just out of reach.

Hands seized her legs, and she knew she wouldn't make it. Flipping over onto her back, she kicked out at the woman holding her, catching her in the face. The mage staggered back, blood pouring from her nose even as the fire snake spat out another ball of flame.

Katrin flipped back onto her stomach and resumed her crawl. She saw Galina, who, having completed the transition to the Volstrum, turned and was now coming back towards her. Her hand reached out, grabbing Katrin's, pulling her through the magical opening.

A gob of fire came through the arch as Galina dismissed it, striking the wall with a hiss to then fall to the stone floor, where it quickly burned out.

"That was a little too close for my liking," said Katrin. "Did you see any of the others?"

"Only briefly. I heard Athgar and Natalia shouting, and the Dwarf was alive last time I saw him, but I can't speak to anyone else's fate." She looked down at her companion's leg. "Let's take a look at that, shall we?"

By the time they bound the wound, the pain had subsided to a dull ache.

"Now," said Galina, "I'll go and fetch us some fresh clothes, and then we'll walk out of the Volstrum as if it were any other day."

"You forget; you've been gone from the Volstrum for nigh on a week. Someone's bound to notice you've returned."

"A matter easily explained. I shall tell them I was gone on family business. Not a complete lie if you think about it."

"And how am I to leave when I can barely stand, let alone walk?"

"I'll use the same technique I did with Natalia. You wait here while I go and find a safe place outside the Volstrum to send a gate for you."

"And how will I know if you're caught?"

"Simple. No arch will appear. It's too bad we have no way of communicating with Natalia. She could just as easily open one herself. I need to give that some thought in future."

"Future," said Katrin. "Now that's an interesting choice of words. It wasn't so long ago I thought I'd die in the mines, so I'm not complaining, but it would be nice to settle down someplace where I felt safe."

"You and me both, but that place is not here nor is the time now." She moved closer, kneeling before Katrin and taking her hand. "We will be safe one day. I promise you, but you must be patient."

"Sure, why not? It's not as if I've any real choice in the matter."

Galina stood. "It's time for me to go. How do I look?"

"You're all covered in smoke and are dripping wet. You might want to change into something more befitting an instructor at the Volstrum."

"An excellent observation. I shall proceed to my office first, change, and then make my exit by way of the stables. With any luck, I'll have you out of here by mid-morning."

"Be careful," warned Katrin. "You know how ruthless the family can be when they get their blood up."

"You'll survive," said Stanislav, hovering over Athgar's leg. "You're lucky it didn't hit something serious, or you could have bled to death." They were in amongst the trees, the burning of Stormwind Manor lighting up the entire area.

"Poor Anushka," said Natalia. "She didn't deserve death."

"Any sign of the rest?" asked Belgast.

"I lost sight of Katrin and Galina. And as for Ulyana, the last I saw of her, she was about to face off against Marakhova. I doubt she survived." Tears came to her eyes. "All those years, I thought Katrin dead, and then I find her only to lose her again. Fate is such a cruel mistress."

The Dwarf snorted. "Fate. It's a word used to explain so much, yet it would seem to suggest our lives are mapped out for us. We Dwarves worship the Gods, and we all know how fickle they can be, but even so, we believe each individual is free to make their own way in life. The deaths of these fine individuals are not fate. Rather, it's the direct result of the family's evil actions. If anyone is deserving of fate's fury, it's them."

"All well and good," added Stanislav, "but we can't just sit here and watch the manor burn. The family will spare no expense to track us down and kill us."

"He's right," said Athgar. "We must leave before they begin hunting us. You take the lead, Stanislav. This is your country."

"Very well," replied the mage hunter. "We'll skirt the edge of Karslev, and with any luck, we'll be well on our way to Porovka by first light."

"I don't know if I can walk that far with this leg. You best leave me behind."

"We'll do nothing of the sort," said Natalia. "We've already lost enough people to this. I'll not lose my bondmate too."

"You sound like Shaluhk."

"I shall take that as a compliment. Now, as for transporting you, I would suggest we find the nearest river."

"To what end?"

"We can't use the roads, not with Marakhova on the lookout for us. A river will lead us to the coast and Porovka. Hopefully, we can hire a boat to take us out of Ruzhina. How many coins do we have?"

"None," mused Stanislav. "What little we had was taken when Belgast and I were arrested. You?"

"I've got a few," she replied. "Although I doubt it would be enough to hire a ship."

"What about a smaller boat?" asked Athgar. "A fishing vessel?"

"It's not likely that a fisherman would be willing to sail far enough for us to be safe."

"I might be able to help," said Stanislav. "I have some associates in Porovka who owe me."

"Do they have a boat?" asked Belgast.

"No, but they might have the coins to buy us passage."

"That sounds risky. Your last 'associate' didn't exactly show herself to be trustworthy."

"I might remind you that Laisa still concealed the existence of the ring. Had she done otherwise, we would never have been able to retrieve that letter of Illiana's."

"Let's not argue over the past," said Natalia. "We need passage, and we need it quickly. Marakhova will stop at nothing to find us."

They began the trip at first light, for stumbling around the forest in the pitch black of night served no one. Progress was slow as they needed to avoid the roads, but by noon, they had a magnificent view of Karslev.

"There it is," said Stanislav. "I doubt I'll ever see its like again."

"Come now," said Belgast. "Who knows what the future might hold."

"Laisa betrayed me, and I don't think the family will forgive me. No, my friends, I shall not willingly return here."

"Then it's good you have a new home in Ebenstadt," said Natalia. "And, I might add, a woman there who loves you."

The old mage hunter smiled. "There is that, I'll grant you. Very well, I'll refrain from further maudlin musings and concentrate instead on our flight from this oppressive place."

"Look at you," said the Dwarf. "Trying to impress us with all your fancy words. Have you finished, or is there something else you'd like to gripe about?"

"No, I'm done."

"Good. Now let's continue, shall we, instead of staring off at an ugly city. If I'm not mistaken, that river down there is just the sort of thing we're looking for."

Katrin sat on the floor, examining the magic circle. She wasn't sure if this was the precise method used to commit it to memory, nor would she until she finally learned the frozen arch spell, but at least it gave her something to do.

Time down here seemed unending, and her lack of a recent meal came back to haunt her. She wished for some roast venison, a particular favourite of hers, but then decided a lighter meal might be more appropriate. A vision of biscuits came to mind, only to be interrupted by a familiar buzz in the air.

Two ice pillars formed, with a top block finishing the arch. The center image shifted to reveal Galina.

"Come," she beckoned. "We haven't much time."

Katrin hobbled through to find herself within a small copse of trees. "Where are we?"

"West of Karslev." Galina pointed. "Over there is a carriage I hired to take us to Porovka."

"And then?"

"With any luck, we'll find Natalia and make our way out of Ruzhina once and for all."

"Hold on a moment," said Katrin. "How are you going to explain my presence to the coachman?"

"That's not a problem. He's a cousin of mine."

"You mean a member of the family?"

"No, I mean a blood relative. Yes, I suppose technically he was born a Stormwind, but he had no magical potential to rely on, so he sought a trade."

"As a coachman?"

"Ah… you catch on fast."

They moved out of the copse of trees, across a grass field where the carriage waited: not the most glamorous vehicle as far as such things go, but it looked well-travelled.

Galina opened the door, climbing in after Katrin. Once seated, she tapped the ceiling, and they rolled forward. The road entered a thickly wooded area shortly afterward, and they finally relaxed.

"We're safe for now," said Galina, "but once we get to Porovka, things are going to get difficult."

"In what way?"

"For one thing, we have limited funds. If necessary, I can probably hire on as a Water Mage, but that may limit where we end up."

"There's still the matter of finding Natalia," said Katrin. "We don't even know if she got free from the manor."

"Nonsense. She's nothing if not resilient, not to mention powerful. If any of us could make it out of there, it's her. The bigger problem will be finding her, especially since she'll be hiding from the family."

"Then how do we find her?"

"Simple, we don't. Instead, we look for her husband, Athgar. As a Therengian, he's likely to draw some attention. Of course, if Belgast is with them, so much the better. I should imagine it's difficult to hide the presence of a Dwarf in these parts."

"I think a ship offers our best chance of escape, but to where?"

"That's a good question," said Galina. "What do you know about the Northern Kingdoms?"

"Not much, I'm afraid. Geography was never my strong suit. Yourself?"

"Let me see, what was that rhyme? Oh yes. Carlingen and Braymoor, hugging the coast, Abelard and Eidolon, angrier than most. Erlingen and just to the south, and poor old Reinwick, the top of the mouth."

"The mouth?"

"Yes, it juts out into the Great Northern Sea. I suppose by that example, Eidolon would be the jaw."

"And where did you get this rhyme from?"

"I made it up, actually. It's a technique I use to remember things."

"It seems to work well for you, but haven't you forgotten one?"

"Which one is that?"

"Andover. I believe it lies south of Reinwick."

"So much for my learning technique."

"Don't worry," said Katrin. "I won't tell."

The carriage slowed, interrupting their conversation. A group of soldiers had blocked the road, and one of them approached.

"Pardon me, mistress," the man said as he drew closer, "but I need to have a look inside."

"Is there a problem?" Galina asked.

He opened the door and peered inside. "A group of renegades has attacked Stormwind Manor. All the roads from here to the coast are on the lookout for them."

"We're not in any danger, are we?"

"As long as you refrain from picking up strangers, you should be fine. Might I ask the purpose for your travel?"

"If you must know," said Galina, "we're on family business."

"Oh? Are you one of those groups of mages sent to track down the traitors?"

"As a matter of fact, we are."

"Then I shan't delay you any longer," said the guard. "You're free to be about your business."

The carriage rolled forward, taking them into the countryside.

"Well, that was interesting," said Katrin.

"Indeed," replied Galina. "It seems the family has given us a convenient excuse for visiting Porovka."

Athgar uttered words of power, and the small fire sprang to life. They were west of the city, where a thick forest sat on either side of the Michutskin River.

"Tomorrow, we'll head downstream," said Natalia. "Although I'm not sure what to expect."

"You still fear the family?" said Belgast.

"I do. They have ways of communicating over long distances, so word of our escape has likely reached Porovka by now."

"We might be better served by sticking to land and following the coast south into Zaran."

"Too dangerous," said Stanislav, "and much too time-consuming. By the time we made it out of there, every court on the Continent would be alerted to our flight."

"Then I suppose we have no option other than to return home," said Athgar.

"No," said Natalia. "That would be admitting defeat. We need to spread word of the family's treachery."

"Why?" said the Dwarf. "They've been doing this for generations. What difference will a few more years make?"

"The family serves Halvaria."

Everyone fell silent as the implications sank in.

"Are you sure?" asked Stanislav.

In answer, she pulled the letter from her belt. "This reveals everything."

Stanislav took it and tried to read its contents, but he could make out little in the dim light. "I'm afraid my eyesight isn't what it used to be. Can you summarize it for us?"

"First off, the family was responsible for the fall of Therengia. We suspected that, of course, but now we have confirmation."

"What difference does that make? The Old Kingdom has been dead for five centuries."

"Yes, but they learned from their failure and applied it to their new conquests."

"Are you suggesting Therengia was a trial run?"

"I doubt it was a trial," said Natalia. "I suspect they hoped it would succeed. In any event, when the time came to repeat the plan, Halvaria was already a growing empire."

"So they infiltrated it, and then what?"

"They took over. It's clear from Illiana's letter, the family controls it and has done so for some time. All their efforts in the courts of the Petty Kingdoms are meant to lay the groundwork for their eventual conquest."

"The problem," said Belgast, "is the only proof we possess is a letter claiming to be written by Illiana Stormwind."

Natalia bristled. "Claiming?"

"I'm sorry, but from the perspective of a Petty Kingdom, it could be a forgery. After all, they've invested fortunes in acquiring the finest mages for their courts, and you know full well the vast majority of them are either Stormwinds or Sartellians. Do you honestly think they'll believe our claims?"

"We have to unmask them somehow," said Athgar. "Now that we know what they're up to, could we lay a trap?"

"Such as?" asked Natalia.

"I can't think in terms of specifics. We'd need to take it one court at a time."

"Or," added Belgast, "the trick would be to start with those courts who don't have a family presence."

"Great," said Stanislav. "Where do we start? Does anyone have a list, because we're talking about a lot of kingdoms and a lot of courts? And it won't take long for word to get around that we're making enquiries."

"Let's not get carried away," said Natalia. "We've yet to reach the coast, let alone sail away to some foreign kingdom. We'd be better served to deal with the present rather than worry about the future. Now get some rest. We've got a long day ahead of us tomorrow."

RETURN TO POROVKA

Autumn 1108 SR

The next day, they kept to the river's southern bank. The terrain here was relatively open, consisting of patches of forest interspersed with fields of long grass.

They were crossing one such open area when Stanislav, who had taken the lead, turned his head to speak to Athgar. His focus soon shifted from the Therengian to where they had just come from.

"That doesn't bode well," the mage hunter said.

Athgar slowed, turning to look behind them. A dozen people were emerging from the distant woods. Not in itself a threatening gesture, but as they watched, one of them pointed at their group and gave a yell.

"They spotted us," said Stanislav.

"How did they find us?" said Belgast.

"Easy," said Athgar. "They have a hunter. If I'm not mistaken, that's Ethwyn."

"It can't be," said Natalia. "I saw her fall back in Stormwind Manor."

"She obviously wasn't as badly hurt as you thought." He scanned the area. "There's a small group of huts farther upstream. You and Belgast run ahead and see if there's anything there that could help us."

"Like what?"

"Maybe a building we can fortify? Stanislav, come here. I'll need your help if we're to hurry."

Natalia raced towards the structures, the Dwarf in hot pursuit. They were sorely disappointed if they were hoping for help, for this area had been abandoned for some time. The buildings themselves were derelict, one so bad its roof was collapsed.

She felt panic rising within her. The thought of making a stand entered her mind, but she quickly dismissed it. Even if they fought, there was no guarantee they would win, and if they somehow overcame their pursuers, there was still the danger of someone getting wounded. She had already lost too many friends. She resolved not to lose any more.

The river beckoned, and she wondered if they might cross over to the other bank. It would be easy enough to bridge the river with a spell, but as she drew closer, it became apparent why this particular location had once been settled, for a natural ford lay just beneath the surface. So much for cutting off the pursuit.

Then she spotted a piece of wood jutting out of some weeds. She rushed over to find an old wooden boat that had seen better days, the bottom seam split.

"That's unfortunate," muttered Belgast. "For a moment there, I thought our luck had turned."

Natalia quickly glanced back toward the forest. Stanislav and Athgar were drawing closer, but their pursuers were catching up.

"Perhaps it has," she said. "Help me get this thing down to the water."

"Don't be daft. It'll sink!"

"Not if I can help it."

Together they grasped the nose and lifted, tearing weeds as they worked to flip the boat over. Then they pushed it towards the river, but Natalia stopped as its end splashed into the river.

"Hold tight," she said. "This may take some time."

"Time," muttered the Dwarf. "The one thing we don't have."

Natalia began casting, but Belgast's eyes were on their comrades who were now passing by the ruined cluster of hovels.

"What's this?" asked Stanislav.

Her spell went off, creating a chill in the air. "Get Athgar in," she called out in haste. "Then push for all you're worth."

Athgar climbed in right before the boat slid into the water, propelled by the others. It took only a moment for the rest to join him, and then Natalia was once more calling on her magic. The water swirled on either side, and they drifted out into the middle of the river, gradually picking up speed.

Their pursuers emerged from behind the huts, and a few stray arrows were sent hurtling towards the boat. Athgar sent sparks flying to land on the shoreline. They exploded as the enemy drew near making them wary of coming any closer.

A final arrow struck, digging into the wood of the boat, remaining there as a sign of how close the encounter had been.

"I don't understand," said Belgast. "How did you get this thing to float?"

In answer, Natalia pointed at the broken seam, now sealed with ice.

"How long can you keep that up?"

"In this weather?" asked Natalia. "All day if necessary."

They spent three days on the river, fraught with panic every time they spotted anyone nearby. As they drew closer to the coast, signs of civilization increased. It started with the odd building or two, and then small hamlets and villages appeared by the water's edge. These they passed without stopping, for they feared word of their escape may have reached the area. Finally, the river widened considerably, the distant cry of seagulls telling them the coast was near.

"Time to abandon the boat," said Natalia. "They'll probably be on the lookout for it."

"We'll go north," said Stanislav, "bringing us to the Porovka road, and from there, we can enter the city."

"Won't they be expecting that?"

"For us to walk in the front door? I doubt it. In any case, I've travelled through here dozens of times. I know what to do."

They left the boat on the bank, taking time to cover it with leaves and branches.

"Are you sure this is necessary?" grumbled Belgast.

"Yes," said Athgar. "The last thing we need is for them to pick up our trail again."

Above them, higher up on the riverbank, Stanislav stood watch. Something caught the mage hunter's attention, for he disappeared from view, returning shortly with a smile on his face.

"What are you grinning at?" asked the Dwarf.

"It seems that once again, luck is with us. I secured us a ride."

"Meaning?"

"Come and see for yourself."

They all climbed up the incline to see a wagon sitting on the roadway, its bed stacked high with hay. Judging from his clothing, a local farmer sat up front, his team of horses snorting in the chilly morning air.

"This gentleman has agreed to take us to Porovka in exchange for a few coins." Stanislav paused, seeing the looks of apprehension on his colleagues. "He also assures me of his discretion."

"Well," said Belgast, "why didn't you say so?"

"I just did!"

The Dwarf ignored him, climbing into the back of the wagon, although admittedly with some difficulty due to his height or rather lack thereof. Natalia joined him and then helped Athgar up with the mage hunter's aid. Stanislav moved to sit beside the farmer while the rest settled into the hay as the wagon moved forward.

"We must be careful," said Natalia, keeping her voice low. "The family's agents will be all over the city keeping an eye out for us. The main thing is to keep Belgast hidden as long as possible. No offence, but Dwarves are rare in this part of the Continent."

"Their loss," replied the Dwarf. "But I'm not sure how long I can remain hidden. I mean, the hay here is fine for now, but sooner or later, I'll need to leave this wagon if we're to sail, not to mention the fact that this farmer, bless his soul, will want to sell off this hay. Where is he taking it, anyway?"

"I have no idea, but we'll deal with that once we're inside."

They fell silent as they approached the city. Stanislav stayed up front but insisted the others remained concealed amongst the hay. It was a tense moment as they proceeded through the gates, but they were spared any attention other than a quick acknowledgement of the farmer's wagon. A short time later, they rolled to a stop.

"Here we are," announced Stanislav. "Now, I'm going to visit an old acquaintance of mine and see about getting us a ship. The rest of you stay here."

"What about the farmer?" asked Athgar.

"Don't worry about him. I gave him some coins to go and get a pint or two at the tavern. You'll be safe enough for now as long as you remain here."

Belgast sneezed. "Great. Just what I always wanted, to be buried in hay."

"Hush now," said Natalia. "You must be patient… and quiet. It wouldn't do for someone to pass a wagon full of hay that was cursing."

"Who said I was cursing?"

Athgar soon dozed off. In his dream, he was trying to run from a torch-bearing mob. To make matters worse, he moved as if he were running through a tar pit, and his pursuers were led by none other than Ethwyn. He awoke with a start, only to see the face of Natalia staring down at him, a look of concern gracing her features.

"Are you all right?" she asked.

"Yes, fine, aside from this throbbing leg, of course. Only a dream, nothing more."

"You mean a nightmare?"

"I suppose that would be a more accurate portrayal, yes." He shuddered. "I have this unshakable feeling Ethwyn is near."

"Then we must take extra care. The last thing we need is for you to have an unexpected family reunion."

"How long was I asleep?"

"Some time, actually. It's well past noon, and Stanislav should be back soon."

"Here he comes now," said Belgast.

The mage hunter strolled down the street as if it were a perfectly normal day. He halted at the wagon, breaking into a grin as he looked up at them.

"You found your friends?" said Natalia.

"Better than that. I found us a ship!"

The road leading into the port city was packed with people trying to enter. Guards wandered up and down the line, inspecting anything big enough to conceal someone. Upon reaching their carriage, Galina informed them they were on family business. They were waved through with no further formalities, and finally, they arrived in Porovka unscathed. They wandered around the city, wary of being recognized, but it soon became apparent they were not the object of everyone's interest. Far from it, in fact, for they found themselves approached by a fellow mage, his magerite ring quickly identifying him as such.

"Greetings," he said. "Have you received your assignments?"

"We have," said Galina, easily slipping into the lie. "They want us down by the docks."

"Might I ask why?" the man responded.

"We have some familiarity with those we seek. That is to say, we know their faces. It's thought they might try boarding a ship, and our job will be to observe the harbour and report any sightings should we be fortunate enough to spot them."

"The docks are down there," he said, pointing. "I wish you well in your endeavours."

"Thank you," said Galina. "Now, you must excuse us. We have work to do."

They headed down the road, the smell of the sea soon drifting to their noses. Before them, peeking out over the tops of houses, was an assortment of masts, and Katrin wondered how many ships were presently at anchor. The answer soon presented itself as they cleared the buildings to see the waterfront.

"By the Saints," Katrin said. "There must be fifty ships or more. How are we ever going to locate them?"

"We watch for the Dwarf, remember?"

"Us and every other member of the family."

"We'll have to be on the lookout for all of them, as well."

"At least no one here knows us."

"So far," warned Galina, "but any recent graduate may know me by sight, so we shouldn't take any unnecessary chances."

"We don't even know if they made it to Porovka, let alone all the way down to the docks. Where should we start?"

"The first step will be to find a tavern, one where they serve sailors. If anything's going on around here, they'll have heard of it."

"And you believe they'd tell us if they were here?"

"Not at all," said Galina, "but if anyone has laid eyes on a Dwarf, it'll be the talk of the town."

That evening they sat in the corner of a tavern, sipping their drinks and listening to those around them. There were all kinds of discussions concerning the fugitives, as people liked to call them, but little in terms of actual facts.

Katrin despaired of discovering anything of value, but then a woman entered the place with a trio of warriors accompanying her. That in itself wasn't anything to make her noteworthy, but as the woman turned, the mage noticed her grey eyes.

"That woman," she hissed. "She's a Therengian."

"What of it?" replied Galina.

"They're scarce in Ruzhina. What do you think the odds are of her being here the same time as Athgar?"

"Too high to be a coincidence. What is it you're suggesting?"

"Let's be patient and listen, shall we?"

They resumed their drinking, listening carefully. It didn't take long for them to hear all they needed to know. The woman identified herself as Ethwyn Sartellian and began asking around the tavern after someone she claimed was her brother. By her description, she obviously meant Athgar. When she mentioned he was in the company of a Dwarf, everything fell into place.

The Fire Mage even walked over to Galina and Katrin, but their claim of knowing nothing was readily accepted, and she soon left, her warriors following.

"Come," said Galina. "It's time we looked into this further."

"How?"

"We'll follow her and learn what she knows."

The city's streets were dark, with only the moon's glow to light their way. Ethwyn made several stops, each time enquiring as to the whereabouts of her brother but came up empty on every occasion. She was becoming increasingly frustrated, for even from their place of concealment, Katrin could hear the annoyance in the woman's voice.

Close to midnight, another individual approached, someone who carried some authority, for Ethwyn bowed her head in greeting before the two of them exchanged words. Their interaction now complete, the visitor turned, and the entire group hurried down toward the docks.

"Something's up," said Katrin. "Do you think they discovered Natalia and the others?"

"I can think of nothing else that would cause them to be in such a hurry, can you? Let's follow and see where it takes us."

The city's docks were extensive, with ships packed together so tightly that a dexterous individual could quite literally jump from one deck to another with a bit of luck.

Ethwyn and her guards took up a position in the northernmost section of the bay, along a stone-walled jetty jutting out into the water. Five ships were tied up here, one a massive cog: the others, smaller merchant vessels.

As they drew closer, Ethwyn pulled her men aside, moving into the shadows of a pile of crates awaiting loading. Katrin held her breath, fearful of giving their position away, even at this range. She and Galina held a similar position farther east and watched with great interest.

A life at the Volstrum had done little to prepare her for this kind of thing, and Katrin's heart beat so fast, she swore it could be heard all along the dock. They crouched there for some time, so long, in fact, Katrina's back started aching. She was about to say something to Galina when she spotted a small group of people heading down the jetty, one of them clearly a Dwarf.

MAELSTROM

Autumn 1108 SR

Athgar halted. "Something's wrong. It's too quiet."

"Don't be ridiculous," said Stanislav. "Everything's fine. It's the middle of the night. What did you expect, a party?"

Belgast grabbed the mage hunter's arm. "No, he's right. I see them."

"Where?"

"Up ahead," said the Dwarf. "No doubt they're well-hidden amongst the shadows, but with my night vision, they're as plain as day."

"How many?" asked Natalia.

"Four at least, possibly more hidden by the crates."

"Keep going and get ready to fight. It's our only chance of getting out of here."

"Wouldn't it be better to head deeper into the city?"

"No," she replied. "They know we're here, else why lay in wait? I'm afraid your contact has betrayed us, Stanislav."

The mage hunter sighed. "Again? I don't seem to have much luck these days. I suppose there's no point in boarding the ship, then."

"Nonsense," said Athgar. "I'm sure the captain will be more than willing to take us out to sea."

"What makes you say that?"

"Because if he refuses, I'll burn his ship to the waterline."

"Here's how we'll do this," said Natalia, keeping her voice low. "Once we're close enough, we'll rush the ship. As soon as we're aboard, Athgar cuts the ropes, and I'll use my magic to propel us into the bay."

"And what of us two?" asked Stanislav.

"Your job is to find the captain as quickly as possible and put a sword to his throat. That should guarantee his co-operation."

"And if he refuses?"

"Then kill him and repeat the procedure with the first mate, but for now, just keep walking as if we don't know they're lurking nearby."

They continued towards a small ship named the *Golden Chalice*—a single-masted vessel with a flush deck forward and a raised aft castle, making it look slightly unbalanced. A pair of crew members lounged on the deck, keeping an eye on things, but as the group drew closer, those hidden in the crates stepped out from behind their cover.

"That's far enough," called out Ethwyn. "Your plan has failed, Brother. Surrender yourself now, and your deaths will be merciful."

Athgar met her gaze. "How generous of you, Ethwyn of Athelwald." The taunt had the desired effect.

"That's Ethwyn Sartellian," she yelled back. "Not that I expect you to understand such things."

"I understand them all too well."

"Keep your hands where I can see them, or my archers will fill you full of arrows."

"You have three archers," said Athgar, "and there are four of us. Who then, shall they target?"

"I've had enough of this," she roared. She intended to attack, for her hands were moving around. Her casting, however, was interrupted by a bolt of ice that sailed past Athgar's group and ripped into the shoulder of the man to her left. He let out a scream and dropped to the ground, blood spurting from the wound, the action breaking her concentration.

Athgar immediately began a spell of his own, conjuring forth a streak of fire and sending it flying.

"Run," shouted Stanislav.

Having noted the ice bolt, Natalia looked behind them to see two people running towards them. She readied a spell and was about to cast when Katrin called out.

Belgast, obeying the mage hunter's command, bolted for the *Golden Chalice*. A wooden plank had been laid across the ship's railing to ease boarding, and he raced across it, screaming out a challenge. Roused by this sudden rush, one of the crew members tried to block his path, only to be bowled over by the Dwarf.

Arrows flew from Ethwyn's two other warriors, one missing entirely while the second struck Natalia, failing to puncture flesh but catching in the sleeve of her dress.

Ethwyn stepped back, keeping her two men between her and Athgar's group and began another spell. Stanislav, meanwhile, crossed the boarding plank, joining Belgast aboard the *Golden Chalice*. Galina and Katrin broke into a run as yelling behind them revealed more soldiers following in their wake.

Natalia was struck with indecision. The ship that would let them escape was near, yet to run now might condemn Katrin and Galina to capture. It took only a moment for her to make up her mind, and then she turned and cast a spell, causing a thick fog to manifest behind her friends.

The effect was most satisfying, denying those coming from using their bows. She spun around just in time for Athgar to push her aside. The smell of smoke and fire raced past her, striking the dock, and then a loud screech echoed along the jetty. Natalia looked up to see a phoenix hovering in the air, its fiery feathers lighting up the area with an eerie glow.

She'd faced one such creature before, back in Caerhaven, and the sight now held little fear for her. Calling forth her inner power, she released a massive ice spear, sending it crashing into the flaming bird. The impact sent tiny splinters of fire flying everywhere, but somehow the thing survived, letting out another screech before it dove towards them.

Knowing fire would do little damage to the monstrosity, Athgar instead chose to dampen the fire, snuffing out the flames and the creature's very existence with them.

Natalia ran for the ship, Athgar following. Once aboard, they turned, ready to cast more spells, but Ethwyn, surprised by the sudden demise of her conjuration, backed up, putting some distance between them.

Belgast, having retrieved a hatchet from somewhere, began cutting the ropes holding the *Golden Chalice* in place. The ship bumped up against the dock before Natalia cast her spell to draw it out into the bay.

Galina ran, throwing herself across the gap as the boarding plank fell into the water. Katrin, not as fast, fell short, her hands catching the railing just before she would have slipped. Athgar ran over, grasping her forearms and lifting her onto the deck where she lay, gasping for breath.

The water around the ship swirled as the *Golden Chalice* eased out of her mooring. Someone started calling out orders, and Athgar looked aft to see the captain yelling at his crew even as Stanislav stood with a sword at the fellow's back. A dozen men swarmed the deck, some to take up ropes, while others began climbing the mast, ready to drop the sail.

The ship was propelled backwards, easing away from the dock. Ethwyn, emboldened by their slow departure, sent a streak of fire towards them, hitting the bowsprit and setting it alight. Athgar got to his feet and ran forward, using his magic to quench the flames, leading his sister to scream out in anger.

The jetty came alive with torches as more soldiers rushed to her aid. Arrows flew forth, but few came close to finding a target, and those that did only hit the hull.

Natalia guided them out, then turned the ship through a ninety-degree angle, aiming the bow for the open sea. The sails were dropped, quickly picking up the wind, and then the Water Mage adjusted her spell to propel them forward instead of reverse. The *Golden Chalice* responded with a sudden change in momentum, sending Athgar crashing to the deck.

They were well out to sea and heading westward by morning, the city having long ago disappeared behind them. It looked like their flight had been successful until word came that sails had been sighted to the east.

"It's Ethwyn," said Athgar. "I'd bet my life on it."

"I hate to admit it," added Belgast, "but she's like a mad dog who needs to be permanently put down. Trust me, I wish there were another way, but the woman is tenacious, to say the least."

"I'm forced to agree, but there's nothing we can do about it at this precise moment unless you're suggesting we turn around and engage her ship?"

Stanislav moved to stand beside them.

"I thought you were guarding the captain?" said the Dwarf.

"And so I was, but he says it's no longer necessary. I'm inclined to agree with his reasoning."

"Which was?"

"He's fled from the family. If they catch us now, they'll likely burn his ship and kill everyone aboard. Like it or not, our fate is his as well."

"Any idea of where he thinks we should go?"

"He suggested Abelard," said Stanislav, "or possibly even Reinwick. Any closer, and we run the risk of coming across members of the family."

"Interesting," said Athgar. "Do we know whether the family is at the court of Abelard?"

"Unknown, but I've heard the Duke of Reinwick had a disagreement with them some years back. His court has been off limits ever since. In fact, it caused such a ruckus, I was specifically told not to recruit mages there."

"How long ago was that?"

"About ten years, I believe. Why? Does it matter?"

"No, I suppose not. It sounds like that might be the better destination for us, but I'd like to see what Natalia thinks."

"Isn't she busy using her magic?"

"Her spell is cast. Aside from refreshing it from time to time, she has only to monitor the results."

"Very well," said Stanislav. "Consult your good wife and come to a decision. The rest of us will stand with you whatever you decide."

Athgar placed his hand on the mage hunter's shoulder. "Thank you, Stanislav. That means a lot to us."

Natalia adjusted her spell, making a slight correction to port.

"You hardly need the sails," said Athgar.

"Oh, yes, I do," she replied. "Favourable seas will help us move faster, but it's no match for canvas."

"It seemed to move us all right back in port."

"Yes, but that was just us backing up. It might have seemed fast at the time, but it pales compared to what we're doing now."

"We have a possible destination. I wanted to see what you thought."

"Go on," she urged.

"It's been suggested we make for Reinwick. Apparently, there was a falling out with the family about ten years ago."

She nodded. "A good choice. It'll give us a chance to get ashore without being pursued. If memory serves, their southern border leads to Andover, and from there, we could go anywhere."

Athgar looked aft. "I swear that ship is getting closer."

"It likely is. It has more sails."

"But won't your magic give us the advantage?"

"There's only so much I can do. A ship's speed depends on many things, including the shape of the hull and the number and configuration of the sails. Remember the *Bergannon*?"

"That's one ship I'd prefer to forget, but I see your point. Still, if Ethwyn is coming, wouldn't we be better off to turn and fight?"

"What makes you think it's Ethwyn?"

"She's not one to give up easily."

"She's a trained Sartellian now," said Natalia. "That makes her a dangerous adversary."

"I'm well aware, but I'm confident I can suppress any fire she throws at us."

"All right. I'll tell the captain to bring the *Golden Chalice* around, and we'll see if our ship lives up to her name."

"Her name?"

"Yes. You've never heard the tale of her namesake?"

He placed a thumb to his chest. "I'm a Therengian, remember?"

"The Golden Chalice was supposed to be the vessel that served wine the first time the Saints sat down together. It's said to bless all with the wine it pours."

"And people actually believe this?"

"They do, although the story first came to light many centuries after the Saints' deaths, so the truth of the tale is in doubt by most scholars."

"Well, let's hope THIS *Golden Chalice* blesses US."

The enemy had the wind behind them, closing the range quickly while the *Golden Chalice* struggled with its change in direction.

"How will we stop it?" said Athgar. "Should I set it aflame once it's close enough?"

"I doubt you'd be able to," said Natalia. "If Ethwyn is truly aboard—"

"She is. I'm sure of it."

"Then she'll use her own magic to dampen any fire, just as you would do to her."

"Shouldn't my power be greater? After all, my magic was unlocked much earlier than hers."

"That matters little in the long run. You're both of the same bloodline, but history tells us that means little in terms of power. The family's past is rife with examples of siblings with uneven potential. Sometimes a sibling doesn't have any magic at all. You also have to account for her training. Her repertoire of spells likely exceeds your own. Remember, she's a battle mage, with all the knowledge that training entails."

The enemy vessel bore down on them with all speed. They were close enough now that there was no longer any doubt as to whether Ethwyn was there, for she stood at the bow of the ship, glaring at them.

The first sign of battle surprised them both. Ethwyn thrust out both arms, sending a streak of flame racing over the sea, striking the *Golden Chalice*. The ship's bow took the brunt of it, and Athgar smelled burning wood. He rushed forward, lest he was needed to extinguish the fire, but the sea had already seen to it.

Another streak shot out from Ethwyn, this one directly at Athgar. He brought up his own counter to the spell, and the two streams met mid-air, sending fire splattering out to either side.

He felt the force of her magic pushing his own fire streak back towards him even as he poured everything he had into it. It became a test of might, a struggle to see who could outlast the other. Athgar forced his mind to calm, concentrating on the flow of magic rather than the target. Slowly, his spell grew more powerful and began pushing back, inching the flames towards the enemy ship.

Ethwyn broke contact, throwing herself to the side to avoid the sudden release of Athgar's power. Flames struck the mainmast, curling up it to lick at the sails while warriors stood waiting on the enemy's deck, weapons in hand, ready to board the *Golden Chalice*.

Natalia released a spell, summoning, once again, the swirling waters that would enable the ship to move against the wind. Athgar cursed as an arrow narrowly missed his head. He'd been so intent on his sister's actions that he forgot about the archers they'd encountered back in Porovka.

The two ships passed each other, going in opposite directions, their hulls so close one could almost jump across the gap. Ethwyn raised her hands as if lifting a great weight, and then a blast of heat washed over Athgar as the deck beneath him caught fire. He turned his attention to saving the ship, letting the enemy continue past.

Natalia, meanwhile, focused her energy on turning the ship, a slow process, especially considering they were moving directly into the wind. As the *Golden Chalice* changed direction, the sails filled.

Ethwyn's ship also turned, the entire encounter like some bizarre dance of death. More fire shot out, setting alight the sails, and in response, Athgar was again forced to suppress the flames. Katrin and Galina appeared on deck, making straight for Natalia.

"How can we help?" asked Galina.

"There's only one way out of here," explained Natalia. "We can't out-sail them, and Athgar's expending all his energy keeping Ethwyn's fire at bay."

"What are you suggesting?"

"The next time we close, I'm going to abandon my current spell. Instead, I shall conjure a maelstrom."

"Are you sure that's wise?" said Galina. "That could spell disaster for all of us. Why not freeze the water? That would hold Ethwyn at bay."

Natalia shook her head. "No. She'll never stop looking for us. The only way to keep Oswyn safe is to end this, once and for all."

The two ships turned to face once again, and as the enemy came closer, Natalia began casting, pouring all the energy she could into the arcane words.

The waves rose higher as the wind picked up. The deck heaved, the clouds darkened, and then Natalia felt droplets of rain. Her litany continued, the wind being whipped into a gale force. Those on deck struggled to grab railings or rope, anything to keep them from being blown into the sea.

A massive swell lifted the *Golden Chalice* on high, holding it there a moment before it crashed down into a trough. Natalia lost sight of the other ship but kept casting, knowing it, too, was trapped within the maelstrom.

The ship shifted to starboard, and then it tilted to her left, revealing the giant whirlpool sucking both ships towards an inky, black doom. Her feet began slipping, and then Athgar was there, his hand around her waist, holding her, keeping her from sliding into the abyss.

Ethwyn's ship tilted towards them, so much so that Natalia feared their masts would become intertwined. Yet, still, she let the magic flow through her, releasing any sense of control.

Even in the midst of the maelstrom, she heard the sound—a great cracking as the enemy vessel's hull split under the stress, suddenly sinking low in the water, then disappearing into the giant maw, leaving only debris.

Natalia collapsed, blood flowing freely from her eyes and mouth. The winds immediately died down, the rain stopped, and then she saw Athgar looking down at her, concern written on his face before everything went black.

EPILOGUE

Autumn 1108 SR

A ngveld Stein looked out to sea on a chilly autumn day. Fluffy, white clouds floated by, born by the west wind, but farther out, they were much darker. Ordinarily, he would have dismissed such a sight, for the weather here was known to be fickle. Still, the distant clouds, as if sensing him watching, dissipated unexpectedly and, before long, were no different from the rest of the sky. He shook his head. This was strange weather indeed.

Later that morning, he had cause to remember the peculiar sight, for as he walked along the beach, he spotted something floating towards him. Halting in his tracks, he once more gazed out across the Great Northern Sea. Barrels, odd bits of rope, and assorted planks of wood all drifted inland, born by the tides in these parts.

Angveld wondered who had suffered such a catastrophe, for it was obviously the remains of a shipwreck. He moved closer until he was knee-deep in the water. If a ship had been wrecked, there was a good chance that whatever it carried might be salvaged. His eyes lit up with the prospect of treasure, for life had been hard on him, and surely this was a gift from the Gods?

A particularly large section floated towards him, and his jaw fell open as he spied a body lying atop it. He rubbed his hands together in anticipation, for it wasn't unreasonable to assume a dead man might have some coins on him.

He moved farther out, the chilly water taking his breath away as it reached his waist. Now close enough to grab the very edge of the flotsam, he pulled it. Much to his surprise, the figure moved, raising its head to reveal the pale face of a woman, her cold, grey eyes staring out at him.

Angveld Stein stumbled back, his heart pounding. He'd hoped for a quick coin or two, but the Gods, seeing his greed, chose to punish him by sending an undead Therengian. He turned and ran, screaming all the way back to town.

Ethwyn slipped into the water and waded ashore. She was battered, bruised, and thoroughly waterlogged but still alive. The stranger's screams faded into the distance as her feet touched dry land.

She turned, looking out to sea and raised her fist in defiance. "I shall find you, Brother," she shouted, "and when I do, I will destroy all you hold dear."

Her curse complete, she held her hands out to the side, intoning words of power. Wisps of smoke appeared where the ring of fire hit drops of water, and then flames leaped up, obscuring the sight of her. Moments later, the fire subsided, leaving only a burned ring to mark the fact anything had ever been present.

<<<<>>>>

ENJOY THE STORY? LEAVE A REVIEW FOR MAELSTROM

CONTINUE THE SERIES WITH VORTEX

If you enjoyed *Maelstrom*, then *Temple Knight*, the first book in the Power Ascending series awaits your undivided attention.

START READING TEMPLE KNIGHT TODAY

SHARE YOUR THOUGHTS!

If you enjoyed this book, I encourage you to take a moment and share what you liked most about the story.

These positive reviews encourage other potential readers to give my books a try when they are searching for a new fantasy series.

But the best part is, each review that you post inspires me to write more!

Thank you!

TEMPLE KNIGHT - CHAPTER ONE

INDUCTION

Spring 1095 SR*
(Saints Reckoning)

Charlaine deShandria stood motionless on the street, her sword resting loosely within its scabbard, ready at a moment's notice. Her fellow initiates were there with her, each dressed in the white cassock of a knight in training, bearing the scarlet waves of Saint Agnes, the colours reversed from that of a full Temple Knight.

Of those gathered, she was the oldest by far. Most joined the order between the ages of sixteen and nineteen, but at twenty-four, she had started much later in life. The Archprioress had assured her that such a thing was not unheard of, but her experience thus far said otherwise.

Charlaine looked to her fellow initiates who were standing nearby, nervously watching the run-down boarding house before them. Their orders had come early that morning. Stand guard and keep any spectators at bay while the knights of the order searched for a criminal.

A Temple Captain of Saint Agnes, resplendent in her plate armour and scarlet tabard, looked their way. "You are only here to keep people back. Do not enter the building, is that clear?"

"Yes, Captain," they echoed back in unison.

The knight, satisfied her instructions were understood, joined the other members of the order as they moved forward, shields to the front with weapons drawn. The captain advanced, kicking open the door as she led her contingent of six into the building.

The sounds of fighting quickly drifted towards them, the ring of metal on metal, the grunting and yells that accompanied such things. One of the other initiates yawned, but Charlaine remained focused on the front door.

Suddenly, a Sister Knight staggered out of the building and fell to the ground, blood pouring from an arm wound. A large man, easily topping the knight by a head or more, followed her out, his bloodied axe raised for a death blow.

Charlaine acted instinctively, drawing her weapon and rushing forward while the others simply looked on in horror, frozen by the spectacle that was unfolding before them.

The axe came down, but instead of sinking deeply into the flesh of the knight, it scraped along a sword blade, deflected at the last moment. Its wielder turned on Charlaine in shock and annoyance, the rage upon his face now directed solely at her.

She backed up slightly, giving herself some room to effectively wield her sword. As he lifted his axe for another strike, she stabbed forward with the point of her blade, a clean, efficient stroke that punctured his thigh. Her attacker cried out in pain as he continued his attack, but she easily avoided the blow as he stumbled. Charlaine immediately struck again, this time sinking the tip of her blade into his stomach.

Her opponent smashed into her ribs with his elbow, trying to rush past, but she reacted quickly and extended her leg to trip him. He fell to the ground with an audible grunt. Charlaine moved in, placing the tip of her blade against the back of his neck.

"Cease in the name of Saint Agnes," she ordered, "or I shall be forced to kill you."

The axeman went still, releasing the grip on his weapon.

Moments later, two armour-clad knights appeared, grabbing his arms and hauling him to his feet. One of them looked at Charlaine. "Good work, Initiate. Do you know who this is?"

Charlaine stared back. "No, Sister, I was only doing my duty."

"That is Taren Ghul, a notorious slaver. We've been hunting him for years. He was the whole reason for this raid."

"I'm glad to be of service."

"What's your name?" demanded the knight.

"Charlaine deShandria, Initiate of Saint Agnes."

"Well, congratulations, Charlaine. I shall be sure to mention this to your superiors."

She sat, waiting beside the door that led into Commander Raphaela's office. As an initiate of the order, it was not unusual to meet with their leader, but she couldn't help but feel that this was something else. Her last assessment had been a mere three months ago, but to be called here again on such short notice did not bode well.

The door opened, revealing the Commander of the Forge. Charlaine chuckled inwardly at the reference. It was said that initiates were raw material, forged into warriors, but to Charlaine, raised and trained as a smith, the allusion struck her as particularly fitting. A forge heated metal, allowing it to be worked into steel, and this place certainly put the heat onto its initiates.

"Come," said Commander Raphaela.

Charlaine rose, entering the office and taking the offered chair.

"This will be an informal assessment of your progress so far," noted the commander as she took her seat behind her desk. Raphaela peered over a stack of papers and books to look her charge in the eyes. "Charlaine, you came to us as a trained smith," she started. "A background that gave you the physical strength and stamina to master the basics of melee in a short time. You could also ride, requiring only minimal instruction in mounted combat."

"And what of my religious indoctrination?" asked Charlaine. "Has it been adequate?"

"You know the teachings of Saint Agnes well," noted Raphaela, "perhaps even better than I do. Your progress has been remarkable, but tell me, what do you know of the other fighting orders?"

"Where would you like me to begin?"

"Tell me about the Order of Saint Mathew."

"They are dedicated to helping the sick and poor. They wear ancient chainmail rather than plate armour, as a symbol of their poverty, and wield the axe, a commoner's weapon, to show their humility."

"Impressive. Anything else?"

"They often work in conjunction with our order since our responsibility, to protect women, often overlaps with theirs."

"Very good," said the commander, "and let's not forget that we have cooperated together since the formation of our respective orders. Now, which order is the largest?"

"That's easy," said Charlaine, "the Order of Saint Cunar."

"And why is that?"

"They form the bulk of the Holy Army, which includes the fleet. They are the senior order."

"Which means?" prompted Raphaela.

"Other orders defer to their wisdom and experience when it comes to battle. Also, when meeting on the road, lesser orders will show deference, moving aside to let them pass uninterrupted. When Temple Knights of mixed orders fight together, it will be under the command of a Cunar Commander, or father general."

"Does that preclude others from commanding?"

Charlaine thought for a moment. "No, a senior sister, say a captain or a commander such as yourself, will still take precedence over a mere knight of any order."

"I see your education has increased significantly since the last time we met, but let's see how deep it goes, shall we? Tell me of the Ragnarites."

"The Order of Saint Ragnar hunts down Necromancers and other illegal practitioners of magic. They will often eschew their green tabards and metal armour in favour of more regional garb, allowing them to carry out their missions in the shadows, where their enemies lie."

"Anything else you can tell me about them?"

"Only that a sister of our order can spend their entire career without ever meeting one."

The commander smiled. "That is not quite correct. Chances are you will meet them, you just won't be aware of it. That's how secret they are. Now, where was I?"

"We were talking of all the orders?"

"Oh, yes," continued Commander Raphaela, "the Augustines?"

"They protect the Holy Relics of the Church," said Charlaine, "and wear white surcoats emblazoned with a black sun, the symbol of their order."

"You wear white, does that make you an Augustine?"

"I am merely an initiate of Saint Agnes. Augustines also wear full plate armour where we, as trainees, wear only chainmail."

"You impress me, but tell me, have I missed any of the orders?"

"You have," said Charlaine, "though I suspect that was intentional. You have neglected to mention the Order of Saint Ansgar."

"And what is their task?"

"To investigate internal matters for the Church."

"Such as?"

Charlaine had to think before answering. "I would imagine such things as corruption or malfeasance? Anything requiring a dispassionate third party, really. Oh, and they wear blue surcoats."

"It appears you have a firm grasp on the organization of the Church, Charlaine."

"Thank you, Commander. Is that all?"

Raphaela smiled. "No, it's not." She consulted her notes once more, then returned her gaze to her initiate. "You came to us later in life than most. I am curious to know how you would rate your own progress?"

"As a smith, I always strived to improve my craft. I see my time here in a similar vein."

The commander made a note.

"This is more than a simple assessment," said Charlaine.

"It is," the commander remarked, though she failed to elucidate further. "Now a final task for you. Explain the ranks of the order."

"The lowest rank is that of initiate," said Charlaine. "Once their training is deemed complete, they are elevated to the rank of Temple Knight, sometimes informally referred to as Sister Knight. Knight is the lowest active rank within the order, initiates being relegated to service only in places of training, such as this."

"And above knights?"

"The next rank is that of Temple Captain, in charge of smaller detachments, typically those of two dozen knights or less. Above that sits the rank of commander, such as yourself. Captains may often be found in staff positions beneath such a rank. Above that is the rank of grand mistress, of which there is only one. She reports to the council of peers that runs the entire Church, along with the Primus himself."

"What about the regional mistresses?"

Charlaine smiled. "Mistress is a position, not a rank. They are senior commanders that carry on the regional governance of the order under the direction of the grand mistress."

"And a Temple General?"

"Such a position does not exist. The Order of Saint Cunar has father generals, is that what you mean?"

Now it was Commander Raphaela's turn to smile. "It is a common misconception that only the Cunars can command armies. There is a doctrine that establishes the position of Temple General for our order, but it has never been invoked, so yes, you are correct, up to a certain point. I commend you for your insight. You have proven to be an outstanding initiate."

She looked down at her notes once more, moving them around until she found what she wanted. "The weapons master feels you can learn no more here at the Forge, and the riding instructor feels the same." Raphaela paused for a moment before continuing, "What are you still doing here, Charlaine?"

"I beg your pardon?"

"It is my opinion that you are ready to join the ranks of the Temple Knights of Saint Agnes. What say you?"

"Me? Ready to be a knight? Surely it takes years?"

"Ordinarily, I would agree, but you have shown yourself to be more than capable in all your studies, and your maturity serves you well. I think you shall do well within the order, Charlaine, you've got a passion for it. The question is, are you ready to accept your destiny?"

"I am, Commander."

"Good, then we shall announce your ascendancy. The ceremony will be held two days hence. Until then, you are to prepare yourself."

"Prepare? How does one prepare oneself for such an honour?"

"Make the most of your remaining time here," Raphaela suggested. "Seek out your instructors if you wish or spend time in quiet contemplation. The choice is yours."

"Thank you, Commander."

"No, thank you, Charlaine, for showing us that our investment in you was worthwhile."

As a soon to be knight, Charlaine had risen early, bathing and eating a modest meal of bread and water, as was the custom. Now she stood waiting in her white initiate robes while Sister Verona, the swordmaster, stood ready as her sponsor.

"Do you know why they call this place the Forge?" she asked.

"Yes," said Charlaine, "you've drilled that into our heads on multiple occasions."

"Good, then I'll never have to fear that you'll forget. Nervous?"

"Does it show?"

"Not really, but I remember my own ascension. It was terrifying, what with all those people watching?"

"Now you're just trying to make me feel worse."

"And did it work?"

"No," said Charlaine. "I admit to some nerves, but I'm not afraid."

"No," said Verona, "I don't suppose you are. You're fearless, I saw it the first day you arrived. It's not often we get people like you, Charlaine."

"You mean old?"

The knight laughed. "No, I mean mature, mentally, that is. You've seen the other initiates, they're all young and timid. You, on the other hand, are fearsome in your own right. You've experienced life, you know what to expect, and yet you don't back down from a challenge. All qualities that will serve you well."

"I certainly hope so."

Sister Verona moved to the door, opening it only a little to peer outside. "Looks like everyone's in place."

Off in the distance, they heard Commander Raphaela's voice echoing, "Bring forth the initiate."

"That's our cue," said Sister Verona, throwing the door wide open.

They solemnly walked forward, down an aisle formed by the members of the Forge, both initiates and staff. Charlaine noticed more Temple Knights off to her left, likely those stationed in Eidenburg, itself.

Her commander stood beside a lectern, on which rested the Holy Book of Saint Agnes. Verona led her forward, then halted, with Charlaine maintaining her position behind.

"Who speaks for the initiate?" asked Commander Raphaela.

"I do," said Sister Verona, then stepped to the side, allowing Charlaine to walk forward, taking her place.

The commander lifted the Book of Saint Agnes from the lectern, holding it before the initiate. Charlaine placed her left hand on the sacred tome, placing her right over her heart.

"Do you swear, by all that is holy, to uphold the tenants of Saint Agnes?" asked Commander Raphaela. "To protect all women, regardless of age, infirmity or religion?"

"I do."

"And do you promise to put the needs of the order above your own?"

"I do."

"Do you swear to keep your word and never lie? To show mercy to enemies of the Church and to be kind, brave, and generous to others?"

"I do so swear."

The commander returned the book to the lectern, then nodded to a nearby knight who stepped forward, a bundle of cloth in her hands.

"Kneel," Raphaela commanded.

Charlaine knelt, feeling a sense of euphoria as if Saint Agnes herself was looking down on her.

The knight unfolded the bundle, revealing the scarlet tabard of the Temple Knights of Saint Agnes. With Sister Verona's help, they lowered it over Charlaine's head.

Verona turned her back for a moment, then faced her again, a sword and scabbard in hand. These she belted in place, a task made all the more difficult by her kneeling position.

"Arise, Sister Charlaine," said Commander Raphaela, "Temple Knight of Saint Agnes."

A FEW WORDS FROM PAUL

When I was writing Maelstrom, I was surprised by how quickly the story came out of me. The characters have a life of their own, and I merely have to place them in a situation to know how they would react.

The actual plot for the tale was created some time ago. I always wanted Natalia to return to the Volstrum, and Illiana's ring was always going to be the thing that led them to uncover the family's big secret. Even back when I was writing Ashes, I knew I wanted to bring Katrin back, along with revealing what happened to those who failed the Volstrum. Thus everything was in place for this new four-book story arc.

The story will pick up again in Vortex, with our band of intrepid explorers arriving at the court of Reinwick, a city steeped in history.

As always, I couldn't have written this tale without the love and support of Carol Bennett, my wife, editor, and best friend. In addition, I should like to thank Stephanie Sandrock, Amanda Bennett, and Christie Bennett for their encouragement and support.

I am lucky to have such a wonderful beta reading team who provided valuable feedback, and so I must thank the following: Rachel Deibler, Michael Rhew, Phyllis Simpson, Don Hinckley, Charles Mohapel, Lisa Hanika, Debra Reeves, Michell Schneidkraut, Susan Young, Joanna Smith, James McGinnis, and Anna Ostberg.

Finally, many thanks are owed to you, my readers, whose encouragement and approval convinced me to continue with the passion of writing. Your reviews and comments keep me going, and I would encourage you to let me know what you think of Maelstrom.

CAST OF CHARACTERS

MAELSTROM CAST OF CHARACTERS
ORCS OF THE RED HAND
Agar - Youngling, son of Shaluhk and Kargen
Artoch (Deceased) - Master of Flame
Gorlag (Banished) - Previous chieftain
Kargen - Chieftain, bondmate of Shaluhk
Kragor - Hunter, Red Hand Tribe
Laruhk - Hunter, brother of Shaluhk, bondmate of Ushog
Shaluhk - Shamaness, bondmate of Kargen
Uhdrig (Deceased) - Shamaness
Ushog - Hunter, bondmate of Laruhk

ORCS - CLOUD HUNTER TRIBE
Azug - Hunter
Gamrag - Hunter, son of Uruzuhk
Grazuhk - Chieftain, sister of Uruzuhk
Morgash - Hunter
Rotuk - Master of Air
Sholar - Hunter
Uruzuhk - Shamaness, sister of Grazuhk
Zarig - Hunter

ORCS - OTHERS
Khurlig (Deceased) - Shamaness, Ancestor
Rugg - Master of Earth, Stone Crusher Tribe
Tonfer Garul - Scholar in Ebenstadt

THERENGIANS
Aswulf - Thane of Thaneford, great uncle of Harwath
Athgar - Fire Mage, High Thane, son of Rothgar, bondmate of Natalia
Cynrith - Thane of Ashborne
Dunstan - Bard, Runewald villager
Faramund - Thane of Farwald
Harwath - Brother of Raleth
Natalia Stormwind - Water Mage, bondmate of Athgar
Oswyn - Daughter of Athgar and Natalia, Runewald villager

Raleth - Thane of Runewald, older brother of Harwath,
Rothgar (Deceased) - Father of Athgar and Ethwyn
Skora - Friend of Athgar & Natalia, Runewald villager
Wynfrith - Thane of Bradon

DWARVES

Bagran Ironwhistle - Fictitious name used by Belgast
Belgast Ridgehand - Entrepreneur, friend of Natalia and Athgar
Harmetia Sternaxe - Female smith, cousin of Belgast
Karzan Stonebelly - Fictitious name used by Stanislav
Kieren Brightaxe - Smith, cousin of Belgast Ridgehand
Targan Hardhammer - Smith, cousin of Belgast Ridgehand
Weylin - Smith, daughter of Harmetia, cousin of Belgast

THE FAMILY

Alexi Sartellian (Deceased) - Son of Ivan and Svetlana, founded the Family
Alfie - Failed Volstrum student
Anatoli Stormwind - Water Mage
Antonov Stormwind (Deceased) - Fire Mage,Illiana's, Natalia's father
Anushka Stormwind - Failed Volstrum student
Balmund Sartellian - Fire Mage, graduate of Korascajan
Corderis Stormwind - Master of Zurkutsk
Diomedes Sartellian - Fire Mage, graduate of Korascajan
Ethwyn Sartellian - Fire Mage, sister of Athgar, Therengian
Felix - Failed Volstrum student
Galina Stormwind - Water Mage, graduate of the Volstrum
Gallus Sartellian - Fire Mage, graduate of Korascajan
Graxion Stormwind - Former court mage of the court of Zowenbruch
Illiana Stormwind (Deceased) - Past Matriarch, Natalia's grandmother
Katrin Stormwind - Failed Volstrum student
Ludiya - Young Volstrum student
Marakhova Stormwind - Matriarch of the Stormwind family
Nezerov Sartellian (Deceased) - Killed by Natalia Stormwind
Nina - Water Mage, Mistress at the Volstrum
Serafina - Young Volstrum student
Svetlana Stormwind - Water Mage, acquaintance of Natalia
Tatiana Stormwind - Water Mage, Grand Mistress of the Volstrum
Ulyana - Failed Volstrum student
Valaran Sartellian - Fire Mage, graduate of Korascajan
Vasili Sartellian - Fire Mage, graduate of Korascajan

Veris Stormwind - Advisor to the Family on military matters
Yeva - Young Volstrum student

OTHERS

Akim Zhukov - Ruzhina warrior employed by the Family
Angveld Stein - Man on beach in Karslev
Ash Biter - Beaver who Natalie befriends
Deiter Heinrich - Duke of Erlingen
Georgi Kulikov - Baron of Raketsk
Grastad - Guard at Zurkutsk
Gruff - Guard at Zurkutsk
Gundar - God of the earth, creator of the Dwarves
Ivan - Coachman in Ruzhina, friend of Stanislav
Karzik - Self-proclaimed king who led an expedition to Zaran
Laisa (Voronsky) Radetsky - Stanislav's former wife, from Karslev
Maksim the Fourth - King of Carlingen
Olya - Servant of Svetlana Stormwind
Rada - Queen of Novarsk , daughter of King Vastavanitch
Rozinsky - Baron in Ruzhina
Sergei - Ruzhina warrior employed by the Family
Sorentis - Life Mage in service to Marakhova Stormwind
Stanislav Voronsky - Former mage hunter, friend of Natalia
Vastavanitch (Deceased) - King of Novarsk
Vicavia - Enchanter who was said to have experimented on children
Yaromir - Temple Captain of Saint Mathew

PLACES:

THERENGIA

Aldhurst - Village
Ashborne - Village, newly rebuilt
Athelwald (Destroyed) - Village near Ord-Kurgad, birthplace of Athgar
Bradon - Village
Ebenstadt (Dunmere) - City
Farwald - Village
Gal-Drulan - Orc Village, Cloud Hunter Tribe
Khasrahk - Orc Village, Stone Crusher Tribe
Old Kingdom - Another name for Therengia
Ord-Ghadrak - Orc Village, Black Axe Tribe
Ord-Kurgad (Destroyed) - Orc Village, Red Hand Tribe
Runewald - Village, home of Athgar, Natalia, and Red Hand Tribe
Scarburn - Village

Thaneford - Village

PETTY KINGDOMS & CITIES THEREIN
Abelard - Kingdom, Northern Coast
Andover - Kingdom, south of Reinwick
Braymoor - Principality, Northern Coast
Caerhaven - Capital, Duchy of Krieghoff
Carlingen - Kingdom, East Coast
Corassus - City State, Coast of Shimmering Sea
Draybourne - Capital, Duchy of Holstead
Eidolon - Kingdom, Northern Coast
Erlingen - Duchy
Finburg - City in Novarsk, northwest of Ebenstadt
Grislagen - Kingdom, near Western Border
Halmund - Capital of Novarsk, west of Ebenstadt
Heronwood - Village in Novarsk
Holstead - Duchy, Eastern Border
Karslev - Great city in the Kingdom of Ruzhina
Krieghoff - Duchy, West of Holstead
Lubenstahl - Kingdom, South of Abelard
Novarsk - Kingdom, west of Ebenstadt
Porovka - Coastal city in Ruzhina
Raketsk - Barony in Carlingen
Reinwick - Duchy, Northern Coast
Ruzhina - Kingdom, Eastern Coast
Ulrichen - Kingdom, borders Erlingen
Zowenbruch - Kingdom, borders Erlingen
Zurkutsk - Mine on the eastern borders of Ruzhina

OTHER PLACES
Baroshka - Secret repository of knowledge in Volstrum
Carcarem Mortis - Dungeon of Death in Karslev
Golden Chalice - Small merchant ship at port in Porovka
Great Northern Sea - North of the Petty Kingdoms
Grimfrost - Dwarven Stronghold, Southwest of the Petty Kingdoms
Halvaria - Large Empire to the west of the Petty Kingdoms
Inner Sanctum - Room in the Volstrum available only to the staff
Kingdom of Shadows - Mythical place said to lie east of Ruzhina
Korascajan - Home of the Sartellian Fire Mage Academy
Kragen-Tor - Dwarven Kingdom, birthplace of Belgast Ridgehand
Laughing Dog - Tavern in Porovka

Michutskin River - Runs through Karslev to Porovka
Restless Hills - Home of the Cloud Hunter Orcs
Volstrum - Water Mage Magical academy run by the Family in Karslev
Warriors Rest - Inn in Carlingen
Windrush - River that forms eastern border of Novarsk
Zaran (The Lost Kingdom) - Area between Carlingen and Ruzhina

OTHER INFORMATION:

Battle of Ord-Kurgad (1104 SR) - Orcs vs Temple Knights near Holstead
Bergannon - Single-masted cog from Carlingen
Frozen Arch - Water Magic spell that opens a portal
Fyrd - Therengian militia
High Thane - Ruler of Therengia, equivalent to a king
Historica Magicae - History of magic, written by a Stormwind
Holy War (1105 SR) - Between the Church (Cunars) and Therengians
River Serpent - Akin to a sea serpent with the head of a dragon
Rygaur - Flying creature with a dog-like face and razor sharp teeth
Saurians (First Race) - Lizard-like sentient beings
Thane - Elected ruler of a Therengian Village
Thane Guard - Elite warriors of Therengia
The Disgraced - Failed students of the Volstrum
The Dragon of Eastholding - Tale told by Belgast to entertain patrons
Tusker - Huge animal similar to a prehistoric entelodont
Umak - Canoe-like boat used by Orcs
Wyvern - Large dragon-like creature with a stinger for a tail

ABOUT THE AUTHOR

Paul J Bennett (b. 1961) emigrated from England to Canada in 1967. His father served in the British Royal Navy, and his mother worked for the BBC in London. As a young man, Paul followed in his father's footsteps, joining the Canadian Armed Forces in 1983. He is married to Carol Bennett and has three daughters who are all creative in their own right.

Paul's interest in writing started in his teen years when he discovered the roleplaying game, Dungeons & Dragons (D & D). What attracted him to this new hobby was the creativity it required; the need to create realms, worlds and adventures that pulled the gamers into his stories.

In his 30's, Paul started to dabble in designing his own roleplaying system, using the Peninsular War in Portugal as his backdrop. His regular gaming group were willing victims, er, participants in helping to playtest this new system. A few years later, he added additional settings to his game, including Science Fiction, Post-Apocalyptic, World War II, and the all-important Fantasy Realm where his stories take place.

The beginnings of his first book 'Servant to the Crown' originated over five years ago when he began a new fantasy campaign. For the world that the Kingdom of Merceria is in, he ran his adventures like a TV show, with seasons that each had twelve episodes, and an overarching plot. When the campaign ended, he knew all the characters, what they had to accomplish, what needed to happen to move the plot along, and it was this that inspired to sit down to write his first novel.

Paul now has four series based in his fantasy world of Eiddenwerthe and is looking forward to sharing many more books with his readers over the coming years.

Printed in Great Britain
by Amazon